SWORD
AND STAR

ROOT CODE, #3

SUNNY MORAINE

Anglerfish Press
PO Box 1537
Burnsville, NC 28714
www.AnglerFishPress.com
Anglerfish Press is an imprint of Riptide Publishing.
www.RiptidePublishing.com

Sword and Star
Copyright © 2016 by Sunny Moraine

Cover art: Kanaxa, www.kanaxa.com
Editor: Carole-ann Galloway
Layout: L.C. Chase, lcchase.com/design.htm

ISBN: 978-1-62649-303-2

First edition
May, 2016

Also available in ebook:
ISBN: 978-1-62649-302-5

SWORD
AND STAR

ROOT CODE, #3

SUNNY MORAINE

ANGLERFISH PRESS

For Rob, still with me now.

TABLE OF CONTENTS

ACCRETION

S ometimes Adam went wandering.

Sometimes he was almost afraid. A great deal of the time he was certain Lochlan was.

But he had learned that there was only so much he could do about their threatening fear. Only so much of himself he could spare for that, for worry. Hadn't they long ago passed the point of no return? If there was an event horizon, hadn't they crossed it? Blown over it like a bullet, like the first shot fired in a storm of them.

Because it was that. It was exactly that. Bullets, shooting, and gone so far that there could never be any turning back.

He could only ever go forward now. The same was true for all of them.

So Adam went wandering through the night that went on forever.

He saw a great deal. Much of it made little sense to him. Much more made no sense at all. But he had grown comfortable with nonsense, as one grows comfortable with a change in gravity, in light, in temperature. You grow accustomed. You acclimate. You adapt.

From his conception Adam had been carefully engineered to be strong in body and in mind, impervious to illnesses both chronic and acute, physically attractive within a rigidly defined set of standards—and adaptable. On the Plain of Heaven, things had been changed inside him, other things stripped away, and now his reflexes weren't what they once were, his strength was no longer so reliable, and he was more easily weakened than he had before. So many small alterations, so many tiny reorderings and reorganizations. So much *movement*.

Things had been taken from him. But other things had been given to him. And above all else he had retained the ability to *adapt*.

He knew how life forms evolved. He knew what time did to them, how it ravaged. How it could be cruel. He knew that the life that survived was the life that could adapt.

As he wandered through the dark and among the traveling stars, he meditated on these things. Somewhere distant, his body rested aboard Ashwina: massive Ashwina, gentle Ashwina, Ashwina the Bideshi homeship and Ashwina the cradle of his first rebirth, Ashwina his adopted home. If he had a home anymore.

Ashwina the machine of war.

He turned and looked back at it, hanging there in sub-slipstream, a little cloud of smaller ships drifting around it like a swarm of flies around some great beast, glittering in starlight. He beheld their fleet, such as it was—all scavenged, many of the ships stolen, some in poor repair, some half-built from the salvaged components of multiple others. He surveyed it with cool detachment, evaluating, briefly seeing it through the eyes of another, an outsider. No one would consider it impressive. No one would consider it a threat, not against any significant military force. No one would consider it formidable, not even with Ashwina's enormous bulk at its center.

Like this, Adam was bodiless. He was consciousness alone. But as he thought these things, he smiled.

It was a tight smile, almost grim. He could take no joy in this conflict they were now part of. It was his doing—his among others—and he knew it, accepted it.

Regretted it. Not that it had happened. But that it had been necessary.

In three months, it was as if he had aged three decades.

He was alone here, but he could sense the beautiful chaos of minds on the small ships, on Ashwina—a strange chorus of life and everything life contained. But for the moment he had left them behind. Now he walked through the night, and as he gazed out into the countless stars and their eons of light, a face he knew coalesced from it and took shape in front of him, like a fantastically complex constellation. He felt no fear as he watched it happen, and he felt no surprise.

He felt no anger as he looked into the coldly aristocratic face of Melissa Cosaire.

She was not there, of course. She was dead, and if any part of her still existed, it was lost to him, and he had no desire to find it. But he gave her a nod, as if she were really with him. Now she was human-sized and human-shaped, and standing before him on nothing at all. Her arms were folded over her chest, her suit as immaculately tailored and pressed as ever, and she wore the same familiar expression of restrained impatience he had seen her adopt every time he'd met her.

Hello, Melissa.

You were my subordinate, she said stiffly. *You shouldn't call me that. Ms. Cosaire, if you please.*

You're dead, Adam pointed out gently. *I don't think it much matters what I call you now.*

Dead or alive, you can mind your manners. I don't imagine you're rude to that Bideshi witch you drag around in your head.

Adam laughed. Without anger, without any desire for vengeance, and with the power this woman had once held over him now gone, talking to her ghost was oddly pleasant. Regardless of the fact that she was imaginary. *Ixchel comes and goes as she pleases. I don't drag her around anywhere. She would never stand for that.*

Cosaire rolled her starry eyes. *Whatever you say, you degenerate.*

Nice to see you, too. Your head appears remarkably intact. What did Aarons call you? Before he blew a hole in it? 'Missy'? There was no malice in his voice. If anything, he was teasing. The dead, Adam supposed, had to learn to thicken their skins.

And indeed, Cosaire didn't seem hurt. She rolled her eyes again and waved a hand. *His manners were worse than yours.*

Mm. Adam moved beside her, and together they watched the fleet. *He misses you. He'd never admit it, but he does. He might not have liked you, Melissa, but he respected you.* He paused. *So did I, if it comes to that. Once I even cared a great deal about what you thought of me.*

She gave him a sidelong look, and her expression was difficult to read. *And now?*

Now you're dead. Adam returned her look with a smile.

If you feel some respect for the dead, you genetic mistake, you could show it.

Adam shook his head. *If I was a mistake, so were you. The sickness was killing you, Melissa. Just like it was killing me. Just like it was killing all of them.* He nodded at the fleet, at the stolen and scavenged and salvaged Protectorate ships full of once-defective defectors. *Just like it's killing the entire Protectorate. You know where the mistake was. You couldn't admit it. That was what killed you in the end, not Bristol Aarons. Not his bullet. You know it. Admit it. You're dead. You have nothing left to lose.*

No, she said softly, and there was quiet regret in her voice. He wondered whether he was truly imagining her.

And then he didn't stop wondering.

No?

No, I have nothing left to lose. There's a freedom in that, boy. You'll know it in time. You and your lover. You and your lover and the rest of them.

We're all for death, he replied. *Each one. You have to deal with the idea when you go to war.*

So it's really to be war, then?

Adam shrugged. *Isn't it already?*

Cosaire huffed a laugh. *A few raids on a few outposts and you're calling it a war? That's a slight overstatement, don't you think?*

It's the beginning of one. We began it three months ago. On Peris.

That was a reconnaissance fleet. Poorly armed, poorly armored. There was no particular heat in her tone, no particular sharpness. *They weren't ready for you. You took the one advantage any inferior force ever has—you surprised them. You continue to surprise them, but you won't forever. Sooner or later they'll be ready for you. Then you'll have to face them.*

She regarded him, and her eyes were full of freezing night. *Then, Adam, you'll see what war is. And I promise you, every battle you've seen—Peris, the skirmish at the detention center, even the Battle of the Plain—will look like a sparring match in a dojo on Ashwina. You haven't seen blood spilled. You haven't seen horror. You haven't seen death.* She gave him a smile, thin but not cold. Sad. *I'm dead. I would know.*

Adam was silent. When one couldn't think of what to say, he had learned—and this before he ever fell from the Protectorate's grace, before he ever found an uneasy home with the Bideshi—that it was better to be silent. And what could he say, in any case?

She wasn't wrong. He knew that much.

I don't fear for you, Adam. Her voice was fading, and she was fading as well. Rejoining the stars, slipping back into the night.

I don't fear for you. But you should fear for yourself. You should fear for all of them.

You should fear.

She was gone. Adam was alone.

He wasn't afraid. Not yet.

But he might learn to be.

CHAPTER

ONE

Ten minutes after the ships entered low orbit and issued their first volley of warning shots, the atmosphere exploded.

It didn't literally explode. But looking on from Ashwina, staring with his mouth hanging slightly open, it appeared that way to Lochlan. A blaze of fire, of detonations, of explosions of flammable gas as holes burst open in the ships' hulls. It was oddly lovely, like fireworks against the brown and blue continents and oceans of the planet, the long glittering snakes of rivers. To the right, a band of night was spinning toward them, and here and there in tiny, shimmering patches were the lights of settlements.

He stood there, helpless, and watched their people die.

A few feet away, Adisa whirled from the primary viewscreen to one of the coordinators who was sitting at her console, staring at her own smaller screen, her fingers poised above her touchpads. Her eyes were wide.

"Report."

"I . . ." She shook her head, opened a window to the left of her screen, and began to pull up strings of text and figures.

Damage reports, automatically compiled. The casualty reports would not be automatic. But they would come.

Lochlan closed his eyes, his hands clenched into fists.

"Heavy surface-to-orbit artillery barrage," called another coordinator. Her words trembled.

"They didn't have any heavy artillery. They didn't have any significant planetary defensive systems at *all*." Rachel, her voice tight.

"They weren't supposed to," Lochlan said quietly. "Clearly we were wrong."

"Kae doesn't get things *wrong*. He hasn't once—that fucking *intuition* of his. You're saying it failed?" She was close to him—he could practically feel the way her presence shoved aside the air in front of him. In the camp where he and Aarons and Adam had found her, she had been impressive. Now she was frightening when she wanted to be. He opened his eyes. On the screen behind her, their raiding ships were dropping out of the sky.

"Don't blame this on him." Lochlan's eyes narrowed. He felt sick, cold; he didn't want a fight, not over this. Not with her. Not while people were dying.

"I'm not *blaming* him." Rachel turned, tugging her shoulder-length braids away from her face—a nervous habit she had picked up recently. "It doesn't matter. Get them all back here, *now*. And what about Kae? Any word?" This to Adisa, to the six coordinators at their screens—possibly also to the five other council members gathered at the edges of the room. The defensive command chamber was reasonably large, but with this many people packed into it, it was positively claustrophobic.

"No, he's—" The coordinator touched a finger to the comm bud tucked into her ear. "He's reporting in now. He says he's lost three—no, four of his wing."

"*Khara*," Adisa breathed, and Lochlan closed his eyes again. Kae alive, but others not, and they didn't have many to spare. And they were people he knew.

He knew all of them.

"What about Bristol?" Rachel's voice was level, but there was clear effort behind it. Aarons was supposedly hanging back on one of the larger cruisers. He would be mostly out of harm's way if the shots were focused on their raiding ships. For the moment. But Rachel loved Aarons with a ferocity Lochlan had rarely seen, and though she would surely keep it in check, it would be boiling beneath her composure.

"He just sent us a report." An older man, dark hair white at the temples, glanced up from his console. "No damage on his end. They're too high."

Adisa swiped a hand down his face. "For now. Pull him back. Pull them *all* back. Tell them to regroup out past the fourth moon. We'll be the rendezvous point." He had been old for a long time, but after the Battle of the Plain and Ixchel's death, he had aged further. Now, three months into a grinding conflict, he appeared positively ancient.

"Yes, sir." A chorus of voices, rapidly moving hands.

Lochlan saw three of the older council members bending their heads together and murmuring, their faces tense. It was unlikely they would say much; the council of Ashwina tended to concern itself with internal matters. They wouldn't make trouble. All their potential troublemaking had been dispensed with when Ashwina separated from her sister ships Jakana and Suzaku and did what almost no other Bideshi homeship ever had. When she left her convoy.

Now there were more losses. And there would be still more. Lochlan shifted his attention back to the viewscreen; there was less flaming debris—fallen out of sight—and their remaining ships were limping away. Even the planet seemed to have halted its fire. In what felt like a matter of seconds, the fight had ended. Only a few seconds to deal them a blow that would be, if not lethal, massively damaging.

To the ships, to the people—and to the spirit.

"Wings are coming. Kae's bringing his people in."

"As soon as they're docked, we go." Adisa clasped his large hands in front of him, his head down. Briefly Lochlan thought about going to him, trying to offer comfort, but knew it would be ill-advised. Ixchel could have done it. She was the only one who ever could.

Though there might be another.

"Adisa," Lochlan said quietly. "I'm going to the Halls. Do you have any message for Nkiruka?" He swallowed. "Or Adam?"

Adisa drew close but didn't answer for a moment. He glanced over his shoulder to where Rachel stood, her arms crossed, her head tipped up to the viewscreen, and her face turned away from them. "No," he said just as quietly, and after another second or two he laid a hand on Lochlan's shoulder and squeezed. "No, son. I expect she already knows everything. Him as well."

Lochlan nodded. Very likely, it was so. When he went to them, he would carry no surprises with him.

And he had to go to them. It was more than desire. Right now, it was the only place he could be.

The Arched Halls were always still and yet always alive with movement and sound—soft whispers, hisses, even music so far distant it was barely there at all, like someone's memory loosed into the world and carried through the interwoven branches by a breeze. Lights danced and shadows shifted, and the paths and clearings were never the same from day to day. It was a place soaked in life, a center of life, a nucleus of the ship. Each one a fragment of a whole that bound all Bideshi together.

Through births and deaths, feasts and famines, gain and loss, joy and grief, they should remain a constant. Unchanging and yet always changed. But as Lochlan walked in under the spreading boughs of impossibly ancient trees, he sensed a difference.

He had since Ashwina left her sisters. Since they chose to wander alone. That much made sense. But this was something else.

For a moment he stood, feeling the change around him. Feeling it breathing and beating like an enormous body—which really it was. Then he began to walk again.

He didn't know exactly where he would have to go, but he probably wouldn't have to go far in. Once he would have been relieved at that; the Arched Halls were supposed to be a place of peace and refuge, but Lochlan had never been entirely comfortable there, and that had had only a limited amount to do with Ixchel and how she had seemed to love to pin him—bug-like—and make him squirm. It was just *him,* was all. His nature—restless, unsteady, unbalanced. Rather than restore his balance, the Halls had merely made him uneasy

But his nature had changed after the Battle of the Plain and Adam's healing, and it had continued to change since his and Adam's marriage. Kae had said that marriage would alter him in ways he could never possibly anticipate, and Kae—a matrimonial veteran of nearly a decade—would know. And he had been transformed. The unsteadiness had become steadier. The lack of balance had begun to right itself. He felt *older,* but more than anything else he felt more like *himself,* like the man who had been hiding under a boy's cockiness and affected carelessness and volatile anger.

So he had come to find a peace in the Halls that had always eluded him. He might not be here for a happy purpose, but he knew that when it came time for him to leave, he would do so only reluctantly.

This place was more than peace. This place was a sanctuary.

But not for Nkiruka. Not for Adam. The Halls did not hold them within themselves. From beyond their bodies, beyond the ship, they would have seen everything. Felt everything.

He found them less than five minutes later—because they wanted to be found, most likely. If they hadn't, they would probably have been able to arrange things so that the Halls hid them, maneuvered anyone else away from where they kept their meditation. They were sitting across from each other in a small clearing, and between them burned a fire. Their heads were up, but Adam's eyes were closed, and Nkiruka's . . .

Nkiruka would never see again. Not as Adam did, not as Lochlan did. Not with her birth-given eyes, which were white and sightless, the skin around them scarred. But no one who knew her—who knew any of the Aalim—was fooled. Her gifts allowed her to see far further and more deeply than a common human.

But when Lochlan approached, she closed her eyes and tipped her head downward. Mingled confusion and anger crossed her face. She wouldn't be expecting him to blame her for what had happened, but she would blame herself.

"Old Mother." Lochlan stopped by the fire and ducked his head. The form of address was customary only; Nkiruka was a young woman, still in her midtwenties, and the glow of the fire on her deep-brown skin somehow made her appear even younger—and extraordinarily lovely. But with an Aalim, age meant little. Her soul was old. It always had been, and then when she had formally been given her place, it had aged much more.

She turned toward him, held up a hand, and beckoned him to sit. As he did, Adam opened his eyes.

They were bloodshot, as if he had been crying. Though there was no other sign of it.

"Lochlan." Nkiruka looked from him to Adam and back. "I assume you know you don't need to tell us anything. We saw it all."

Lochlan nodded. "But I thought I should come." He glanced at Adam again and pain stabbed at his heart—a complex pain, deeper than mere sorrow. Adam and Nkiruka had both been ready to be present with the minds and spirits of the raiding party, to give them focus and strength, but their powers were limited to that. They wouldn't have been able to stop weapons.

"You did well in thinking so." Nkiruka was silent a moment, and Adam said nothing. He simply gazed at Lochlan, a terrible kind of helplessness twisting at his features.

Lochlan wanted to go to him, but he shouldn't. Not yet. Adam was still returning to himself. And he was returning wounded.

"We don't yet have a full casualty report," he started, but Nkiruka cut him off with a raised hand and a shake of her head.

"Twenty-seven dead. Kae lost four ships of his wing, which is two singles and two doubles. Six. I knew them. I knew them all, but those . . . Somehow it's worse. Maybe it shouldn't be, but it is. The others were on . . ." She sighed deeply, but before she could continue, Adam spoke.

"Eight ships. In all." His voice was low and flat, and his eyes were slightly unfocused. "We can give you their names. Someone should notify their people, someone should—"

"That's not necessary, *chusile*," Lochlan said gently. "I'm sure they already know the names by now."

"But they—" A hard edge of desperation sliced into Adam's voice, and for an instant the look in his eyes was both sharply focused and stricken. Then he shook his head and seemed to pull back into himself. "Yes. All right."

"There's little else we can tell you from this end," Nkiruka said quietly, almost as if Adam hadn't spoken. "Once we rendezvous with the others and the fleet can confer, I should be able to issue a word."

Lochlan ducked his head again, close to a bow. "Thank you." He paused. "Nkiru."

He saw her start. He had swung abruptly from formal address to deeply informal—not only her true name but its abbreviated version—and he hadn't known her well prior to her taking the place of Aalim. She had always been Kae and Leila's friend. But now she was mother to the whole ship, and he cared for her.

He couldn't not. They all had to care for each other these days.

That was all any of them had.

He thought she might be offended. But her face softened, and she reached for his hand. "I won't tell you there's nothing wrong,

Lock," she said softly—and in her words he heard the woman she had been before she had become so much more than herself. "But we'll do what we must. This won't kill us. Something else might, but it will not be this."

He gazed down at her hand in his, and thought of how different she was from Ixchel—Ixchel, who had appeared to enjoy living up to Lochlan's term for her. *Mad old bat.* Nkiruka carried a sadness about her that Ixchel had covered with the years she had been given. Nkiruka was young, and she kept it so close to her skin. Raw and painful.

Ixchel had lost Adisa long ago. But it had been barely three months since Nkiruka had given up her future with Satya. With the woman she had intended to make her wife.

"Thank you," he said again, in a whisper.

She gave his hand a squeeze and released him, turning to Adam—whose attention seemed lost in the dancing fire. "Go with your love," she murmured. "Walk away from death for a time. It'll be waiting for you when you're ready to return."

Adam looked up at her and his brow furrowed. Then he got unsteadily to his feet. Lochlan rose and laid a hand on his shoulder—more like a comrade than a lover. There was no way to be sure what Adam would need. Lochlan could assume nothing.

Adam took a breath, and when he met Lochlan's eyes, he was more *there.* He managed a smile—it was tiny and pained, but it was something.

"I'm all right," he said. "Really."

"Okay." Lochlan grazed his fingers across Adam's cheekbone—his one concession to his own need for physical contact—and turned to leave the clearing. He felt Adam close behind him.

He also felt Nkiruka's blind gaze on them, gentle, like a warm hand on their backs.

They were nearly out of the halls when Adam collapsed.

Lochlan knew it was coming a split second before it happened— saw the wobble, the beginnings of a stumble—and was already moving to catch him, but Adam stopped his fall with a hand on a trunk and leaned there for a moment, sucking in huge breaths. Lochlan stared at him, briefly and horribly helpless, and saw that Adam was shaking, trembling all over, like a man in the grip of deep cold.

"Adam . . ." Lochlan went to him and touched him, laid a hand between his shoulder blades, and Adam stiffened, shuddered harder, as if to pull away. Then Adam twisted—a single violent movement—and fell against him, groping for him, and Lochlan realized the shaking was caused by sobs.

It was beyond second nature to curl his arms around his husband, to cup the back of his head and gently press Adam's face to the hollow of his throat. Adam went loose in his arms, beginning to slide, and Lochlan took them both awkwardly to the ground, cradling Adam in his lap.

He had held Adam like this once before. On the Plain, with the battle raging all around them, with death like a storm and them the eye. Then, he had been certain they were both as good as dead, and when he held Adam close, he had believed they would die together.

This wasn't like that.

This was somehow worse.

"I *felt* them," Adam whispered. His voice was surprisingly steady, given how hard he was still trembling. "I felt them die. I was *with* them. Nkiruka was . . . She was deeper. But she's stronger. I wasn't ready. Lock, I *wasn't ready.*"

"You can't be ready for that, *chusile*." Lochlan combed his fingers through Adam's hair—which was damp with sweat. Adam was hot, burning like fever. Like a star. "There's no way to ever be ready for that."

"No, you don't understand." Adam pulled away and gazed up at him with wild eyes, brilliant, mismatched blue and green. "*I have to be.* I have to be ready. I don't have the *luxury* of not being ready."

"Adam . . ." But Lochlan was at a loss, and Adam gave him no chance to answer. He laid his head back down on Lochlan's chest, though his eyes remained open. Open and staring at nothing.

Or at everything.

"This is only the beginning." His voice was calm again, but there was a terrible relentlessness in it, and it sent a finger of ice running down Lochlan's spine. "Three months ago . . . Peris . . . She was right.

That was nothing. *This* is nothing. It's going to get so much worse before the end."

It was difficult to tell if this was fear or prophecy. Before she died, Lakshmi had referred to Adam as a prophet, but it had been unclear whether she'd meant a guide or someone literally capable of foretelling the future. Lochlan didn't think the latter was likely—Adam might be extraordinary, but he wasn't an Aalim. This didn't have the feeling of genuine foresight; there was no real certainty in Adam's voice.

Merely terror.

In any case, it was a good guess. Lochlan didn't honestly expect things to get *better*. Not for a while.

"If it does, we'll stand together. We always have. You've seen that we can."

Adam nodded. "But there's— We should have had some idea. Nkiru and me." He curled a hand into the front of Lochlan's shirt and gripped until his knuckles were white.

Here it comes, Lochlan thought.

"We were there. We should have seen it coming. We *should have seen it.*"

"You're not *gods, chusile.* Even Ixchel never saw everything clearly. She—"

"I *know that.*" Adam actually gave Lochlan a little shake. "But we were close. We should at least have known a few minutes ahead of time. Enough to warn everyone. We should have *felt it coming*, and we *didn't.*"

Lochlan didn't answer immediately. He simply held Adam close. He had always been gripped by a desire to repair what was broken. With Adam, he was beginning to learn that sometimes all he could do was simply be there—be there while the storm raged, and be there for the calm in its passing.

So for a time they were both silent, and the Halls whispered around them.

At last Adam stirred and pulled back, swiping at his face in an oddly childish gesture. He might still be in the grip of what had happened, and Lochlan was sure there would be nightmares, but he resembled himself again. Weary, grieving, but himself.

"I'm sorry," he murmured, and Lochlan shook his head.

"Cut that out."

"No, I . . ." Adam took a hard breath. "I can't lose control like that. Wrong place, wrong time . . . It would be dangerous."

Lochlan arched a brow. This was new. "Dangerous *how?*"

"I'm not sure yet. Just . . . dangerous." He looked away, off into the shadows, up into the branches, back the way they had come. "Something's happening, Lock. I don't know exactly what. Not yet. There's a lot that isn't clear. But something's happening to me. Something that started on the Plain. Before, it wasn't moving fast enough for me to notice, but now . . ."

Now. Lochlan had sensed it. He hadn't wanted to, had hidden it from himself, but he had. "It's moving faster."

Adam nodded. "Faster every day. I don't know where it's going to end. I have no idea. And there's more." He swung his gaze back to Lochlan, and Lochlan almost shied away. Adam might look like himself, but there was something about his *eyes.*

Still that bright blue and green. But there was something even brighter behind them. Something burning like a young sun, and then he realized that was exactly it; there was a star inside Adam, many stars, so distant they were barely visible but approaching.

Approaching rapidly.

My God.

"What is it?" he breathed, and he was uncertain what he was asking about.

"It's how we missed it," Adam said. "How we didn't see the attack coming until it came. Lock, I don't think that was just a fuckup on our parts. I don't think it was just us being *human.*"

He sat back in the packed dirt and moss, his hands clasped in his lap, and then he lifted his head and gazed up at the stars shining through the interwoven branches. "Something was blocking us," he said softly—coldly. "Somehow. Someone pulled a curtain over our eyes, and they did it without us even noticing."

He paused a moment, and Lochlan let it sink in, the idea of it and every implication that came with it. Yet more to fear. All unknowns, all speculation, and there wasn't any reason to assume Adam was right . . .

But he was. Of course he was.

"Something didn't want us to know." Adam blinked, and just for an instant Lochlan would have sworn his eyes were literally glowing, burning with that awful internal starlight. "Some*one*. Someone found a way to stop us."

Adam stared down at him. Yes, his eyes were glowing. God help him, they were.

"Which means that whoever they are, they have the power of an Aalim."

CHAPTER

TWO

Isaac Sinder flung the pad on the desk—the report still scrolling by in a stream of text—and turned away toward the window and the streaked white of slipstream beyond. Everything had gone off without a hitch. He should be pleased.

He wasn't.

The truth was that he wasn't pleased very often these days, not in himself. Once he had taken pleasure in his every success, every job well done; it made sense to do so. If one couldn't take pleasure in the proper execution of one's responsibilities, what was there to take pleasure in at all? At least for him. But his feelings were inconsequential; the glorification of the Terran Protectorate was its own reward. Its ideals, its philosophies and truths—things that, more and more, he had elevated to something akin to holiness, which he knew made the people around him a little uneasy.

Well, if they didn't share his feelings, that was their concern. In the meantime, he would do what he must. He had watched the people around him closely, and he was beginning to wonder whether *any* of them truly grasped what was at stake. What the Protectorate had already suffered.

Peris. The defeat at Peris. The *indignity* of Peris, the utter *insult* of it. The abomination. It hadn't been as foolish or as costly as the massacre on the Bideshi planet, but in its way worse. The massacre had been a mistake on both sides: Melissa Cosaire and her hapless forces had attacked, the Bideshi had stood and defended, and the result had been like something from ancient Terran history, from the time when two armies would meet in a valley and simply hurl themselves together until one of them had outkilled the other and was declared the winner.

On Peris they had been outstrategized. The Bideshi—and their own defective people who *refused to be dead*—had taken them on in inferior numbers with inferior firepower, and had bested them.

It should not have happened.

And it could not be borne.

Perhaps it would become necessary to wipe out the Bideshi in the end, whether or not in punishment for that insult. But in the meantime, the only true concern was Adam Yuga. The leader. The figurehead. The guiding star. Never mind the intelligence that indicated that the rebellion's military leaders were Rachel Garroway and Bristol Aarons—a defective and a traitor, of all people, and the defective woman with no high status, no history of distinguished service to anyone or anything, nothing to indicate the command ability she had displayed. That *she* would possess that ability was nonsensical—so incredible, it turned his stomach. It was *offensive*. And then there were Kyle Waverly and Eva Reyes, defectives and traitors to both the Protectorate's commercial and military arms. But the true leader would be the man who started everything. Adam would be the lifeblood. The heart.

There was a knock on the door. No chime—Sinder had disconnected it, finding its soft tone annoying. The truth was that he hadn't been sleeping much—not that it was anyone's business—and sudden sounds were more distracting than usual. Jarring.

Sometimes he couldn't figure out what had made them.

"Come."

The door slid silently open and in stepped a young ensign, features twisting with discomfort—a familiar sight since they had taken their new passenger aboard. Sinder hadn't been on the battle cruiser *Relentless* for over a week, but its crew's discomfort was obvious to him.

He couldn't have cared any less.

"Sir?" The ensign shuffled her feet, and though the room was dim—there was essentially no illumination but for the white light through the window—Sinder could detect a flush in her brown face.

He was unimpressed. The propensity to be that intimidated should have been both bred and trained out of her. He hadn't even said anything yet.

And he still didn't. He merely nodded, indicating that she should continue.

She did, evidently finding her spine. "Sorry to disturb you, sir, but our . . . guest is asking for you."

Sinder arched a brow, though he had been expecting this. Had in fact been waiting for it. This was the only report he truly cared about, the one that would decide a great deal, because it would give him a clearer picture than he yet had regarding what was possible.

"Very good. Tell him I'll be down directly."

"Sir." The ensign hesitated for a few seconds, but when only silence greeted her, she turned and was gone without another word.

Sinder waited a while longer, staring at the point in space she no longer occupied. He wasn't truly seeing it. He wasn't truly seeing any of the room at all—the simple fixtures, the spare furnishings, the basics of an office without luxuries or hints of the personal. He was seeing the deal he had made and what it had perhaps cost him. Would still cost him. It was, he knew, a kind of blasphemy, but he was willing to do whatever was necessary to protect what made the Protectorate great. His faith was unshakable.

So what did this say about him?

What it said was just that. That he would fight. That he would do whatever was necessary.

That, when needs must, the devil himself would drive.

The cargo bay was also dim. Their guest preferred it that way.

Sinder stood in the doorway, waiting to be given leave to enter. He would have expected the same in his own quarters; again, this was about mutual respect. Regarding this man as his equal—very few people were. A decade ago, perhaps even less, he would have been shocked to see such behavior from himself. But things had changed.

"Mr. Sinder." The voice that emerged from the low light was smooth, pleasant, and as Sinder's eyes adjusted, he saw the man seated cross-legged on a wide, cushioned mat, though his face was still hidden in shadow. He held his body straight and appeared strong, his shoulders broad and his frame powerful—and that strength was no illusion. But this man was old beyond reckoning. Old, and he had doubtless forgotten more than anyone on this ship had ever known.

Including Sinder himself.

"Old Father," Sinder said, inclining his head. Not quite a bow. As he stepped into the cargo bay and the seated man leaned forward, the hard, craggy lines of his face left the shadows and came into view. His short-cropped, salt-and-pepper hair. His unnaturally pale skin.

His white, sightless eyes.

"You should call me Julius, Sinder. I told you. I am no longer an Aalim, and the title no longer applies."

It wasn't a slip on Sinder's part. He remembered what the man had said when they first met, when their first overtures were exchanged, when their first understandings were arrived at. That felt like a lifetime ago, though it was barely a month, and they had spent no significant time together until both of them had boarded the cruiser. Sinder had never once forgotten who he was dealing with—what this person had been, and what he no longer was.

Those would be foolish things to forget.

He didn't want to allow Julius d'Bideshi to forget it either.

That surname would also have been abandoned. All ties to the Bideshi were cut when they cast one of their own out. The exiled were no longer one of the family; they no longer had any claim on anything that made them part of that family. But Sinder understood enough to keep him from truly believing that claim was gone, and if the Bideshi did, they were deceiving themselves.

You couldn't change your blood.

"Julius," he said, and the man lifted a hand and beckoned him closer.

He was clad simply in plain, loose-fitting pants and tunic of an off-white that, a little disturbingly, was close to the hue of his skin. He was otherwise unadorned except for his left wrist, where he wore a slender bracelet made from a leather thong and long, narrow beads of what appeared to be bone, carved with elaborate shapes and symbols.

Anyone who looked at it would almost certainly assume that it was animal bone.

Sinder was prepared to make no such assumption.

"Things appear to have gone well," he said, approaching Julius but stopping a few feet away. "Reports have come in. The damage was mostly confined to their raiding party; the other ships were out of range. But they took heavy losses."

Julius nodded, sitting back and resting his hands on his knees. They were disconcertingly smooth, nearly unmarked—the hands of a much younger man. "I already know it. Though I appreciate you coming to deliver the news in person."

"You asked for me."

"I did. I also wish to deliver news in person." Julius gestured to a cushion across from him. "Please. Sit."

Smoothly, Sinder did so.

"You are aware, then, that I successfully concealed the presence of the extra firepower you ordered installed."

Sinder nodded; in fact he *was aware* of nothing of the kind, but he was prepared to suppose it was very possible. Again, another in his situation would have reacted differently—they would have scoffed, declared such a thing impossible. Bideshi magic was all tricks, illusions, sleight of hand. Everyone knew that.

Except Sinder no longer trusted what anyone *knew*.

"There was no great difficulty. They went in under the assumption that nothing had changed since their scouting run. That was their arrogance. It required nothing on my part. The bad news is that they're not fools. They wouldn't be, surviving as long as they have. And with Adisa helming Ashwina, as I'm certain he is . . ."

Sinder nodded. "They won't make that mistake again."

"Indeed. The good news is that my supposition was correct. My powers *can* extend that far. Obviously you already know that, but what you don't know is what's possible under those circumstances. Which is . . ." Julius shrugged. He didn't appear disappointed. Indeed, he looked distinctly self-satisfied. "Not a great deal. I can essentially do what I did—nudge a few sensor readings in the wrong direction, cloud a few minds for just a few seconds. It was enough. But at that distance you should expect no more, and possibly less. Depending."

Sinder cocked his head. None of this was particularly surprising, but it was interesting. "And if you were closer?"

Julius smiled, wide with hints of teeth. "Aha. That's the best news."

Sinder returned the smile, albeit in less than a fraction of its width. "How good is 'best'?"

"I can't be sure without making a proper test. But given our . . . *resources*, I suspect my power might be quite effective indeed. Highly destructive. Highly *persuasive*. I believe I could potentially exert an extreme degree of control over . . . Well." He laughed, short and soft. "Everything."

Sinder made a quiet, thoughtful noise and folded his fingers in front of his mouth for a moment, closing his eyes. Julius could be exaggerating his own abilities—to himself as much as to Sinder. He would have reason to do so. Exile could generate anger, resentment, a thirst for revenge—and it could also mean shame. The man might have good cause to tell himself he was better than he was.

But Sinder didn't think so.

"I want a test."

Julius inclined his head as if he were a monarch bestowing a great favor. "Name the target."

The defectives—Sinder refused to consider them *rebels*, a term that to him denoted a species of nobility—were long gone, and would now be in hiding. But there were any number of backwater planets, colonies, stations that could be utterly obliterated, with few people missing them. It would be an easy task. It wouldn't even take them far out of their way, most likely.

But.

"There's a planet which has been proving . . . troublesome," Sinder said slowly. "Specifically a group of insurgents has been making themselves a nuisance. Radicals, calling for the *purification* of their world." He spoke this last with sharp scorn; it was a perverse use of the term, but he wouldn't expect anything else. "There aren't many of them, but they've been doing a fair amount of damage at some mining facilities, and thus far they've eluded capture or destruction. It would be advantageous on a number of levels if we could eliminate them."

"What is the planet?"

"Koticki," Sinder said, and waited for Julius to respond.

He did, with a slight widening of the eyes. "That's one of your more prominent holdings. Are you certain a direct strike there would be advisable? To be perfectly frank, I know I could command considerable power at close range, but what kind of control I would be able to maintain over it . . . Let's just say we might be dealing with a sniper rifle or we might have a plasma cannon, and I won't know for certain until the moment of truth."

Sinder waved a dismissive hand. "Koticki is somewhat significant as a source of natural resources and minor manual labor. It has no value beyond that. Its inhabitants are primitive. We've been dangling the possibility of full Protectorate membership over their heads for a while now, but only to keep their *government* easy to handle. If it's collateral damage you're worried about . . ."

"And the potential harm to your standing if it should go badly wrong?"

Sinder smiled thinly. The man would think in political terms. Sinder wouldn't want it any other way. "My standing is secure. I've done a great deal since Peris to make it so. With you as an asset, it would be unshakable. I just want to know exactly what manner of asset I have." His smile grew a touch. "I'm sure you do as well."

Julius was quiet a moment, his head lowered. Sinder could practically *feel* him thinking, a soft humming in the air. It might not even be his imagination. Things like that—sensations that seemed to drift to him from nowhere—were more and more vivid these days.

"Set a course," Sinder said at last. "At your convenience. Let me know when you're ready to brief me, and we can go into final consultations. In the meantime, I would like to remain undisturbed. I must meditate. What I did was not untaxing, and I have strength to recover."

Sinder nodded and rose. "I thank you, Julius. Clearly this is a mutually beneficial arrangement, but it's also— Honestly, it's a pleasure to watch a skilled man at work."

"You haven't seen me at work," Julius replied quietly. "Not yet. My friend, you will."

"I have no doubt of it." He turned to go, but as he reached the bay doors, Julius called his name, and he looked back.

"Yes?"

"Send down some food, if you would. Something simple. Oh, and." Julius glanced over his shoulder at the far corner of the cargo bay. Sinder had been trying to avert his gaze from what was there; he wasn't squeamish, not especially, but this was still distasteful.

Albeit fascinating.

"I'm finished with it," Julius said. "Have it removed."

CHAPTER

THREE

"It's shit."

Eva felt Kyle's hands on her waist, but he didn't try to turn her from where she leaned against the railing of the long gallery that circled the great central chamber of Ashwina. He didn't try to pull her closer. He merely stood there, making his presence known, and she was grateful for that.

Grateful beneath the pain.

"We knew things like this were going to happen," he said quietly. "They *have* happened. We saw them. Together."

She hesitated a moment, her eyes closed, then gave him a weary nod. He was right. More than right. There was a way of striking at the truths that hurt badly, that cut. It was calling up memories that twisted at her, memories that sometimes sent her tumbling into thick, roaring nightmares. Bodies strewn across the gray, dusty ground. The injured crying out for help, for water. People missing limbs. People burned. People cradling slaughtered lovers, parents, children, comrades. Protectorate and Bideshi in equal measure. Seeing it and trying to face her part in it, however small. The blood in the dust had also been on her hands. None of the Protectorate present there had been blameless.

Ironic that such a slaughter had taken place on a planet named the Plain of Heaven. The Bideshi didn't think that way; they knew it for what it had been to them, for what it still must be even after all the blood spilled into its dust. Sometimes she wondered how Kyle stood it. How Aarons did. But she didn't know how to ask them.

"I thought." Her hands tightened on the railing. "I thought maybe that wouldn't have to happen again."

"No, you didn't. At least, not all of you did." Kyle lifted his hands from her waist and smoothed them through her hair, pulling it away from her face. It was getting long. Leila had taken to braiding it for her, plaiting it into complex and lovely patterns, occasionally weaving beads into its strands. "You're not a fool. You wouldn't be here if you were."

In spite of herself, Eva smiled. Maybe she should have been annoyed with him, and at another time maybe she would have been, but his voice was gentle and so were his hands, and in any case he was right. As right as she had been.

"I wanted to believe, then."

"So did I."

She hesitated before closing a hand around his wrist, tugging her to him. He folded his arms around her and pulled her close, then kissed the back of her neck. One hand slid down to her belly and rested over the slight swell. Barely noticeable, still. But there. She rested a hand over his and leaned back against him.

"I wanted to believe because of this," she said softly. "And instead I walked into the middle of a war. How's that for foolish?"

"You did what you thought you had to do." He kissed the side of her neck. "I love you for that. It was one of the first things I loved about you."

"And now I can't pull out of it."

"You could. We both could." He held her a little tighter. "If you wanted. Are you thinking about it?"

"Maybe." But she hadn't been. Not until that moment. Even through the horror, the fear, the understanding that what they had seen the day before was probably the first taste of much more to come, she hadn't considered leaving. "But I . . . How can we just pick up and run like that? What kind of message would that be sending?"

"That you're sane? That you understand how sometimes priorities change? You think anyone would blame you for that?"

Eva shook her head. "There are children on this ship, Kyle."

"And after we make the next rendezvous with the convoy, there won't be."

She fell silent again. Again, he was right. That was the end result of a long and excruciating ship-wide conversation, its timetable accelerated by what had happened to the raiding party. A Bideshi defensive ship always carried families, but the situation had changed, and if anyone had doubted it before, those doubts had been blown out of the sky.

So to speak.

Jakana and Suzaku were still flying, awkwardly absorbed into another convoy until a more permanent solution could be found. Bideshi families were often spread out among the three ships in any given convoy; there would be homes on both Suzaku and Jakana to receive every one of the children on Ashwina. Those who had no families on either ship would find families more than willing to take them in.

They would do what they must. All of them.

"Do you want us to leave?" She asked the question softly, though she knew he would hear her.

When they met with the convoy, she and he could go with the others. The children, the older men and women, those who—for one reason or another—had made the decision not to fight any longer. They could look for a life elsewhere.

"I don't know," he said at last. "I'm sorry. I just don't know."

"Do you think they would understand? Adam and Lock? Rachel? Aarons? All of them? Would they blame us?"

"Of course not." But he didn't sound entirely convinced, and she didn't feel any more certain. Her stomach twisted, and she sighed and was silent.

If she left, if they *ran,* it would feel like cowardice.

Even if it wasn't.

"We stay." She gave his hand a soft squeeze. She knew he wouldn't argue. She also knew he wouldn't simply go along with her. They were of one mind, and they had been since the beginning. At the Battle of the Plain, Kyle had gone to the surface of the planet to do what he could do. To help Adam. To help his friend. It had been the next thing to suicide, but he had gone and she had gone with him. It hadn't been that difficult a decision.

It had been the right choice.

"I know." He spread his palm across her belly, and she thought of the tiny life growing there, a warm little star getting brighter and hotter every second. "Because of this. Because . . ." He took a long breath. "A galaxy where this just *happens* and we don't do whatever we can to stop it?"

"Isn't one where I want our child to live." She nodded. Someone else might think giving birth in the middle of this kind of fight was irresponsible. Even cruel.

That was their business.

"So what now?"

Eva made a confused little *mm?* and opened her eyes. "Now . . . I don't know. We have a briefing in about eight hours, and I guess after that we'll have to see what we—"

"I don't mean that. Not the briefing, not after. What do we do *now*?"

"Oh."

She tipped her head to one side and looked up at the enormous hall's transparent ceiling. The sky was white streaks as Ashwina plunged through slipstream. Before all of this, she would never have thought she would be risking her own life to help Bideshi. Now she was making a home on one of their ships, and while she didn't think she would ever feel like one of them—and she was almost certain the place would never truly feel like a *home* . . .

It was something. It was beautiful, in its way. If she was going to give birth, going to bring new life into the universe and try to help it grow, maybe she could do worse than Ashwina.

She turned in his arms and kissed his jaw. "I'm tired. We have some time. Let's just . . . go to bed."

He nodded and laid his hands on either side of her face and tilted her head up to his. His hands were large, strong, but there was also something elegant about them—long, graceful fingers. He could be so gentle. When she needed him to be.

"We'll come through this," he said, and pressed his lips against her brow. "We have before. All of us. Or . . ." He looked down at her again, and his mouth twisted into a sad smile. "Obviously not all of us. But we will. One way or the other."

"One way or the other," she echoed, and he took her hand and led her to the lift that would take them to the level where their quarters waited.

And then there was love, slow and just as gentle as his hands, and afterward he fell asleep against her, his hand between her breasts, close to her heart. But Eva lay awake for a long time, gazing up at the shadows on the ceiling, and wondering.

Could you ever know a choice was the right one?

When the Bideshi dead had been transported from the surface of Takamagahara back to their homeships, there had been many, but they had been spread out between ships, and no one ship had significantly less than any other. Adam didn't think this was worse than that terrible aftermath.

But it was the only other time he'd lived through something so horrible.

Not even that many, he thought as he followed the long procession through the fields toward the Arched Halls. *Only twenty-seven. Nothing at all. If this is the worst loss we suffer . . . I would never believe it. I would think it was the dream of a madman.*

Twenty-seven bodies, wrapped in white shrouds—though some of them were wrapped effigies, surrogates for the sake of farewell. Not only Bideshi dead but all the dead of their fleet, including those formerly Protectorate—and those who'd considered themselves still so, and had been fighting to save something they believed in—were to be given rest here.

Even those who weren't Bideshi must feel the quiet, gentle, ancient power of that place when they set foot beneath those trees.

Lochlan walked beside him. They weren't holding hands, but now and then Lochlan's came into contact with his. His fingers, knuckles. Just enough to let Adam know he was there.

It had been two days since the failed raid. Adam hadn't needed to tell Lochlan that he wasn't recovered. It had to be plain in every word, every movement. Every nightmare.

Now you are haunted. You were before, but now you really know what it means, don't you? It wasn't his own voice, he realized, but Cosaire's. *You understand what it is. You understand how, given enough time and enough ghosts, it can drive one mad.*

He wasn't going to argue with her. He knew. He understood.

He understood her better than he'd ever believed possible.

The procession snaked over the little hill that led to the Halls, following the plain dirt path. At the front of the procession walked Nkiruka, unguided, her head up. She was dressed all in white, her many braids woven with small, pale flowers. They stood out brightly in her black hair, and Adam thought of stars.

The procession was silent, but as the shrouded bodies were carried beneath the trees, a song began, gentle and soft. There was no particular structure in it, and even the words were difficult to make out, but as more and more Bideshi mourners took it up, it began to shape itself, each individual part slipping into a harmony that nevertheless retained some of the incoherence of its beginning. The words were clearer, though not all of them were in Standard.

But enough were that he could understand the song. It was about dusk, about the setting of many suns on many worlds, the stars that shone down on them all and touched them with light. It was about lights from each world reaching back, rising to meet them. Returning, for each creature in existence was made of the stuff of stars.

There was deep melancholy in it, but also a deep sweetness, and if it encouraged tears, they weren't tears of despair. As the last people moved into the Halls and the thick trunks flanked them, Adam could hear weeping, but none of it sounded wrenched. None of it was agonized. Agony was there, and when they left this place it might return, but here there was a kind of peace, even if the peace was heavy with grief.

The song rose with the story it told, and Adam wasn't surprised to find tears running down his face. Not just for the twenty-seven being carried to their rest, but for everyone else who had died, and for all the death still to come.

But the heaviness in his heart had lifted. And when Lochlan found his hand and took it, a warmth spread through him, and he leaned against Lochlan's shoulder and was supported. He had this. Whatever else happened, he had this man by his side. This odd, beautiful man who had given every impression of hating him when they first met, who had danced with him in the light of a bonfire, who had taken him roughly when he needed to be reminded that he was real and alive, and who had been far more gentle with him under the shelter of a glowing flower on Klashorg. Who had fought for him. Faced death with him. Promised himself to Adam on a distant world under strange moons, and was with him now.

Adam doubted so many things. Feared so many others. But this . . .

He didn't doubt this. And if this fight ended badly, if he came to be one of those lights rising to join the stars, Lochlan's spark would rise with him.

They came at last to a large clearing, the same clearing in which his own Naming ritual had begun—in what seemed like another life.

In a very real sense, it had been.

The clearing now appeared much larger, however, as if it had grown to accommodate the gathering. No fire was set at its center, but instead a ring of twenty-seven lit torches. The bearers brought a body to each of these and laid it down, a torch at its head, so that the wrapped bodies looked like the spokes of a wheel of light.

All around them, glowbugs danced.

Nkiruka stepped easily into the center of the ring of torches, and as she raised her hands, the mourners fell silent.

For a moment there was no sound. Even the whisper of the breeze and the low creak of the branches seemed to have ceased. Then Nkiruka began to speak.

"We have lost," she said. Her voice was low, but somehow it carried over the heads of the people and into the trees, the branches, filling the clearing as it would an enormous room. "That word is insufficient. All words are insufficient for this. Pain is unapproachable with words. It can only be felt. And in the end the only thing that can make it bearable is knowing that we do not feel it alone."

She fell silent again and let the silence settle. Her words seemed to hang in the air, and then faded. As Adam watched, the glowbugs began to cluster around the bodies, began to land on them.

He had seen this before. But there was something different about it now.

"Loss comes to us all. That doesn't mean one can be prepared for it. One can never be prepared, nor can one easily bear its weight. Some offer words intended to comfort, and sometimes they do so, but in the end there is still the loss. In the end we must face it and what it means."

She spread her hands, palms down, as if bestowing a blessing on the circle of bodies, and lowered her head.

"I am the one who must offer those words. But I cannot. I stand in the face of this loss, and I have no words but these: they were loved. All of these people were loved. Love is a force in the universe as powerful as any. It cannot be seen or measured or marked, but it guides each one of us from our births to the day when we rise to meet the stars from which we came. There is that love, and so there always shall be. Whatever becomes of our bodies, that love is deathless and unending."

She raised her hands and head together, and her eyes were wide and seemed to glow with their own clear light. "We send these, our brothers and sisters, to the stars. Our love goes with them. May it be that, somehow and in some way, we find them again."

Once more there was silence. Then, so softly it was nearly inaudible, the song began again. One by one the bearers emerged from the crowd and moved toward the bodies, which were now bright with glowbugs. As soon as the bearers reached the bodies, the glowbugs took wing, but they didn't fly away. They hovered above each one in a cloud, and as the bearers lifted the bodies onto their shoulders, the insects stayed with them.

Spreading out in all directions, the bodies were carried from the clearing.

What would come next was sacred and attended only by the dead's loved ones. The bodies would be taken deep into the Halls, to places set aside for them. Final farewells would be said, and then the dead would be left behind. What came after that, no one was certain, for no one ever returned to search for their dead again, but no shrouded bodies reappeared after they were laid to rest. Not even bones. If decay took them, it was decay of the most complete kind.

Adam stood for a time, watching the bearers and mourners depart—though not all of them. Some of those remaining would go soon. Others, like Adam, would linger. In the fields, a bonfire was being set and food and drink were being laid out. There would be a feast of sorts in honor of the dead, but there would be no music and no dancing.

Adam wasn't certain he wanted to be there for it.

Lochlan touched his hand. "You all right, *chusile*?"

Adam took a breath and nodded. It wasn't exactly true, and of course Lochlan would know that, but maybe it was true enough. Nkiruka had said she didn't expect her words to bring significant comfort, but at least to him they had. This was her task, and she performed it well.

She was an Aalim to her bones. To her blood.

She was coming toward them now. She wouldn't oversee any of the final rituals; she was a leader of the ship as a whole and a counselor to individuals, but there were limits even to her place and her position. As she approached, Adam took her extended hands.

"I'm glad you came," she said quietly. "I know you didn't have to."

"Yes, I did." He gave her hands a squeeze, and felt even steadier than he had, as if some of her strength was passing into him. "I had to say good-bye. Same as everyone."

"And you needed to be reminded of those left alive. Yes." She released his hands and moved to stand beside him, and Adam could feel her scanning the clearing and those who lingered with her unique kind of sight. "Somehow this is so much worse than what happened on the Plain. Yet the dead are so many fewer."

"Because it's the beginning." Lochlan laid a hand on Adam's shoulder, and Adam covered it with his own. "What comes next?"

"We regroup," said a gruff voice. "We consider that exact question."

As one they turned. Bristol Aarons emerged from the shadows, his scarred face somehow appearing more scarred than ever. Rachel was at his side, her face somber. Aarons continued without waiting for a response. "In a few hours we'll link up with the other homeships. After that . . . We've marked a system about three days from here, riding high. Unpopulated. No habitable planets. Nothing much at all. It's not out of the question that someone might find us there, but it's about as unlikely as it's going to get."

"We just got word that Jakana is willing to replenish our food stores," Rachel said. "Which is good. We're low. Very low. And Suzaku is willing to help with basic supplies. Medical, among other things."

Her mouth twisted wryly. "Evidently they're not so displeased with Ashwina that they'll leave us high and dry."

"We take care of our own." Nkiruka's voice was quiet, firm—and somewhat amused. "Even in the face of hurts done to us. I know you haven't exactly been taught to expect that."

"Well, either way." Aarons sighed. "We can come back from this. But . . . We'll be making the decision when all the captains meet, but I don't think the raids can continue."

Lochlan shook his head. "They *were* working. They were giving us ships. We were actually getting people out of some of those camps. We were building our forces, we were—"

"We were setting ourselves up for what happened." Rachel's tone was even but clipped. "They've learned to anticipate us now. If they knew we were hitting that place when and how we did . . ."

"Wait." Adam's attention had been drifting, moving up into the branches and the stars beyond, but all at once something that had been troubling him since the raid reared its head. "How *did* they know? We were careful. I know careful doesn't cut it forever, but—"

"I dunno." Aarons rolled a shoulder. "Maybe they figured out how to spot our recon runs. It doesn't really matter. We have to assume we won't have the element of surprise anymore, and that means we've lost our primary advantage. You can't conduct guerrilla warfare without the ability to strike from cover."

There was a footstep, and Adam glanced over his shoulder to see Kae coming to join the group. He had been a bearer for one of his wing, and his tone was weary. "He's right. And there's another problem."

Lochlan moved aside to make room for him. Everyone else had fallen silent. Kae had been a wingleader three months back. He still was, but—though the change had been mostly informal—he had since assumed leadership of all of Ashwina's wings. The Bideshi had no military ranks, but they did possess a sense of hierarchy, and Adam supposed, in Protectorate terms, that Kae was now essentially a commander.

As such, he was afforded everyone's ear. More even than before.

"The raids are growing our forces, yes. But not fast enough. We're adaptable. So are they. Every time we hit them, they learn.

What happened was inevitable. It's all well and good to do what little we can with inferior numbers, inferior firepower, and never truly engage, but sooner or later this is going to become a real shooting war. A *war*. One we can't run from. If we're not in a position to fire back by then . . ."

He shrugged. The implication was clear enough.

"I didn't want this to become a war at all," Adam said softly.

Rachel stared back at him, impassive. "I'm not sure what the hell else you expected it to be."

Lochlan frowned—he already had been, but the frown deepened, became stony. "Ease up."

"It doesn't matter what anyone expected," Nkiruka said, still quiet but a bit harder than before. "What matters is what we're dealing with now. And at the moment there's nothing we can do about it. In a few days, we'll see."

She laid a gentle hand on Adam's arm. "I need to steal you. Can you come?" Before he could respond, she turned an apologetic expression to Lochlan. "Alone. He'll be all right. I just need to talk to him."

For a moment Adam wasn't sure why she felt the need to specify; then he got it. The last time he had been with her, he had been hurt. He would have to return to those mental exercises at some point, but now might be too soon.

Lochlan hesitated. But at a glance from Adam, he reluctantly nodded.

Adam leaned in and kissed the corner of his mouth. "I'll be okay. Wait for me at the fire. I'll come find you."

In truth it was with relief that he allowed Nkiruka to lead him into the trees. He hadn't liked the direction of the conversation, and he wanted to be away from it. He might once have been the man who was good at solving problems. Untangling puzzles. And yes, perhaps in a significant way he had begun all of this.

But he had done so as a healer. Despite his relative skill when he had flown those two times with Lochlan and Kae's wing, he wasn't a fighter. He certainly wasn't a *warrior,* and he wasn't a general.

It was no longer clear what he was.

He followed Nkiruka down a path until the lights and the low voices in the clearing entirely vanished, and only the Halls rose around them, ever-whispering. Adam half closed his eyes and let himself slip into the semitrance the Halls often put him into these days. He could walk, talk, respond as if he was awake, but part of him was detached and floating, freed from everything.

He wondered why he hadn't come here sooner. Except he knew. Fear had kept him away. Fear of what he might see. Might feel.

But he couldn't let fear rule him forever. He couldn't let it rule him at all.

At last she stopped, and he stopped with her, still partially hypnotized by everything. The clearing they had halted in was small and dominated by a stone shrine slightly taller than Adam. The stone itself was a deep green, and it was a single piece: a low altar above which rose a bizarre figure, sporting wings and eyes and eight spreading arms like a spider. In each of its cupped hands was a silver flame.

He had never seen it before. He stood for a moment, marveling. "What is it?"

"No one knows. It's been here for as long as anyone can remember. Sometimes one can find it. Sometimes the paths which lead to it seem to be blocked. It's as if it can be found when it wants to be found."

Adam shot her a questioning glance. "How did you know it wanted to be found now?"

Nkiruka returned his look with a small smile. "How do I know anything?"

It was a fair point. Maybe he shouldn't even have asked. Rather than responding, he walked closer to the statue, and as he did the strangely sinuous carving appeared to move. There were letters intertwined with its lines. Script he couldn't read, didn't recognize. "A god?"

"Perhaps. As I said, no one knows. We remember many things, Adam, but we have forgotten many more. When a ship carries as many stories as Ashwina does—as our people do—nothing is retained forever."

He took a slow breath. "That's sad, isn't it?"

"I don't know. I take a kind of comfort in it. Everything dies, doesn't it? Everything has an end. Even the night that goes on forever.

Sooner or later none of this will be left. The death that accompanies forgetfulness is gentle. What's forgotten just . . . slips away. Burns itself out like a little flame." When Adam next looked at her, she was still smiling. "Any of us might wish for such a death."

Adam's mouth tightened. He would have preferred not to think about death at all. "Why did you bring me here?"

"Because it came to me that I should." Nkiruka stepped forward and laid a hand on his shoulder. "Because I can feel you pulling away, Adam. What happened . . . I know it wounded you. I know it wounded you more than you showed me. I knew it because I was inside you, as you were in me. You try to hide things reflexively, but in that state, you can hide nothing. And you've had to hide things for a great deal of your life, haven't you?"

Adam said nothing. He didn't have to. She was right; she had been inside him, had seen everything. In their connection on Peris, and every time they'd connected since then, in every exercise he'd taken with her and every time they'd worked together to give their ships an extra edge in their raids. She had seen what his life had been before Ashwina, before Lochlan. She had seen it all.

She knew what he had suffered.

"The habits of a lifetime often take a lifetime to unlearn, and your habits are born of fear. When we failed in the raid, it was an old fear that gripped you, and one that runs deep. You need to understand where it came from. What it is. *Why* it is. Not so you can combat it, but so you can face it squarely, embrace it. Accept that it's now part of you who are."

She hadn't removed her hand from his shoulder, and she gave him a gentle squeeze. "What do you fear, Adam? Above all else? It's not the loss of your love. You *do* fear that, but you also accept it. Before you entered this fight, you knew it was possible that he might die. You knew you might lose him. It would destroy part of you, but you would survive. As for your own death, you accepted that long ago. So what is it, this fear? What's its nature?"

Adam gazed at the statue, at its faceless, chaotic form, its many eyes, its wings. Its flames. Yes, it was a god, or something close to it. He believed in no gods, no deities; the universe was a great deal stranger than he had ever suspected, but despite that, he'd seen no evidence for a conscious entity guiding events. There appeared to be an underlying logic, yes. But that logic needed no God or gods to exist.

Yet he couldn't take his eyes off the figure. It was both terrible and beautiful, and as he stood here under the trees, captivated, it was not so difficult to believe that such a thing might once have existed.

Its eyes. Seeing him. Penetrating him. Eyes that were nevertheless unseeing. Like Nkiruka's.

"The Plain," he murmured. His nightmares, terrible in the first few weeks after the battle, lingered even now. "Everyone dead. Because of me."

Nkiruka was quiet for a moment, and she lowered her hand. Adam stood in the quiet, let it gather around him, and wasn't certain whether he found it comforting.

"You realize," she said at last, "that they all made their own choices. To be there. To help you."

He shook his head. "All of them? How could they know they would be attacked? There were *children* there. Did they make a choice? Did they understand what might happen? What did happen? The ones who even survived—do *they* understand it?"

"Adam. You are not responsible for the choices of others." Nkiruka's voice was low, even. Gentle as her hand had been.

He smiled thinly. "Apparently that doesn't mean I can't blame myself for them."

"This is arrogance." Still low, still even, but now there was a core of steel in it, and the steel was chilly. Not without sympathy, but without mercy. "You're not that important. Maybe you started this, in some capacity, but you didn't start *all* of it, and whatever the damned fools who lead your people think, you're not the center of it. You never were. You aren't the hero of this story."

Adam turned to her, stung. "I never said I was the—"

"You didn't need to. You think it, even if you don't realize you do. You're fixated on one story, on *your* story, as if it were the only story and everyone else merely characters. It isn't so. You need to release the idea that you *are* that center, that somehow you could control any of this, because as long as you hold on to it, you'll blame yourself for everyone who dies. And more people *will* die."

Her voice, which had risen slightly, hung in the air, and Adam stood silent, feeling it sink into him. He wanted to argue. He wanted to fight back. But he could find no weapons, nothing that wouldn't make him feel small and petulant and childish.

He couldn't fight back because she had already won.

And it wasn't even about winning.

Nkiruka turned him to face her, and she fixed his eyes with hers—her essential blindness only making them pierce deeper.

"Adam." Her voice was soft again. "I love you. You love and you are loved, and such a thing is powerful beyond measure. But everything ends. Every story is ultimately forgotten. And on the scale of time on which the universe moves? You are *nothing.*"

He expected that to sting too. It should have. And yet it didn't. He gazed at her, let her gaze back into him . . . And everything in him loosened. Released. Tension he half sensed, tightness so deep inside him it had become simply part of his existence.

He knew his insignificance. He had felt it. When he was Named, when he fell into himself, he had caught a glimpse of the sheer *size* of everything, and his own insignificance in its face. Of how much he mattered, and how little.

He was nothing. And that was a fine thing to be.

Her presence quieted him, to a greater degree than the Halls themselves. He might not know her well, not nearly as well as he had known Ixchel, though he and Nkiruka had already been close — intimately so—in ways he had never been with her predecessor. But he knew enough. He knew all he needed, at least for now.

At last he took a breath and raised his head. "What should I do?"

"Simple. Don't give up. Don't pull back. I can feel you doing so, and it's that fear driving you. What you are, what you might be . . . You're not an Aalim. You never will be. You *shouldn't* be. The Bideshi have more than enough. We don't need you. The ones who need you are your own people. And yes, they are your people still."

She cupped his face, and her hand was soft and cool as her thumb stroked down his cheek. "You're a bridge, Adam. Ixchel saw it. She saw it before anyone else. You're a tether between us and them. A hybrid. That's what you must be. And you can't be that if you're hiding inside yourself. What you and I have begun, we have to continue. You have to discover the depths of who you truly are. Maybe you were Named . . . Maybe you went through the *ceremony*. But what starts in that ritual is only the beginning of a much longer journey. Often it's a journey which runs the course of a lifetime. You don't yet know yourself." She smiled. "You will."

He returned the smile, a smaller iteration of it. "You'll help me?"

"Of course. What else am I here for?"

"Lots of things."

"Lots of things and singular things. They aren't mutually exclusive. Your story is your story. You'll follow it to its end." She lowered her hand and stepped back, and Adam felt the conversation drawing to a close. "Go now. Find your rest. I think you'll need it for what's to come."

Adam nodded but didn't yet turn to go. His attention was once again fixed on the shrine, on the wings, on the eyes that seemed to stare and see. "I still don't understand what *that* has to do with it all."

Nkiruka's smile remained, and now there was something secret about it. Almost mischievous. "A forgotten story. Perhaps it'll come to you, if you meditate on it."

Before he could say anything else, she appeared to melt into the trees, and in a few seconds it was as if she had never been there at all.

CHAPTER

FOUR

Koticki was a large world, mostly covered by water. Its single continent was sizable, though still dwarfed by the vast ocean that surrounded it. It was mostly grassy plains with a band of thick forest near the equator, a long mountain range that ran north to south along its western edge, and a small patch of desert in the range's rain shadow.

In short, it looked like nothing much at all. Until one noticed the countless oil drilling platforms in the ocean, and the enormous refineries that lined the coasts.

Sinder gazed down at it as they slid into low orbit. He had only been to Koticki four times in his career. The place hosted a range of climates, but he found the climate in which a number of the refineries sat far too hot for his tastes, and hadn't made the visits lengthy ones.

But now he was pleased to be here. He was anticipating what he might see, regardless of how the crew might react. If it worked . . .

Well. One couldn't argue with results.

"Captain Archer." He shot the man a quick glance—short, powerfully built, hair graying at the temples, Captain Archer exuded an air of quiet, dignified authority, but though Sinder should have liked him, he didn't. Not particularly. Something about the man's manner gnawed at him. More than once Sinder had been certain Archer was staring in his direction, only to find he'd redirected his gaze when Sinder looked. "You've informed central command of our presence?"

"Sir." Archer's voice was smooth, level, but cold. He clearly didn't like Sinder either, which was vaguely pleasing. "They're informed and awaiting further instructions."

"Command authorization codes transmitted?"

made contact with surface command. Sinder waited, and although he wasn't exactly worried, apprehension trickled down his spine.

It wasn't entirely unpleasant.

Captain Archer leaned forward in his chair. "What's the word?"

"Sir." One of the comm officers turned. She looked puzzled . . . And something else. Fear, yes—that had been there since Julius walked onto the bridge. But this was a different kind of fear. "We have reports from the central detention center. As you requested."

Archer's mouth twisted impatiently. "And?"

"All of their Kitchit separatist prisoners just . . . They appear to be dead. All of them. They aren't yet sure of the cause, but . . ."

"Aneurysm," Julius said quietly. Placidly. "Not really that difficult. Though that many at once . . ." Although Julius was holding his erect, strong stance, he was wavering. He was tired, probably more than he was letting on even now. "If they aren't all dead, enough of them are that their organization will be in shambles. Long before they recover—if they ever do—your people will be able to clean up the last of them."

Archer shot Sinder a look. "The ones in the detention centers? I hardly think they were in a position to—"

"You misunderstand." Julius smiled, and it was ice. "Not just the ones in the detention centers. All of them.

"Everywhere."

There was no way to confirm it, obviously. There were separatists who were in hiding, who had been in hiding for a long time, who would likely never be found. But there on the bridge, watching Julius—and considering their exchange later in the privacy and quiet of his own quarters—Sinder was sure the man hadn't been lying. He could do what he claimed. And he had.

In any case, he had little reason to lie. All he had to maintain was a relationship. Sinder—and through him, the Protectorate, even if the few remaining authorities who oversaw him were unaware of this arrangement—had offered Julius nothing but room, board, transportation . . . and the opportunity to increase his power, which it was safe to say primarily motivated him. Which in itself was something to watch, with which it made sense to be concerned. If the man became sufficiently powerful, what might he do with that power?

As far as Sinder could tell, Julius maintained no feelings of allegiance to the Bideshi as a people, or to whatever individual ships had been his convoy. Neither did he seem to bear the Protectorate any ill will. He seemed to feel no true obligation to anyone but himself, which was reassuring and relatively easy to manage—but which also in some ways made him a more difficult man to manipulate.

Why he had been banished from the Bideshi, Sinder didn't know. But he could make some educated guesses.

"Were you impressed?"

Sinder had been seated in a chair before the window, toying with a palm-sized tablet. Now he started slightly and swiveled the chair around, maintaining his calm with measured care. "I didn't send for you, Julius. How did you get in here?"

Julius smiled, his hands clasped loosely in front of him. "I'm surprised you would even ask me that, after what happened."

"It's not very polite."

"I only care about courtesy so long as it serves me to do so. As do you." Julius regarded him for a moment, then moved farther into the room. The indirect lights were on but only softly lit, and in the dimness Julius looked a great deal younger than he was. "Let's not mince words, Sinder. Isaac. You said you had a specific job for me. You never specified what that job was, but I can draw my own conclusions. I might have been on a swampy backwater of a planet when you found me, but that doesn't mean I wasn't keeping my ear to the ground." He smiled a little wider. "So to speak."

Sinder arched a brow. "Meaning?"

"Meaning you marked that insurgent fleet as a target. That much makes sense. That a Bideshi defensive ship is leading them also makes sense. They—*we*—tend to stick together, but that doesn't mean none of us ever go rogue, and in some circles resentment of the Protectorate is running high. Higher, since you killed a bunch of them."

"I wasn't there," Sinder said with just a touch of stiffness.

Julius waved a dismissive hand. "Whatever. The point is, I can see why you'd want to deal with the *problem*, and I can see why you'd want to do so decisively, in ways your own personnel don't seem to be capable of doing. I understand why Ashwina is acting as flagship. That particular ship is one of the best, but she's also known for, shall we say, slightly unorthodox leadership. Even by Bideshi standards."

He had been circling the outer edge of the room, passing shelves on which stood a collection of delicate Klashorg wood carvings—abstract and sinuous and suggestive of life forms that were neither flora nor fauna but some hybrid of both. Now he turned and faced Sinder, his eyes blind and his gaze keen.

"It's that defector of yours, isn't it? Adam Yuga. I know he's at the center of what happened on Takamagahara, though I haven't been able to determine exactly why. But it's not just about the massacre, is it? It's the insurgency itself. He's there. I could feel him."

Sinder's eyes narrowed. He had been almost certain this matter would come up before he was ready to introduce it. Julius was no fool.

The man would know about Adam. At the very least, he would know that Adam existed.

But *feeling* him.

"On Ashwina?"

Julius nodded. "At first I wasn't sure *what* I was feeling. Then I got it. Like a glimpse of something through a curtain. He was with their Aalim—young girl. New. Strong, though. It'll be interesting to see what happens to her, assuming she doesn't die."

"But he wasn't clear?"

"No. That . . . I'm not sure why. He should have been. Everyone else was." Julius moved a little closer, and now he was frowning, half thoughtful and half—seemingly—genuinely perturbed. "Or everyone who rated my attention. But him . . . There was that curtain. And he was different. He's no mere *defector*, is he?"

Sinder regarded Julius coolly. "To be honest, I can't say at this point what he is."

"Your people want him alive."

"That's the official stance."

"You don't."

Sinder didn't answer, not at once. Slowly, smoothly, he rose and turned away. He had come here to be alone, and now, looking out at the stars through which they drifted, he again felt that he was.

At some point he had slipped into a solitude that maintained itself even in the midst of a crowd.

"We tried to take him alive on more than one occasion. That was . . . misguided. Perhaps once interrogating him, making an example of him, might have served a purpose, but those days are long past. Now he—he and everyone who follows him—has to die. Whatever the cost."

"But that . . . That's all you, isn't it, Sinder? That's your decision. The rest of them, the people to whom you answer . . ."

"Are few and far between these days. And for the most part they're otherwise occupied." Sinder smiled to himself, small and thin. "There are times when one can rise in power absent formal promotion. This I've done."

"And in such a short time."

"Indeed."

There was a long silence. Sinder could sense Julius considering him, probing him with that uncanny sight. How much Julius could see, he didn't know, but probably it was a great deal. His mind. His heart. His eyes half-closed—could he literally feel it? A tickle against the inside of his skull? Yes... Yes, he could, and he gritted his teeth. He could resist it, could make it far more difficult than it had to be, or he could do what any wise strategist did and pick his battles. And he was wise. Wiser all the time.

"The Protectorate," Julius said at last. "The sickness. It's true."

Sinder let out a slow breath. "It is."

"He was cured."

"So it seems."

"So why wouldn't you want to take him alive? Why wouldn't you want to discover the logic behind his *cure*?"

That little knife-edge smile returned as Sinder glanced back. So this was some of the truth of it. Not all. "That's one of the areas in which I was hoping I could count on your help."

Julius actually looked surprised. "Oh?"

"We're working on it from our end. Subjects at the quarantine camps have proven very useful. But I think the time has come to employ less conventional methods."

"That doesn't explain why you won't get what you can out of him."

Sinder's jaw tightened. This was a sore subject. It was getting sorer all the time. Sometimes it came to him and gripped him, shook him, made it difficult to be still. Even now his muscles were twitching, trembling, and he wanted to throw things. He began to pace. "His way is an abomination."

"His way seems to *work*," Julius said dryly. "And if you call what he does an abomination, what exactly do you call what I do?"

Sinder didn't answer. Not right away. He turned back to the window, considering everything in a half-conscious way. The fact was that, purely from a pragmatic standpoint, Julius wasn't wrong. He was irritatingly correct. But this wasn't only about pragmatism. There had been an *insult* dealt, a deep one, one he couldn't allow to stand. The man's very existence was an insult.

Sinder didn't want to depend on Adam Yuga. Didn't want to need him. The feeling was irrational. That didn't mean it wasn't strong. Strong enough now to be overwhelming. It was like a dark, pounding thing in his mind, getting closer and closer, looming over him.

Sometimes, if he was perfectly honest, he worried a little about his own sanity.

"You haven't sided with the people who would just as soon destroy us."

"I haven't sided with anyone. Unless you count myself. I'm not in this for idealism. I don't care about your threatened utopia."

"I can respect that."

"And not Adam Yuga? A man who fights for a cause? However abhorrent it is to you, you have to allow that there's a kind of honor in that."

Sinder whirled on him, fists clenched, suddenly and dangerously angry. The man could probably end his life at will, without any need for bloodletting. He didn't care. He was Isaac Sinder, protector of people and worlds who had no real idea he was there, a mighty hunter before the Lord, and he was not going to be argued with by one of the *Bideshi*.

No matter how right Julius was.

"Honor isn't an escape from a deserved death sentence," he said, lowering his voice into a tense growl. "If we can take him alive, all the better. But it's not my first concern. It isn't even about him anymore. It's about all of them. We end them all at once. None of the mistakes we made on that wretched little planet. No stay. No reprieve. No one gets to live."

Julius studied him for a few minutes. Sinder allowed it, let him see the man with whom he was dealing.

"Very well," he said finally, and shrugged. "As I said, I take no sides, so it's none of my concern. You give me a target, I'll take care of it for you. Whatever logic you may be using . . . I won't trouble myself with that." He turned to go, but paused by the door, glanced back.

Sinder didn't like his expression. It was all cool amusement.

"I'll be your rope, Isaac. I'll be that much. But in the end you'll be the one who decides whether to hang yourself with it."

Slowly, Sinder nodded.

Hanging. Yes, someone would swing.

CHAPTER

FIVE

S o the children took their leave of Ashwina.

It hurt Nkiruka to watch them go. They gathered in the cavernous open space of the main docking bay, saying their farewells. The ones old enough to understand what was happening looked somber, and held on to their younger siblings if they had any. The younger ones were merely confused, a few upset, and the youngest were clinging to their parents and crying.

No one had sugarcoated anything. No one had pretended that this situation was anything other than what it was. Such wasn't the way with Bideshi children. From the earliest moment, where possible, they were told the truth.

This was a dark time. There might be light at its end, but for now they would all have to be strong and bear the hardships ahead. They wouldn't bear them alone. No Bideshi on a homeship was ever alone.

Nkiruka stood in the high gallery that ran along the wall of the bay, her hands on the railing, and let the sadness of the moment wash through her. She didn't want to, would have rather done almost anything else, but she was an Aalim. These were *her* children, and as such she had to stand witness. When she accepted this role, she had known on some level that it might include things this difficult, but she could never have been prepared for it, and now she wondered if that was her failing. At not even thirty years of age, she was no Old Mother. Every Aalim began somewhere, most of them not much older than her, but in times like this? When so much was at stake?

She wouldn't have been called if she weren't strong enough. Most of the time she believed that. But then there were times like these, when she was shaken by an awful helplessness, and a sense that she could no longer reach the people she was watching over.

Dark times indeed. She could think of no other time in Bideshi history—though it was true that there was much that had been lost—when it had become necessary to separate families this way. To send them away from the convoy, given that it had proven impossible—at present—to reach Suzaku and Jakana.

They were having to become more and more flexible.

"They'll be all right."

A quiet voice behind her—deep, solid, from a large and solid man despite his now-considerable years. Nkiruka felt a warm, heavy hand on her shoulder for a moment and smiled, though the smile was still pained.

"Hello, Adisa."

"I thought you might be here. And I thought you could probably use some company."

He drew up beside her, a presence she found instantly grounding. Since long before she took her place as Aalim, she had looked to Adisa as most people on Ashwina did: he was a leader, though mostly an informal one; a wise and just man; a kind man; a friend. He had come to her when she had been struggling with the choice—and in the end it had not been so much of a choice—between accepting the role of Aalim or keeping her life as it was, and the love of the woman she had meant to marry.

He hadn't forced her hand. He never would have done that. But he had told her truths. His own. The love he himself had given up in order to be the leader his people needed, and so that the woman he loved could take her place as Aalim.

If there was one man on the homeship who understood the terrible price of doing the right thing, it was probably him.

"It must be done," she said softly.

"Yes. And other things must as well. Things we won't regard any more favorably." In her mind, his gaze was both warm and penetrating. "You're ready for the meeting?"

"I've *been* ready," she said, a little dryly. And so she had. For the last two days she'd been preparing herself—meditating, consulting sacred texts, and considering the movements of the stars and what they might reveal.

She couldn't see a future, not clearly. It had always been difficult for her, but now it was practically impossible. That doubt attacked her again—she *needed* to see. That was why she was here. That was her purpose, what she had been called to do—what she had sacrificed a future of love and companionship for. That she might not be able to find her sight now . . . It gnawed at her. Now she said as much, and she sensed Adisa's mood alter subtly. To concern . . .

And recognition.

"You're not surprised."

For a moment he didn't answer. The hum of voices below them continued, and she felt the turmoil in their owners—the pain, the worry, the fear, the loss. The hope, desperate and fierce, that everyone might be reunited in the end. She let it flow into her, and let the silence play itself out. He would answer her when he was ready.

"Ixchel," he said at last. "Before Adam came. Some time before. She told me the future was hiding itself from her. Or . . . not hiding. But there were complexities. Greater ones than even she could untangle. It was part of why she was certain the situation was approaching a—a point of reckoning." He let out a soft breath that was almost a laugh. "And she was correct."

"This fight began on the Plain. The point is still ahead." She knew. She knew it to her very bones.

Adisa gave her a tight smile. "Yes. I'm beginning to see that."

"As time goes on, possibilities will foreclose on themselves," Nkiruka murmured. This, too, she saw. Felt. "We open some doors and we close others. Paths branch, extend, and grow, and at present it's difficult for me to see even a few steps ahead. Everything is in flux." She took a breath. "But things will narrow. Rapidly. After that point we'll be locked into whatever comes. No choices except to do what we can with what's in front of us."

She sensed Adisa's smile as if she were touching his lips, the stretch and the change in his affect. "We've been there before."

"Yes. But not like this." She was silent another moment, then gathered herself and turned. "There's nothing more for me to see here. I should meditate before the meeting."

She was near the short corridor that would lead her to the stairway down when Adisa called her name, and she halted and swung around.

"What is it?"

"Ixchel," he said, and hesitated. Then, "She tried to keep a balance within herself. She had a way of making it look easy. But she struggled.

Few knew it, but she did. At the end she couldn't hide anymore. When Adam came to us, when she began to see what was coming . . . She was afraid. She was strong, and she was certain of what was right, but she was still afraid, and I think she felt the confrontation on the Plain as a burden on her shoulders. She carried more than her share of the weight."

He moved toward her, and once again laid a hand gently on her shoulder. "I know you as an Aalim now, Nkiru. But I also knew you as a woman. A young one. You're still finding your balance. It's the way of an Aalim to take on heavy responsibilities, heavier than most can bear. And you will find that balance. I have every confidence in it. But take care of yourself. I already see Adam bearing that same weight, in pain because of it, and I fear for him."

She stiffened—or not quite, but a brief wave of tension rolled through her.

"I'm helping him." She laid a hand over Adisa's and squeezed, giving him a soft, sad smile. "He has a true heart. That's part of the problem. And he thinks he should have more control than he does. He's not good at letting go."

"Neither are you."

"No. Never have been." She gave Adisa's hand a final squeeze and slipped free, turning once more to go. "We'll all care for each other, Old Bear." She used the name with a touch of warm amusement, and again she could feel his smile. "That's the only way we'll survive. Any of us."

She left him and went to her meditations.

The meeting took place in Ashwina's council chamber, and it was total chaos.

It was made up of Ashwina's council—now four women and four men, including Adisa and Nkiruka—along with Leila and Kae, Rachel and Aarons, Kyle and Eva, Adam and Lochlan as more general leaders. The others were the nineteen captains of the ships of the fleet—a somewhat motley crew made up of a Protectorate civilians and peacekeepers alike, with wildly differing levels of training and experience.

Many of them didn't especially like each other. Now, in even more dire straits and with even more to disagree about, the tension was getting ugly, and it was giving Nkiruka a headache. She sighed, rubbing her temples with her fingertips, and felt the sympathetic looks from all of them, especially from Adisa.

Satya had always known how to massage these away.

"Should just pull back," someone snapped. "This is pointless, we can't—"

"—for a while now," someone else cut in, voice rising. "We've been lucky, but we—"

"—just need to hold fast. They got us this one time, but that doesn't mean—"

"—every time we hit them, we're stronger for it. Doesn't it make sense to keep—"

"—we're *weaker* now. Do you really want to wait and see what happens when we lose others—"

"—I have angry people on my ship. They want to know when we're going to—"

"—how many more funerals before—"

"*Enough.*"

Silence, profound and immediate. For half a moment Nkiruka wondered who had spoken. She had always been possessed of confidence, as any Bideshi defensive fighter needed to be, but she had never been the kind of person to take hold of an entire room like this.

Then again, she had changed. Had grown. She'd been questioning how much, but the worry and the frustration had transmuted themselves into a weary strength. Not the best source of power, but she would take whatever she could find.

She dropped her hands away from her head and rose to her feet. She was not a tall woman, but now it was as if she towered above the rest of them, and for the moment her own doubts faded into the background.

"How do you expect to do *anything* useful when you can't even speak one at a time? Like squabbling children. Worse, even. We could bring the children of Ashwina in here and accomplish more in five minutes than we have in ten of listening to you all carry on. Get yourselves together."

She said this last with hard scorn, scorn that she felt fully . . . and it seemed to come from somewhere beyond herself. Somewhere older, wiser, and of different temperament.

It seemed that Ixchel had still not left her. Not entirely. Regardless of whether she was strong enough to do this on her own, evidently she *wasn't* entirely on her own.

"I know we've taken a blow. But if we can't hold fast in the face of that, then I'm not sure what we're all doing here. Honestly."

She dropped back into her seat, radiating disgust—intentionally. She *was* disgusted, and also resolved not to speak again unless she had to. Her headache was getting worse. She had played her role, but what good had it done?

Daughter, sometimes you simply won't know.

"All right, then," Adisa said presently, getting to his own feet with a soft rustle of his robes. "So. Let's try to actually *accomplish* something."

The meeting proceeded in a much more orderly fashion after that, though clearly with grudges held on multiple sides. Some wanted to continue the raids. Others—Kae and Rachel and Aarons among the loudest—were pushing for new strategies. More than one person brought up Kae and Aarons's point: the size of the fleet and its meager firepower were problems that would likely not improve fast enough.

As they continued, Adam's presence grew heavier and heavier at her back. She tried to reach for him, tried to lend him some strength, but couldn't tell if it was working. Often she could sense things like that, sense *him*—such was the nature of the bond they appeared to be developing—but whatever strength had come into her was slipping away. At last she heard him rising, heard Lochlan rising with him, heard them heading together for the door.

She was troubled. There was cause for it. There was also little, at the moment, that she could do.

The discussion wore on, and the argumentative atmosphere subsided. Slowly, as usual, Rachel and Aarons emerged as the dominant parties, and, like sanding down a block of wood, consensus emerged. The fleet needed to rest, recuperate, and take time to plan its next move. They also needed more information, though scouting trips into Protectorate space seemed like questionable moves. They could draw supplies from the other Bideshi homeships, but only a limited amount. That left them with essentially only one choice.

The frontier.

This was a specific stretch of space on the outermost edge of the Protectorate's sphere of control, far enough from anything that that control was thin at best. It contained a fair number of colonized worlds—but humans maintained no supremacy whatsoever. They were simply one more species.

The inhabitants were rough, frequently violent, without much in the way of principle, and usually loyal to themselves and perhaps a select few others. But one thing united most of them.

No one liked the Protectorate.

Yes, it was the kind of place people in their situation would go. It made sense that they might be hunted there. But, Aarons pointed out, that would be true anywhere. At least out there they might find aid, and people who might be willing to hide them. For a price.

"Well, about that," a captain said—Tamara, one of the women who had escaped the quarantine camp in that first great liberation. One of the smarter captains, Nkiruka knew, even though she wasn't closely acquainted with the woman. Apparently the captain was good at weighing costs and benefits. "They'll want payment. What do we have to pay *with*? I've heard they mostly stick to gold and ore out there. Do we have either?"

"We have *ships*," Aarons said calmly. "We don't need to cannibalize 'em. A little judicious scavenging here and there, some trading for parts . . . Anyway." He smiled. "Remember what I used to do before all this. Contacts in low places were always a plus. I know people."

"You trust these . . . people?"

Aarons gave her a look. "Captain, out there I wouldn't trust anyone. Doesn't mean we can't deal with 'em."

This was met with dubious muttering, but no outright argument. What else was there to do?

The meeting broke up with a plan of action: remain in the system for two more days to rest and recuperate, then ride in slipstream to one of the less populated frontier systems and see what they could trade for in the way of supplies and information.

Nkiruka watched them file out of the council chamber, as they went to the meal that had been prepared for them in one of the lower-level halls.

"I think we might lose more," she murmured. Kae and Leila, Aarons and Rachel, Kyle and Eva, and Adisa had drawn closer to her. Rachel and Aarons had been talking quietly together, but they fell silent when Nkiruka spoke. "They're mad enough, some of them. They didn't leave with the homeships, but they might leave for a station."

"You think just people?" Eva sounded tense. No wonder.

Nkiruka shook her head. "I think maybe entire ships."

"But you don't know."

"I don't know anything. Not for sure. What I'm telling you . . . Tell me you weren't thinking the same thing."

"Yeah." Kae sighed. "We can only do what we can do. Leila and I will check on the wings, make sure they're getting the repairs they need." He turned. "Get in touch if there's anything else I need to know."

"I need to *sleep*," Rachel muttered. "Shit, I have no idea when I last *did*."

"We all need to." Aarons's voice was heavy. There was a shift and shiver in the air as his hand moved, settling against Rachel's back. "C'mon. At least we can lie quiet for a bit."

Then it was just Kyle, Eva, Adisa, and her.

"Adam left," Kyle said quietly.

"I know. I felt him go."

"Everyone's worried." Eva touched Nkiruka's arm, and her worry pulled at her, at both of them, flowing between them like a tight muscle gripping another.

"I'll talk to him. We'll be talking a lot." Nkiruka took Eva's hand, gave it a squeeze. She knew about the child, had known since she met the woman, but wasn't her place to say anything about it. Not yet. If ever. "For now I'll let him be. It may be he'll come to me in his own time."

"I hope so." Eva drew gently back and raked a hand through her hair. "Because when it comes to time . . . We're running short."

Adam turned over and stared at the ceiling's soft, ambient glow.

Lochlan stirred beside him and pushed himself up onto his side, his head leaning on one hand. He had been dozing, judging by the depth of his breathing. Now, caught by that soft light, his dark eyes were bright and aware.

"*Chusile.*"

"I'm fine." Adam sat up and pulled his knees against his chest. "I mean . . . No. I'm not fine. You know I'm not fine." He rubbed both hands down his face, and the light, comforting weight of Lochlan's hand landed on his back.

"Look, you can't keep beating yourself up over—"

Adam shook his head. "It's not that. Not this time." Maybe, if he was honest, this tension had been here for a while. Selfish, but Nkiruka had implied that he should be a different brand of selfish now. "Lock . . . When I married you, I did that for a reason."

"Because I'm devastatingly attractive and amazing in bed and you can't bear the thought that I might ever slip away from you?"

Adam smiled. It felt good. It felt *tethering.* They hadn't lost the past or its joys. It was with them still, and he could still reach it within himself. And in this man. "Well, *yeah,* but there were other reasons too."

Lochlan wrapped his arms around Adam's middle, chin on the ridge of his shoulder. He was solid and warm, and Adam relaxed against him. "All right. Tell me."

Adam took a breath. This   Perhaps when he had made the decision to say those vows, to take that step, he hadn't really thought of this. Not consciously. But watching the children leave, knowing that they might never come back . . . He had confronted the future's essential fragility. Futures were endlessly changeable. Sometimes plans seemed like the most profound foolishness.

Yet what else were promises and vows but lines drawn into the future? Lines held fast.

"I never thought about the rest of my life," he murmured. "After I got sick. After I ran. It was all . . . just day to day. Surviving. I knew I wouldn't even be able to keep it up for that long. By the time you found me, it was . . . it was habit. I wasn't thinking about why I was staying alive. I didn't have anything to live *for.* But then there was you, and I . . ."

He sighed and leaned back a little further, and Lochlan held him, listening in silence. Letting him find his own way to what he needed to say.

"I want a future. Now. Isn't that hilarious?" And he laughed thinly. "I don't know what *kind* of future. I don't know if I want a family . . . I don't even know how that would happen. Or if I just want to try to make a home. Find something stable. Real. I know this *is* a home, and I know I have you, and that's amazing, but . . ." He closed his eyes. Like this, he felt almost weightless. "Lock, I still feel like I'm living day to day. We all are. We have to, I'm not saying we call this off or back down. But I'm tired. I'm just so tired."

"I know." Slow kiss to his shoulder, and soothing warmth spread out around it. What was looming behind his tension wouldn't be chased away, but Lochlan had a way of pushing it away. He always had. Even in the beginning, when he had been rough and maddening and basically an asshole, and had put up a valiant front of not liking Adam much at all.

Somehow, even in the midst of all that, he had managed to make things better.

"I never thought about that either." Lochlan took a long breath, settling further, leg sliding along Adam's. "I mean . . . *the future* was this idea for other people. Maybe I was afraid of it. I dunno. But you . . . you changed a lot. Guess that's fair." Adam felt him smile. "Sure as hell never thought I'd be getting *married, chusile.*"

"You asked me."

"I did."

"What did you want, when you did?"

"I . . ." Lochlan hesitated, but Adam didn't for a moment think it was because he hadn't thought it through. Lochlan might have once been impulsive, but that had changed since the Plain. He would have a reason. *Did* have a reason.

"I wanted to be with you," he said, still soft. "That simple. Not just—not just then. Not just the next day, not the day after that. I don't know if people get to be together *forever*. I rather fancy they don't. But I want to be with you for as long as we have. However long that is." Again that smile, and though Adam couldn't see it, he sensed something bittersweet in it. "I hope it's the same reason you said yes."

"It is." Adam's eyes were still closed, but lights were swelling into being and dying away again behind his lids. They were coming more frequently now. He didn't know what they were or why they were happening, but they were grounding. Even as they frightened him, as they tugged him somewhere distant and unknown. "But there's also . . . Look, assume we make it through this. Assume we live, whatever happens. Assume everything doesn't end in ruins. What do you want then?"

Lochlan was quiet, and the quiet stretched out. Though Adam had no obvious reason for it, a thread of unease tightened in his middle.

"I told you. I never really thought about it. I'm—I'm not sure. A life? A life with you. I don't know about a baby and boring sex once a week and early to bed, but . . ." That familiar grin was working its way into his voice as he spoke, but to Adam it sounded a little desperate. "I'm not saying I'm not open to those things, mind."

"Except the sex part."

"Of course."

Another stretch of silence, and the thread of unease loosened. Adam began to float toward drowsing. Then, in a low rumble at his back, Lochlan spoke again.

"You want something to fight for, don't you? No . . . not want. You need something."

Adam stirred, though he didn't open his eyes. It was as if he was being pierced—gently, slowly. No pain, but Lochlan was touching something deep inside him, and his aim was good. "You don't think I already have something?"

Lochlan breathed a laugh. "*Mitr* . . . I'm not a fool. And I know you. You want to help. You've always wanted to do the right thing. You know that drives me crazy. But you're also pulling away. I feel it." His tone sobered. "I feel . . . Adam, you're holding on, but I think it's getting harder for you."

He paused again, and Adam knew what was coming. Lochlan had already said it in several different ways, and even if he hadn't . . . Adam knew him too.

"*Chusile*, I'm afraid for you. You're—you're going into something. I can feel it. You're becoming something different. I'm with you sometimes, and I . . . I feel like you're far away. Getting farther. I don't know if I can follow you there. The truth is . . . Adam, this is changing all of us, but I think it's changing you more than anyone. I don't know who you'll be, if we make it that far."

Lochlan was always blunt, but it could be hard to get truths out of him. Now they were coming easily. But Adam could hear pain in them.

"I don't know either," he murmured, and said nothing else.

So much of the change was due to Nkiruka and what he was doing with her. What he felt compelled to do, even though it frightened him. Ever since the Plain, ever since he had found something in himself that was like an Aalim, if not exactly the same, he had been drawn to this. Healing. Visions. What he had done on Peris, flying with the fighters and lending them strength and focus. What he had done with the raids since then. What he had decided to continue doing, what he felt he must.

He had changed when the Plain had healed him—when he had healed himself. For a time, he had believed the change was over.

It wasn't. He no longer felt like a man from the Protectorate. He didn't feel like he had become someone adopted and Named by the Bideshi, someone who might be assimilating, despite his doubts.

He was becoming something neither. Other. He was coming unmoored and drifting into the dark.

Lochlan held him tighter. "I'm not saying you should stop. I wouldn't say that. I just . . . I'm afraid."

"I am too," Adam whispered, and he turned in Lochlan's arms, pressed his face into the hollow of his throat, and let the embrace push it all back. Just for a little longer.

But I'll fight.

I'll fight for this.

CHAPTER

SIX

Terra was beautiful.

It hung in the dark like a jewel, like a pearl plucked from the wide oceans of Juno. Sinder stood beside Julius, gazing at the viewscreen and watching as soft clouds swirled across its surface, highlighting its blues and greens and bronzes. Once it hadn't been the way it was now: stricken with storms of increasing intensity, heat and rising sea levels, felled forests, bad air and water. It had been a garden trashed and ruined by foolish children, brought nearly to the point of no return before the children had been swept away by the ascendant new order, the gardeners. Lovers of beauty for the sake of beauty, of life and sustainability. And maybe now what they had made was threatened, maybe it was teetering and might fall, but the foundations were not lies, and he would *not* see them saved by a traitor. By someone who had consorted with those whose treachery dated from the beginning.

The time when this world was saved.

And if he was doing a little consorting of his own . . . Surely it wasn't the same. He owed Julius no allegiance. The man was a tool. Nothing more.

In the end Sinder would wash his hands clean and all would be well. He could *make* it be well through the sheer force of his will. And some good fortune had come to him regarding that task. Some additional information, which he intended to make use of as soon as possible.

"It's exactly as I thought it would be," Julius breathed from beside him. He sounded disturbingly eager. "How soon until we make planetfall?"

"We'll dock with New Horizon Station and take a shuttle down from there. There are customs procedures to follow." Sinder shot him a look. Customs was going to be an interesting process. He wasn't worried about his ability to get Julius through and onto the planet, but it would take a deft hand. "Obviously we're rather particular about who gets to come here."

"Even among your own people?"

"Of course. At least when they come in from outside."

Julius regarded him with his usual penetrating gaze—which Sinder was liking less and less. It felt like tiny fingers skittering along under his skin. "You're concerned . . . About what? Disease? Are these procedures new? Aren't you all supposed to be engineered to be immune to practically everything?"

"Practically." Sinder couldn't entirely keep the chill out of his voice. "As I said, they're customs."

"Ah." Now Julius sounded positively amused. "Customary customs."

Unspoken, but as clear as if he had: *You don't question these things. Well, I'm going to be rude enough to do so. Because I can.*

Customs did end up requiring a deft hand, but Sinder's hand was quite deft. Plus, he hadn't been lying when he said he had managed to amass a fair degree of authority in the three months since Peris. Subtly, without anyone even noticing, he'd traded favors for favors, put people in his debt, and whispered in the right ears. Peris had been an embarrassment, and for anyone else it might have damaged their career, but he had managed to spin things to his favor and shift the blame to Captain Alkor—he had done what he could to stop her foolishness and had convinced her to pull back, avoiding greater losses. What he had seen had only strengthened his resolve, and didn't he now understand the psychology of these rogue defectives? Wasn't he the best positioned to hunt them? Thrown for a considerable loop and eager to move on, people had tended to agree.

In the pursuit of this, he had begun communicating regularly with the ancient, senile lords who made their home here. He had familiarized himself with the workings of what remained of their minds, and how to use them to his best advantage. He had discovered other methods of manipulation regarding the people around him— because everyone had their weaknesses. Pride. Greed. Envy. Lusts better kept secret. Or merely weakness of mind and will—and those were appalling. The defectives were one thing, but Protectorate citizens who were weak in that sense sickened him to his marrow.

He had discovered just how to get his way. He had practiced these skills. And he hadn't been unskilled to begin with.

A small favor. I know it's irregular but I have special dispensation . . . I wouldn't come to you if I didn't know you were the only person I could trust. Times being what they are . . . Yes, we must all be flexible. Perhaps more than is strictly comfortable. I won't forget this. I have the ear of certain people. There are things that would make your job easier, surely. Tell me and I'll see what I can do. No, I don't want anything now. Just remember we had this discussion.

And, when necessary: *It would be very unfortunate if the wrong people were to find out about this. Wouldn't it?*

It became clear to him that the networks of Protectorate authority were beginning to break down, through growing unease and an increasing awareness that something was wrong. This was the greater illness, for a healthy network of power should be able to withstand the disease they faced. This weakness of spirit was the real sickness that Adam Yuga and his people had threatened them with, and they hadn't taken care of it when they had the chance, because of some—in hindsight—foolish perceived need to take Adam alive.

As if he could tell them anything that wasn't already plain to see.

So with the right application of convincing and subtle threatening, Julius d'Bideshi was allowed through customs, and less than two hours after that, he, Sinder, and an escort of four Protectorate peacekeepers were seated in a shuttle, dropping swiftly and smoothly toward the planet's surface.

The shuttle was compact but luxurious in an understated way, the seats plush and many small, internal, decorative features made of rich, glossy wood where it would have been easier and cheaper to make them from something else. A cabinet set into the bulkhead at Sinder's elbow would, he knew, open to discharge a crystal decanter full of Albaran brandy and several glasses.

It wasn't even as if the larger commuter shuttles that ran to and from the surface were shabby things. Terra was, if no longer the true seat of political power, the center of Protectorate wealth and culture— the Protector who had first established the empire. However, real political power, everyone knew, now rested on the mining planet Kolyma due to its rich Trithosite deposits, which allowed space travel of the magnitude the Protectorate required. Gradually authority had slipped away from Terra to a planet which, if it weren't for its natural resources, would have languished in total obscurity.

But Kolyma was a desert world. Possessed of its own stark beauty, yes, but in his short time there, Sinder had decided that he didn't share his colleagues' enthusiasm.

He wanted Terra. Yes, he wanted power and position, but most of all he wanted the heart of this majestic society he believed in so utterly. And now, looking out the shuttle window at the glittering swaths of cities that stretched across the land beneath them, that desire hit him in the chest like a physical blow.

He was home. His blood and heart and soul were here.

The planet and everything it meant.

"You seem preoccupied," Julius said quietly. Sinder started—and was immediately annoyed with himself for doing so. He couldn't allow himself to slip like that. Not with this man.

He turned his gaze away from the window and directed it at Julius seated opposite him, who sat with his hands clasped in his lap, his expression bland. "I was just thinking how good it was to be back."

No reason not to be honest.

"I see." Julius inclined his head and regarded Sinder with obvious interest. "That's fascinating to me. It always has been. You know those I once considered my people call you *raya*. Or at least the less polite among them."

"I do. And before you ask, yes, I do know what it means."

"I would have been surprised if you didn't. You seem like the kind of man who makes it his business to know things." Julius smiled and looked out his own window—or seemed to. For a second Sinder could see the shining towers of the enormous metropolis below reflected clearly in the man's blind eyes. "You know *why* the Bideshi call you that?"

"They feel scorn for anyone who calls a singular place a home."

Julius shook his head but didn't turn back to Sinder. "It's not that simple. They interact with many species who hold one planet as home, and feel nothing but respect for them. It isn't a rejection of a general way of life, Isaac. It's a specific rejection of *yours*."

Before Sinder could think of a response, Julius smiled again—a good deal less pleasantly. "If you asked them, they would say they regard your inflexibility as a weakness—your inflexibility. Something they shed a long time ago. But if you remember, they practically *fled* this world. Maybe they made the choice to leave, but they were running from a place that was losing its tolerance for who they wanted to be. They didn't *choose* to leave. All they chose was when and how they left."

Sinder arched a brow. "Your point?"

"My point, Isaac, is this. When they call you *raya,* they're expressing contempt, scorn . . . absolutely, all those things and more. But those things are coming from a place of *envy.*" Julius leaned forward, and that unpleasant smile was still playing about his lips. "Terra is their endgame. They want it. That weakness in all of you, in everything the Protectorate is . . . They see it. They'll exploit it. They'll seize their chance, and they'll come."

There was a moment of silence. Sinder met his gaze—met it and held it. Julius might be blind, at least in every technical sense, but Sinder would be damned if he looked away. It would be betrayal.

At last he returned the smile. "Well. It's a good thing we have you, then."

Julius sat back, his steepled fingertips just touching his lips. "Indeed."

Although the more ceremonial officials and administrators of Protectorate government made their homes in nearly every city on Terra, the capital, for all intents and purposes, was the ancient city of Beijing. Immense, covering many hundreds of miles, Beijing was also dense with cloud-piercing towers stacked together. Groundcars filled the streets, while aircars hummed overhead in regular, carefully maintained lanes. The city should have been chaos, and on another world it might have been, but instead it was orderly, lovely, and gleaming, even elegant. Large, meticulously arranged gardens spread over many of the rooftops and descended from step-like terraces. The towers themselves were crystalline, possessing all the pristine beauty of cut diamonds, delicate in many places despite their size. Each building, each room, had been designed and constructed with the goal of catching every beam of sunlight possible.

Standing before a floor-to-ceiling window, Sinder gazed at the city from the office that had been set aside for him in one of main administrative buildings. He was entranced. Enthralled. Love gripped him by the heart.

He wouldn't see this place sullied. He wouldn't see it poisoned by uncleanliness, unholiness. What there was would be purged. Whatever else had to be done . . .

He would darken his own spirit to protect this world. He would make of himself a sacrificial lamb, his sacrifice all the greater and more profound because of his spirit's fundamental purity.

Sinder smiled to himself, darkly amused to be thinking in such mystical, religious terms. It was almost blasphemy.

But he was already guilty of that. If one could be *guilty* of taking on the tasks of a savior.

"It's a great deal more impressive than I imagined," Julius said from behind him. He was seated in a chair before Sinder's broad and semitransparent desk, his hands once more clasped in his lap. He was still wearing the loose clothes he had traveled in, and it was becoming apparent that he had the ability to make himself comfortable even when he was out of place.

Sinder laid a hand on the glass, his attention remaining on what was beyond it. The sun was going down, turning all the towers gleaming shades of pink and red and gold. Like flames rising above the city.

"And what did you imagine?"

"I'm not sure. Perhaps I imagined nothing in particular. I try, where possible, to enter new situations with as few preconceptions as possible. I find it allows me a greater degree of flexibility."

It was a good philosophy. Sinder would allow that. Flexibility was its own virtue. He might know that better than most people.

He and Julius had that in common. Life had forced the knowledge on them both.

"So what's our business here? You haven't been exactly free with that information."

Sinder didn't immediately answer. He had his own ideas, his own goals, and to him they were clear ones, but he had yet to decide how to articulate them to others. In truth, he hadn't anticipated that he'd need to.

It made sense that Julius would want to know, and he wasn't a man to be easily brushed off.

"There are some people I need to speak to," he said slowly. "People I need to consult."

He turned just in time to see Julius arch a brow. "You couldn't communicate with them at a distance?"

Sinder shook his head. "I have to meet with them face-to-face. We have to be in the same room, feel each other's presence. Surely you of all people can see the advantage in that."

Julius inclined his head. "Granted. But why else? Because you have other reasons. I can feel it in you."

Of course he could. Perhaps it was an ability he didn't even need to consciously deploy anymore. Perhaps it was as intrinsic to his strange, given sight as any other part of it.

"I wanted you to see this place," Sinder said after another brief pause. "I wanted you to *know* what I'm protecting. What's at stake for me. I know you don't value it the way I do. I didn't expect you to, and it makes no difference—as far as I can see—in terms of the end result. But I wanted you to know all the same. What I'd do to see this preserved. How far I'd go."

"As far as bringing me to it," Julius murmured. "Blaspheming against it with my very presence. You really are a curious one, Sinder."

"There's more than one kind of blasphemy."

"That you people conceive of any kind is fascinating to me." The corner of his mouth twitched. "You look down on *superstition*, but you have your own superstitions. Your own conceptions of the sacred. The profane. Me being here should make no difference at all where the well-being of your society is concerned. I'm a single man. Yet to you—to any one of you—it matters deeply."

Sinder didn't argue. Instead he nodded over his shoulder. He had his own questions, his own fascinations to explore. "What do you see? With those eyes that were burned into you? What do they reveal?"

Slowly, Julius rose and came to the window, standing beside Sinder. And as Sinder had done, he laid a hand on the glass and closed his eyes.

"I see light," he said after a moment. "A tremendous amount of light. Brilliance. Radiance. Your world is a world of light, Isaac Sinder." He paused, frowned, then went on. "I see structures. Towers. The physical towers of this city, and others too. Towers within the towers. The true structures that make all this light possible, that hold it up. They're beautiful. Intricate. Profoundly complex. It's as if I'm perceiving a tapestry, one whose threads are woven into the past."

His frown deepened. "But those structures are weakening. Not too severely yet, but greater severity is coming. Their foundations are wobbling. Cracks are running through." He opened his eyes, and though he didn't look at Sinder, Sinder could feel his gaze. "For all the skill of your people, all their technique, all you *know* . . . These foundations are built on faith, aren't they? As gods need devoted worshippers or their existence is threatened, if enough of your people lose faith, suspect that these foundations are built upon sand . . ."

Sinder's gut clenched, sudden cold flooding through him. He was prepared to tolerate a great deal—had already done so—but there were some insults he wouldn't bear in silence. "They aren't built on *sand*. Those *foundations* have held our world up for centuries."

"Regardless. All of this is in danger. All this light. All this life." Julius paused again, brow furrowed thoughtfully. "And you maintain that there's nothing to be gained from considering whatever Adam Yuga did to heal himself and so many others?"

"We'll find our own way. We always have."

"Yet if you make use of me . . ." Thin amusement crept into Julius's voice. "Is that really so different?"

Yes, it was. The difference was crucial, and Sinder's jaw tightened with irritation; Julius should be able to see it. "You're not a traitor."

"To your people? No. To my own . . . I think some of them might disagree. But then, I doubt you care very much what they think."

Sinder felt his lips pull into a humorless smile. "You're correct."

For a few minutes neither of them spoke. Sinder was sure his affect was calm, neutral, but inside he was full of swirling thoughts, ideas . . .

Doubts?

Doubts were a luxury he couldn't afford at the moment. One of the few. And in any case, he wouldn't entertain them even if he could. He was above them. Doubts were for lesser men.

"Do you find it entertaining," he asked, "to question everything I do?"

"Not everything. I simply like to know what I'm dealing with." Julius turned away from the window and returned to the chair, but didn't sit. He stood, one hand on its back, and appeared to be looking around the room—which was spacious, furnished simply, devoid of any particular decorations, and utterly without personal effects. It rang with even the smallest sound and encouraged a kind of quiet. Nearly all its surfaces were at least somewhat reflective, sending light flying everywhere.

Light, indeed. Light permitted nothing to hide. It exposed. It was merciless. There was a great comfort in that lack of mercy. He felt a certain kinship with it.

"What would you have me do next?"

"Currently?" Sinder shook his head. "Nothing. I have work of my own to attend to. If you have any . . . meditations, any rituals you need to perform to strengthen your *skills*, you could—"

Julius laughed. "Even now you find it distasteful."

It *was* distasteful. But Sinder was tired of the argument. "We've established apartments for you in one of the best hotels in the city. I'll have you escorted there, and I've assigned some people to you who'll see to it that you have everything you desire. Within reason, of course. And," he cleared his throat, "I would be appreciative if you could . . . keep to yourself. To the extent that it's possible."

"Hide, in other words." Julius held up a hand before Sinder had a chance to formulate a response. "Teasing aside, I understand. I do. It would be awkward for you if my presence here were generally known. It would be awkward for me as well. I have no desire to cause trouble."

Sinder ducked his head, nearly a bow. "I'm grateful, Julius. I truly am. I've assigned aides to you, and they'll be waiting for you in the hall. I've given them everything you need to know to contact me. Anywhere, anytime."

"I take it this is your polite way of suggesting that I go?"

"As I said," Sinder replied, keeping his voice cool and level. "I have things to attend to. The sooner I do so, the sooner we can move forward."

Julius turned to go. But he had just reached the tall door at the far end of the room when he paused and faced Sinder again.

"Isaac."

Sinder disliked being called by his first name, and especially by this man. It smacked of a familiarity he hadn't initiated. "Yes, Julius?"

"I'm sure your aides are there in part to spy on me." Once more he held up a hand. "I'm not insulted. Not at all. I would do the same in your position. Do whatever you need to do in order to feel secure about me." He smiled faintly. "That said . . ."

Sinder sensed him shift his attention toward the desk. For a moment there was nothing at all. Then the air itself seemed to shiver, almost to warble, something between a vibration and a sound that cut through Sinder's head and made his eyes water. He blinked, dizzy, and was about to ask Julius what the hell he thought he was doing when the desk cracked down the middle and shattered, glittering shards of it flying, bouncing across the floor, hitting the windows with noise like ringing chimes.

Dazed, Sinder stared at them as they settled, as the room fell silent. The shards were cloudy gray, and dimly he could see the outlines of the screens that had been set into the desk's surface, fragments of a darker shade. They caught the light and were lovely, lovely as anything else in this place.

Something warm trickled down his cheek. He lifted a hand to it, and his fingers came away slicked red. He turned to Julius again, speechless.

"Look," Julius said quietly. "But don't touch, Isaac. Don't you dare touch."

He went out.

CHAPTER

SEVEN

E va leaned back against the ancient bulkhead and sighed, pushing her hair out of her face. She was tired, but that made her neither special nor unusual. The entire fleet was tired. Everyone who could was working on the ships, removing components and fitting new—or at least better—ones into place, taking inventory and figuring out what they could afford to lose. Afford to trade.

Here she was on what was essentially a garbage scow refitted as a barracks ship with guns strapped to its underside, helping with one of those inventories, and she got the distinct feeling that no one on board was especially fond of her.

Or at least, no one on board was fond of this. It wasn't her fault. Surely they knew that. They had *agreed* to this. But they seemed to be looking for someone to blame.

Well. She couldn't spend the next two hours trying to argue them out of doing so. She had already gotten into one heated argument with a technician about the state of the ship's CPU, and was licking her wounds behind a stack of crates, wishing she simply cared less.

"Eva?"

Kyle. She sighed again and closed her eyes. She was mostly taking a few moments to hide from the people they were supposedly assisting, but the truth was that she was also hiding from *him*, just a bit. He was worried about her, increasingly so since they had decided to stay, and she knew it came from the best part of him, but it wasn't helping her feel less worn down. She loved him, she did—but she was beginning to understand, in a way she hadn't, even when they had both been ill almost to the point of dying, that loving someone doesn't make them endlessly tolerable.

"I'm here," she called softly, and he came to her around a bend in the corridor, his brow furrowed.

"You all right?"

"Yeah." She gave him a smile, and it was small and a bit wan. "I just needed a few minutes. How long have we been here?"

"A couple hours or so. Listen, if you want to head back, maybe check out the station or something. I can take over here. There can't be that much more to do."

"I'm fine." She pushed away from the wall, squaring her shoulders and drawing herself up. It was a long time since she had served in the Protectorate starfleet—it felt like half a lifetime, easy—but there were parts of her training she hadn't forgotten. How to hold herself, how a certain stance would make her feel stronger. More focused. "Really, Kyle, I just . . . Someone has to do it."

"I want you to take care of yourself, is all," he said quietly as she made to pass him, to head back to the cargo bay where they had been going through storage.

A surge of irritation twisted at her gut. Hormones? Maybe. She was hesitant to blame body chemistry for this. She was *tired*, and that had been going on for a while now, though it was only in the last week or two that it had become impossible to ignore.

"I'm not *sick*," she said—snapped. "Shit, Kyle, even when I *was* sick you weren't doing this. I can handle work. I can handle what I have to do. So let me do it."

He stared at her, abashed, hurt and surprise and confusion evident on his face, and she unbent. A sliver of guilt jabbed her. She lowered her head and went to him, laid her hands on his shoulders and kissed the corner of his mouth. "I'm sorry. Like I said, I'm tired. But I'm all right. I really am. I know you're worried, and I know why, but . . . I am."

"No, I'm sorry." But he didn't sound as though he completely meant it. What she heard in his voice wasn't resentment, not quite. "Okay. I'll back off. You just *know* why I—"

"I do." She looked up at him, this kind, handsome man who never would have been able to be with her if they hadn't left the Protectorate—given how he outranked her, because in the Protectorate there were still differing degrees of perfection—and she was grateful for him. She was.

But irritated.

"I'm not sure I want to know what you'll be like in the third trimester," she said, all dry amusement. "So far you're handling it worse than I am."

"I'm just worried," he echoed, stepping away. "Should we go, then?"

They did, but as they walked back to the cargo bay, Eva stole a glance at him, noted the set of his jaw and the thinness of his mouth. He wasn't happy with her. He wasn't happy with anything.

Even in the first phases of a war, she thought wryly, there was time for trouble in paradise.

In the end she did go to the station, catching a lift on one of the smaller ships in their fleet, which was making a run there anyway. Eris Station wasn't large, but it was the center of commerce for the entire sector. It was crowded with sentients of various species and races, there to exchange news and goods, to drink and gamble and settle debts—with blood if not with goods or services, though she had it on good authority that the station's administration was draconian about controlling violence.

It suited the entire fleet just fine.

Kyle had returned to Ashwina, and there had been something pointed in the way he had allowed her to go off by herself. Nearly since the beginning of their relationship, he had kept close to her side almost every waking moment. His clinginess, she thought, came from long months on the run together, and then weeks of increasing illness, trying to take care of each other, depending on each other for survival of the spirit as well as the body. That closeness had lingered even after they had both been healed, and she hadn't thought anything of it.

If he was begging off accompanying her now . . .

It might be nothing. He might, like her, simply be overworked and overtired. But she didn't think so.

Oh, well. There was little to be done about it now. And she did want to see the station. Ashwina was massive, hardly claustrophobic, but it wasn't her home, they weren't her people, and now and then she felt penned in.

Pleasures were going to be few and far between for a while. Better take advantage, even of the mundane ones, while she could.

As she stepped out of the corridor and into the main part of the station, she scanned her surroundings. She was standing on the top of a double-leveled promenade lined with vendors and shops and people seething to and fro, heading into and out of the centers of business, the two large bars, and the docking rings. Kae and Aarons were with her, for the same reasons she had come, and she shot them something close to a grin as they exited the corridor that led to the docks and surveyed the scene in front of them.

"I'm heading right for the goddamn bar," Aarons said, and in his own gruff, restrained way he sounded eager. "Already got some contacts I think I can make there, and besides, it's been a while since I was in anything like what I'd call a *real* bar."

Kae gave him an amused look. "Noise and engine oil in glasses and occasional death threats, eh? I'll come with you. It's been a while for me too. Too bad Lochlan isn't here. Those always were second homes to him."

Eva went to the railing and surveyed the first level, considering the vendors and shops. Weapons and armor and ship parts, yes—and no doubt they would be dealing with those as much as they could afford to—but there were other things. Clothing, assorted curiosities, food. All of them of potential interest.

"Think I'll pass." She glanced back and indicated the lower level. "I'm going to take a turn down there. See if I find anything worth finding."

"Suit yourself," Aarons said, already turning to go. "Just make sure you're back in three hours. I didn't get the sense that the captain was inclined to stick around, and it would be a hassle if they left without us."

They parted. Eva headed down in one of the lifts, pressed between the cool, slick tentacles of a Sepiod and the hard carapace of a Koticki. They all spilled out when the doors opened, and Eva was happy enough to be caught in the flood. This was, in truth, one of the reasons why she had joined the peacekeepers in the first place: to go to new places, to see new people. To experience things she wouldn't otherwise have done. Terra had been lovely and comfortable, but growing up there, none of it had been novel by the time she hit her teens, and wanderlust had stirred in her.

But when she joined the peacekeepers, what she found instead was bland routine, little excitement, and for the most part the clean, gleaming, sterile interiors of battleships and cruisers. Aside from the occasional leave . . .

Now her life was, if not easy, at least interesting. And how ironic that when she first realized who Adam was and what he might mean, it had been when she was serving on the ship dedicated to pursuing him, finding him, and very possibly killing him.

It was difficult to predict where events would lead.

Without any specific goal in mind, she made her way down the rows of shops, examining the items in the windows and around the wide doors. Intense, conflicting smells wafted through the air, and a confusion of music beat gently but relentlessly at her ears. She also heard a wild mixture of languages: Standard, of course, and others most people spoke as close seconds, the Kotickis' clicking chatter among them, but there were more she only vaguely recognized, and several she could pick out but didn't know at all.

There was something weirdly comforting about it.

She had turned to look at a display of strange jewelry made of cut green stones when the shots rang out.

She whirled without thinking, hand on the small pistol strapped to her hip—violence was forbidden on the station but weapons were not.

The shots were coming from the upper level. Once again Eva's training reasserted itself and she was off and sprinting for the staircase she had seen on the far end of the chamber, shouldering her way past the frozen crowd. They were already heading toward cover when she reached it, and doing so with practiced calm; they all must be acquainted with gunfire, even if not in this context.

They weren't her concern. She tore up the stairs, her gun drawn and cocked. The lift would be too slow, and while she had no reason to be certain that the shots were directed at Kae and Aarons . . .

She was. Completely.

As she reached the top, she saw them hurrying toward her, their own weapons drawn. Kae turned, still running backward, and fired.

At a small group of men and women, following close on Kae's and Aarons's heels. They were dressed in plain clothes, clearly meant to hide their identities, but she marked the way they moved. The way they aimed and fired. It was unmistakable, drilled into their bodies.

Peacekeeper training.

If it had been by chance, they would probably have been in uniform. This was a surprise attack. An ambush.

They knew the fleet was here. In the sector. They knew the exact *station*.

She had no time to wonder how. She fired round after round and one of the men fell, a patch of blood spreading across his chest.

"Go!" she cried. "I'll give you covering fire."

"Who's going to cover *you*?" But Kae was already sprinting past her, Aarons in tow, and after a few seconds Eva followed them, still firing. The peacekeepers had ducked behind cover—a stack of crates, a couple of beams that extended from the wall, but Eva knew they wouldn't stay put, wouldn't be shaken off so easily. They would pursue.

And there was no telling how many more of them there were.

She lunged into the corridor, plunging down it, turning once and then again. A bullet ricocheted off the bulkhead to the left behind her. She skidded, almost fell, and Kae gripped her arm and kept her on her feet, pulling her along. They were close to their airlock now, and even that might not be safety, because it couldn't be that easy, but at least they could take a breath.

And Kae gave a hard hiss of pain and surprise, and his hands slipped from her.

She grabbed him, one arm around his chest and wedged under his arms, heard his cry of pain and saw blood blooming high on the right side of his chest.

Oh fuck, oh fuck oh fuck oh fuck. He was starting to go limp. Ahead, Aarons was punching the airlock open. He extended a hand, took hers, and dragged them both inside. There was a sharp ringing of ricochets just behind her, and then beside her head—and Kae jerked violently.

The airlock hissed closed. The opposite side opened and they stumbled into the main passenger compartment.

Aarons left them immediately, and Eva knew he must be heading for the cockpit. The ship was already lurching as the docking clamps disengaged. Eva lowered Kae into one of the seats and knelt in front of him, turning his head this way and that, trying to look at all of him at once.

And she didn't have to look for more than a split second to confirm what she already knew. Blood was soaking his shirt from the wound in his chest, and that was bad enough.

But blood was pouring down the right side of his head. And that was so much worse. As far as she could recall, there had been no collisions. She hadn't hit his head against anything as they ran.

Kae had been shot.

He was completely limp, his head lolling. With a horrible, numb calm, she took his wrist, felt for a pulse. The ship shuddered, rattled, and it was impossible to miss the sound of something impacting it.

She couldn't feel anything beneath her fingers. Not even a flutter.

A dull sob tore out of her and she held on to him, hands on his shoulders, trying to keep him upright in the seat. But the ship shuddered again, and Kae dropped into her arms. A cry came from the cockpit, surprised and pained. Eva closed her eyes.

There was nothing to pray to. And she wouldn't have prayed even if she could.

CHAPTER

EIGHT

Adam was sprinting to the docks when he nearly collided with Lochlan.

Lochlan briefly gripped him by the shoulders, but then they were both running again, running together. Two things drove them: that the fleet was clearly under attack, and that the ship bearing Kae and Aarons and Eva had docked—and there were casualties.

"Are we scrambling the wings?" Adam gasped as they skidded around a bend, heading down the central corridor that would take them to the docks. Others were rushing past them, faces drawn, frightened.

"*Mitr*, I don't know any more than you do."

If Kae was— Adam couldn't let himself think about it. But there was a chain of command. Someone else would take the wing if Kae—if he couldn't.

Adam shoved everything away and ran.

They burst out of the corridor into the main docking bay. The shuttle was scorched from multiple hits and what looked like small external fires—gases ejected into vacuum and burned off. The hull showed impact dents . . .

And holes.

"Line and orbit," Lochlan breathed, stepping forward, pushing his way through a clot of people. Adam slid through behind him. Not far away there were cries of "Ying! Ying's here, make way for her, for God's sake," and he knew the ship's healer must have come as fast as she could. That was good. That was—

A scream.

Lochlan skidded to a halt. Adam stumbled into him and caught himself with a hand on Lochlan's shoulder. Everyone around them had frozen, all looking in the same direction. Everything was still except for that scream—shocked, *anguished*—and then a name, cried by the same voice, cut through the air.

"*Kae. Kae*, no, oh my *God*, no."

Leila.

"*Fuck*," Lochlan hissed, tight with panic, and shoved his way forward again. Everyone had started moving, sound rising, voices, but Adam was barely aware of them. He hurried after Lochlan, not bothering to mutter apologies, and half stumbled through a wall of people and into the open space beyond.

Ying and four of her assistants were kneeling around two forms lying on the deck. Rachel and Kyle were standing nearby, Kyle's face twisted with agony and fear. Rachel's was a mask, stony, hard, but she was trembling, a deep tremor that ran from her shoulders down to her clenched fists.

And Leila. It had to be Leila, though Adam could barely see her. She was just a huddled shape, cradling one of the forms in her arms. Memories washed over him, almost powerful enough to physically rock him back. How he had been pressed into service when Ashwina was first attacked by Melissa Cosaire's peacekeeper fleet, shortly after the convoy had taken him in. When Kae's gunner had been killed. Taking his place in the turret, firing with uncanny precision. Solving equations of flying and trajectory. The hit on their ship—Kae, burned and bloody. In the clinic—Leila's bloodless cheeks, her red and swollen eyes.

Full circle, he thought dimly, stopping beside Lochlan and staring down at the two bodies on the deck. To his left, Rachel was dropping into a crouch. Bending forward to touch Aarons, fingers trailing through the blood painting his scarred face and matted in his graying hair.

And then there was Kae, who had much more blood on his head. Far too much. A neat hole high on his brow.

"No," Lochlan breathed. "No, that's . . ."

Leila's wails died into heavy sobs as she pulled Kae further into her arms, holding his head to her chest. Her hands, her face, her clothes, all stained red. Adam stared. Why couldn't he feel anything?

"Let me through." Ying, gently pushing him and Lochlan aside to kneel opposite Rachel. Lochlan teetered, nearly fell, and Adam caught him with an arm around his waist and bore him up. He was heavy, and Adam wondered if he might really fall. As he tried to tug his husband back, he saw Eva standing there across from Kae's and Aarons's bodies, staring blankly at the two of them.

No, not blankly. Her expression was numb. Exhausted. Her face was streaked with tears.

"Eva." Kyle rushed forward and pulled her into his arms. "You're . . . Are you—"

"I'm all right." She spoke low and dully, and it seemed strange that Adam could hear her over Leila's weeping. "I didn't . . . Kae got hit. I'm all right."

"I need you to get out of the *way*." Ying, quiet but hard, and Kyle looked at her as if seeing her for the first time. "*Now*, boy. If you can't, I'll have you removed."

"Kyle, c'mon." Eva taking Kyle's arm, Adam noted, as if from a distance. Lochlan was shuddering against him. He might be crying. Eva was gently ushering Kyle away even though her shoulders were slumped with weariness and her jaw was tight, the set of her mouth pained. "Let's . . . I need to sit down."

Clearly dazed, frightened, with tears in his eyes, Kyle allowed her to lead him off. As they passed, he met Adam's gaze and looked as if he might be about to say something. Adam stared silently back at him.

Then he was gone.

"*Chusile*," Lochlan whispered. "I have to go to him. I have to—"

"No, you don't. You can't do anything for him. Stay with me." The words came out flat. *Only two dead here*, he thought. *Only two dead, and how many times that have we just buried?* What did it mean that this felt so much worse? Was it just that he loved these people? Was that all?

Ying was bending over Kae, trying to tug his body free from Leila. Leila was holding on, shaking her head furiously. Leila the death dancer, so cool and collected that even her anger was normally both wild and controlled. He had never seen her like this. Never believed he would.

One of Ying's assistants was pressing Rachel back and kneeling beside Aarons, touching his face and turning his head, feeling for a pulse. The man frowned, snapped his head up.

"He's not dead. He's . . . distant, but with us."

Ying's head had been bowed, her hands framing Kae's bloody face as best she could with Leila clinging to him. Now she raised it, and her expression was impossible to describe.

"So is this one."

A new silence crashed down on them. Lochlan stumbled again and sucked in a harsh gasp.

"He's barely there, but he still is. We'll lose him if we don't get him to the clinic now. *Move.*" This time when she shoved Leila, she wasn't even remotely gentle, and Leila fell back, catching herself on one hand, her eyes wide and her mouth open in shock that seemed to transform her into someone Adam hardly recognized.

Still with us.

"Adam."

There was a soft touch on his arm. He turned his head, struggling to focus, and saw Nkiruka beckoning him. At the same time Ashwina shuddered and klaxons began to blare.

"I have to go," Lochlan murmured and stepped away. He was unsteady, but he was on his feet. Relief surged through Adam—and in fact it was a relief to feel *anything*—and a sharp ache under his breastbone that might have been any number of things. "*Chusile*, I have to—"

"I know. Go." Adam curved a hand over the nape of Lochlan's neck, pulled him in, and kissed him. "I'll be here when you get back."

Lochlan laughed, an awful, hollow sound, and spun. In seconds he was lost in the rush of people heading toward the fighters.

Adam turned to Nkiruka. The numbness was once again descending. Aarons was being lifted into a stretcher. Kae had already been carried away.

"They're coming out of slipstream," Nkiruka said calmly. "Too many of them. I need you. Can you help me? Can you do this?"

He might have hesitated. He might have needed time to think, time to work through his uncertainty. He might have needed time to confront his doubt. His fear.

But all he could see were the bloody faces of two men he had come to love.

"Yes," he said softly. "I can."

CHAPTER

NINE

There were too many.

Their fighters had been here before, Lochlan thought as he spun and wove and dove, evading fire and sending out his own. The rest of the wings had scrambled, and in spite of the circumstances, they had remained focused and they were all flying well. Picking targets, bringing them down where they could. Several small white Protectorate fighters had already dropped out of their formations, either in pieces or too badly damaged to continue fighting. *So perfect,* Lochlan had thought more than once with grim amusement, *so supposedly perfect and perfectly bred for what they are doing, yet our pilots can routinely fly all over them.*

But there were too many.

No more than he had seen at the Battle of the Plain. But perhaps as many, several larger cruisers and a couple of warships coming out of slipstream, carrying complements of smaller fighters. And Ashwina had a fleet on her side, to be sure—but it was a ragged fleet. Many of its ships had not originally been designed for combat, and in truth Ashwina had for a long time been *their* defender against any attackers.

And there were just too many.

Nothing's right. This shouldn't have happened. Lochlan went into a darting spin, dodging around a Protectorate fighter—which was better armed and armored but far more cumbersome—and blew off its primary guns. *Someone,* he thought vaguely as he arced back toward the rest of his wing, *someone must have told someone something.* Whispered in the correct ears. One of Aarons's contacts, perhaps. He said himself that he didn't trust them.

All of this was going on in a small part of his brain. The rest of him was lost in the fighting haze, the veil that gave the battle crystalline clarity. He rejoined his wing and then broke off again with three of the others, flying in a loose formation that would allow them to draw smaller ships out of their own groups and pen them in, pick them off—a common tactic when dealing with superior numbers.

Another Protectorate fighter pulled away from its fellow, tempted into chasing Lochlan as he made himself out to be an easy target, flying unsteadily, as if he had sustained damage. *Come and get me.* The other three speeding in from where they had been hovering, faster than the Protectorate ship could hope to outrun, one of them disabling it and the other two blowing apart the side of its hull. Lochlan saw two white-clothed bodies fly out into the vacuum and get lost in the debris.

The fleet had to get to slipstream. They had to. But they were too close to the station for that; they would have to pull back far enough, and all together. Share coordinates. They had planned for quick getaways, but not with a station as complication. Not with a third of their ships half dismantled.

Fuck.

He returned to his wing, which was prepping for an attack run on one of the cruisers. "Targeting secondary guns," came the word over the comm. Something to do. Something to focus on. Their job was to provide cover now. He could do that. It was something he could do.

All he could do.

The Arched Halls had meant peace to him.

Not anymore.

It had been during the first raids, when Nkiruka had suggested that what he had done at Peris—joining with her and the exiled Aalim Lakshmi to lend the Bideshi pilots focus and strength—might be done again with her help. He had been doubtful. He had been afraid. But he had gone with her and had done what he could, and had discovered that it was indeed possible.

The Halls were still a place of peace for many, but deep in their darkness, close to the impassible tangle that was their heart, they also became a place of war. And it was into that place Adam now followed her.

She set a fire—more for their mutual focus than anything else. Then she sat and he sat across from her, closed his eyes, and let himself sink into the negative colors of the flames that danced across the insides of his eyelids. Into the small heat, into the way it caressed his skin, into the way he could practically *feel* the shiver and the wave of the fire's movement.

He sensed her joining him in the burning dark, and together they bled through Ashwina's hull and flew into the fray.

Things slammed into him, with the impact of bodies: fear, panic, anger. Things the Bideshi pilots were controlling, but felt anyway, buried under their mental training, and now he could sense that behind those walls, all those emotions were threatening to break through.

He had to shore up those walls. Beat back the panic. Give them clear thinking, clear seeing. But shoring them up meant touching them. Feeling it. Letting it seep into him.

And he could only see Kae's bloody face. The hole in his head. The horrible pale limpness of his body.

Focus. Nkiruka pulled back, swirling around him, covering him like a blanket. Like an embrace. *Shore up your own walls, brother. You can't afford to fail. This is your way of fighting.*

Fire everywhere around him. Jets of burning gas, burning fuel. Debris as Bideshi fighters went spinning off into the void. Others breaking into smaller formations, chasing Protectorate ships, being chased. A larger wing swooped down and across the long hull of a cruiser, low to avoid gunfire, strafing. He felt Lochlan there, in among them, felt his fear, felt his anger, and nearly fell again. Adam almost went to him and him alone, to hold him, protect him however he could. Finally his own numbness was swept away and the walls began to crumble.

No. Nkiruka, this time holding him back. *You can't. If you do, you'll never come out. You'll follow him to whatever end. I know you want to. I know, Adam. But you mustn't. You can't.*

You can't afford love now.

Falling through the night, he moaned. But she was right.

He rose with her and spread himself out once more.

He wasn't strong. Not like her. But she gave him her strength just as she shared it with her people, and he could hold fast. The other fleet ships were nearing the distance they needed to be. Protectorate ships were no longer emerging from slipstream. The wings had managed to cut down the numbers of the smaller Protectorate fighters. On one of the cruisers, the secondary guns exploded in bursts of flame. As he passed through the Bideshi fighters, he heard orders crackle across the comm: "Fall back." Return to Ashwina. The final preparations were being made. Slipstream, and wherever they had chosen as safe haven.

As he turned and made ready to follow, he saw Bideshi ships drifting in pieces. The torn and scorched bodies of their pilots. There would be no time to recover them. They would be left behind, only symbolic funeral rights for them.

Somehow that was the worst thing.

Now, Nkiruka said and touched him. *Come. We've done all we can.*

Adam let her guide him. At his back, he felt rather than saw the Protectorate ships massing, delivering barrage after barrage. Ashwina's hull lit up as the shots struck home.

The numbness returned.

They weren't ready for this. They hadn't been ready. They had been at their weakest.

Someone had known.

Lochlan limped home.

He had taken hits, several of them. Not enough to disable the ship, but enough to come close. He was exhausted, hurting; one of the impacts had hurled him to the side, and his hip had slammed against the edge of the console. It was just bruised, and nothing Ying couldn't take care of, but he felt the pain, what must be one more piece of much greater pain, shared among them, and the weariness crushed him.

Out. They had to get out. They were going to. Then they could come together. They might still be all right.

He told himself this with utter desperation. With the fear and horror of a man clinging to a ledge, trying to keep himself from falling. They weren't all right. Nothing was all right.

Adam. He had felt him. But only at a distance.

He could guess why Adam might have stayed clear of him, and sensed no anger. Only even greater weariness. What Adam was becoming, the tasks he had to perform because of it . . . It would consume him. His own damned sense of responsibility in this fucking war—it would keep pushing them apart. This man, whom he loved more than his own life, was turning into something he might one day no longer recognize.

This could destroy them without ever killing them.

Nothing to be done about that now though. He had to return. They were retreating. They had done that when Cosaire was chasing them, and he had been so angry. The indignity of it. Fleeing from those fucking *raya* bastards. He had gone to Adam, had fucked that anger into him, and then it had become something else when Adam let go beneath him. Something softer and gentler, something needy.

It had taken him a long time to realize that Adam loved him then. It had taken Adam a long time as well.

Now Ashwina was running again.

It all comes back around. It comes full circle.

Ashwina opened to them and they swarmed into her. He was barely docked when the homeship's immense engines cycled up for the jump into slipstream. He sat there, hurting and tired, sensing chaos around him but seeing nothing.

Somewhere, Kae might be dying. Dead. And they were running.

He hadn't felt so alone since he watched his parents murdered in front of him. *Chusile.* He realized that he was breathing hard. Panting. Weeping. *Where are you?*

He dragged himself to his feet and stumbled out of the fighter and into the docking bay. All around him people seethed, rushing to stations, loved ones, family. But as he made his way to the clinic, he was moving slowly. Almost plodding.

Not to the Halls. Not to Adam. Perhaps Adam would come to him when he was ready.

Or he wouldn't. And that might be the future, now. The horror of that wrenched at him. Out of everything, all the fear and the pain, it was the worst.

Eva sat in the clinic, staring at everything and at nothing.

One of Ying's assistants had put her in the larger, main infirmary—bright and airy and reserved for less severe injuries. The smaller intensive care ward had been closed off to anyone who didn't absolutely have to be there. At first Aarons and Kae had been the primary focus of attention, but now more people were being brought in—pilots, mostly, returning in fighters that had taken fire. Burns, bruises, lacerations, and several with seriously mangled limbs from where they had been pinned against broken equipment and crumpled hulls.

"Eva." Kyle was kneeling in front of her, taking her hands in his. Looking up at her with his dear, worried face, and she sort of wanted to punch him in it. Not for any fault of his own. He hadn't done anything wrong. His only sin was loving her more than anyone ever had or probably ever would. It was the worry; it was too much. She didn't want that from him. She wanted him to fold her up in his strong arms like some kind of romantic hero, tell her that everything was all right—lie to her, and she would believe it gladly. Wanted him to do something she normally would never tolerate and treat her as if she were weak. Give her the space to be weak in, just for a moment. Just to pretend. She recognized that she wanted that vulnerability, and she hated herself for it.

And she hurt.

"Are you all right? Can I—"

"I'm fine." The words brought him up short, and his face took on a gray tinge.

Frightened.

"Water," she said, more to give him something to do than anything else. A way of feeling useful. "Please just . . . get me some water."

He nodded, rose, and was gone. Eva leaned over her knees, her face in her hands, and tried to breathe.

Aarons and Kae. She knew nothing about what had happened to them since docking, and knowing nothing might be best at the moment. Like this, they were in a state of superposition: both alive and dead and therefore somehow neither. She could exist in that uncertainty and try to rest in it.

"Eva."

There was Adisa, standing tall and broad and solid over her. He looked as tired as she felt, and lowered himself onto the bench beside her without being asked. Sensing, probably, that it was what she wanted. He had a way of doing that. Sensing that someone wanted something, needed something, and he would then, if possible, give it to them.

For friendship. For kindness. For the sake of connection with someone. He was a leader, and these were things a good leader did.

"Do you have any news of Kae? Of Aarons?"

Eva shook her head. She didn't really imagine that, if there was any news to be had yet, Adisa would be unaware of it. He was likely just making conversation. Trying to distract her.

If she was perfectly honest with herself, this was already what she truly wanted. What Kyle couldn't or wouldn't give her. Not necessarily the space to be weak, but simply someone to sit beside her in quiet, steady strength.

"Last I heard they were both alive. Going into the ward. Nothing since." She gave him a wan smile. "That's good, right?"

Adisa grunted softly. "It's something. You know what they say about no news." He was silent a moment, looking down at his hands. Eva noticed how every eye in the ward seemed to be on him, yet no one approached him. No one seemed inclined to interrupt the two of them. In another setting and at another time, she might have thought they feared him. Now she knew better.

There was fear, yes, but not of him. Concern. Curiosity. Respect. Most intensely—and somehow clearest—hope. They saw him and they felt hope.

"You're doing all right?" His expression was open and gentle, and his eyes were keen. So she started to nod, and then hesitated and gave him a half shake of her head.

"I don't even know what *all right* means anymore."

"You're conscious. You're making sense. I heard that after the ship pulled in, you walked out of it. Carried Kae." Adisa gave her a small, sad smile. "I'd say you're doing better than a lot of people at present." He paused and gazed toward the wide, curtained doorway that led to the next ward. "And we'll need you now. If you can find it in you to help us."

Eva looked at him, surprised. "What?"

"Rachel is with Aarons. Leila is with Kae. Rachel seems to be holding herself together, but she's not. At least, I don't think so. Leila lets out her feelings, allows herself to be open and raw, but Rachel shoves them away. She does her best to keep moving, regardless of what's happening around her. When she first came to us, she wasn't so much like that—maybe you remember. But command has changed her. The last three months have changed her. You know they've changed all of us."

Eva was beginning to get the sense of what he was saying. What he was asking of her. As with the fighter wings, there was no official chain of command in the leadership of the fleet, but there was a logic to it that people were aware of and generally accepted.

She was Rachel's subordinate. As was Kyle. If Rachel became incapacitated . . .

A shudder ran through her. She wasn't fine. She was so tired.

"Why can't it be you? Nkiruka?"

"They aren't our people." Adisa shook his head. "We could try, and we'll support you however we can, you and Kyle. But we aren't what's needed to hold the entire fleet together. Our children are Ashwina's people. Much of the fleet still doesn't entirely trust us." He paused, looking into her eyes, his own both dark and bright. "If you truly can't, I understand. Some sort of solution will be found. But if you can . . . I can't think of anyone better."

"What about Kyle?" Because he had mentioned Kyle, but she felt—strongly—that he was talking about her alone.

Adisa shrugged. "No disrespect to him, Eva. I swear it. But I think we both know that you're the stronger one."

She was quiet for a long moment. He wasn't telling her anything she didn't already know.

She could do it. She knew she could. She could be a point of solidity. A touchstone, if the fleet needed one.

Slowly, she nodded. But then she said, "I don't want to."

"I wouldn't either. Only the people who don't want to lead are ever suited for it." He was quiet for a moment. "I heard a story once, from ancient Terra, about a time of war in a great empire. A man was chosen to lead the people through the conflict, to hold the empire together. He was a simple farmer, but he proved to have a talent for the kind of leadership he was called to do. He led his people with both strength and justice."

There was something about Adisa's voice that caught Eva's attention and held it, even through the chaos around them. It was almost lulling. She listened and felt herself calming. "What happened?"

"He saved the empire. Won the war. And when the conflict was over, he gave up all his power, all his wealth and luxury and authority, and he returned to his farm and his fields."

He paused again. Then he took Eva's hand between his own gentle and large and warm ones. "I don't think I'm asking anything of you that you can't give. I'm certainly not asking you to forever take on a role you didn't choose. But I just received preliminary reports. We lost three ships. Nearly a hundred and fifty people. Ten of our fighters. Twelve more docked, and they won't fly again for a while. Two other ships were barely able to make the jump to slipstream without being torn apart. We're in far worse shape than we were before. People are frightened, questioning everything, and they can't be forced into staying. We won't become the people we're fighting. But we can't afford to lose anyone else. We need strength. We need *calm*. I believe you can provide that. And as I said, Nkiruka and I will be behind you. The entire council will be behind you. Daughter."

The last word should have felt like an afterthought. It didn't. He had said that only the people of Ashwina were his children, and perhaps she shouldn't feel included in their number. But Eva had loved her father. Had joined the peacekeepers in significant part to make him proud. She loved him still.

And Adisa reminded her of him. More than a little.

She hesitated for a moment, then squeezed his hand and felt him squeeze back.

"All right," she said softly. "All right. I'll do what I can." She swallowed heavily, lifted her head, and pushed her weariness away.

I'll do what I have to do.

CHAPTER

TEN

The Terran capital was famous for its botanical gardens—among many other things. They were extensive, the largest on the entire planet, and boasted not only specimens from around the world—from every Terran ecosystem human beings had touched and studied, which was all of them—but also rare species from other Protectorate worlds, the beautiful and unusual and remarkable. Hybrids as well from carefully engineered and managed matings between those alien life forms and Terran natives. The results were often wonderfully strange and intensely beautiful, as well as robust and adaptable, though Sinder had always found it awkward that Protectorate scientists were so willing—so *eager*—to do with these forms what they would never do with people. Now he strolled through a rose garden and contemplated this paradox—which he regarded as an amusing hypocrisy—as he waited for word of the mission he had arranged.

The ambush.

When he had planned it—thanks to the information they had received—he hadn't expected it to destroy the entire fleet, and didn't expect that to be the result now. Instead he wanted to weaken it, to sow doubt and fear, and lay the groundwork for long-term panic. He understood well the strategic value of terror.

And in fact he liked the idea of proceeding that way. It might not be entirely efficient, it might not be what he should want, but these days he was wanting all kinds of things he probably shouldn't, and events continued to work out with relative smoothness. His life was charmed—more than charmed. Gods were a ridiculous fiction, but he felt positively blessed. He was amassing all sorts of advantages.

It was nearly time to take the next step.

The aircar ride to the Hotel Tian was swift and pleasant. The car was spacious and done up in the same simple luxury as the shuttle here had been. Unlike most, the car wasn't self-driven, and the presence of a human being to do the work that could be easily done by a rudimentary AI was a mark of status. Sinder relished it quietly and coolly, just as he did all such marks.

Likewise, he enjoyed traveling at higher speeds than usual, thanks to the private airlane they were flying in. He wasn't in a mood to spend any more time than necessary in moments of transition. He needed to be where he needed to be. The hotel was a golden tower spiraling up into the sky, like a conical seashell made fluid and then frozen, all swoops and swirls. There was a harmony about its construction, a sense that every element of it existed in perfect concert with every other. It was common knowledge that the greatest living architect on Terra had been pressed into service to design the building.

It was relatively new. Made to be the triumph of yet another century of Terra's careful maintenance of its Protectorate. In spite of the fact that everyone knew one slightly uncomfortable truth.

Terra might still rule in name, and the ancient ones who had been among its first great leaders might technically still hold the highest authority. But the Protectorate itself—its administrators, its military—in short, everything and everyone that had been meant to control territory *off* Terra . . .

They now controlled the entire Protectorate. Including Terra itself.

So when people spoke of power, of authority, of the people who really ran the entire machine, they spoke not of Terra but of the Protectorate. Everyone accepted this. It wasn't even a new idea. Terran history told of old nation-states that established democratic governments while keeping up the appearance of monarchies, though the real power didn't truly rest with them. Few had dissented. The system had been stable, and everyone who participated had benefitted—at least, everyone who mattered. Sinder appreciated how it all functioned, appreciated its logic and its current applicability.

He had also, in the months since the battle at Peris, come to appreciate what a quiet little abomination this state of affairs was. It had to change.

He was the one who would change it.

The car pulled up at one of the docking platforms and hissed open, a short stair unfurling itself like a gleaming flower. Sinder walked down it, adjusted his suit, and stepped through the wide glass double doors into a lobby just as flowing and golden as the building itself.

Julius d'Bideshi had been given a suite on one of the upper floors, where rooms were both fewer in number and more opulent in every respect. Sinder nodded to Julius's aides, a placid-faced pair of women who flanked the door, and walked into the suite's main living room.

To find all the furniture cleared away, leaving only the muted colors of a fabulously expensive carpet and the soft blues and silvers and crystal of the room's other decorations.

Sinder closed the door behind him and stood for a moment, glancing around.

Julius was seated on the floor in the center of the space, a few cushions scattered here and there, his eyes closed in what appeared to be meditation. Sinder wasn't fooled; Julius had almost certainly been aware of his presence before he even passed through the door. He cleared his throat, and Julius opened his eyes and smiled.

"What a pleasant surprise." He arched his back into a slight stretch and let out a breath. "I trust your business was fruitfully conducted?"

"Indeed. That's what I came to talk to you about." Sinder crossed the room and nodded at the floor in front of Julius; Julius returned the nod and extended a hand, beckoning him to sit. Sinder did so. "And I trust you've been made comfortable?"

"Very much so." Julius's smile widened, though it maintained its essential thinness. "I appreciate how willing your aides were to indulge my desire to have a little more . . . floor space. I hope you'll forgive me—an eccentricity, perhaps, but there's something about sitting elevated from the floor which I find . . . discomfiting."

There was a great deal about Julius that was discomfiting too, if it came to that—increasingly so—but there would be many more allowances made. Putting on his own faint smile like a gracious mask, Sinder inclined his head. "We all have our eccentricities, don't we?"

"True. But tell me, please. What can I do for you?"

Sinder leaned forward. So far he had asked the man for assistance in dealing with the raid, and for a demonstration of his power that had turned out to be assistance of its own kind. But this was another thing, and like the things before it, it would give him a better idea of the resource he truly commanded. This was deserving of his complete attention.

"I've just received word that a surprise attack on the insurgent fleet has been . . . marginally successful. We destroyed three of their ships and several of their small Bideshi fighters, damaged many others. They took heavy casualties. They jumped into slipstream before we were able to fully eliminate them, but I never really expected that would be possible. I aimed to cripple them, not destroy them outright."

Julius cocked his head. "I congratulate you."

"Thank you. It's certainly gratifying." Sinder hesitated, brows drawn together, letting himself—he assumed—appear to be thinking something through. For a fraction of a second his vision wavered, shivered, and the floor tilted. His gut lurched—but in the literal blink of an eye the world was steady again, as if it had never happened. Which . . . well, perhaps it hadn't. Surely Julius had detected nothing, since there was nothing to detect. He squared his shoulders.

"But now I'm faced with the question of what they'll do next. I was hoping, with your insight into how they think, how they move, you might be of some help."

"They aren't entirely Bideshi. They aren't a Bideshi convoy." Julius arched a brow. "Ashwina might be their defensive ship, but there are any number of other personalities at play, and they're . . . How far away was this?"

"At a small station on the frontier."

"Then they're much too far away for me to get the slightest touch of them. Even with all the *bolstering* in the world."

Sinder shrugged. "Nevertheless."

"Hm." Julius looked at him for a long moment, his expression cool and thoughtful. "You don't need me for this. You have your own plant with them."

Ah.

Sinder cleared his throat. "What makes you say that?"

"How did you know they were on the frontier?"

"We're the most powerful society in human-explored space." There was no reason to discuss the source of that knowledge yet, so Sinder wouldn't—but an odd jumping sensation had seized his middle, something that absolutely could not be anxiety. "We have eyes and ears everywhere."

"Obviously. But I think there's more to it than that. You were able to predict the location and time of the raid. From the reports I've reviewed, it appears you've become very good at predicting their movements in general, even when you don't attack them directly. Eyes and ears everywhere indeed? The sensory organs in this case seem extraordinarily well placed, if I may say so."

Sinder should have expected that Julius might pick up on his secret. And in fact he had. Julius's actual powers of perception might be limited, they might be unreliable, but the man wasn't a fool. He hadn't survived this long by being so.

"You're correct," Sinder said at last. "We do have a plant. A minor one, not in a position of any particular power. But they've been with the core Protectorate insurgency since the beginning. They've had time to cultivate relationships, to get close to certain people. To gain trust. They've become extremely well versed in gathering information, and they've been very useful to us thus far."

"And they've avoided detection."

"Obviously."

"Good. But how are you maintaining their loyalty? How are you making certain that the information they're feeding you is reliable? Because it seems to me that there's a significant problem there, given how you've done what you've done."

Sinder frowned. "Explain."

"Well." Julius stretched again, leisurely. "You've uprooted these people. You've dragged them from their homes. Many of them have seen their closest blood relatives taken as well. You've seized and liquidated their assets. In short, you've left most of them with a tremendous grudge against you and not much to lose. Surely I shouldn't need to point out how dangerous that is."

"Ah. Well." Sinder allowed himself a smile. There were elements of what he was doing that he enjoyed talking about, not because they were complex or made him feel especially clever, but because they were simple, fortunate, and elegant.

"This plant isn't in that situation. Their position isn't unique, but it's rare. They had no close blood relatives. They had children, but not by blood; they married a partner who had already produced offspring. There was no need to take them. They're still here, on Terra, and they're still free. Still alive." His smile widened. "For now."

Julius reflected the smile, his own stretched and hard. His own kind of pleased. "Somehow I didn't see you as the type to take hostages. I should have known. I respect your willingness to do whatever needs to be done."

"I thought I had already proved that, given what I've provided you."

"Yes," Julius mused. "Yes, you have done that. You of course know that I was never given an especially complimentary view of you—in aggregate—but it was only when I came to know you better that I gained a full appreciation for the cruelty of which you're capable."

"Not all of us." Sinder expected to feel affronted. He didn't. Nothing Julius had said was inaccurate. He was more than ready to own it. "Only the most determined. Like myself. And I don't know that I'd call it cruelty. Cruelty implies enjoyment in the acts. I take no pleasure in what I do. I do it simply because it's necessary."

"Do you." Not a question. Again, Julius cocked his head, smiling faintly. "I think we should all take pleasure in our work. I don't see anything wrong with that. Especially when the work is necessary. Skills are fortunate things. For some of us, they are the only true opportunities for pleasure we'll ever have. In my opinion, we would be best served to take advantage of those opportunities. Don't you agree?"

Sinder said nothing. He had nothing to say.

"In any case." Julius drew himself up a bit. "You want my advice. I suspect you want it in order to compare it to the information you'll be receiving—or have already received—from your little turncoat. Very well."

He closed his eyes for a moment. "Let's assume that although your insurgency contains people from your own ranks, the Bideshi themselves are the ones guiding strategy, and they'll be the ones primarily determining what they'll all do next. The Bideshi are clannish and prefer to rely on themselves. There are many reasons for this, most of them to do with past experience. You may think of those people as superstitious, irrational, but in fact they're highly rational people. They learn, and they learn quickly—and they can be remarkably adaptable. It's part of how they've survived for as long as they have. Maybe in most cases they would favor clannishness over adaptability, but you have in this case a homeship that has split itself off from its convoy. By choice. That's almost unprecedented. Clearly these particular people are willing to resort to tactics far outside what one might ordinarily expect." He opened his eyes and narrowed them. "Don't underestimate that, Sinder. Doing so could ruin you.

"If you've damaged them as much as you say, one of two things will happen now. Perhaps degrees of both, in fact, depending on a variety of variables. Either the fleet will fall to frustration and fear and infighting and break itself apart, or . . ."

"Or?"

"Or they'll seek outside assistance."

Sinder blinked. Of all the possibilities, this frankly wasn't one he had considered, though it rankled him to admit it, even to himself. How many people or species were beyond Protectorate control who were ready and able to lend assistance to such people? But he thought of what Julius had said about them—*clannish*—and the other thing—*adaptable*. Maybe it would make sense to write off the idea, if they were dealing with Bideshi in the conventional sense. But these weren't conventional Bideshi, if such could even be said to exist.

And in fact, now that he considered everything he knew about Ashwina and about the long, strange chase she had led the Protectorate, there was one faction that might be a possibility. An unlikely one, perhaps, depending on what the Bideshi—and the insurgents—asked for.

But an unsettling one, regardless.

"I think perhaps they'll seek help from the Klashorg."

Julius's eyes widened slightly. "Really? Of all . . . Why would you single them out? They're not exactly outgoing, you know, despite their willingness to sell you their woodwork. And their diplomatic relations with just about everyone are—"

"*Frosty.*" A touch of impatience tightened Sinder's throat. "You're not telling me anything I don't know."

"I was going to say *distant*, but I suppose *frosty* works just as well. Regardless, you must also know, then, that their relations even with the Bideshi aren't especially close. I would say they aren't much friendlier with them than with anyone."

So another thing Julius didn't know. Hidden away on that sullen little peat bog of a planet, he might have done a fairly good job keeping abreast of galactic developments, but he appeared to have missed this.

"Ashwina is something of an exception."

Julius's brows drew together. "How so?"

This, Sinder had always felt, was an extremely interesting story. Troubling in some minor ways, but fascinating. "When they were first on the run from us—when Cosaire was directing her small fleet—they took refuge in Klashorg space. The information we received was so minimal as to be nearly worthless, but we do believe from what we have that Adisa—one of the most prominent leaders on the homeship—has a relationship with a prominent Klashorg government official. A friendship, in fact. One of the few humans to possess such a thing. No other comes to my mind."

"And you expect him to leverage it."

"I can't think of anything else it would make sense for them to do. If you're correct about them seeking outside assistance, then who else would be powerful enough to offer them shelter? Who else would even be willing?" That jumping sensation in his middle surged again, extending tingling tendrils into his muscles, and Sinder could no longer remain still. He got carefully to his feet—forcing his muscles into composure with a violence that was almost painful—and began to pace slowly across the room. "The question is what *kind* of assistance the Klashorg'll be willing to offer."

Julius was quiet for a moment, then broke the silence. "Surely just repairs and supplies. And time to rest and tend to their wounded. I'm guessing that's what they offered before?"

"Near as we can tell. And an escort to their border, though that was likely as much for their own security as the convoy's. Whatever relationship Adisa has with one of them, the rest of them would still be wary. Inclined toward extreme caution. Especially given that the convoy was being pursued."

"The Klashorg have never displayed any indication that they're interested in direct conflict with the Protectorate."

Sinder shook his head. "None whatsoever. They leave us alone and we leave them alone. We allow them to trade and work in our territory with relative freedom. We don't harass them. We don't try to control their migrant workers beyond what they seem willing to accept, and in return they provide labor of extremely high quality and command considerable rates of pay. The arrangement is mutually beneficial."

"Mm." Out of the corner of his vision, Sinder saw Julius take on a speculative expression as his gaze followed him back and forth. "And that's all it is, yes? Mutual benefit? That's why you haven't made any attempt to subdue them the way you have almost every other species you've encountered? To get them into full *accord* with the true benefits afforded by being part of this galaxy's Protectorate?"

Sinder stopped and looked squarely at him. "They have no need of us. And they wouldn't thrive in our hands. We saw that at once. They're better served if left alone."

"Because you're always primarily concerned with the well-being of the species you bring in from the cold."

When Sinder smiled, he showed his teeth, just an edge, and it sent fresh steel into his spine. This was at once a truth as deeply held as any he possessed, and something he recognized as a convenient justification. Neither was mutually exclusive. "Benefit to all explored space is and has always been our primary concern, Julius."

"And it has nothing to do with the fact that in every war in which the Klashorg have been involved—the *vanishingly* few—they've wiped out or nearly wiped out their enemies."

Sinder pulled his lips back further. He thought of a wolf pacing, an apex predator lurking inside himself until needed. "It would be an enormously destructive conflict on both sides. We command overwhelming military resources. If they were fully brought to bear in an interstellar war, we would likely do as much damage to them as they would to us. Do you have any knowledge of Terran history, Julius?"

Julius shook his head, brow arched. "I can't say that I do."

"It's something of a hobby of mine. I find that it helps me to bring current events into greater perspective, and makes me able to predict the future with a small degree of accuracy. In order to understand the present, I think it's necessary to have some knowledge of the past."

Sinder approached Julius and dropped into a crouch, his hands clasped between his knees. This was another favorite story of his, one that increasingly occupied his thoughts when he lay fighting the tremors that came and went in waves, staring into the dark and feeling threads of the possible future winding themselves around his mind. "Long ago, two great states were engaged in a war that never truly became a war at all. It was mostly confined to espionage, planning that didn't come to much, the posturing of leaders, widespread fear and hatred through demonization of the enemy. Occasional proxy wars. And the primary reason it never exploded into a shooting war was the fact that each side commanded a massive arsenal of weapons so destructive that they could have destroyed this entire planet several times over."

He cocked his head. "The term for such an *arrangement* was an interesting one. Can you guess what it was?"

Again, Julius shook his head. His expression was mild, revealing nothing, but his eyes were keen. Penetrating. Opaque, milky drills, whirring softly.

"It was 'mutually assured destruction.' They even made it into a rather appropriate acronym: MAD. It was recognized by leaders on both sides, you see, that although for political and deeply held ideological reasons, neither side could back down from the state of potential war in which they had locked themselves, actual war could never be allowed to happen. In such a war there could be no possible victor. There would be no one left to claim victory. And even if anyone survived, there would be no spoils worth the fighting."

Julius let out a low, incredulous laugh. "A hugely irrational state of affairs. What happened? Clearly it never did descend into the kind of conflict you describe."

Sinder shrugged. "One of the states turned out to be politically or economically unsustainable. The regime collapsed. The war ended. There continued to be distrust on both sides, but nothing like what had gone before ever existed between the two of them again."

For a moment the men regarded each other without speaking. Then Julius leaned forward and folded his hands. "An interesting tale,

Sinder. But I'm not sure I fully understand what it has to do with the Protectorate and the Klashorg."

Sinder smiled thinly. "Why, simply this. Even if that *cold war* never became a hot one, and even if no one with any real power ever wanted it to be so, it was still apocalyptically dangerous. Several times the two sides were almost forced into war anyway. As you say, it was profoundly irrational. Even rational people can be pushed into madness in an irrational situation."

He paused, letting the words sit in the air between them. Julius's figure was blurring in his vision. "Since we first made contact with the Klashorg, since we first gained an appreciation for their history, our leaders have known that we can't allow that between the Klashorg and the Protectorate. It would be the height of foolishness. Better to allow a world to rule itself than to risk such a thing. Is it something we're proud of? No. But we haven't maintained dominance of this society by losing sight of what's practical."

Julius looked at him for a long moment, and while Sinder couldn't gauge the direction in which his thoughts were moving, there was something about the feeling of that movement that he didn't particularly like. His own mental fingers, slipping through the air and caressing Julius's skull—the sensation was so clear that his palms tingled.

Finally Julius shifted, relaxed backward, and leaned on one hand. "So what if the Klashorg do offer military assistance to the insurgents?"

"I think that's *highly* unlikely. They're aware of the risks of conflict just as much as we are."

"But still." Julius rolled an idle shoulder. "Indulge a hypothetical. What if they did?"

A hypothetical. Well. He should have considered this. He'd been sure he had thought all eventualities through carefully, but now he saw a new possibility: not that the Bideshi might seek assistance from the Klashorg—that was, of course, a fresh revelation—but that anything might happen to place the Klashorg and the Protectorate at odds.

He had been good at hypotheticals from his earliest days studying philosophy in university. Preparing for his career, beginning to delve deeply into Terran history, he had melded the two disciplines. What if this had gone differently? This battle, this diplomatic engagement, this scientific discovery, this election. What if these crucial moments had proceeded in another direction? What meanings would have changed, what forms of knowledge, the course of history, humanity itself?

What if the Protectorate had never come to be at all?

What if it was destroyed?

"If it were to happen, I would handle it. Diplomacy has worked at every crucial moment in our history. Perhaps it hasn't always prevented conflict, but at moments of potentially apocalyptic disaster, it has never failed. I know it wouldn't fail us now. Not while both sides remain reasonable."

"Really," Julius said softly. His pale, blind eyes were like compressed photon beams. Focused and direct. "You'll handle it. You."

Sinder's mouth tightened. He had been certain, but that certainty had taken damage, and now he wondered whether Julius felt that damage, sensed it, *noted* it. Had he tipped his hand? Did it matter? Wouldn't he have to bring Julius in on his plans anyway? Wasn't his involvement crucial to their success? Julius would know his secret sooner or later, and Sinder would see his way through it, whatever difficulty it presented. He would untangle any potential issues just as he always did.

But was it too early?

He could play the middle. He had become skilled at that.

"Yes," he said. "Me. I'm well positioned. I know the history. I know the present. And I may not have your sight, respected Aalim, but I can make an educated guess regarding the future."

He slapped his hands onto his knees and pushed to his feet—And wobbled slightly. He closed his eyes as dizziness swept over him—and passed, just as quickly.

Stood up too fast. And he was tired. He would have to take better care of himself—his body was ultimately of little consequence, but it would have to carry him for the present, as reliably as it could. Especially given what was to come.

"I thank you for this consultation," he said, his tone brisk. Businesslike. He owed nothing else to Julius, and the tension that had wormed its way into him was intensifying. "I can't tell you how valuable it's been. Once again I want to express my sincere appreciation that you're with us now."

Julius inclined his head. "I'm only too happy to help, Isaac. Please come to me as soon as I can assist you with anything else. And . . ." He hesitated, and his attention appeared to shift to the door. "Send for me, perhaps. It would be nice to *see* something besides these walls, at least for a bit."

Yes, he would go to Julius, Sinder thought as he left the suite and headed back into the gilded hall, his footsteps echoing softly off the polished walls. As soon as he had reviewed some hypotheticals. Nothing could be neglected.

And then, when he was ready, he would make his move.

CHAPTER

ELEVEN

"I need to see him."

Lochlan pulled out of Adam's grip and stumbled down the corridor. Adam's grip had been weak anyway; only ten hours ago he had left Nkiruka and barely made it to his quarters before he collapsed into a sleep so heavy it probably had more in common with a coma. Lochlan had been there when he woke up, sleeping just as heavily, and at first Adam had thought he was simply tired as well.

Until he'd smelled the lovina on Lochlan's breath.

Lochlan must have passed out drunk, for he had woken up that way; for all Adam knew, he hadn't been there more than an hour. Now he regretted waking Lochlan in the first place, because he had shoved Adam away and staggered out of their quarters, slurring something about how they hadn't let him see Kae before but he was fucking well going to see him now, and *fuck* anyone who stopped him, those fucking piece of shit *duraks*, he was going to beat his way through them if he had to because this was his fucking *brother*, and didn't they know that he—

Adam was pursuing. But not well. Lochlan possessed the unsteady, lurching speed of someone drunk enough not to care how they threw their body around. Adam was merely exhausted, still, and physically weak in a way he hadn't been since . . .

Since the last time he healed someone on his own.

He hadn't done that since the battle at Peris. He hadn't needed to. Everyone else knew how at this point.

Lochlan was doing a lot more than slurring now; he was ranting. And as Adam followed as quickly as he could, now and then pausing to lean a hand against the wall and fight the despair twisting in his chest, he realized he had never seen Lochlan this drunk before.

Never.

"Lock. Lock, just slow down, we can talk about—"

"Nothing to *talk about*." Lochlan whirled on him, and while once Adam would have been skeptical that the term *eyes blazing* was anything but hyperbole, now he realized that he would have been wrong. "He's *there*. Kae's *there*. What's to talk about? What the fuck are we gonna *discuss*?" He was still wobbling, still a bit unsteady, but the slur had somehow—for the moment—left his voice, and he sounded nearly sober. "You *saw* him, Adam. You *saw* him. You think you're gonna stop me getting to him? You think you're gonna slow me down?"

He took a step toward Adam then, and there was something about that step and about the fists clenched at his sides and about the blaze in his eyes that made Adam take a step back.

He had never been afraid of Lochlan before. He wasn't now.

But he saw how he might be. In the distance, like a terrible mirage, he saw it.

"I'm not trying to slow you down," Adam said softly and held out a hand. He wasn't sure what for—he didn't imagine that Lochlan would take it. But it was all he could think to do. "But Lock . . . you're drunk. You can't go see him like this. Even if they would normally let you, there's no *way* they will when you're . . . ." Helplessness joined his despair. All he wanted—all he had wanted ten hours ago—was to curl up in Lochlan's arms and forget everything else. How, so many times before, Lochlan had given him the space and the safety in which to forget.

"You can't fucking stop me," Lochlan said, and the drunken belligerence had returned. Once again he seemed to be having difficulty focusing. "*They* can't fucking stop me. I'd like to see 'em try."

"So you're going to, what, punch your way through Ying? Lock, she *raised* you."

"That's my fucking *brother* lying there with a *hole* in his fucking head," Lochlan shot back, and there was a choked sound to it, as if he had crashed through the belligerence and was now, though it lingered, also about to cry. He was cycling through moods, through emotions, faster than Adam could follow, and he wondered if Lochlan had only taken too much lovina or if there had been something else in the mix.

He shook his head. "Lock . . . he wouldn't want you to."

Lochlan froze, eyes narrowing, sharp again. Everything sharp. And Adam knew, without knowing why or how, that he had crossed a line.

"You have *no fucking idea* what he would want." Lochlan took another step toward Adam, and while Adam held his ground this time, unease shivered down his spine. This was dangerous. He still wasn't afraid, but Lochlan, this man he loved more than he had believed he would ever be able to love anyone, this man he would die for and who would happily die for him . . .

He wasn't sure where that man was. Not now. This man . . .

This was the child, he realized suddenly, who survived the massacre on Caldor Station. Who hid for days in the air ducts, crawling around like a rat while his parents bled out on the floor and the screams of the dying and wounded faded away. The little child who'd made himself cold inside so the fear and the rage and the grief wouldn't eat him alive.

He had never seen that child before. He was seeing him now.

"Lock," he murmured and stepped toward him, holding out his hands—his *arms*, as if to reach for that child and embrace him, because abruptly that seemed like the only thing that mattered anymore. "Come here. You don't have to—"

"Don't you fucking touch me." Lochlan recoiled and bared his teeth. "You have no right. You have no right to say—" He stopped and cocked his head, and a hard, mean look swept across his face, thin as the blade of a knife. "Oh, but I'm sorry . . . You're *used* to this, aren't you? This is no big deal to you. Seeing as how you put him in that bed before."

Adam's chill of unease became a needle of ice. He dropped his arms. "You don't mean that," he said quietly. "Don't say it, Lock."

"Don't say *what*?"

"*This.* What you're saying." The corners of Adam's eyes were beginning to sting, and he was unsurprised to see Lochlan's eyes shining as well. "You know I love him too. You *know* that."

"You said back on that shithole planet, in that camp . . . You said you were never gonna be one of us. I remember. You said it. You *kept* saying it. You're not Protectorate, no, but now . . . Now you're turning into something . . . You're *not like us*. You said it. I don't know what you are now, but you're sure as shit not like us. You feel *wrong*. So he's not your brother. He never will be. Why don't you just fuck off? Why don't you just let me take care of my own?" Lochlan shoved his whole body forward, all aggression, his lips pulling back in an expression that looked too much like a sneer. "Get the fuck out of here, you fucking *raya*."

He blinked, took a breath, and in the time he took to draw it, horror passed across his face. "Adam," he whispered, but Adam shook his head and backed away, tears finally spilling over and running hot down his cheeks, washing the feeling from his body. They had held each other up. He had believed they were something worth fighting for. A future. He had been sure.

But Lochlan didn't know what Adam was becoming. And Adam didn't know either.

Maybe he didn't belong anywhere.

"I can't." He shook his head again, palming clumsily at his cheeks. "Lock . . . I just can't."

He whirled and walked swiftly back down the corridor, not looking behind him. If Lochlan called after him, he didn't hear it over the roar of the blood in his ears.

Raya. It wasn't what Lochlan meant, he knew that, because . . . "*You're not Protectorate*." It was hate. The only word Lochlan could find in that moment. Planet-bound. Grounded. Held in place.

If only.

He had no idea, later, how long he walked, or even how far. Ordinarily he might have gone to the Halls, meditated, searched for anything there that might give him peace, but now the thought of heading up to the top of the ship twisted his gut and made his heart quail. He couldn't go back there. It was a poisoned place for him now, given what had happened there and what had happened after. After everything he had done, after the horrible moment of knowing that he could help Lochlan, *had* to help him, and knowing that he couldn't enter him or he might lose himself, might not be able to help anyone else . . .

He halted in the dim, narrow corridor he'd been wandering— little more than a maintenance passageway in one of the lower parts of the ship. Halted and stared at nothing, his fingers pressed against his mouth.

Maybe Lochlan had felt him. Had known. Had felt him close, and had felt him turn away again.

That alone didn't explain Lochlan's behavior. Lochlan, in a calmer and more rational and most of all more *sober* moment, would be able to understand, with little difficulty, why Adam had done what he did. Why he *hadn't* done what he might have. It wasn't abandonment for lack of love. Even without an explanation from Adam, ordinarily Lochlan would probably never have assumed something that made so little sense.

Ordinarily.

But nothing about this was ordinary.

There was the lovina, and whatever else he had taken. Kae. The things he kept buried most of the time but which were never truly gone. The fear he had already talked about, the fear of what was happening to Adam. Where it might be going.

"I'll always be a little bit of an outsider. I'll always be a tourist. No matter how much you love me, you can't change that."

He hadn't expected this. He had always thought it would be the past that dogged him, that kept him apart from his friends. He had never expected to be ripped away by the future. To become neither Protectorate nor Bideshi. Something that didn't fit anywhere.

Adam kept walking. Heading steadily deeper and deeper.

He had never been in this part of the ship before, and the corridors were alternately as narrow as the one he'd stopped in and wide, almost cavernous, spaces big enough to move heavy equipment through. This must be where the engines and other fundamental workings of the ship were maintained, and although the place was reasonably clean and the air was clear, it was hot, and sweat began to bead on his brow and trickle down his temples. Pipes and ductwork weren't as smoothly integrated into walls and bulkheads as they were above. The entire place had a decidedly more industrial feel.

None of it was made for comfort or beauty. Everything had a job and was engaged in doing it. Frequently loudly.

Despite that, there was indeed something comforting about this level. Maybe that it was so profoundly different.

While he passed a few people wearing muted-color overalls, there weren't many—it must be the night shift—and he was left alone. No one asked him who he was or what he was doing there, for which he was grateful. The Bideshi might be communal, might maintain close social bonds, but they also knew about the value of minding one's own business.

As he descended even deeper, closer and closer to the engines, the thrum around him seemed to work its way beneath his skin and into his flesh, vibrating gently, lulling him. Calming him. The beating heart of the ship. No more or less than the heart represented by the Arched Halls, but different.

Why hadn't he come down here before? Here, he was discovering, lay a form of meditation, and with every step he felt calmer.

Then the thrum began to stutter, to become uneven, and he exited a long passage and found himself in a chamber that had half fallen apart.

He had been aware that Ashwina had taken damage, of course. There was no way she would have escaped unscathed. This must be one of the worse hits. Wires lay tangled across the floor, some of them sparking. A series of panels in the bulkheads had obviously fallen—or been blown outward, judging by their bent and warped states—and more had fallen from the ceilings. A few small fires burned. People were attacking the fires with foam extinguishers, while others cleared away the worst of the debris and prepared patches for the exposed components. They were oblivious to him, and for a few seconds Adam stood and merely watched them, half-entranced.

Then another panel exploded in a jet of flame, throwing a woman across the floor.

It seemed to happen in slow motion. For a moment no one else moved. The woman was on fire and she flailed, dropped to her knees, beating weakly at herself. She must be screaming, but Adam could hear nothing, and as the others rushed toward her—still in that strange slow motion—he realized why.

He realized what he had to do.

They were running to her. He ran too. He had been tired, weak, but suddenly energy surged into him—from where, he didn't know, and couldn't take the time to figure it out—and he shouldered his way to her. They had dragged her away from the burning hole and beaten out the flames, but her skin was blackened and cracked, blisters rising, and it was doubtful she would survive long enough for Ying's people to get there. Or for the time it would take to get her to the clinic.

He dropped into a crouch beside her and reached for her.

She screamed when he touched her face—rough and hoarse, and there were shouts behind him. Hands pushed and pulled at him, but he ignored them all. He closed his eyes and found the center inside himself, *the roots*, and by now he knew how to do this even if it had been weeks upon weeks since he had. One never forgot something like this. He plunged *into* her, into her body, and she convulsed— for a split second he was sorry, because this must feel, on some level, like a violation. But he had to.

This time he wasn't going into her code, so it would be easier. It wouldn't drain him as much. He flooded into her damaged cells and found how they should be properly arranged, found where they were burst and torn open, and with every piece of himself he began to knit them back together. To discard the ones too damaged to be salvaged and raise new cells in their places. Growing new flesh, new skin. Healing.

Was this what Ying did? Or was this something else?

Again she convulsed under his hands, heard her suck in a choked gasp, and felt her pain—but the pain was lessening. Her body was no longer screaming panic and agony, her muscles were loosening, and she was slipping slowly into exhausted sleep.

At last he had done enough, and he flowed out of her and fell back, catching himself on one hand, as the world spun gently around him. Hands were still on him, on his shoulders, but now they were supporting him rather than trying to pull him away. Faintly, as if from a distance, he heard a jumble of voices.

"Any idea who he is?"

"None, must be—"

"Not one of Ying's. What happened—is he hurt? Here, leave him here. You, are you all right?"

He managed a weak nod. He was all right. And he couldn't stay, couldn't get tangled up in what would follow now. He rose and took a shaky step, another, shrugging off the helping hands, clutching at his head and making for the nearest exit, ignoring the confused cries behind him and the calls for someone to get Ying.

He was all right. Now he needed to figure out the rest of what he was.

CHAPTER

TWELVE

Nkiruka sat by Kae's bed.

He looked bad. She knew that even if she couldn't see him. The wound in his head had been tended to as best Ying could, the swelling against his skull reduced, the bleeding stopped, and his additional wound had been cared for as well. It would heal—and if it weren't for his head wound, he would have been all right.

But he hadn't woken up. And Ying, when she had gently pulled Nkiruka aside, had admitted that she didn't know if he ever would.

Or, if he did, how much of him would be left.

Nkiruka sat now and studied him in her way, his bloodless face half obscured by the machine that was helping him breathe. Other machines fed medicine and nutrient into him, worked to keep his body stable. Ying said he would live, at least for the moment.

But they didn't yet know what *living* would mean.

This happened, this abandonment of the body. It wasn't even that infrequent. Injury sometimes caused it, or simple old age. The body remained, but the mind and spirit—or however one preferred to think of them—were already gone, leaving only a shell. The question was always whether to keep the shell locked into a kind of twilight life, or to let the night finally fall. For many patients' loved ones, it wasn't a difficult question. Often people had made their wishes known beforehand.

But sometimes it was very difficult indeed.

Leila sat by the opposite side of the bed, her hands curled around one of Kae's and her head bent, her hair hanging in her face. It was tangled and unkempt, and her face was flushed and blotchy with weeping, her eyes swollen. Somehow that was almost as distressing as

Kae's condition, for Leila was always elegant, even tired, even angry, even pushed to the extremity of stress and frustration. There was a fire in her that glowed through her skin, and it had never been difficult to see why Kae had apparently begun to fall in love with her the moment he set eyes on her.

That fire was still there. Nkiruka could feel it as if it were a real flame. But it was flickering. Threatening to gutter.

She knew the two of them had both been here before, and that now Leila must look back on that time and see it as merely a prelude to this.

A warning, perhaps. An omen.

"Leila."

Leila didn't answer, but her rough breathing caught and her shoulders moved.

"Leila, you need to rest."

"I'm not leaving him," she muttered, head still lowered.

"You can't do any more here." Nkiruka was calm, calm and weary, far too weary to be impatient. "It's been hours, Leila. You'll be no good to him if you collapse, and if you do, you'll be occupying a bed next to him, which Ying needs. When we come out of slipstream and take in wounded from the other ships, I doubt the empty beds she has now will be empty for long."

"I'm not leaving him," Leila repeated, and though her voice was low and quiet, there was a harder edge to it.

"Ying is prepared to have you removed."

"Let her try." Leila finally raised her head, and Nkiruka felt the flush in her face, the pounding in her head, as if these things were in her own. "I'd like to see that, Nkiru. I'd like to see her try."

This is being said elsewhere, Nkiruka thought vaguely. *Or was a very short time ago. Or will be very soon. What is this man before me, that he's loved with such depth and such fire?*

Love was love. Love would go where it would, and thank whatever God or gods there might be that it wasn't a thing that had to be earned by deeds or virtue.

It was given. And Kae d'Bideshi had been blessed.

"No, you wouldn't. You wouldn't, and more importantly? *He* wouldn't, and I think you know that." Nkiruka sat forward, her hands clasped in her lap. "You're heartsick. You're frightened. But more than anything else, you're *tired*, and being tired will magnify everything you're feeling. You're not stupid, Leila. You know this."

Her voice was still calm—even gentle, and she still sensed no anger. She saw and sensed and *felt* a woman who had become a dear friend, who was already mourning a man who had become the same, and in her heart she mourned as well.

Even though . . .

"He's still there," she said softly, and reached across the bed—not touching Leila, because the distance was too great, but reaching for her nevertheless, and even in that act she felt stronger. "I can feel him. For now, at least, he's still there. Weakened, damaged, but waiting to heal enough to emerge. Go and rest and let him heal."

Something in Leila seemed to falter. She let out a sound that was close to a whimper and shook her head, looking back at Kae with a shiver of pain. Satya had not died when Nkiruka left her, but it had been a good-bye all the same, and a good-bye forever. This pain was a greater echo of her own, and she took it into herself as one would take in anything familiar.

"If he's there, how can I leave him?"

"He is there, and he's likely to remain so until you return." Nkiruka couldn't offer Leila the comfort she deserved, not as she would have before. Because nothing between them was the same.

"Leila, I can . . . There are still empty beds, as I said. You wouldn't have more than a few hours in one, I've heard we're soon due to come out of slipstream, but I think Ying could probably—"

There was a commotion across the room. Leila and Nkiruka looked up—Lochlan was coming toward them, shoving his way past three of Ying's aides, his eyes wild. He was staggering slightly. Nkiruka could feel his anger, his grief, his profound confusion of mind—natural but exacerbated by substances. Inwardly, she sighed. Of course he would do this. She knew Lochlan. Knew that he had matured considerably in the last year, but he still was who he was.

She wasn't ashamed of him or for him. She simply wished he had not done it.

Leila was already getting to her feet. Lochlan stopped and laid a hand on the shoulder of an aide, gripped, leaned.

With a helpless glance at the others, Leila stopped trying to fight him back.

Even at a distance, Nkiruka heard his desperate murmur. "Help me get to him. Please."

Leila moved forward to take his hands, his shoulders. As she reached him, the aide let him go, and he collapsed into Leila's arms, his whole body trembling. As she took him in, Nkiruka was certain that this was the first time he had truly released his grief this way. The first time he had allowed himself to feel it to its full.

Which implied he hadn't done this with Adam. That was troubling.

But not entirely surprising.

She rose and left them together without looking back. There might be more trouble with Lochlan, with them both, but probably not. What they couldn't do for themselves, they would find a way to do for each other. In the meantime, she had her role to play.

Gathering her robes around her, Nkiruka went to find Adisa.

It was important—vital even—to the mental and emotional well-being of the Bideshi to be able to see the stars, and as such there were many places on Ashwina where one could do so. There were the High Fields, and the great transparent ceiling at the top of the central hall, but the ship was also dotted with public viewing chambers, lounges, places for meditation, observatories, and gardens walled with starlight. Now, of course, there were no stars, only the streaked white of slipstream, but that provided its own kind of meditation. In one of the star lounges, Eva sat in a large, plush chair, staring out its enormous window, her eyes unfocused and her hands in her lap. There was a gentle hand on her shoulder. She lifted her own and covered it, giving it a slight squeeze. Kyle, come to check on her. At the moment she deeply wanted that.

Even if she wasn't sure how he was going to take what she had to tell him.

"You're all right?"

"I'm fine." She wasn't fine. She was terrified, had barely slept in the last few hours, and most of all she was lonely. Because maybe Kyle was technically in this with her, but Adisa was also correct: there were things here in which she would be mostly on her own. And not all of them would have to do with the fleet.

"What about you?"

"I thought you might come back to our quarters. You need to rest, Eva."

"I know." She pushed a hand through her hair and squeezed her eyes closed. "I haven't been able to. You know how sometimes you get so tired you can't sleep at all? It's like you had a chance and you missed it."

"You could go to Ying. I bet she has something you could take to help."

She shook her head. "That stuff gives me nightmares. I have enough reasons to have them right now."

"She could probably cook up something that wouldn't."

"I don't want to. I wouldn't anyway. There's thinking I have to do."

She practically felt his frown. "What kind of thinking?"

Eva sighed again and patted the seat beside her. Outside the window, the quantum flow of slipstream continued ever onward. It wasn't clear to her—and never had been—whether it would be fair to say that the ship moved through this bizarre and half-nonsensical version of space-time, or whether it remain stationary and space-time moved around it.

It didn't matter, but she wondered anyway.

Kyle sat down and turned to look at her. "Eva . . . what's this about?"

She didn't quite meet his eyes, and cursed herself for a coward. "Adisa spoke to me. Not long after we got away."

"Concerning what?"

"Everything. What happens now. What happens next. What we have to do for the fleet." She did look at him then, looked at him squarely—though it was an effort—and was uncertain if she was being fair to him, worried as she was about telling him. "You know Aarons is out of commission."

He nodded. "Ying briefed me. You were gone, but she said . . . concussion. More than a concussion. Not a head injury as bad as Kae's, but worse than she can heal with her skills. She put him in a coma until he heals enough to be awakened."

Eva nodded. "And Kae . . ."

"Yeah. She doesn't know if he'll wake up at all."

"Have you seen Leila and Rachel?"

Kyle frowned. "No."

"Neither have I. But Ying filled me in on them too. Leila is . . . She's in no state to lead anything. Perhaps in a bit, once she's had a chance to rest and get herself together, but now . . . She's barely functional. They almost had to force her to leave Kae's bed."

"What about Rachel?"

Eva shook her head. Rachel was a greater problem. "Holding steadier. But she's . . . She's holding too tight. Or that's what Adisa thinks. Holding tight like . . . Brittle." She bowed her head for a moment, and spoke more softly. "We're all pushed to the edge, Kyle. You know that. The ragged edge. They're both strong, Rachel and Leila, but they've been carrying a lot of this on their backs—the fleet, not Ashwina—and they were never going to be able to do it forever. So . . . Adisa wants us to take over."

Kyle blinked at her. "Us."

"Us." She took a breath. There were things here that she could say, and other things she shouldn't. "Not permanently. Not officially. But he said someone needs to hold the rest of the fleet together, handle those of us who used to be Protectorate. He said they wouldn't respond as well to Bideshi leadership—him and Nkiruka and the rest of the council. He was right. I know he was right. Kyle." She took his hands, because the alarm on his face wasn't fading. "It has to be one of their own. One of *our* own. Aarons and Rachel were good leaders because they were suited for it, but the others *let* them lead because of who they used to be. Leila and Kae worked well as their seconds because of who *they* are. It all worked."

She swallowed and took a breath. "But it's not going to work anymore. At least not for a while. Things are changing. We have to help Rachel. We have to step up. More than we have." She gave his hands a squeeze. "Are you with me on this? I need you. I need you with me."

His alarm had finally faded. But now sadness had taken its place. A calm sadness, and she could tell he was trying his best to hide it. But he had never been good at hiding anything from her.

Why sadness? She was feeling it too. She had said it herself, hadn't she?

Things are changing. Who are we going to be when this is all over? If we live through it?

"Of course," he said quietly. "Of course I'm with you."

"All right."

Eva closed her eyes then and took a deeper breath, as if she could draw strength from the very air. Because if this little bit had hurt him, what she had to say next would hurt him even worse.

It was probably a terrible time to say it. But likely there was no *good* time. Not anymore. And if she didn't say it now, she wasn't sure when she would be able to.

And with this, time was a factor. At least as far as her heart went.

"Kyle, I . . . There's something else."

The alarm was back, just a flicker of it, but then it faded again and he merely looked tired. As tired as she felt. There was only, she thought, so much disaster someone could take, and responsibility had a way of shoving some of it to one side. "What?"

"It's the baby." *The baby.* She had hardly begun to really think of it in those terms, that actual word, and now that she had said it aloud she didn't know how to feel.

That was the problem.

"Kyle . . ." She thought she might have to break eye contact. But she didn't. She wasn't going to. "I'm not sure I want to keep it."

He stared at her. She stared back, miserable. She hated this, hated that she was saying it, hated that she was in a position where she would even feel like this. Hated all of this. Hated, just a little, the people and the events that had thrown them together all those months ago. Hated that they had ever found each other. Hated Melissa Cosaire.

Hated Adam Yuga.

Her life had been dull and not terribly fulfilling when she was still with the Protectorate, but it had been something. It had been easier than this.

But you would be dead now, a voice whispered. *You would have sickened and you would have died with no one to help you. Probably in one of those camps.*

You and him.

The thing she was beginning to truly understand was that sometimes there weren't any good options. Sometimes no good ending was possible. The *happily ever after*s of her childhood had been a lie. People were often lucky to get as much as *happily*.

"Why not?"

A fair question. One she thought she could answer. But if this came down to reasoning, to arguing . . . She wasn't sure how that would go. And she didn't think that was an argument she was even willing to have.

"I don't think it's time. I don't know if I *can*. Kyle, this is . . ." She lowered her head at last, but it didn't feel like cowardice. She was still holding on to his hands, and he was holding on to hers. "In the middle of this? With what we have to do? When we don't know when it'll end? When we don't know if we'll live through it? It's not that I don't want a family—I do—it's just that . . . I don't know. I don't know." Something in her collapsed and she finally pulled her hands back, dropping her face into them. She had told herself she wasn't going to cry. She had been determined.

"You do want one?" he asked softly. "You want a family?" She heard him take a breath, and then his hand was on her shoulder again, on her back. There was no tremble in his voice. No anger, no horror. Only quiet strength.

What she had been needing all along.

"Yes," she said just as softly, and she allowed her own voice to shake, and that was a relief. "I do. Swear it, Kyle, I . . . I do."

She did. She hadn't been so sure of it before now.

"I do too." Gently he tugged her hands away from her face and tilted it toward his, and she didn't resist him. He leaned their foreheads together and ran a hand through her hair, and the clutching hand that had gripped her gut loosened. Released her. "Even if you didn't, I . . ." He paused. Maybe there was strength in him, maybe he had found that and was giving it to her, but she could sense something else. Inner tension. Inner . . . She couldn't quite put a name to it.

But she wasn't going to dig for it.

"Even if you didn't, I would want to be with you. You know that." She nodded, but he was already continuing. "If you don't feel ready now, I don't want to . . . I don't want to push you. I don't think I can. Eva, all I'm asking is . . ." He lifted his head, lifted hers, and that quiet strength was still in his eyes. But also that other thing. Far back in the shadows of him, barely visible.

Doubt?

"Sleep on it. That's all I'm asking. You're exhausted. We just got punched in the gut. Sleep on it. Don't make the decision immediately."

She hesitated. But he was right. She should rest. She couldn't address it now anyway. She'd rest for a few hours, and then think about it fresh.

Think about everything fresh.

"Still don't know if I can," she whispered and gave him a wan smile. "Sleep on anything, I mean."

"Sure you can. You can sleep on me." On the other side of the room, there was a long couch, and he took her hand and led her to it, sat, and tugged her down beside him. "C'mon."

It was better than their quarters, somehow. Better than their bed. She stretched out and settled her head on his thigh, and he stroked his fingers slowly through her hair until she started to drift, her eyes unfocused and the rush of slipstream oddly lulling.

She might sleep. Eventually.

And eventually she did.

CHAPTER

THIRTEEN

Nine hours later, the fleet came out of slipstream in empty space and took stock.

Adam watched it all from the huge window in one of the upper corridors near what had been Ixchel's quarters. For a while Nkiruka had also made a home there, but not long after taking her place as Aalim, she had moved, saying—with a faintly wry smile—that although it was good to have Ixchel's ghost looking over her shoulder from time to time, it was possible to have too much of a good thing.

But Ixchel wasn't the only one with ties to this place. She had brought him here, the first time she spoke to him at any length. Brought him here to this place with its curved wall of impossibly thin transparency and chided him about perfection and his people's obsession with it, about the fundamental emptiness of his life. About the lines he had to find and seize, and orbits into which he had to fall.

About how—though perhaps not in so many words—he would have to consider the possibility of faith in something beyond what he could see and touch.

Standing here, watching the fleet assemble around Ashwina like scattered, broken toys in the dark, he missed her more than he had in weeks. Months. He hadn't seen Lochlan. He hadn't seen Kyle, hadn't seen Eva. Hadn't felt that he could go to Adisa. Hadn't seen Kae or Leila.

It had been a long time since he had last felt truly alone.

When? On the run in his scrap heap of a ship after he sold all his assets and cut himself off from the Protectorate that had raised and then betrayed him? Living hand to mouth, slowly dying, reduced to theft? Becoming everything he had once scorned, and in truth dying in his heart quicker than in his body?

He hadn't felt like this since he met Lochlan.

Time, he had learned, was not linear, and now he had been thrown backward along its flow. Back upstream to old rapids. It was almost as if he had never met Lochlan at all, never loved him, never lived with him and been determined to live *for* him. Could one argument—one stupid, drunken argument in a fit of grief—really destroy all of that? Except the argument wouldn't destroy it.

The fault lines for this conflict weren't just about the Protectorate. They weren't just about where he came from, what his loyalties were. Used to be. Might still be. They were about who both of them *were*.

You fucking raya.

He laid his hand against the window and closed his eyes. Somewhere far below him, the captains and the council were preparing to meet and take stock of injuries and damage, and to plan whatever their next move might be. Whatever they might be able to do.

Be able to do.

He opened his eyes then, lifted his hand away, looked at both of them. What he had done for the woman still felt like a dream. He hadn't told anyone, not even Nkiruka, and he didn't think she had sensed any change in him. Was there any change? He didn't think so. This had probably been there all along, just like the rest of his abilities. Just as the potential for healing lay in everyone, and it was only a matter of bringing it to the surface. What was doing so in this case? There might never be a way to know. Fear. Panic. Grief. The extremity of his mind and heart and body. Afterward he had wondered if he might use it to help Kae—but he didn't think so. He had gotten to the woman quickly, seconds after she had been hurt. Her body had not yet fully settled into its new state. Kae—and Aarons—had been lying wounded for some time. By Adam's own guess, what he could do now wasn't much more than what Ying could do—if he even approached her level of skill. And as far as he knew, Ying hadn't been able to heal them.

But now he considered the possibility again. Was it really something he shouldn't try? Would he lose something in the trying?

Don't be a coward, Yuga.

Cosaire. He turned his head sharply, and there she was, indistinct but unmistakable. He wasn't drifting now but was, as far as he was aware, fully awake.

Yet here she was, as immaculate as ever, regarding him coolly with her arms crossed over her chest.

"I'm..."

You're what? Those are all the right questions. You got handed a tool and now you aren't using it. You're probably correct, it probably won't work—you used it, you felt it, so you already understand it in ways that have nothing to do with the rational and everything to do with instinct. But you're never going to be sure unless you try.

His mouth tightened and he looked away from her, back toward the window and the stars. "I'd be giving Leila and Rachel false hope. They've been through enough."

And you'd have to face them. You'd have to face Kae, such as you can. Leila, I think, might be the one you're truly afraid of.

He glared at her. "What the hell are you talking about?"

You don't think some part of you agreed with that husband of yours? She said *husband* with no particular scorn, as she would have done in life—there would have been acid contempt, in fact. Instead she sounded merely bemused. *You remember how it was the last time he was lying in that bed. You remember how much it hurt. Lochlan blamed you then. You both knew it wasn't fair, but he still did, and that was the beginning of a lot of things. You forgot it after, didn't you? I was keeping you so busy.*

She gave him a dry smile.

But you didn't really forget. You've never forgotten the people you believe were hurt because of you. Died because of you. Every minute of every day, you flog yourself for it. You're like one of those idiot god-worshippers back in the ancient days who believed that if they just suffered enough, they could atone for the sins of all humanity.

She faced him, and then—to his shock—she touched his jaw, and her hand was cold and very solid. *If you won't listen to that witch, maybe you'll listen to me. Stop it. Stop it now. It's arrogance. You're not that important. Your husband thinks you are, because he loves you and to him you're his world, for better or for worse. But this is so much bigger than you. So do what you can do, learn what you can learn, test what you can test, and stop your stupid dithering.*

You probably can't heal them. But maybe this isn't about whether or not you can. Maybe this is a different kind of kick in your ass. Go see them. Do it. Do it, and then move on.

He had been certain, since she started appearing to him, that she was simply a figment of his imagination. A powerful figment, to be sure—powerful and vivid. But just himself talking to himself, a ghost that was only a memory. After all, Cosaire had hated him, had been willing to sacrifice countless numbers of her own people to kill him, in a fit of diseased, mad despair.

She couldn't be real. She couldn't be there.

But now he wondered.

In spite of himself, he almost smiled. It would have been a sickly smile. But there was something about this that he didn't hate. He had never liked talking to her even before she got it into her head that he needed to die, and he wasn't sure he *liked* it now, but that didn't change the fact that what she was talking sounded an awful lot like good sense.

Good sense he'd been running from.

"People keep telling me to let it go. Awfully hard to do that when it's all around you."

When what's all around you? Blood? Death? That was going to be there anyway. I've got news for you, Yuga: this was going to happen sooner or later even without you. It was always headed here. The situation was never sustainable; look at what's happening to the Protectorate without any outside pressure. You just happened to get to the root of the cure before anyone else, and when and how you did. That's all you are in this. You're the first. You'll never be the only one. Maybe you're turning into some new creature, not quite human, and maybe you aren't. Maybe you're the culmination of something set in motion a long time ago for reasons you'll never understand, and maybe you aren't. Maybe you're a tool the universe is using to course-correct itself, and maybe you aren't. But you need to at least ask yourself whether any of that matters.

Remember what the witch on Peris said to you? She called you a prophet. But she also told you what that meant. Not so much telling the future as reminding people of the things they already know, but forgot. Because people are stupid, Yuga. You learn that when you try to manage them. They forget things. Important things. Sometimes you have to prod them.

Sometimes you have to prod them hard.

Go read those books they have. Take a look at their gods. Especially take a look at the desert ones. The ones who kept insisting they were the only real deal. They had to do a lot of poking. And most of the time, that poking involved spilling some blood. One way or the other.

She turned away from him and started to walk up the corridor, heading toward Ixchel's old chambers. *Get out of here. I have all the time in the universe now, but you don't have a lot of it, and you've been wasting your share.*

Adam stared after her, hand pressed against his jaw where she had touched him, and as he watched, another shape emerged from the shadows and took Cosaire's arm. It was difficult to see clearly, and the shape itself was hazy . . .

But as the two forms walked away together, fading into the air, Adam was certain.

Melissa Cosaire had been walking arm in arm with Ixchel.

Kae and Aarons were in adjacent beds. Rachel was seated by Aarons's bed, leaning back in a chair, with her head lowered and her hands loose in her lap, and Leila seated by Kae, in much the same attitude.

And standing beside her, a hand resting on her shoulder, was Lochlan.

For a moment, watching from a few feet away, Adam didn't move.

Then Leila lifted her head. Lochlan looked up at the same time, and there were no words for the expression that passed across his face.

Leila was already rising, coming toward him as he went to her. She appeared exhausted, cried out, but there was also a weary peace on her face that, having seen her before in the docking bay, he might have believed was beyond her. She opened her arms and folded him into them, and as he held on to her, one hand combing through her tangled hair, he remembered when he had first come on board and how kind to him she had been. How kind she and Kae had both been. Far kinder than Lochlan, who had seemed to feel their relationship ought to consist of insulting and swearing at Adam.

Something horribly between laughter and tears pressed against his eyes, the top of his throat.

He loved them. All of them.

"I was starting to get worried," she said, giving him a weak, watery smile. "I mean . . . I'm sure you were tired. Lochlan said he left you sleeping."

Adam's gaze flicked from her up to Lochlan still standing by the bed. And he was certain, somehow, that this wasn't about Lochlan protecting his own ass so much as it was about keeping something painful and difficult, private. Adam shouldn't have to talk about it if he didn't want to.

It was kindness, mostly. Even an olive branch. At least, in that moment, it made sense to take it that way.

"Yeah. I mean . . ." He returned her smile, just as weakly, and it wasn't pretense. "I think I slept through to about an hour ago. I should find Nkiruka after this." A lie he might be caught in, but Leila likely wouldn't care if he was.

"Then you should come see him." Leila stepped back but took both of his hands in hers and tugged him toward Kae's bed.

He went. And when she released him and he looked down, really looked, the rest of the world bled away and all he saw was Kae, the man who had been so kind to him, who had been there when he first woke on Ashwina and who had showed him the ship and taken him to the Arched Halls and given him his first taste of its power and its peace . . . This man, lying ruined in a sickbed. Not just injured like that last time, in the battle with Cosaire's fleet. Ruined.

He tried to swallow and couldn't.

"Nkiruka was here," Leila said softly, standing at his elbow. Somewhere behind them Lochlan also stood, wordless. "She said *he's* here. His mind. His spirit. However you want to think of it. He's buried deep in there, and he might not be able to come back, but he's still here."

Finally able to move, Adam covered Kae's hand with his. It was cool and boneless, and the skin was oddly smooth. The power came to him all at once—what he had done to Protectorate refugees and what he had done to the burned woman—and he didn't have to push very hard. He barely had to press through the surface of Kae's being. He felt that immediately.

Kae was indeed there. So far down he was almost impossible to see, like the shape of a creature lurking in very deep water.

And Adam couldn't do anything for him.

So what was the point of this? he thought, all frustration and despair, and in answer he heard Cosaire's voice once more.

You probably can't heal them, no. But maybe this isn't about whether or not you can. Maybe this is a different kind of kick in your ass.

And even if he couldn't help Kae . . . He was still *there*.

"She's right. I can feel him." He looked up and saw Leila staring back at him, eyes wide.

"Really? You can do that?"

"Perhaps not as well as her. But yeah, I can." He sighed. There was no excitement in this, no pleasure. This wasn't some child's story. Greater levels of being, greater *powers* . . . He had a much better idea now of what they meant, of what they did to someone's life. To the lives of the people around them. "So now what?"

"Ying said we try to keep him comfortable. Keep him alive. And we wait."

"She doesn't know how long?"

Leila shook her head.

Adam's mouth tightened. It was the answer he expected. But no one knew anything. For a people who, he had been raised to believe, were supposedly immersed in the arrogant superstition of fortune-telling, every Bideshi he had ever met was extremely forthcoming about the impossibility of knowing a fluid and highly unreliable future.

It would be nice if that superstition had turned out to be correct.

"You should go." Leila laid a gentle hand on his shoulder, and he felt her old strength. She was tired, grief-stricken, but—like Kae himself—that strength remained under everything. "There isn't much more you can do here. If he can still feel anything, I'm sure he felt you. I'm sure that helped." She paused, then nodded to Aarons's bed. "You should see him too. See Rachel." Her voice dropped. "She's putting on a brave face, but I think she's struggling. She's exhausted. She has been for a while."

"So are you." Adam took her hand and squeezed it, and with his other he cupped her face. "I don't even need to see you. I can feel it on you. Promise me you'll take care of yourself."

"I promise." She gave him another smile, and now it was a little less weak. She inclined her head at Lochlan, who was once more focused on Kae. "He'll make sure I do."

Adam nodded, gave Lochlan one last quick glance.

Lochlan gave him a slight nod of his own. Adam couldn't be sure what he saw on his face then, but he thought it might be an apology. It wasn't what he had hoped for. But it was something.

There wasn't any taking back what Lochlan had said.

He walked to where Aarons lay. Aarons looked better, but not by much. Bandaged head, ugly purplish cast around his eyes. His lips were lax and bloodless. A couple of tubes protruded from his arms. Rachel lifted her gaze as Adam approached, and her lips twitched, as if she was almost giving him a smile.

Leila had been right. She was holding herself together. But the weariness behind her eyes was far deeper than Leila's. She had carried so much on her shoulders for the last three months since Peris. Maybe even before. Adam remembered the camp, how she had taken a leadership role without being asked, how she had seemed to view the other prisoners as her people, how she—like Adam—had wanted so badly to see them all freed.

And then he remembered her children. He hadn't thought of them in a while. He hadn't seen them in a while. While they had still been on Ashwina, they had been kept away from everything martial with a series of people who amounted to foster parents. It was a common practice for multiple people to share the responsibility for caring for children, since multiple marriages weren't uncommon— but her children weren't Bideshi.

And now they were gone. Sent to the other ships in the disbanded convoy. Had she even given them a proper good-bye?

Just how deep did her pain go? What would this do to her? Losing this man, who in spite of his gruffness had become a place of softness and safety for her?

Rachel was strong. She was one of the strongest people he knew. But even strong people could be pushed to a limit, pass that limit, and crumple.

"Hi," he said softly.

"Hi." She did manage a smile, then, and he took comfort in that. She nodded to another chair across the bed, and he took it, his attention moving from her to Aarons and back again.

He didn't need to touch the man to know he was unneeded here. Aarons's injuries might not be nearly as serious as Kae's, but there was little he could do, especially if Ying hadn't been able to do much. Trying would be . . . Perhaps his doubt should feel like giving up. But it only felt like pragmatism. And what he had said to Cosaire about false hope was likely true.

Still.

"What does Ying say? What should we expect with him?"

Rachel shrugged. "She's not sure. The injury to his head . . . it's serious. She put him in this coma to give him a chance to heal. She seems optimistic that he'll come out of it all right, that it won't even be long, but . . . she doesn't know." She swiped a hand down her face and sat back with a hard exhale, her dark skin slightly gray. "No one knows anything."

"I've noticed." Adam paused for a moment, considering. There were questions that needed asking. Questions he hadn't asked Nkiruka. Hadn't had a chance to ask Lochlan. Hadn't felt it appropriate to ask Leila. Now might not be the best time to ask either of them, but there probably wasn't going to be a good time, and for the moment they had space and some unoccupied time and relative quiet, but for the murmur of a busy ward.

And it felt important.

"How did this even happen?"

"How did they get ambushed, you mean? How did *we* get ambushed?" Her mouth tightened. "Aside from the obvious. Aside from who it was."

"Yes."

"We're not sure yet. Eva's told us what she can, but she doesn't know much more than anyone else. I wish we could talk to Bristol." She nodded at Aarons, her face briefly tighter. "He might have a better idea about how it went down. Because I think it's pretty obvious that one of us tipped someone off."

"Are you sure?"

"How else can you explain it? And it must have been before we even arrived. After the decision was made. There's no way the

Protectorate could have come in such force so soon after we did. We were barely there a day. As far as we were able to tell, there was no significant Protectorate presence in the entire sector. In the sectors *around*. They couldn't have gotten there that quickly unless they were ready. Unless they knew exactly where they were going. I know I could be wrong, and there's always a chance we missed something, but Adam . . ."

She leaned forward, her hands clasped tight enough to squeeze the blood out of her knuckles. In seconds she had gone from weary to all cold fire. "They had *force*. They were ready to hit us hard. It was like they knew how many of us there were. That wasn't a recon group, and it wasn't there on patrol. They were on a mission."

Adam got it before she was done speaking. Really, the conclusion was obvious.

Regardless of how horrifying it was.

"One of us."

She nodded. "Someone highly placed. High enough to have been in on the decision relatively early. Or someone with connections. So either news traveled extraordinarily fast—which it could—or . . ."

"One of the people who knew first."

She nodded. "One of the captains."

Adam paused, then dropped his face into his hands. "We're going to make a decision soon," he said, lifting his head after a moment and pressing his folded hands against his chin, elbows on his knees. "About what to do next. They're all going to know the plan. They're all going to *help make the decision*, for fuck's sake. How can we . . .?"

"I really don't know. I have no fucking idea." Rachel looked at Aarons again, and for a moment her calm, poised mask slipped and her grief and her exhaustion and her anger were violently clear. "Maybe we should have expected this. We shouldn't have assumed none of us had anything left to lose. That was one of the biggest things we were banking on. That was one of our biggest advantages."

"Banking on people," Adam murmured. What else did they have? What else was there? But he saw the weaknesses in that strategy. The risks. All these variables, this many people, and how to be sure that they could depend on them? How to give people the freedom to do what they needed to do, to hold on to themselves and what they believed in, let them decide for themselves, and be sure?

If one didn't do that, what did one become?

If we're going to fight monsters, we can't become them.

Rachel nodded again. "Greatest asset. Greatest weakness. So what do we do now?" She closed her eyes and pinched the bridge of her nose. Adam knew that her approach was usually pragmatic and strategic. She was clinging to that now, because even strategy in the face of dire odds was better than simply staring at the man lying in that bed. It was better than merely watching someone you loved in danger, in pain, and knowing that there was nothing you could do to protect them.

Not in the end.

And once more he wondered if this last thing would break her.

"I don't know." He looked at Aarons again, thought of him—strong. Aarons had once been a tool of Melissa Cosaire, an enemy . . . Except now Adam understood that Aarons had never been anything of the kind. He had been given a job to do. He tried to do it to the best of his ability. When it became obvious that it was the wrong job, he stopped. Ended it. Ended it by killing the woman who had employed him. And Adam was certain that with her, as when Aarons had been chasing Adam, there had been no personal malice.

It had just been a job.

His part in this fight hadn't been a job to him. That much had been clear when he saved Adam and Lochlan from Sinder's detention cells. This had been something he actually believed in. Was willing to fight for.

Die for.

Likely not out of romantic idealism. He wasn't a romantic man. Simply out of a pragmatic understanding that it was necessary. It was the right thing to do, in the most basic possible sense.

One didn't have to love justice with all one's heart in order to uphold it with everything one was.

"I remember," he said, still quiet, still looking at Aarons. "I remember when we were in the camp. When we first met you. You were so strong. I was sure immediately." He nodded at Aarons. "Like him. You were willing to do whatever you had to do. You cared that much. Because you came so close to losing everything."

"Saw everyone else losing everything too. People who were proud once. People who believed in what was killing them." She passed a hand over her face, her fingers pressing briefly against her closed, swollen eyes. "*I* believed. We were fed poison and told it was medicine, and we ate it up. Sucked it down. Coded into us before we were even born." She leaned further forward and looked down at her hands. "You think you ever escape what you were, Adam? You think you ever get away from it? Can you really change, or do you just carry that person around on your back for the rest of your life? Trying not to look at them, trying to shake them . . . And you never do."

"We can change." He didn't have to think. Because he believed it. He believed it completely. Despite everything else he doubted, there was still that. "We have to be able to change. There's no point otherwise. There's no point to any of this."

"Adam, I'll be completely fucking honest with you. That's what I'm wondering. The point. That's what I'm not sure of."

"He believed."

"I know he did. Look at him now."

"That wasn't because he believed. Someone betrayed him. Kae, Eva, all of us. We're going to find them." Anger swept over him, unexpected and terrible, and he clenched his fists at his sides, blunt nails digging into his palms until there was pain. He didn't like anger and didn't often feel it. It burned in him. It hurt.

She gave him a wan smile. "Even if we don't know how. Even if we only have hours."

"That, we can fix. We can stall. We can tell Adisa what we think—he's probably already thinking along the same lines. He hasn't led these people for as long as he has without being sharp as a knife. He can find a way to postpone the meeting. At least for a day or two."

"That doesn't help us much." Rachel's mouth thinned. "And you're that sure you can trust him?"

"Yes." However unreliable people in general might be, there were some he never doubted even for a second. "I trust him, Rachel. I know you still don't know him that well, but I do. I already have. Many times. I'd trust him with my life."

"With everyone's lives?" Rachel let out a slow breath. "No, no, I get you. I do. Anyway, I can't think of any reason why he would be beholden to the Protectorate. Or anything working for them. I think . . ." She gritted her teeth briefly, a grimace that was almost painful to see. "It has to be one of ours. Has to be."

Adam said nothing. She needed no agreement from him. She would already know it was there.

For a moment they sat in silence. Then Adam pushed himself up, feeling his aches, his weariness afresh. *Getting old*, he thought. He was barely into his thirties, but what was time anymore? What was age? *This business makes you old.*

"I should . . ." He didn't know what he ought to do. Or he knew what his next move had to be, but nothing in front of him felt as real as it should. None of it felt as solid, as meaningful. He examined those possibilities now, laid out in front of him, threads intertwined in a massively complex, terrible, *beautiful* tapestry, and felt them all slipping through his fingers.

He didn't have the option of stopping.

He looked helplessly at Rachel and she nodded, waved a hand at him with a kind of gentleness. *Go. It's all right. Go.*

"I'll come back and see him soon," he said quietly and left.

He had one more person to see.

He found Ying in her private office, slumped in the chair behind her desk, her face in her hands. He was sure that she wasn't asleep, and she didn't appear to be weeping, but for a moment he waited in her doorway to see if she would call him to her or wait for him to come in.

It seemed like decades since he had first been here, come to be examined by her in his early days on Ashwina, when it fact it had been barely a year. Yet it also seemed like it might have happened only the day before. The place looked the same—bright, open, spacious, and decorated with a simple elegance. Light colors. Clean, spare surfaces. It was, he had thought then, somehow a mixture of the Protectorate's austerely pristine approach to cultivating surroundings, and the Bideshi's beautiful, organic chaos.

It was a good place to be. Healing in itself. He was sure it had been designed that way.

But now even its brightness seemed dulled, and even the open space felt like it was closing in on itself.

"Ying?"

She raised her head immediately, and though her eyes were red-rimmed, they were dry. "Adam." With a faint smile, she gestured to the low couch near the desk. As he went to it, she rose, brushing aside a pad and some papers, and joined him, sitting down in an equally low and comfortable chair opposite. "What can I do for you?"

He returned her smile, just as faintly—but warm, warm as hers had been. From the beginning she had been kind to him, one of the few who had been kind and welcoming before he was ever Named and made their *brother*. She had healed him of the illness that had driven him from the Protectorate, even if that healing hadn't been permanent, and she had been one of those who supported his being allowed to stay and take refuge.

She cared for people. It was the core of her being.

"You look tired, Ying."

"We're all tired, dear heart." She swept a strand of silver-streaked red hair out of her face and leaned forward. "You didn't come up here to tell me that."

Adam shook his head. "I came to see Kae and Aarons." *Among other things.* "Rachel and Leila filled me in a bit, but . . ."

"Then you know as much as I do already." She sighed. "Aarons will be well. Eventually. I'm fairly certain, anyway. Kae . . . I don't know. I won't know for a while."

"I know you're doing everything you can."

"Would for anyone, equally. Isn't that why I'm here?" Her smile returned briefly and then was gone again. "But in truth, between us . . . I love that boy like my own. Him and Lochlan, like brothers from the beginning. Seeing him like this . . ." She closed her eyes, and her expression was pained—gone quickly, like her smile, but intense. "I can't even tell you what it does to me. I'll fight for him. Adam. I'll fight with everything I have."

He nodded. Ying's determination, her strength . . . They radiated from her, washed over him and sent a little more solidity into his spine. But everything still felt distant. Even what her presence was doing to and for him—it was almost as if it was happening to someone else.

This sensation of separation from himself . . . It was new.

He didn't like it.

"There's something else, though."

She cocked her head. "Oh?"

"Yeah. Look, did you— Did you get word of an accident down on the engine level a few hours ago?"

"I . . . Yes, I did. Why?"

"What did you hear?"

Ying frowned. "Well, I . . . It seemed mostly straightforward: there was a coolant leak somewhere there shouldn't have been, and it mixed with something else that ignited it—which should *never* happen, by the way. There must have been more damage than they thought. But there was a fire. Some people received minor injuries."

"Really." Adam couldn't hide his surprise; he had been wondering why Ying hadn't begun by questioning *him* about it. "Is that all?"

Ying's eyes narrowed very slightly. "It was strange, actually, how chaotic it was. Some people were swearing up and down that they'd seen a woman on fire healed minutes later. Others were insisting she wasn't on fire at all. And there were other conflicts between the two of those claims. The woman herself . . . She just seemed confused. I figured she took a knock on the head. We were busy, so I pretty much dismissed it." She studied him. "You know what happened, don't you?"

"I know," Adam said quietly. "I was there. There *was* a woman on fire. She was burned. She shouldn't have survived." He took a breath. "I saved her."

Ying blinked—but she didn't look nearly as startled as she might have. "You healed her. Like one of my assistants."

"I—I think so. Yes."

"And the people there didn't know who you were." She paused, her brow furrowed. "That's strange. You'd think they would."

Yes, you would. But hadn't he felt different in that moment? Hadn't he felt something *more,* and more intensely than he ever had before? For a while now, he had been thinking of his *changing* in vague terms. Maybe it was becoming a lot less vague.

"Everything was— It was chaos. I barely knew what was going on myself. Could be that no one got a good look at me." He drew in a breath. "As far as what I did, I don't know if it was more than your people could do or about the same, but . . ."

Ying was silent a moment. "It really depends," she said finally, clasping her hands between her knees. "Our abilities aren't nearly as exact as you might think. All kinds of things dictate what we can and can't heal. Sometimes healing is easy—usually easier the more recently the injury was suffered. Sometimes even simple things are surprisingly hard: viruses, bacterial infections, injuries. You've seen how much we do with other . . . I suppose what you would consider *conventional* methods." Her smile returned, and now it was a touch sardonic. "It's not all hand waving and spell casting. A burn that should have killed might be something we could handle, if it had just happened. How quickly did you get to her?"

"Quick. Seconds after."

"That might make all the difference." She was silent again, the tips of her fingers drumming together. "This was the first time it happened? Like this, I mean?"

Adam nodded. Now that he was talking about it, now that she was asking him simple questions . . . He didn't necessarily feel better. But he did feel more grounded. "There's what I could do before, but that felt different. I don't know how to explain what this was. It wasn't *unlike* what I've done before, but it definitely wasn't the same."

"No. It wouldn't be. What you were doing for your own people . . . No one has ever done anything quite like that before, Adam. Not that you were somehow *more powerful* than any Bideshi healer. Not that you were more skilled. But it's a particular ability, and you have to know that there are those of us who believe it was given to you for a particular purpose. By who or what, we don't know—the workings of the universe are persistently mysterious. But if you buy in to the idea that there's some kind of greater intent behind all of this, we aren't able to do what you do because, to be blunt, it was never intended to be our job." She arched a brow. "If you'll permit me to talk like your husband used to, *you people* appear to have been tasked with saving yourselves."

"I don't know what's behind this." Adam's voice was soft, and he looked away. Among the Bideshi, it was a widely held belief that there was Something, some logic behind it all, perhaps sentient and aware and perhaps not.

But Adam still wasn't sure he believed. There was some underlying logic, maybe. But no gods. Only people.

People they still had to depend on.

"Regardless. There has to be a reason. The question is what it is." She glanced toward the door. "You tried to heal them, I assume."

"I tried with Kae. At least I went—I went far enough *in* that I could tell I wouldn't be able to. Aarons, I could tell without having to go in at all. Even though he isn't as badly off."

Ying nodded. "Not surprising. Injuries to the brain are some of the most difficult to treat." Her mouth twisted. "The complexities. There are so many levels damage can occur on. I'm sure you felt that."

She rose and began to pace slowly. "What this means, I don't know. It suggests a lot of things to me. Everything is in a state of flux right now. Nothing can be depended on to go the way it usually does. That may well include you."

"Yes." Adam captured his lower lip with his teeth, bit down, and the flash of pain centered him. Here it was—what he had kept from almost everyone. "Ying, I . . . I think I'm changing, and I don't know what I'll become, and I don't know . . . what it's for. Why. You say there's a reason. I can't see it. But everywhere I go, there's death, and I . . ."

He swung his gaze away. It was difficult to look at her. She was his friend—a close friend, even. But not so close that he had confided anything like this in her before.

She didn't answer. Not at once. But she stopped pacing and faced him, and in his peripheral vision he saw that her expression was steady. Calm, and when she spoke, her tone matched.

"Your former people know about evolution. If anyone does, they would. Yes?"

Still without looking at her, he nodded.

"Well," she said quietly. "I don't pretend to understand. Perhaps I'm not meant to. But, Adam . . . it's possible that you're evolving."

The words settled into the air, and in his mind Adam approached them. Stared at them. Circled them, tried to feel his way through them. *Evolving.* Everyone he healed had followed him in that ability. But he was going further. Moving away from everyone.

For what? And *into* what?

He turned his attention back to Ying and she was squaring her shoulders, businesslike. Brisk. "As I said, I don't know why it's happening to you. What we can *do* with your ability—if anything—is more of an immediate concern. I know you're currently employed by Nkiruka in a variety of tasks, but may I place you on call for the clinic? Not for you to spend specifically allotted time here, you understand, but to come when we badly need an extra pair of hands? If you can?"

A pang of doubt hit him. The idea of telling her no was abhorrent. But still. "I'm not certain I could do it again."

"Oh, yes you are." She gave him yet another faint smile, the kind of smile a mother might give a child who has just said something silly. "And even if it turns out you can't, you could still assist those who can." Her expression became serious. "Please say yes, Adam. I think the time is coming when we'll need everyone. Everyone together, everyone lending every ounce of strength they have."

"We aren't there already?"

She shook her head. "You know we aren't. You know we haven't yet reached the peak of our extremity."

He didn't answer. He couldn't think of an answer. She was right. One way or another—whether the fleet ripped itself apart, Kae didn't survive, or there *was* a traitor in their midst—things were going to get worse. "I'll do it," he said at last. Really, it wasn't such a hard decision. "If you need me, send word. I can't promise I'll come, but—"

"The possibility is all I ask." Ying returned to her chair and sank into it, pushing her hair back from her face. The animation had slipped away from her, and she was only tired again. "Now you must leave, dearest. I'd like to talk to you more—and I'd like to see these new abilities of yours in action—but I need to sleep, at least a little. Or I won't be fit to help anyone."

Adam nodded and rose.

He was almost at the door when he stopped and turned back. It wasn't necessary to say this. She must already know. But things like this shouldn't go unsaid now. They were more important than ever. Where there was love, anyone and everyone should know.

That too was part of survival.

"You're like family to me, Ying," he said softly. "I know we haven't known each other for . . . hardly at all, really. But even so. Like family. Few people have ever been so kind to me."

The brief smile Ying gave him was still strained, but full of warmth. Full of affection. "I know, sweet boy. I know it." She nodded at the door. "I'll speak to you soon."

Adam left.

Outside her office, he passed a hand over his face, pressing his fingertips against his eyelids. What he *wanted* to do was to sleep again. But he had to see Adisa. Perhaps he should wait until Rachel could accompany him, but there wasn't time. If they wanted a prayer of success, they had to move now.

He had just stepped through the clinic's wide doors and into the equally wide corridor when he heard someone softly call his name.

Not *someone.* He knew who it was. Slowly he turned, his heart rising into his throat, tight and aching.

Lochlan met his gaze then his eyes dropped away. He said nothing else.

"What do you want, Lock?"

He had expected to feel relief when Lochlan spoke to him. Maybe a powerful urge to forgive. And in fact he did feel them, but more than anything he just felt numb.

He still didn't know what to do. It should have been merely a stupid argument, fueled primarily by exhaustion and drink, but it wasn't.

It just wasn't.

Lochlan shook his head. "I'm sorry," he murmured—and everything was in those two words. They were wrenched. Ashamed. Sorrowful.

Frightened.

Adam wanted to go to him. Hold him. Wanted it so much it was a physical pain, massive, sending shudders through him. Worse even than when Lochlan had been hissing abuse at him. This man was everything he wanted. A man who had given so much for him, come through so much, been so strong, done so much growing. It wasn't fair.

It wasn't fair that now Adam looked at him and felt so much distance.

If he came through this, if they both did, he didn't know who—or what—he would be. And now he was realizing that he didn't know who Lochlan would be either.

On that desert world, before they were taken into the camp, he had said that he didn't know if love was enough. Then he had faith it was again. Now, standing here . . .

He just wasn't sure.

"I know," he whispered. "Lock . . . I know. I am too. I'm . . ." He lowered his head, his eyes, and squeezed them shut against sudden tears. He wanted to say that it was all right. He *could*. He could say it, and it would be a lie, but maybe he could make himself believe it; believe it, and at least for the present it might be enough.

But there had never been lies here. Not even at the beginning, when everything was difficult and he'd been certain Lochlan hated him. And if he lied, Lochlan would know. It wouldn't work. It wouldn't fix anything.

"I can't do this now," he finished. "I want to. I promise, I do. But there's too much. Do you understand? There's too much right now. Later maybe we can—"

Lochlan put up a hand, shook his head. He still wasn't looking directly at Adam. Pain twisted his features. "Later," he echoed, and managed a weak smile. "I'll be here. I'm not going anywhere. Promise."

"Promise." Adam hesitated. He couldn't stay. He had been telling the truth—he couldn't do this now. But he also couldn't go. Not like this.

He could move, go to Lochlan, slide into his arms. But instead he raised his hand and laid his fingers against his breastbone, over his heart. It was an odd gesture, one with no prior significance to them, but it felt right. He sent it across the space between them and trusted that it would be accepted.

"*Chusile*," he said, soft. A word he hardly ever used. Lochlan's word. But he meant it. He felt it.

My dance. My heart.

He turned and walked away, and he didn't look back.

CHAPTER

FOURTEEN

The official story was that no part of the grand Terran capital was impoverished. No part was uncared for, unmaintained, or anything less than gracefully lovely. No part was inhabited by people who were anything less than the pinnacle of genetic engineering. It would never be allowed.

Isaac Sinder descended into the lowest levels of the city—into the evidence that belied the official story, in order to maintain that story.

The aircar dropped and dropped, and traffic thinned. He was still being chauffeured today, but by a different man—a man specifically sought out and chosen for his willingness to go where few other people went, and to be highly discreet about it. Top Protectorate and Terran officials made use of him, and of people like him, to convey them to places where they could satisfy particular interests. Particular proclivities. Not all of them carnal in nature, but all of them strange, and for things that would be more difficult to obtain in the higher, more respectable, more *visible* parts of the city.

As the car continued to drop, the light faded, though it was only midday. The buildings crowded in and were less clean, less scrubbed. Deeper and deeper, and the mortar and concrete was stained here and there with exhaust and dirty water, and the metal was tarnished, the glass and crystal in need of polishing. There was still a stateliness about it, but it was the stateliness of old grace and fallen majesty.

In his studies of Terran history, Sinder had come upon the story of the ancient city of Troy—a place of myth and legend and power. And how it had not been one city but *many*, one built atop the ruins of the other.

So it was with the Terran capital. So it was, in fact, with many of the greatest Terran cities. The greatest civilization the galaxy had ever known advanced incredibly, not in thousands of years but merely hundreds, and so new and better structures had been built to reflect that advancement. That great progress, accompanying a great and noble work.

After another fifteen minutes or so, the ground finally became visible. It rose up to him out of the gloom like the swell of a dark sea. By then gloom was indeed what they were falling through; much of the remaining sun had disappeared, throwing them into a heavy twilight. Here lights burned: windows, lamps, the multicolored glow of screens and signs. Below them were streets, actual streets—the original streets of the original city, or as close to it as they would ever get. The streets were lined by lamps on high posts, orange-yellow, staining the black pavement with pools of illumination. Along these streets groundcars hummed—more evidence of the older period this place was trapped in.

And who lived down here? Someone might assume monsters, mutants, twisted and misshapen things that had been cast out of the world above, mistakes never admitted and not euthanized at birth.

No monsters down here. Merely people who—for one reason or another—had fallen into disfavor, or who hadn't been terribly well off at birth and hadn't improved their station. There was no overtly violent lawlessness to speak of—which wasn't to say there was no crime. It wasn't to say there was no poverty. Simply that the truth of this place wasn't nearly as dramatic as one might assume.

Even here, the dignity of the Protectorate maintained itself. Even here, its bonds and structures and ways couldn't be destroyed.

That gave him hope for their future beyond anything he saw in the world above.

The aircar set itself down in a small alley with a soft hiss, and after a pause the hatch opened silently. Sinder rose, smoothed a few wrinkles out of his suit, and with a nod at the driver he emerged from the dimness.

He smelled them immediately: smoke, exhaust, the sour-sweet smell of decaying garbage, faint but nevertheless perceptible. He stood for a moment, getting his bearings, and observed a tavern across the street, a groundcar dealership a little way down, and a few people passing by, moving as if in no particular hurry. In his experience, the inhabitants of the city's ground level were never especially hurried and never under any obvious stress. The reason for this was simple: the work they did was rarely of real importance. It was something to do. They were solidly mediocre—by Protectorate standards—and lived lives untouched by any true responsibility.

Sinder was sure some of those above might find such an existence desirable, if they were aware the people here possessed it. But he didn't think much of that attitude. It was necessary, for a true Protectorate citizen, to find a purpose and hold to it. Everyone should have a task. Everyone should contribute something vital—no matter how small— and *know* that they did so, and take pleasure in the knowledge.

If they didn't—to any significant degree—it was yet more evidence of a slow, subtle decline that he was seeing more and more clearly and that he was finding more and more disturbing.

Squaring his shoulders, he headed across the street toward the tavern's green-and-blue glowing sign. He paused to look at its subtly shifting color, oddly beautiful. The name of the place.

The Crooked Spine.

An odd name, he'd thought when he first saw it, and now too. Somehow perverse. People down here tended to possess a wry sense of humor.

Inside, the tavern was all dark, polished wood, and it was in many respects a reproduction of taverns from Terra's distant past. The decor was more out of place, dating from a past unique to what had then been called the West. He was aware of the phenomenon many had disparagingly termed *colonialism*—back when it was primitively understood—and the presence of an aesthetic that had belonged to a dominant culture in a place where it was essentially foreign was pleasing to him.

It was almost like a subtle tribute to one of the Protectorate's forebears. For would the West have been so dominant if it was not, in some profound way, superior?

The place was quiet and only a few people were hunched over its tables, toying with half-full glasses. Those who sat with companions were leaning close together and talking in low voices. The tranquility was another feature of the bar; one might assume it would be ill-mannered and raucous, but again, the carefully bred Protectorate gentility reached down easily. These people still had that breeding. They wouldn't abandon it.

For many of them, it was one of the only significant things they had.

He already knew where he was going. He headed toward the back of the place, which was secluded by half walls, corners of it completely out of sight. On his way, he nodded at the bartender—a tall, slim woman with carefully coiffed white hair and a bearing only slightly less aristocratic than any he had seen above. She returned his nod and returned to polishing glasses.

The space was empty except for a single middle-aged man seated in a large chair upholstered in maroon leather. He looked up as Sinder approached and motioned for him to sit. Sinder did so. He didn't greet the man by name; he didn't know his name. It was better not to, given what he was here for.

"Punctual as always," said the man, leaning forward over a glass of what appeared to be dark, thick beer. His gray eyes were bright. "I appreciate that. As always."

Sinder nodded again. "It's the least I can do, considering."

"The least you can do is see that I'm paid promptly. Which I have no doubt you'll do." The man smiled. His mouth was already thin, and now it nearly vanished into a line. "Again, as always."

"Shall we get down to business, then?"

"In a moment." The man raised his glass. "I'd like to finish this first. It's excellent. Shall I ask Gail to bring you a glass?"

Sinder waved him off. It was better—in these transactions—to keep his wits fully about him. "You're very kind, but I shouldn't. I'm afraid it doesn't agree with my digestion."

"Something else, then?"

"Thank you. But no. Beer in general doesn't agree with me, and I try not to drink at all past a certain time."

"Suit yourself." The man took a swig and closed his eyes in quiet satisfaction. "How goes it in the world of love and light?"

"Bright and loving. Busy. As I'm sure you know, the peacekeepers have been addressing a little problem of late."

"Yes." Another grave sip of beer. "Your insurgency."

"Hardly mine. But yes."

"And how is that going for you?"

The barb was difficult to miss, even if it was subtle. Because here was the final—and in many ways the most fundamental—truth about the people who lived in this shadow world. They had been raised in Terran society—under the wing of the Protectorate, a wing that both covered and lifted. They maintained its conventions and its ways and the surface of its ideals. But the surface was as deep as any of that allegiance ran.

Some of these people likely still considered themselves true citizens of the Protectorate. But many more did not. Citizens of what, then? Of a world they themselves governed, even if they paid official lip service to the Terran government and to the highest authorities of the Protectorate. Down here, he might as well be in a different country.

He was a visitor. And while this man worked with him, their concerns were not the same.

"It's going well enough. Better, after we take care of certain matters. I trust you have them ready?"

Sinder's contact sat back and nodded, his face relaxed, placid. A careful placidity. What they were discussing was something about which one was either placid or wasn't able to do at all.

The man suddenly pushed back his chair and got to his feet, stretching. "They're upstairs, as a matter of fact. You'd like to see them before we make arrangements for transportation?"

Sinder rose as well. "Please."

Together the two men walked through a narrow door at the very back of the room and into a short corridor. It ended in a flight of steps illuminated at intervals by yellowish lights even dimmer than the ones on the main floor of the tavern. These stairs led them to another flight, and then to another—an unusual number, in a world in which lifts were ubiquitous. Finally they came out onto a floor that might have been as many as six or seven stories above street level, and he found himself standing in a brightly lit hallway.

It also didn't look anything like the tavern.

Gone was the feeling of antiquity. In its place was a far more familiar aesthetic: clean white walls and floor, the kind of spareness that managed to keep from being sterile, and a sense that they had somehow jumped forward in time by climbing up into it out of the past.

Which was true. Maybe not exactly here, but in the whole of this world, it was.

Here and there along the length of the hall were doors—plain, unmarked, and though they had the appearance of polished silver, Sinder knew better. These were reinforced doors, strong enough to withstand any attempt to open them that didn't involve explosives or heavy equipment. From the outside—and, more importantly, from the inside.

The man gestured to the left and began to walk. "It's down here."

Sinder followed him. The man stopped at the second door on the right and touched his fingertips to five small depressions on the wall, which had been invisible from a distance. There was a pause. Then the door slid open with a barely audible hum.

The room beyond was large, just as bright and just as clean as the hallway. It was lined with shining steel tables—twenty in all, ten on each side.

On each table was a person.

One might, Sinder supposed, assume they were dead. They certainly *looked* dead—grayish, bloodless lips, their bodies lax. They were naked, and rather than a cloth, they were swathed in what looked like a spun-steel cocoon. A cocoon—or a spiderweb.

Little flies, caught. He needed what was inside them.

The man stopped in the center of the room and turned to face him, hands clasped behind his back. "So here they are. Are they to your satisfaction?"

Slowly, Sinder began to walk down the rows. The truth was that any live human would do—perhaps any sentient—but Julius had made it clear that some subjects worked better than others. Young ones. Strong ones. People in generally good health—not difficult, anywhere on Terra. In particular—and this, he had said, was most vital—they mustn't show any signs of the disease slowly burning its way through the citizenry. That they already had it, he knew, but he suspected it would only be an issue if it was manifesting symptoms.

Young and strong and healthy. Man or woman apparently didn't matter, so Sinder had arranged for ten of each. He looked them over now—they had a range of skin tones, hair colors, and doubtless eye colors. But all of them relatively similar beneath these surface differences.

All attractive, of course. But noticeably attractive, even by Protectorate standards.

Sinder was sure that a great number of the selection criteria were necessary. But he wondered, now and then, how much of this was about what Julius required. And how much was about his pleasure.

It probably didn't matter. It might be that there was no meaningful difference between the two.

He made his way up one row and down the other, to give the appearance of looking over what he was buying, when in fact he was simply lost in meditation. Meditation on what he was doing. On what it meant. On what else he was willing to sacrifice, on how much more of his soul he was willing to chip away.

Because here, gazing down at these faces that looked dead already, it was perhaps easier to be honest with himself than anywhere else. These might be denizens of this lower world, and they might indeed be the Protectorate's version of castoffs, but they were still technically his people.

His people, and he was delivering them to . . .

Needs must.

He turned back to the man. "They've been appropriately sedated?"

The man nodded. His expression was still deeply placid. "Of course. If you arrange for transportation now, we'll make sure they don't wake up until . . . Well. Until you want them to."

"Good," Sinder murmured absently. The truth was that there were details of this transaction—of what its goal entailed—that he didn't know, and was happier remaining ignorant of. "Transportation . . . I would need it taken care of immediately. You can do that?"

The man nodded. "Shouldn't be any trouble. We already have people making runs up and down right now, but there are several others who are free for the moment. Provided you don't want them taken too far."

"No." Sinder smiled faintly. "No, it will be mostly a straight rise."

The man gave him a sharp smile. "My favorite kind. Oh, and there's the last thing you requested." He reached into his pocket and produced a small box, rather like a jewelry gift box. He held it out to Sinder, who took it, opened it.

Inside lay a tiny glass vial full of a clear liquid. Sinder gazed at it.

"Exactly what you specified. Don't be fooled by its size. It'll get the job done for you."

Sinder closed the box with a snap, looked around a few moments more, and nodded. "I think we can call this officially a deal. I'll see the rest of the payment is sent directly to your account."

"Good." The man jerked his chin toward the door. "Then we have other matters we should discuss."

Obviously. A thin thread of pleased warmth snaking through him, Sinder was turning to follow, when a soft rustling behind him caught his attention. Curious, he turned—and froze, that thread sharpening into a blade of ice.

Every one of those bodies had turned its head toward him. Each head's eyes were open, staring at him. And they were black pits, holes of nothingness, the space between galaxies where no stars shone.

As he stared, all the feeling dissolving out of his nerves, their blue lips peeled back from their teeth in something between a grimace and a horrible smile. They couldn't move, no—surely they couldn't; the cocoons were designed in part to be a safeguard against that. He was safe from them, these ghouls, *looking* at him with those terrible, accusing eyes. But he didn't feel safe. His testicles were pulling into his body cavity, his breath suddenly shallow, adrenaline pumping in spite of his numbness. Ready to run, and not certain that he could.

But he blinked, and the vision was gone. Everything was as it had been. The bodies were silent and still on the table. And his companion was touching his shoulder lightly.

Sinder managed to keep from jumping.

"Are you all right?"

"I—" Sinder cleared his throat. "Yes. Yes, I'm fine. Just . . . considering the future." He spun briskly and jerked his head toward the door. "I shouldn't linger. Let's go."

He was overtired, as he had been before. That was all, and it was understandable. There were things he could do to mitigate it. He would see to it.

Together they returned to the stairwell, and this time the climb was considerably shorter. When they emerged into the next corridor, it looked a good bit like the tavern on the ground level, but newer, somehow cleaner. The carpet was a deep green, only a little threadbare, and softly glowing lights lined the walls, along with framed paintings. Several of them were genuinely expensive. The man led him down the hall to a door at the end—more dark wood and subtly elegant carvings—and opened it.

The room beyond was small and comfortable, with two plush armchairs in front of a fireplace, a series of tall bookshelves lining the walls, and a writing desk, beside which sat a drinks cabinet. The mantel above the fireplace was cluttered with objects: small statuettes, a few books, an empty tumbler, the skull of what might have been a cat. A fire was burning, and the only other illumination in the room was from a green-shaded lamp on the desk.

"My fondness for antiques," said the man, heading to the cabinet and producing a bottle full of something rich golden-brown. "I have to confess that it doesn't stop downstairs."

"I appreciate it." Sinder took a seat in front of the fire and crossed his legs. The shock of the waking dream had almost completely left him, and now he was calm, even relaxed, muscles steady and vision clear. "I'm a fan of history myself. Not so much its aesthetics, but aesthetics are part of everything, I suppose."

"They are," the man said gravely, returning with two glasses. "Now please, at least take a drop or two. To seal our arrangement."

Sinder hesitated only a moment before taking his Surely a little wouldn't do any harm, and it would be unwise at this point to be impolite. It was remotely possible that the man was trying to poison him . . . but poisoning him would make no sense, at least none that Sinder could see. It would confer no advantage, gain the man nothing. He hadn't even been paid.

True, there were always things you couldn't anticipate. But it didn't seem likely that this was one.

He waited until the man was seated to sip. The taste was strange—sharp and smooth at once, with a bitter aftertaste that was, nevertheless, not unpleasant. He let it rest in his mouth for a moment, then swallowed.

"What is it?"

The man smiled faintly. "I think I'm going to keep that my secret. A man must have secrets."

"Because you have no others at all." Sinder arched a brow but was willing to let it go.

"So, then." The man stared into the depths of the tumbler as if it could tell him something, and lifted his gaze to the fire. "This place is secure?"

"There's no place more secure in the entire building."

"Good." Sinder was quiet a moment longer, then pushed ahead. It was best to be as direct about this as possible. "I'm going to create a situation of civil unrest. I need you to exacerbate that situation as much as you can down here. To the extent you're able, make *down here* bleed into *up there*."

The man didn't answer immediately. He was still staring thoughtfully into the fire. "How much unrest? How severe?"

"Severe. Not too much so. I need things unstable, but I don't need them to come crashing down. I would prefer that they didn't, actually. I intend to be on top when they stop wobbling."

"So that's your game."

"It's not a game."

"Of course not." The man took a sip of his drink and closed his eyes briefly. "You've paid me for your merchandise. Or you shortly will. So that business is concluded. Very straightforward, very clean. Uncomplicated. What you're asking . . ." He fixed his gaze on Sinder, a thin smile pulling at his mouth. "It's complicated. It involves putting people in danger. I maintain order down here, Sinder. Me and people like me. Chaos is the polar opposite of what we do."

"Order can hide in chaos." Sinder slid his fingers around the cool glass of the tumbler. Yet where the liquid touched it, it seemed warmer, though in his mouth he didn't detect it. "I'm not asking you to put any of your own people in danger. Surely there are those down here who are expendable. I mean, clearly there are." His smile was wry. "You just sold twenty of them to me."

The man was quiet again. Then, "How exactly will you *compensate* me for this? Compensate more than just me. This would involve coordination on a fairly considerable scale. It would be expensive. It would make what you just paid look like the purchase of a pet. A sofa."

"I have ways. Once this is all over, I'll have more ways than you can imagine."

"Surely you don't expect me to do this for you on credit."

"I don't. We can settle on a price and I can pay you half up front. Same as this. You clearly don't feel that you can trust me; fair enough. How am I to be certain I can trust you?"

"Fair enough," the man echoed softly, and paused. "I'll consult with my colleagues and we'll send you a quote. Just so you're aware, there won't be much room for negotiation here. I would count on there being none."

Sinder nodded. This wasn't unexpected, and it was always comforting to have things play out as your logic and intuition told you they must. "I think I don't have much else to say, then. Send me your quote, I'll send you my details, and we can proceed from there."

"I hope you'll finish your drink. I promise you, it wasn't cheap."

Sinder nodded and took another sip. It really was excellent. He gazed into the fire and allowed his mind to unfocus. Rest. All was well. And when a faint tremor ran through his hands, he tightened his fingers on the glass and it passed quickly. His control over it was pleasurable, and the sensation of warmth returned to him.

"One more question," the man said after another short silence. "What's your timetable? How soon are you planning to move?"

"Oh." Sinder didn't turn head away from the fire, but he smiled "Soon.

"Very soon."

CHAPTER

FIFTEEN

Nkiruka made it through the next morning with the aid of deep meditation. Not much else could have been any help to her.

Adisa had come to her, told her what Adam reported to him. A traitor. Likely highly placed. No idea how they might be discovered before the next plans were made. Someone in the Protectorate side of the fleet, but even that couldn't be concluded with certainty. It was, in other words, a disaster. People had died. Probably, no matter what happened next, more people would.

Two things were unspoken—though clear—and Nkiruka was reasonably certain that neither Adam nor Adisa had made these suggestions to anyone else. Though Adisa would likely make one of them. If someone else didn't suggest it first.

The first: Could she help? Could she send out feelers, touch minds, discover whatever she could discover? Any hint, any clue, no matter how small? She wasn't certain; her powers were considerable, had been tested at the battle on Peris and revealed as much, but used like this, so deep and focused, wielded like a scalpel . . . She didn't know. She would try.

And second—and terrible, but she had already thought of it: they could give up. Retreat permanently. Either dissolve the fleet and let everyone go where they would, or band together, depart for the furthest reaches of space, and try to find a new home. Raise families. Start their own colony. Be satisfied with saving these few members of the whole society they had been trying for. Live.

For some, it might seem like a far better choice. People with children. People who hoped to see those children again. See them grow, have children of their own. Who with children didn't want that?

So much pain, and so much more to come.

She took refuge in the Halls now, kneeling before her fire and running a length of beads through her fingers. Ixchel's. She had made such things—bracelets and anklets and necklaces and things to be woven through hair. She had given them as gifts, in accord with her own mysterious whims. Beautiful things of multicolored glass and multifaceted crystal. Things that seemed to have their own meaning, deep and ineffable, and their own secret purposes. Doubtless, they did. Ixchel had never done anything without meaning, without intent.

The piece Nkiruka was holding now had no obviously specific purpose. It was simply a braided length, a series of strands woven together, with no clasp or hook to suggest it was to be worn in any way. To someone who didn't know Ixchel or her ways, it might look unfinished. It was one of the last items she had ever made. Woven on Takamagahara, perhaps completed mere hours before the battle and the wounds that eventually killed her.

She had known. In the end, as the wave functions collapsed, it had all become clear to her. So she had accepted it. She had gone to it with the grief anyone feels upon seeing loved ones die and with the sadness that accompanies leaving a world and a life one holds dear, but she had prepared.

She had known, Nkiruka sensed, about the woman who would take her place. So she had made this thing for that woman to inherit. It was something Nkiruka was meant to use.

Not a big thing. Not a weapon or some item of great power. But important. Something she should hold close. Something to solidify the ground beneath her.

She did so now, fingering each line of the braid and each bead. As she did, her mind calmed, eased, and she both sank into herself and was lifted higher. Separating. She had touched the universe like this, of course—had practiced, sending herself out into the night, stroking and caressing the minds she found there, giving them solace and strength. In small ways she had been doing it since the fleet had exited slipstream. There was much pain, yes—so much sorrow and fear. None of their people had been prepared to lose so much.

You never could be. You might know it in your head. But there was a universe of difference between knowing it in your head and feeling it in your heart.

She had power; she had wanted to use that power to put everything right. But now she was truly learning that she could only do so much in her role. The others in the fleet, those of Adam's people . . . She couldn't rule them in the way they should be ruled. She wasn't one of them. It wasn't her place. Someone else had to fill that role.

But she could love them. She had enough love for all of them. Even if it drained her. An Aalim was a scholar, an advisor, and a sage, but an Aalim was first and foremost a caretaker. And to care for someone was to love them. There was no other way. There were elements of life that persisted no matter what else happened, and this was one of them. It was beyond her. But when she faltered, this also might give her strength.

She began to rise, slowly, gently, spreading herself like wings. She would look, yes. She didn't think she would find anything— that wasn't the kind of touch she performed—but Adisa had asked, and what was happening was terrible. What they had to do might be terrible as well.

Sometimes love required terrible things. Adisa understood that. Ixchel had understood that.

A footstep on the path—soft, nearly inaudible. She returned to herself and her hands stopped their movement, and she looked—in the way she looked—toward the approaching presence.

Adam. Weary. But determined. She could feel the strength in him, the desire to continue. To not give up. To not fail.

He would come through this, she knew at once. Had known. He might die, yes—they all might die. It might be so. But even if one died, one might not be broken. And Adam would not break.

She extended a hand to him. "Love."

His smile was palpable to her—again, weary, but meant. He came to her and sank down beside her, laying his hand in hers. She felt him—the trembling of every part of him, the sadness in him. A newness, which she would learn to understand, but also such deep age. The war was changing him in ways he might only discover years hence. If he lived that long.

"Sorry I waited to come to you."

"You had to take care of yourself. Now more than ever, I think you need to make a practice of that."

He laughed, a little hollowly. "So far I think I haven't been doing a very good job."

"Why not?"

For a long time, he didn't answer. His hand tightened around hers. She might have touched his mind and helped him articulate what was troubling him, but he should be allowed to reach it on his own.

At last he spoke. "Lock and I . . ." He sighed. "I don't know. We fought. He said . . . he said some things. He said some things I'm not sure he can take back."

"Did he mean them?"

"I don't know. I don't think—" He broke off and was silent for a minute. "I don't know if he meant the actual words. But what was under them . . ."

"I see," Nkiruka said softly. "Yes. I see."

"He doesn't know what I'm going to be when this is all over." Adam became briefly darker, more afraid. "*I* don't know what I'm going to be. Who I'm going to be. Back on that planet, where we were in the camp? I told him that—that I don't belong here. Not completely. I can't. You took me in, you were all so kind to me—kinder than I ever thought anyone could be, and everyone sacrificed *so much* . . . But it's true. I don't belong here. I'm not one of you, and I never will be. And Lochlan . . . He wanted me to be, and he still does, but I don't think . . . I can't go back to the Protectorate, I can't be one of the Bideshi, and I'm caught in the middle—I don't know *what* I am. And it's not just about not belonging. It's deeper. You know that. It's about what's happening to me, what I might be, what I might have to do, and there's so much I don't understand and I feel like I'm losing him. And I *can't stop it.*"

The dam had clearly broken now, and she let the waters flow. He needed to say these things, things that perhaps he hadn't admitted even to himself. They were things he had been afraid of, *was* afraid of . . . But they were things he shouldn't ignore.

Things he couldn't afford to ignore.

"You can't forgive him?"

Adam sighed again. "I don't— You know, I don't think it's about me forgiving him. I love him. I always will. I think it's about him forgiving the *Protectorate.* Forgiving *me.*" Once again, everything in him tensed. "Forgiving himself. Because what he said, the places it came from . . . I think he hates those places in him just as much."

Slowly, Nkiruka took his other hand in hers. The words that came were like words she was speaking to herself, and they gripped her. "Remember how I told you that you weren't the center of this? That you couldn't hold yourself responsible for what happened? Only for the things you can control?"

Adam nodded.

"Adam, this is one of those things you *can't* control. You love him—good. That's good. You can forgive him, if you think you need to. You can open your heart to him, open your arms, make sure he *knows* they're open. But as to whether *he* can forgive anyone . . ." She shook her head. "You have no say in that. That's for him and him alone. You may have to wait. And in the end . . . Yes, he may not be able to. I believe he will. He's not a weak man. He's a good man. I know you know that."

She smiled and released one of his hands, laid her palm against his cheek. "And I know you know he loves you too. He loves you more than he thought he could ever love anyone. That also means a lot. But you can't make that decision for him."

Adam smiled, and she ran her fingertips over its curve. It was thin. Wan. "I want to."

She laughed sadly. "I know. Believe me, I know. Love is terrible. There were times—" Pain stabbed her, though not as intense or as sharp as once it would have been. She would always carry the wound with her, but it had surprised her how quickly she had begun to heal. "There were times, once, where I honestly thought the universe might be better off without it."

"It would definitely be simpler."

"Yes." She smiled her own wan smile. "But none of us would be here. And that would be a shame."

He nodded and was quiet again. She let him go and folded her hands in her lap, allowing herself to fall into meditation again—though not so deep nor so far as before.

"The traitor," he said at last. "The one feeding information to the Protectorate. You've heard?"

"Yes. Adisa told me. He told me *you* told *him*."

"I did. But Rachel figured it out. She's sure. I am too." His hands whispered over each other. Dry washing. "And I have *no fucking idea* how we're going to find them. At least not before it's too late. We can't tell the captains why we're stalling if we don't know who it might be, and we can only stall so long before they get impatient. Suspicious. Start making demands. Even what we're doing now could spook whoever it is, put them on their guard."

"Adisa asked me to see what I could do."

"How?" Then he pushed ahead, and she felt a ripple of realization in him. "No, wait. I . . . You can do that?"

Nkiruka shrugged. Tension was edging into her gut, but less than before. She didn't have to worry about putting on a brave face, not here and not with him. If there was one man who might understand uncertainty in general, it was Adam. "I don't know. Searching for someone like that . . . It's so far outside what I normally do. I was just trying when you came to me."

"Should I—should I help?" He didn't want to. She could sense it clearly as a physical touch. Yet he also *did* want to. Perhaps because if he could do something, bring something actually under his control—even a little . . .

"Maybe." She hated to say it, but it was true. To bring him into this now was an uncomfortable thought, in part because she felt she should be able to do it alone. "As I said, I don't know if I can. If I had someone with me . . ." But then she stopped, put up a hand. "You should tell me something first. If you can."

This time the ripple in his core was rapid, tight. "What?"

"There's more to what you said before, about becoming something new. About not being able to stop it. You knew it, I knew it too, but now something has happened that's bigger than anything we've done together. Can you tell me what it is?"

He hesitated. For a long moment, she wondered if he actually would tell her. Then he shifted, and something in him solidified. There was still fear in him, but she knew he would push through it.

He wouldn't be broken.

He told her the truth. And when he was done, she marveled at it. But then again, perhaps she wasn't so surprised.

When the news came, it came fast, and reached Eva as she was dressing. Not a pounding on her door, nothing in person, but a *ping* on the room's comm.

From Rachel. A location. Two words.

got her

She was out the door in minutes, still pulling her shirt on, Kyle at her heels.

Adisa had come to tell her a few hours previously, and she had listened with bleary disbelief, half-certain she was dreaming. That level of betrayal, on the part of someone that highly placed and that close to all of them . . . It was nightmarish. But as she had listened, as she had turned it over in her mind . . . it had made sense.

It made terrible sense.

But she had slept again. She hadn't been able do anything else. Everything in her was collapsing.

It still was. Her. *Her.* Who? What would it mean? What would it require of them?

She traveled down the corridor to the lift that would take her up several levels to the council chamber. The captains would probably be gathered there. What next? A trial? Had the Bideshi ever done that? The Bideshi dealt with criminals, punished them, exiled them—the worst fate, and so terrible that it wasn't unheard of for the exiled to choose suicide instead—but had they ever confronted this kind of treason? If it was one of the Protectorate, the Bideshi would take no responsibility for it. Adisa had said they couldn't take control of the entire fleet that way.

It would be up to her people. And how they would handle it . . . She didn't know.

The council chamber was full when she arrived. More than full; people had spilled into the corridor, and she had to push past them to get inside. In there was just as bad, with people packed shoulder to shoulder, but she made out the Protectorate captains, the Bideshi council members, Nkiruka and Adam. Not Lochlan. Not Leila. She noticed these things, filed them away, and let them be.

Forgot them, even. Because she turned her attention to the center of the room and saw Rachel.

Rachel, wearing her sidearm, and the woman with her, whose hands were cuffed behind her back.

Eva's mouth went dry. Not all the captains were there. Not all. One was missing.

"Oh, fuck," Kyle whispered beside her. "It's Tamara."

Tamara. Copilot of the one transport ship that had made it off-world, the one the survivors of the first liberated camp had escaped in. The woman who had taken Rachel's children to safety during the battle on Peris. Close to her. One of the closest.

She was standing there, staring only at Rachel. From where she was, Eva couldn't see her face clearly. But she could see that Tamara was shaking. Hard.

"Rachel." Adisa spoke from the doorway, and as everyone's eyes turned to him, he moved toward the center of the room.

And Rachel didn't look right.

Her eyes were at once hollow and blazing, every muscle in her face tight, every muscle in her *body* tight. An animal ready to attack. Adisa was still approaching her, one hand held slightly out as if to placate her, and Nkiruka also was rising, but Eva's belly was cold and heavy. These events felt inevitable. Something had been set in motion, and it was too late now to stop it.

Perhaps it had been too late for a long time.

"Rachel," Adisa said again, his voice low. The room had suddenly gone almost silent, and it wasn't hard to hear him. "Talk to us. You're certain? How did you come by your proof?"

Assuming Rachel had proof. Eva actually wasn't sure . . .

Everything is collapsing.

"Repairs to her ship." Rachel's voice was flat and dead. "Her comm system. I sent someone over to take care of it. Their own man was incapacitated. Going through it, he found logs that showed evidence of attempts to purge them. Clear evidence. But whoever did it hadn't known how to do a total purge. We probably never would have found the logs otherwise, but it was all there. All of it." She shot Tamara the coldest stare Eva had ever seen anyone give. "Names. Times. Locations. Our numbers. Our weapons and arms. Plans for raids. That's how they knew we were coming. That's how they found us on the frontier."

Adisa's gaze shifted from her to Tamara. Eva had shouldered her way a little further through the crowd and closer to Adam. From here she could see Tamara's face—absolutely drained of blood. Stunned. Terrified.

"Is this true?" Adisa's voice was somehow both gentle and hard. "Tell me now."

Tamara said nothing. She merely shook harder, looking frantically from Adisa to Rachel, her lips trembling.

Rachel backhanded her across the face and she cried out, stumbled. Rachel grabbed her viciously by the arm and held her up, twisting it in the process, and Tamara cried out again.

"It is," she whispered. It cut through the air in the room, seemed to drain it, and a sigh followed the sound: very quiet but heavy, mournful, afraid.

"It was my family," she went on louder, her voice harsh and shaking as badly as her body. She was weeping now. "My children. I didn't want to. They said they would—I was afraid—I didn't—"

It was as if it happened in a fraction of a second and in an hour. The movement of Rachel's hand down to her hip and back up.

Rachel shot Tamara in the face and she went down without another word.

This time the silence was complete. No one even breathed. There was a vacuum, a void as everyone stared at the body crumpled in the center of the room, the blood pooling beneath its head. And Rachel standing there with her gun in her hand, now loose by her side, staring down with wide eyes.

Eva had no idea how long the stillness went on. Every part of her was numb. Time no longer seemed to mean very much. But then Adisa was turning, his face calm, gesturing to the rest of the room.

"Everyone not part of the leadership here, please leave."

He didn't have to say it twice. They began to file out, suddenly orderly. The Protectorate people who followed them might have done so simply out of herd mentality. Or it might have been the sheer quiet power Adisa commanded.

Regardless, in the end, the chamber was left empty except for Adisa, Nkiruka, the rest of council, Adam, Kyle and herself, Rachel . . . and Tamara's body.

Kyle went wordlessly to the doors and closed them. And then for a moment longer there was nothing at all.

This time it was Rachel who spoke. Two words only.

"I can't."

The gun clattered to the floor and Rachel sank into a crouch, her face falling into her hands. "I can't do this anymore."

This time it wasn't Adisa who went to her. It wasn't Nkiruka. It wasn't Kyle, and it wasn't Eva herself. Adam crossed the room to her, knelt, and pulled her into his arms.

CHAPTER

SIXTEEN

S o this was really where they were.

Lochlan wandered the docks alone. No more ships were coming in, and none were going out. Elsewhere in Ashwina's halls and chambers, events were moving fast. By now, everyone knew what had happened: a traitor found and killed. Executed, publicly. Nothing like that had happened on Ashwina in their recorded history. The Bideshi punished. They exiled. They didn't kill. But this hadn't been his people. This hadn't been a sanctioned punishment, arrived at via a fair trial.

This had essentially been murder.

So there had been rearrangements in command. He knew the basic outlines of how they had been done and what the results were to be. No one else had to die, and no one was to be exiled. Everything going forward was to be handled as calmly as possible. There was to be no panic. No more blood spilled.

He didn't care.

Or he did. But there was only one question in which he was truly interested. Only one thing he wanted to know. He had satisfied himself of the answer and gone on his way.

Adam wasn't involved. Not anywhere in it. At least not directly.

His absence hurt, and it was pain Lochlan had no idea what to do with.

He had caused his own share of pain. He knew that, though he only partly recalled what he had said. With the amount he had drunk—laced with something like shala but a good bit more illicit— he shouldn't have been able to remember any of it at all. But he remembered enough. It was terrible. He cringed at the memory of every word. Poison pouring out of him, thrown in the face of someone he loved more than his own life.

And he wasn't sure he hadn't meant it. Maybe not the specific words. But the feelings behind them. He remembered those most of all. An old wound that had never truly healed had been reopened.

He was so afraid. He was so lost. He was so angry.

He had been all three for such a long time.

Faces blurred as he passed. He moved out of the halls and corridors where people appeared to be congregating. When he had left the clinic, Kae was still lying motionless and silent as death with Leila asleep beside him, her head on his chest. Ying had finally allowed her to stay—it might be the only way she could rest. Kae was as good as lost to him—at least for now. Adam? He had no idea. Didn't know where to begin to look for him, and even if finding him probably wouldn't be difficult, he didn't want to.

Couldn't.

One fight, he told himself as he wandered. *One fight.*

Except it wasn't.

He thought about when he had first met Adam. Saved him. Running from the peacekeepers on that little trashball of a station. Saving the Protectorate from the Protectorate. He might not have realized what was he was doing then, but he appreciated the irony now. Still did. This Protectorate *raya* he had fallen in love with—and once he had used that word more in teasing than anything else, even when relations between them hadn't exactly been friendly.

He had never wanted to hurt Adam. Never. It hadn't taken him long to want to help him. Defend him.

Hadn't taken Lochlan all that long, really, to love him.

On some level, perhaps, Lochlan had expected that love might fix everything. He never would have considered himself much of a romantic, but there was a practical side to love as well, and wasn't love enough in the end? Didn't it have to be?

Wasn't it all there *was*?

He couldn't lose himself in these thoughts now. His friend was possibly dying. There was a war to fight. If Kae was out of commission, that meant that Lochlan's responsibilities would increase exponentially. He would have to take over leadership of at least part of Kae's wing, and there was every probability that the wings would be needed again, and soon. He had to be ready. Needed his head in order. He couldn't control whatever was happening to Adam. He had no way to determine what it meant. He didn't know anything.

Suddenly he looked up and found that he had made his way to the lock which had once been reserved for *Volya*, which had been abandoned in the bay of a Protectorate cruiser. Since then he had tried to think about his old ship as little as possible. She was probably scrap now. No *probably* about it; she *was* scrap, and it was better to accept it. But God, she had meant so much to him. Had been with him for years. She had been his friend and companion in the night, when he had no one else. She had carried him home with Adam. She had taken them from Ashwina on that fateful journey to the borders of Protectorate space—where he had lost her forever.

He looked at the place where *Volya* would once have rested, and he closed his eyes.

"I don't know how I knew you would be here," Adam said softly behind him. "But I did."

Lochlan didn't turn. "You knew because you did," he said, equally soft, and felt his mouth stretch into a pained smile. "You always do."

"There's a lot I don't know. Didn't you always tell me? I don't know anything. Not really."

Lochlan finally turned. "Then I don't either."

"We deserve each other."

"I don't deserve you." Lochlan struggled against it, the weight of despair on his chest. He still didn't have the words, would *never* have the right ones, and maybe his only hope was to accept that. To accept that he was hopeless. He had believed Adam was the hopeless one, early on, and maybe that was also true.

But he was worse.

"Lock . . ." Adam sighed. "Don't."

"Don't *what*? *Chusile*, I'm—" *Sorry* sounded stupid in his head, felt utterly inadequate on his tongue. "I don't know what to do here. Tell me what to do."

"I don't know what you should do."

"*Adam.*"

"Lock, what?" There was no force in the words. No anger. Only weariness. Lochlan wasn't sure if it was better or worse that way, if he would have preferred the energy and the passion true anger would require. "I can't fix this. And I can't tell you how to fix it. I can't help what I am. I know this life is not what we thought it would be, I know we don't know what it *is* or why it's happening, but even if you think it's taking me away from you, even if you think it's going to mean I can't be with you anymore . . . I can't help it. I can't stop it."

He lowered his head, paused, and dragged in a ragged breath that hurt to hear.

"I talked to Ying. She said this might be evolution. She doesn't know. *I* don't know. Nkiru doesn't know. I don't know if this is *for* something, and I don't—I don't know if that *purpose* could mean anything good for me, if it's there. I'm *scared*, Lock. Worse. You think you're scared? I'm fucking *terrified*." He pressed a hand to his chest, eyes wide. "But it's *happening*. I'm not Bideshi, I'm not Protectorate, I'm not sure I'll be *human* when it's done, but I need you with me. I can't do this without you. And I have to. I *have* to. Whatever happens, I need you with me to the end."

"To the end," Lochlan echoed softly. He didn't need to have that clarified. He had imagined it. Of course he had. Knew death was possible. Knew there might be nothing they could do to prevent it. That was always the way, in peace or in war. It could come for you at any time. But not like this.

There was more than one kind of casualty.

"I said I would trust you with my life," Lochlan said. Slow. Halting. "Back when we were trying to convince everyone. Do you remember that? How hard we had to fight? I fought for you. I *fought* for you." His voice rose, but like Adam's, there was no anger in it. "I would have run with you, if you hadn't been Named. If you failed the ritual. Do you remember *that*? I was ready. I would have done it in a moment." He laughed, a little incredulous. "Line and fucking orbit, I still don't understand why. I mean, I do. I do now. But I didn't know then how I felt. I didn't know, and I was still ready to do it."

He took a step closer to Adam, his gut clenching, knotting in on itself in a tangle of misery. What was in him wasn't just that knot of pain but a deeper knot, older, all scar tissue, and where it came from. What it meant.

"I hate your people, *chusile*. I *hate* them. I don't know if I'll ever be able to stop hating them. I can't help it. What I saw, what they took away from me . . ." He shook his head, hard. "And the Plain— Ixchel—and now Kae? How can I *not* hate them?" He was choking on the words. "I told you I'd move past it, that I wouldn't let myself lose you that way. Now I might lose you like *this*. It's getting worse, whatever is happening to you, and I know it might take you from me. I look at everything, and I don't— You don't know what it means. I don't either. But I've never loved anyone or anything the way I love you. I have no idea how it happened, but I *love you*, and I can't stop doing that. And I know you told me love might not be enough, but it's *all I have*."

He fell silent, breathing a little hard. The knot in him had only tightened, and he ached for it to be loosened. But how that would happen . . .

"It's all I have," he repeated softly, and his voice broke on the last word.

For a long moment Adam said nothing at all. His face was a mask, even his eyes clouded, whatever lay behind them obscured.

Lochlan was silent, motionless. And at last Adam spoke.

"Will you fight for me now?"

It was so soft that for a second or two Lochlan wasn't sure he had heard Adam correctly. It wasn't anything like the answer he had been expecting. Just a simple question. A question that held within it a hundred other questions. A hundred other meanings.

He had to answer it, and he couldn't lie.

Not even to himself.

"Will you?" Adam repeated, his face still unreadable. His eyes. "Will you fight? Will you die? It might come to that. Will you stay? No matter what happens to me?"

There was only one answer. It wrenched at him. But that one answer remained.

"Yes." He met Adam's clear, mismatched eyes and didn't look away. "I would. I will."

For another moment Adam didn't move. Didn't speak. Lochlan waited, barely breathing.

Then Adam came forward. Came to him. Framed Lochlan's face with his hands and kissed him, kissed him hard, all the force of love and anger and despair in it, and a terrible, reckless hope. It sucked the air out of Lochlan's lungs, and at first he couldn't respond. Then he shoved himself into the kiss, combing his fingers through Adam's hair and pulling him close, so close he imagined crawling inside Adam's skin. Erasing the barriers between them. Everything that kept them apart. Everything in both of them. Everything in him that he wanted so much to be able to change.

Even if it was true, it fixed nothing. He wasn't so great a fool as to think that. This promise fixed nothing at all.

It might simply be damning them both.

CHAPTER

✴

SEVENTEEN

The night after Sinder descended into the depths of the city, he took Julius d'Bideshi to the very top of the hotel's spire—at least, the highest one could go without mountaineering equipment and a death wish—and they gazed out over the glistening towers at the last of the lowering sun, and were silent. It was windy up here, and neither of them had dressed for it and for the chill the wind brought with it. Sinder hugged himself and didn't try to hide his shivering, but Julius stood as if it didn't bother him in the slightest: head up, shoulders straight, a statue standing tall and erect. One of the gargoyles on ancient buildings, but beautiful. In his way.

Julius might pass as Protectorate, if the truth wasn't known, given his fine bone structure, aristocratic features. Only his eyes gave him away.

"I feel them," Julius murmured after a time, and raised a hand. "All of them. So many voices. So many lines, so many orbits, so many paths walked. Branches followed. Choices made and not made. And of course, to refuse to make a choice is still to choose." He glanced at Sinder and gave him a sardonic smile. "You've made a choice, haven't you, Isaac? But not recently. This is a choice you made long ago."

Sinder inclined his head, said nothing. He wouldn't agree. He wouldn't disagree. In truth, he didn't view it as a choice. He was what he was. He could only do what nature required of him. Therefore he really couldn't be blamed for any of those actions. Especially not when they were made with such goals in mind. Such means for such ends. When the time came, everyone would see that. For the moment, what they might think mattered not at all.

"Do you know the story of your namesake, Isaac Sinder?"

The question startled him—it seemed to emerge from nowhere—and for once, Julius had Sinder at a loss. He shook his head—Julius would sense the movement.

"That surprises me. You have such a love of history. Then again, this is not so much history as myth. Legend. Some of it may be true. Once there were people who regarded it as absolute truth. But like all legends, it's likely that most of its truth has been carved away by time and repetition, and replaced with whatever people wished to put there."

He paused a moment, as if waiting for a response. The wind was rising, and odd shapes flickered at the periphery of Sinder's vision. He ignored them.

"Isaac was the father of a nation. A great nation. He was promised to his father by his father's god, long after his father and mother should have been able to produce any children. He was the child of a miracle. But his own childhood was, shall we say . . . fraught." Julius smiled and paused again, turning his blind eyes on Sinder, leaning against the small viewing platform's railing.

"His father was close to his god. Very close indeed. But his god was rather capricious. Acted according to his own mysterious whims, and often didn't make the logic behind those whims clear to his own children. Perhaps he didn't feel they needed to know. Perhaps he didn't consider it their place, these tiny creatures who couldn't begin to comprehend his magnificence. Or perhaps he genuinely enjoyed the deception. Perhaps it made him feel clever." Julius shrugged. "Who can explain the ways of gods? To be honest, I think your people were wise to abandon them. More trouble than they're worth, if you ask me.

"In any case, although this man—Abraham was his name—was never anything but faithful, this *almighty god* got it into his divine head one day that he should set a test. See how far Abraham would go for the sake of obedience. So he told Abraham to take his son up on a hill, bind him, and sacrifice him."

He paused another beat—probably for effect—and obligingly Sinder widened his eyes. Those little dancing shadow-forms had begun to intensify, to close in, but as he shifted his focus, they vanished.

"Abraham agonized over what he was being asked to do. Commanded to do. This was his god, after all. This was a being who had performed the miracle he most desired, given him a beloved son to carry on his name, his lineage. Abraham had been promised that his descendants would number the stars in the sky. Isaac was his hope for that. His *only* hope. For how could he expect such a miracle to be repeated?

"Besides, he loved his son. What father wouldn't?

"But in the end, he obeyed his god. He took his son up the hill, bound him, prepared to kill him. How must he have felt, then? What must that pain have been like?" Julius shook his head, and while Sinder thought the sorrow on his face might be an act, it didn't seem entirely so. "Yet he made his choice. The worst choice that can be given to any parent, I think. At least, any parent who also goes in fear of their god."

He stopped again, his brow slightly furrowed and his mouth curled at one corner. Sinder sensed that, once more, a response was expected from him. Well, once more he would oblige. And the story *was* rather interesting.

It was a distraction from the vertigo creeping into him.

"What happened?"

Julius shrugged. "His god was satisfied by his mere intention. Just in time, he sent a sign that Abraham shouldn't go through with it. He provided a ram instead for Abraham to use as sacrifice. So the ritual was completed, and Isaac lived. He went on to be the father of a nation, as I said." He stopped again, and that faint smile returned. "But that isn't the only side of the story.

"Before Abraham's wife was made pregnant by their god, Abraham was driven to somewhat desperate measures. Though perhaps in those days they weren't so desperate. He so greatly desired an heir that—with the consent of his wife—he took one of his wife's handmaidens to his bed. She became pregnant, and had a son, who she named Ishmael. But then Isaac was born, and Abraham's wife changed her mind. She was angry, for what reason now did she have to tolerate this bastard child in her home? Why should she allow any other heir? So she demanded that this handmaiden and her son be cast into the wilderness. And Abraham . . . How could he stand against his wife? As the story goes, she was quite a formidable woman."

Julius's smile widened just a touch.

"So the handmaiden was banished with her son. They ran out of water in the desert, and their deaths seemed certain. But once again, this god acted according to his whims and sent a spring to the handmaiden. Water in the desert. A powerful thing.

"And the handmaiden was made a promise by this god. That her son *also* would father a nation. Another nation, separate from that of Isaac. That her son would be a wild man. An outsider. You see, the two boys had been set against each other from their births by fate and circumstance. So their destinies would ever proceed, and all their children would ever be set against each other. The sons of Isaac would never have peace with the sons of Ishmael." Julius was quiet a moment, and he turned back to face the city. "So one version of the story goes.

"But there is a coda. Again, in one version. That in the end, when Abraham died, the sons came together one last time, as family, to bury him."

A final silence. Sinder let the silence rest and turned the story over in his mind. Over and over, seeking the deeper meaning of it.

He could feel that it was there. But he couldn't find it. The vertigo shifted closer and settled into him, and he had to close his eyes, pinch the bridge of his nose, and breathe deeply until it stopped.

It did, and he looked up, found his focus. "So what?"

Julius didn't turn. "Mm?"

"Why did you tell me that?"

"Oh." And this time Sinder could hear the smile in his voice. It wasn't a pleasant smile. "No reason. I just think it's an interesting story. That's all."

Later that night, the delivery was made.

Not to Julius's hotel suite. Sinder had set aside another room for this. Deep in the bowels of the building where he kept his office—still nowhere near ground level, of course, but many floors down. It was a large room: clear, featureless, all cold tile. Sinder wasn't sure what it had been used for originally. Some sort of storage perhaps. The tile was indicative, but he wasn't sure of what.

Twenty crates were laid out under bright overhead lights. The people who brought them in on grav-lifts left as quickly as possible, and then Julius and Sinder were alone.

Julius moved toward the double line of crates, laying his hands on the first one. "You checked them yourself?"

"I inspected them, as you requested. I think they'll more than meet your requirements."

"Excellent." But Julius stayed still, hands on the crate and his head tipped back. "I'll need equipment and the other items we discussed. Soon, if you intend to move quickly. I'll have my own preparations to make."

"Of course." Sinder remained where he was. He had no reason to walk among the crates himself, and in fact he preferred not to. The odd waking dream he had experienced in the lower city was no doubt unimportant, but if he was being honest—and he should probably be honest with himself if with no one else—the images had lingered. It was better to keep his distance. And in any case, the arrangement *was* rather distasteful. "And yes, I do intend to move very soon. I've made most of the final arrangements. The last piece to move into place is you." He smiled thinly. "Before myself."

"So when you're ready, you'll proceed to the central command building."

"The Palace, we call it." Glancing at the crates, Sinder folded his hands behind his back. It was steadying. "Yes."

"And signal me."

Sinder nodded. "I don't anticipate any problems, but there's always a slight chance. So I'll need you with me in some capacity to do whatever you can to turn the tide in my favor."

"And you're certain you want to be there? You know if I made full use of what I had here, it would be simple to take care of it at a distance."

Sinder shook his head. He had considered that. Considered and immediately rejected it. "No. I have to be there myself. It's going to be the beginning of everything, Julius. I have to be the one who begins it."

Not him. Not Julius. Not a Bideshi. This was *his* story now, and he would be at the core of it. At the root. The visions he was having of this grand narrative were increasingly vivid, increasingly intense. They crowded into his dreams, filling them with light, and at times, even when he was awake, he could almost feel those lines and branchings under his hands. Like the limbs of a graceful, elegant tree.

With that kind of near-physical reality, his task was as good as done. All he had to do was be there when his plan was set into motion.

Julius made a small *mm* noise and proceeded down the row, trailing his fingers over the tops of the other crates. "Up to you, of course. I'll do what I must. Has anyone ever attempted anything like this before?"

"In the history of the Protectorate? No. There has been no perceived need." Sinder's smile widened just a touch. "Which is one of the reasons why I don't anticipate any major problems. None of them are prepared for it. To many people, I imagine, it would be completely unthinkable." He paused, meditative. "It's always the things we can't imagine that kill us in the end."

Julius nodded. "Survivors tend to have the best imaginations." He looked up, his scarred eyes narrowed. "And the Bideshi have truly impressive imaginations. They always have. It's one of their strengths. When you turn your attention to them, you should bear that in mind."

"I can do some imagining of my own. I know one can't always foresee every possibility, but—"

"I have every confidence in you." Julius turned back to him. "But we need to discuss what I want in return for this. Because I *do* expect to be compensated."

Sinder cocked his head. Now was as good a time as any for this conversation. "I thought we had discussed that? Just a bit?"

"Just a bit. But now I think we should address it in greater detail."

Sinder crossed his arms over his chest. "Address away."

"We Aalim . . . we have always been counselors. Leaders, yes, but in our own special way. Our roles . . . They aren't ones of direct power. We don't command. Nothing so blatant. We stand apart, we see, and we gently manipulate. In the interests of our own people, of course."

"Of course."

"You'll be in a position of considerable power once this is all over." Julius paused. "I'll have considerable power as well. More than any Aalim in history. But power is useless unless it has a purpose. You will command. I would be at your side as counselor, as companion and seer. I believe I can be very useful to you in that capacity. Especially if you keep providing me with more, ah . . ." He gestured around at the crates. "*Materials.*"

Sinder frowned. This wasn't entirely unexpected, but it was somewhat troubling. There was what was necessary, however distasteful. And then there was what one did after the necessity was past.

"I don't know how possible that would be. My people . . . that you helped save them all, that you no longer consider yourself Bideshi . . . I don't know how much that would mean to them. I don't know to what degree they would accept you. Especially in such a high position."

"Surely you could convince them."

"Once this is over, the situation will still be delicate for a while. Unsteady. It will take time to rebuild and shore up foundations. The wrong move at the wrong time could upset some very fragile balances."

"Then I'll wait until things have stabilized."

"Even then." Sinder shook his head slowly. "Julius, I'll do what I can for you. I've already given you extraordinary power. You could use it anywhere, to rule anyone. You could take command of the remaining Bideshi; I doubt we'll be able to eliminate all of them. Certainly not at one time. And under a firm hand, one friendly to the Protectorate . . . That might be the most advantageous position for you."

Julius smiled again. It was sharp and unpleasant. And not in the least shaken. The smile of a man undeterred. "But that is the position I want, Sinder. That is my price. You can deny me my materials, you can put a stop to my ascension, but only temporarily. One way or another, I'll have what I want. It's in your hands to decide whether we're trusted allies . . . or something else."

So.

This also wasn't unexpected. Julius was a threat; he had known that from the beginning. Anyone who could wield such power was a threat, because power was a drug. More led to more led to more. It created endless desire. Some was never enough. Power for its own sake was a trap—didn't he know that perfectly well? Hadn't he felt that temptation when he first began to imagine what he was about to do? Naturally he had conquered it. But regardless, he remembered.

And the man was correct. He would make a bad enemy.

There will be time. First things first.

"I believe it might be done," he said quietly. "I believe I might *make* it be done. But when we turn our attention to your people, you must be seen to attack them. To destroy them. There can be no question whatsoever about your loyalties. You must appear to be above reproach. You must *be* above reproach."

Julius nodded, a single, slow bob of his chin. "I see no reason to argue with that." He sighed and turned his head away. "They were once my people, yes. But they decided that I was no longer one of theirs. That was *their* decision. I was only doing what I had to do. To perfect myself, to serve them as best I could. They decided that my work wasn't a thing of value, or a thing to respect." Now an air of coldness came over him, and it lingered. "I owe them nothing. No allegiance. No mercy. Give me a target and the means to see it done, and they die."

Sinder pointed at the crates. This had gone better than he expected. Julius didn't trust him. But that was of no consequence.

"I've given you the means," he said. "Or the better part of them. I'll see that you get the rest in a matter of hours. Make your preparations, and let me know immediately if you require anything else. When I'm ready to move, I'll send word." He smoothed down his suit. He had his own preparations to make.

The branches under his hands . . . His fingertips tingled.

"I want to thank you, Julius. Maybe this alliance is not one many would understand, but I know—believe me—that I never could have come this far without you. And these final few steps will be impossible without your aid."

Julius bowed slightly. "I thank you in turn. For letting me know that I'm appreciated. What more can someone with a talent ask for?"

Sinder took his leave. Out in the corridor, he leaned against the wall, looking up at the sharp, clear lights that ran across the ceiling. He closed his eyes and focused on the red inside his lids, and when dizziness came to him and buzzed like tiny electric shocks into his nerves, it was pleasant. It wasn't weakness. It was the future itself, touching him.

Soon. Very soon now, he could truly begin.

CHAPTER

✳

EIGHTEEN

A s Nkiruka observed from a seat in the corner with her hands folded under her chin, and she meditated. Not deeply, but enough to give her the sense of calm she sorely needed. The meeting proceeded as planned. Or almost as planned. But there was a core of chaos in it that held despite Adisa's attempts to bring the room to order.

Nkiruka was undecided as to whether or not she would say anything. She was a counselor, an advisor, and a person who held the rank and respect of an elder though she hadn't yet reached her thirtieth year, but she still didn't feel it was her place. This matter was for the council and the captains to decide together. And there were enough voices there to fill every potential gap in conversation.

The large council chamber was closed to any but the fleet's leaders, but the room still felt packed. Many of the Protectorate captains had personalities larger than their bodies. And after Tamara's death—murder, really—and Rachel stepping down as fleet commander, no one was entirely certain who was meant to keep everything in check. Eva and Kyle had been given fairly central places on the Protectorate side of the table, but they both appeared uncomfortable, and as far as Nkiruka was aware, no official announcement had been made regarding their new places of authority.

They likely hadn't expected to officially assume them. They had been told their strength would be required behind Rachel, as she worked without the help and backing of Aarons. They probably never expected her to be gone.

No one had.

Adam wasn't there. Neither was Lochlan. She had left Adam in the Arched Halls to do some meditation of his own, and when she inquired about how he and Lochlan were doing, Adam had merely shrugged and looked away. She could feel something there, something still not quite right. But it wasn't the time to ask.

Whatever the case, they would work it out themselves. Or they wouldn't.

Voices were rising; some were questioning whether Tamara had truly been a traitor, demanding evidence, wondering if the Bideshi had been behind it, if one of them might be next. Nkiruka closed her eyes—useless, since it blocked none of her senses—and pushed back weary despair.

Or not exactly despair. Despair implied hopelessness. She was holding on to hope, but this was a time for frustration, and perhaps for the energy frustration could provide. She needed energy from wherever she could get it.

Adisa rose and struck the table with the flat of his hand, and Nkiruka could feel his own frustration radiating from him like heat from a star. "Enough!" he bellowed in a ringing baritone, and the room abruptly fell silent.

Adisa was a big man, broad-shouldered, and the robes he wore often served to make him look even bigger. He generally used reason rather than force, but when he wanted to command attention . . .

He was formidable.

Warmth flooded her. Here was something she could find some hope in. Strength for her, and by extension for all of them. Leaning her chin on her clasped hands, Nkiruka smiled, gratified.

"It seems every time we gather like this, no one can be trusted to proceed in an orderly way. Neither I nor any of my people have any desire to exert control over you, but if you persist in behaving like children, it will be difficult to keep from treating you like them. God's sake, even our children can sit down and be quiet and speak in turn."

He was quiet, and the silence stretched out. Nkiruka sent out feelers of awareness and perceived that a few of the captains were chagrined. Embarrassed. They weren't children. They were scared and angry, and they were tired of seeing their people die for a cause in which some of them had lost at least a bit of their faith.

"We're not going to discuss the decision Rachel made regarding Tamara. Not because we want to close off discussion, but because that frankly isn't the most pressing matter at hand. Rachel did not act without evidence or cause, no matter how inappropriate her reaction was. If you want that evidence, we can provide it to you. We've verified that it's legitimate, but you can judge for yourselves. If, after that, you still have doubts, no one will stop you from voicing them. Certainly not my people. We didn't make the decision to kill Tamara, and I think we would prefer to have as little to do with it as humanly possible.

"Along those lines, we arranged this before Rachel stepped down," he continued, more calmly still, "but we had no time to have her formally announce it, so will have to do so now. Eva Reyes and Kyle Waverly have elected to take positions of authority over the fleet, and were meant to support Rachel while Aarons is still recovering. Of course, that's no longer an option. They're still willing to take on those roles—as leaders and advisors to you—provided you accept them. We can obviously hold formal elections if you would prefer. It's entirely up to you."

Adisa nodded at Eva and Kyle. "I'll let them address you, if they wish. They have more to say to you than I do."

He sat down with an air of finality.

Eva and Kyle glanced at each other, and she felt the discomfort between them. That was good. It was good for people to take power who didn't especially want it. They were far likelier to give it up when the need for their leadership had passed.

There was a rustle of shifting bodies in the room. Finally Eva cleared her throat and stood, and the strength in her was also palpable, solid and true under her nervousness. Yes, she had been a good choice. Both of them, but her especially. Additional people Nkiruka could depend on, people who could hold her up when she faltered.

An Aalim might stand alone, but was also—in the most fundamental way—*never* alone. She had forgotten that. She couldn't afford to forget it again.

"I know this isn't where any of us wanted to be." Eva's voice was shaking slightly, though that underlying strength flowed into it with every word. "It's definitely not where *I* wanted to be. Where Kyle wanted to be. Rachel was a friend—*is* a friend. What happened . . .

I don't support it, and I don't condone it, but she has my sympathy. She's exhausted, and she's lost so much. We all have."

She paused, Eyes briefly downcast as she took a breath.

"I know you all want answers, and you'll get them—I want them too. But we can't focus on them right now. Tamara is dead. There's nothing we can do to change that. What we *can* change is what happens next. The way I see it, we have three options.

"Option one is to continue as we are. Maybe not exactly as we are, because clearly what we were doing wasn't working. But now we know that was in part because Tamara was feeding information to the Protectorate. Obviously she won't be doing that anymore. I suppose it's possible that there's another mole working somewhere among us, but we have no way of knowing, and a witch hunt isn't going to help anyone. We have to hold together. Now more than ever. So we can formulate different strategies and keep raiding, keep hitting and running, keep scavenging and try to build our numbers as much and as fast as we can.

"Option two is to disband. Call this a failed attempt and go our separate ways, or at least stop trying to do what we've been doing as a united force. Cut our losses, take what we can, and try to make a life somewhere safe. We could do that. Maybe no one else would have to die. Maybe. At any rate, it's an option.

"Option three is to go on as a fleet, but stop trying to do this on our own. Look for allies. See if we can strengthen ourselves all at once rather than bit by bit over a long period of time.

"I think there are advantages to each of these, and there are problems. If you don't mind, I'll lay them out, and then we can discuss them. Maybe," her tone was just a bit wry now, "we can even come to a decision, if we can keep our shit together."

Once again she paused, and Nkiruka felt her gaze moving around the room. There was a little more shifting, a cough or two, and a couple of murmurs, but otherwise only expectant silence.

"All right." Eva took a breath. "Option one . . . Like I said, that way has real disadvantages. We've taken heavy losses doing things that way. There's nothing that says we won't continue to do so. Though Tamara no longer presents a danger, as I said, we have no way to be sure she was the only one. And regardless of what the Protectorate knows or doesn't know about where we'll be before we strike, they now almost certainly know a lot more about us than they should. They probably know our full numbers. They know what our complement of ships is. They know what kind of firepower we have. They likely know all about our command structure. In short, they know everything they need to know to keep carving away at us. So I don't think this is a good option. But you tell me.

"Option two is a lot easier, and again, it would mean no one else has to die. We get our families back and we get to have lives again. Or we get a shot at that." She laid her hand against her belly, and Nkiruka felt a soft flush of light and warmth. Of course, Eva had her own reasons.

"But there are also problems. I don't think the Protectorate is going to just let us be, regardless of whether or not we're still hitting them. I don't know, obviously, but I have a feeling they would keep searching for us. And even if we run, we can only run so far. Their reach is probably farther. It might take years, but if they don't collapse first—and they very well might—the chances that they'll find us are greater than I'd like. Maybe we could build up defenses in the meantime, maybe we could be in a position to fight them off . . . but I don't know. I wouldn't want to bank your lives on it, or the lives of our families.

"Option three: we look for help. That's hard. I'm not sure where we would look. But I know the Protectorate has a few scattered enemies, even if those enemies wouldn't be willing to strike back at them alone, and maybe we could . . . I don't know. Form some kind of alliance? That would grow our numbers quickly, it gives us much more in the way of resources, and it potentially puts us in a much better strategic position. I think so, anyway.

"But there's . . ." She stopped and Nkiruka sensed her pull inward, briefly frustrated, worried. Eva had been worried the entire time, but now the anxiety swelled in her, along with a helplessness that made Nkiruka ache for her.

She would have to speak to Eva afterward. Make it clear that her help was available. That she was there to offer strength. Comfort. And there was no weakness in accepting it. She had always gotten the feeling that Rachel thought that way.

"We've been trying to save people. We've been trying to make things so difficult and unstable that the Protectorate stops imprisoning people and starts looking for other options, and this is our first step. But there are some options I think we need to decide on before we can take it. We need to have them clear. As far as I can see, in terms of a goal, we have two choices. Either we cut our losses, like I said, and run, and try to make what kind of life we can. Or."

Eva let out a long breath. *This is it*, Nkiruka thought, and her entire body became a prayer. A benediction of sorts, but also a plea. For the mercy of whoever was listening. For salvation. Because this was a dark road. Ixchel had known that, and she had been so afraid. It had tormented her at the end, and while her last moments had been peaceful and full of love . . .

The moments before that had been anything but.

"Or," Eva continued slowly, "we go all in. We try to bring the whole structure down. We stop skirmishing and we go to war."

For a long time there was no response. Nkiruka felt the words sinking in, settling over everyone.

At last Yvette, one of the younger captains, stood. She crossed her arms, and there was solidity in her stance. Command. It was good that she had elected to speak first, and Nkiruka could already sense what she was about to say. That it was her was a testament to how well Eva had laid out their choices.

"I'm not sure how much more discussion we even need. It seems our choices are fairly clear. I think the only thing left is to vote on it, and then decide where we go from there. And whatever we decide on . . . Whoever wants no part in it, who wants to split off, they should still do so. After everything that's happened, I don't imagine it would be a good idea to force anyone to do anything against their will."

Another pause. Then, starting slow and quiet, mutters of assent. Some of it grudging, but no one seemed especially inclined to argue. Unity at last. Unity hard-won, maybe, but they had all found it again. Right when they needed it.

Perhaps some greater hand *was* lending them aid.

"Let's have an anonymous vote. No one should feel pressured. This is a choice . . ." Yvette laughed softly. "This is everything, I believe."

Things proceeded, and now they were calm and orderly, though there was a pall of discomfort on the room. Of tension. Because yes, this *was* everything. This was the moment on which the rest of this—to whatever end—turned.

Votes were written on slips of paper and put into a porcelain bowl that Adisa had brought in. Yvette—who seemed to have appointed herself aide to Eva and Kyle for the moment—carried the bowl to Eva and set it down on the table. One by one, Eva read out the votes and tallied them. And in the end, it was fairly simple.

Seven votes in favor of running.

Thirteen in favor of going to war.

There was a break. It wasn't a long one, and when the captains were assembled again, Adisa rose. A murmur ran around the room, and after a moment or two of waiting for it to die down, Adisa spoke.

"So we're losing three ships," he said. "I obviously have no right to command you from a position of authority on that point, but if you'll permit me to speak simply as a captain like the rest of you . . . I'm saddened. But I understand. As was said before, no one should be forced to fight in a war they didn't choose.

"The rest of us clearly have a decision to make. Who do we go to for help? Eva said the Protectorate has enemies. So it does. She also said they're scattered. So they are. We can try to unite them, try to bring them into agreement to the point where they're willing to fight by our side. But to be honest . . . I'm not sure I like that idea. As with the proposal to continue with the raids, I think it might take too long. And time is something we don't have much of. So instead, let me make a suggestion. It's a strange suggestion, and I wouldn't be surprised if some of you aren't in favor of it. Or if all of you aren't. But here it is, nevertheless.

"Back when Adam Yuga was first a refugee on Ashwina, the Protectorate forced us and our convoy to flee. They pursued us, and we went to the only place we believed was safe, that we could reach. The only place the Protectorate wouldn't follow. We fled into Klashorg space."

Another murmur. A ripple of disquiet ran through Nkiruka. She had seen this coming; it was a logical plan. But he was right. The Klashorg were feared within their own space. Powerful beyond what anyone wanted to test. There was a reason why the Protectorate had always left them alone.

"I know, I know. But hear me out. The Bideshi and the Klashorg—I wouldn't say our relations are *warm*, exactly. But they're civil. And I know one of their highest governmental officials. Or at least, last I heard, he was still holding that position. He's a friend of mine, from days far back, and he has never forgotten me. He managed to convince his people to take us in then, and I think it's worth asking them to do so again. I know they have a reputation for being dangerous to outsiders, but I truly believe that with Ashwina heading the fleet, the worst they would do is turn us away from their border. It's unlikely that they would harm us unless we pressed." He smiled thinly. "And obviously we wouldn't press."

One of the captains—an older man with a particularly commanding voice and a presence to match—rose and glanced around at his comrades, eyes narrowed skeptically. "And you think they might, what, lend us a battle fleet? Come in and take care of the whole thing for us?"

"I don't know what specifically I think they might do," Adisa said coolly. "Aside from not harming us. Personally I'm hoping they'll give us a good, hot meal. They're known for their woodworking, but their cuisine is really something special."

From across the room, Nkiruka felt the captain's indignation as intensely as if it were the heat of his life. And she felt Adisa's wry amusement and took pleasure in it, hiding her smile behind her hand. No doubt he knew she could feel it; no doubt he was hoping she might enjoy it.

"This is no time for jokes."

"I'm not joking. Best-kept secret in this part of the galaxy." A twitch at the corner of his mouth like a plucked string. "It would be, given that it's kept by them."

The captain glared and opened his mouth, but Yvette stood once more. "I say we trust Adisa. He has the experience, and I don't see why he would lead us into certain death. And the Klashorg? We know their reputation."

Another captain piped up, a younger woman with slightly haughty manner. "We also know that they're reluctant to involve themselves in any matters outside their borders. They prefer to be left alone. I actually can't think of a time when that hasn't been the case, except for when they fought their two interstellar wars, and that was centuries ago. Adisa, I see the logic in the idea, but why should they help us? I do think we need to consider that."

Nkiruka felt a smoothness flowing into Adisa's mind as he adopted a tone of quiet respect. "Indeed we should. And I'm not sure, to be perfectly honest. It's entirely possible that they won't. But these are extraordinary circumstances. They've never been fond of the Protectorate, though they maintain civil relations with them. But to date, the Protectorate's crimes against other worlds haven't been severe enough to force their hand. The Protectorate has been cruel, they've been a destructive force, and they've taken planets using sometimes violent coercion, but on the whole they haven't done very much to give the Klashorg cause to be directly concerned with them. Not when the result of conflict between the two could be so massively destructive.

"But things have changed. Things have gotten much worse. They know about what happened on Takamagahara, and I promise you, they marked it very well. This . . ." He paused, brow furrowing in thought. "The Klashorg may not care for interfering in anything outside their homeworld, but they're a justice-loving species, and they know what civil war means. And they have always felt a special kinship with us. They know our history, where we originally came from. What's happening now . . . I think it might be enough to draw them out. Especially given that Bideshi have died. Especially given that many more will die if this is allowed to continue."

Nothing else was said. Not immediately. Nkiruka could feel skepticism still lingering—skepticism and anxiety. This was more of the unknown, and while those raised in the Terran Protectorate were raised with an inherent sense of superiority over other species, everyone was aware of the Klashorg's reputation. It was fearsome. So much so that only twice had other species engaged them in warfare.

Nothing much was known about those conflicts. Or about the species with whom they had gone to war.

Nothing remained to be known.

Finally Eva broke the silence. "We need to discuss it. I'm not saying we should do it—I'm not even sure what I think—but we need to discuss it as a real possibility. Look, we're— As it is, we're broken. We're in bad shape. We're literally in pieces. And one advantage I can see with the Klashorg is that we have nothing they want. Probably not, anyway. If they decide to help us, I don't think they'd try to cheat us or manipulate us. It's not what they do.

"The people who might be willing to go up against the Protectorate? Pirates. Mercenaries. People chased away from their homes, who turned criminal to survive. Mostly, anyway. You think they'll just join us out of some sense of idealism? Even if they do want revenge, they'll be looking for an advantage. No. Like I said, I'm not sure, but . . . From that end? I do think the Klashorg are our best option."

She sighed and there was a feeling of friction, vibration, as she squeezed her eyes briefly closed.

"All right. Let's talk."

The talk went on for some time. After a while Adisa rose and came to Nkiruka, took the empty seat beside her. She laid her hand on his, and his weariness flowed into her like water into a depression in the ground.

"They'll agree. Eventually." She gave him a faint smile. "You said it wasn't your place to convince them, and you convinced them anyway. Sly Old Bear."

He shook his head, but turned his hand under hers, wrapped his fingers around it, and squeezed gently. "Eva will do the majority of the convincing. She has already. She claimed she didn't know if she could, I think she believed she couldn't, but she did. She's wise in ways she isn't even aware of. Not yet."

"She will be."

"Yes. Another one of us, changed."

"What do you think of Kyle?"

Adisa was quiet for a moment. Then he shifted, rearranged his robes, and turned his attention toward the man still seated by Eva's side. "One doesn't have to obviously lead in order to do so. You know that better than anyone. He'll have her back. Be her foundation. Calm her, comfort her. And when the time comes, he'll stand with her, and no one will doubt his strength."

"When the time comes," Nkiruka echoed softly. "Yes."

And it would.

Soon.

CHAPTER

NINETEEN

It was dawn when Sinder made his move.

It was quiet at first. It had to be. He rose before light, bathed, made himself a cup of strong coffee, and stood in front of the immense window that made up one wall of his bedroom, gazing out at the city. Its lights still glowed and twinkled like stars, shimmered, gleamed, reflected over and over in endless facets of glass and crystal.

He loved it with a ferocity that caused him physical pain, spasms of it rolling through his trembling body. He loved it more than his own life. He had loved it his whole life, but after Peris, after tasting that shameful defeat, after looking Adam Yuga in the eyes and knowing that—then—he wouldn't be able to catch the man, let alone destroy him . . . That love had grown tenfold. He understood what was at stake now. It wasn't just about avenging a slight, and it wasn't just about seeing an enemy of the Protectorate brought to justice. It wasn't even about uncovering the details of some potential conspiracy, or discovering what kind of threat the Bideshi now posed, seeing the darker shadow of the immense tree-like form that the future had become in his endlessly keen and far-seeing mind.

It was about everything. It was about the greatest civilization the galaxy had ever known being beset on all sides, by barbarians without and by creeping weakness within. Eaten away by parasites who had too long been allowed to cling to its body. It was about purging and reordering and seeing things repaired. Put right. The Terran Protectorate returned to its full glory.

And Terra once again taking her rightful place as the true center of it all.

Sinder pulled in a deep breath. The air was cleaned, scrubbed of impurities, and should hold no scent whatsoever—unless he wanted one—but to him it seemed sweet. Everything around him was lovely in a way that gripped at his heart. Beauty flowed into his soul and set it alight. The elegant form of the future, unseen but so keenly and viscerally felt, was smooth and cool against his skin like spun gold.

He wouldn't be corrupted by this power, because he was only an instrument of a greater purpose. He sensed his own greatness, his own strength of will, and his fundamental purity, perhaps the closest anyone in the Protectorate had come to what every one of them sought to be, but he was nevertheless only a vessel. History might revere him in the end, but he himself—Isaac Sinder—was nothing.

He was no more than the means by which a world would be saved.

He closed his eyes and that tremendous power swirled around him, stroking against his skin. It swelled in him, made him want to weep with the sheer intensity of his exaltation—but suddenly his hand began to shake. Only slightly at first, but then with increasing severity. The coffee slopped over the edge of the mug. The mug slipped from his fingers, fell to the floor, and shattered.

He barely noticed. It was of no consequence.

The ride to the Palace wasn't a long one, and as the car hummed through the air, Sinder fingered the little tube in his pocket and looked out at the sunrise and pondered.

He had been to the Palace only four times in his career. Many people of high rank—administrative, commercial, and military—never set foot inside it at all. Part of the reason was that it was a place of great ceremonial importance, and a tremendous privilege and mark of honor to be summoned there, but—most of all—it was that there was little need any longer for anyone to go. It was, again, a place of enormous ceremonial importance, and that was truly most of the importance it now possessed. The finer points of Protectorate rule took place elsewhere, in rooms and halls less hallowed and more modest and generally better for conducting business.

It was as it should be. He knew that now as well as anyone. Doing that kind of business in those kinds of places was how he had come to be here. But it offended him. It offended him deeply. Genuine power shouldn't be ceremonial. The greatest power should rest in a place like the Palace, and it should do so in the most profound sense. When people looked toward the Palace with awe, that awe should be genuine. When people regarded it with respect—even with fear—they should have a real reason for doing so.

After this, they would. And as he had told Julius, he expected nothing significant to stand in the way of what he planned. By the time they truly realized what was happening, it would be far too late to stop it, and there would certainly be no one to stop *him*.

The Palace loomed in the morning sun, all brilliant gold and noble spires, enormous and graceful. Its sides were dotted with many landing platforms, some grand and some much more humble, and it was to one of the humbler ones that the car headed. It lowered itself slowly onto the platform, and Sinder descended the extended stairway with barely a nod at the driver. This wasn't one of the careful drivers, but he didn't need one of them. Not this time.

It didn't matter who knew he was here.

The platform ended in a set of tall, narrow double doors of frosted glass that swirled with subtle rainbow hues that intensified when the sun touched them. They swung open at Sinder's approach, and he stepped into a relatively modest entrance hall of what looked like polished gold, which was dominated by a desk, behind which sat a tall woman with a crown of braided chestnut hair and a small but extremely pleasant smile. Likely she wore the same smile for every visitor she greeted, carefully and expertly practiced as a step in a dance.

Sinder nodded when he reached her, and she nodded back and leaned forward. "You're Mr. Isaac Sinder."

"Yes." He also leaned forward as a small scanner unfolded itself from the smooth surface of the desk, extending a retina reader and a place for him to lay his hand for both fingerprint and DNA identification. Regardless of whether true power lay within this place, security was still tight.

The woman consulted a screen as Sinder let the machine scan him. "You have an appointment with the Founders. Congratulations, I'm impressed they found a spot for you. They're usually booked weeks in advance."

"It was a matter of immediate importance. They made it a point to carve out time for me." As if the Founders were even capable of managing their own affairs any longer. The time-carving had been his own doing, pulling those threads he had so carefully woven into a web to catch what he needed. "But it shouldn't take long."

The woman was nodding as she tapped her console, but he could tell she wasn't listening. The Founders dealt with nearly constant meetings every day, but few of them really mattered. Despite what he had told her, his would just be another one of those. All the better.

She ceased her tapping and gave him another iteration of that practiced smile. "You're set, Mr. Sinder. Do you need directions, or can you find your own way?"

"I've been here before. I'll be all right. Thank you." He nodded a farewell. She returned it and lowered her head, and immediately he could tell he had been dismissed.

In fact, although he had been to the Palace before, he had never had a personal audience with the Founders. But he could find his way. The night before, he had finished his preparations by engaging in a close examination of a map of the entire structure, memorizing all its passages and hallways and chambers, all its lifts and stairways, to the point of intimate familiarity. He was heading to a set of those lifts now, set against the back wall of the room, and he knew the way well enough to proceed on autopilot and turn his conscious mind to other matters.

The ride up the thirty floors past which he needed to rise was smooth and swift, the soft, warm lighting of the lift somehow lulling. It was probably intentional—to ease the nature and mood of any visitor to the Founders, lest anything upset them—and he allowed it to wash over him. Tranquility would probably be of more help than harm. He didn't need to be agitated to do what he had come to do.

The lift hummed to a smooth halt, and the doors opened on a wide, gleaming, brightly lit entrance hall. Like most of the finest Protectorate spaces, it was elegantly and sparsely furnished: a tall silver fountain in the center boasted a series of flowing, abstract figures, down which water ran. A few benches. Glowing orchids of purple and white and blue and pink were set into recesses in the walls—examples of the latest and most advanced engineering and genetic management. A single crystal chandelier hung from the high ceiling. And directly before him, two enormous golden doors.

The room itself radiated wealth and grandness and—yes—power.

Appearances weren't everything, but they could be close.

There was also no desk here, no receptionist, no guards. Everyone who came here knew what lay beyond those doors, and that knowledge was enough to command respect and care.

The Founders. The first authorities of the Terran government, and the mothers and fathers of the Protectorate. The authors of the most fundamental ideals of their entire civilization. Perfection, order, and, above all, the march ever onward toward true perfection, which was total mastery over one's own being. One's own body and mind and life. No sickness. No infirmity. Immunity from once life-ending injury. No weakness. No *death*. What more superstitious people had once thought of as divinity.

The ideals were still worth fighting for. They were the only things that truly were.

As with the doors that had admitted him into the Palace, these opened silently before he even reached them, and he stood for a moment, blinking in the light that streamed through.

The room beyond, like the entrance hall, was large and simple. The lighting was equally tasteful, delicate, and the surfaces gleamed. But there were no chairs, no seats of any kind, and there were no windows whatsoever. No art. No decorations. Nothing that marked this place as either a dwelling or a room of state.

Because in truth it was neither.

When Isaac Sinder stepped forward, he stepped into an infirmary.

Or something much like an infirmary. The medical technology that kept the twelve Founders alive was kept as out of sight as possible. Some appearances still had to be maintained; if nothing else, a facade of dignity of the twelve creatures before him had to be preserved. But really, they were beyond the point of proving anything to anyone. Long ago they had turned inward, selfishly abandoned the greatness and might of their empire, and given themselves over entirely to the project of prolonging their own increasingly pointless lives as long as possible. They heard arguments and delivered judgments, they communicated with leaders on distant worlds, and they passed laws and issued decrees, but Sinder was certain that they had ultimately rejected their once-sacred trust.

This was an obscenity. If the Protectorate was going to be saved, this problem had to be addressed.

For the first time, he sent out a thought to the unseen and unfelt presence he was certain was with him.

Almost time.

He stepped forward.

Twelve beings floated in twelve vats of thick, colorless, slightly cloudy fluid. Everything was in that fluid, everything needed to keep them fed and oxygenated and to rebuild them cell by cell every time one died, inside and out. Every part of their bodies was being constantly replaced. A thin spiderweb of wires ran through the fluid and beneath their skin at intervals, which were stimulators that kept their muscles from completely atrophying. More wires—impossibly delicate filaments—extended into their bald scalps; by this method their brains were kept from degrading, though given their vagueness and distraction during his conversations with them, it wasn't working especially well anymore.

Once it had. But it had been centuries now since they had left their tanks, and despite the machine's attempts to maintain their muscles, they barely looked human anymore. They were wasted, hairless, pink things, their eyes wide but unfocused, their mouths opening and closing slowly, rather like fish. They were alive, yes—but what kind of life was this?

What kind of perfection?

A wave of nausea rolled through Sinder as he bowed. He had known it would be like this. He had known all about the dirty secret of the Terran Protectorate, the fact everyone knew and away from which everyone turned their eyes. Everyone else seemed content to ignore it.

But now he was here. And he had no intention of ignoring anything.

"Isaac Sinder." A united murmur, though the union wasn't perfect, and the words were slightly slurred. "You wish to speak with us."

"I do, honored Founders." He folded his hands at his waist, and as he did so, he palmed the vial. "A matter of great importance, as I said when I requested the audience."

A low hum, not quite words. Three of the figures stirred in the tanks, blinking owlishly. "Speak, then."

Their tone conveyed no particular urgency, no particular interest in something so significant. Freshly obscene, but also a thing that would work in his favor.

"It concerns the entire Protectorate. A prevalent sickness, an illness that threatens to afflict every single one of us."

Another murmur. "We are aware. We have the matter in hand."

Of course you do. Sinder smiled thinly. "Yes, Founders. I wouldn't presume to waste your time by telling you what you already know. And I'm grateful for how you've been managing the crisis. We are, all of us, grateful. But I'm talking about a different disease altogether."

He slipped the vial into his fingers and felt its smooth coolness. It was barely larger than his fingernail, but it seemed to thrum in his hand, hot like a tiny star. That wasn't so far from the truth.

"This is a much older and more pervasive sickness, and I think it's been at work among us for much longer. I think it's far more dangerous. I think it threatens to destroy the very foundations on which our civilization is built. I think so far you have all remained unaware of it," his voice was rising, and he made no effort to stop it, "and I would like that to change. Now."

This time the murmur was disapproving. Somewhat taken aback. He could feel them focusing—and there was something delightfully, amusingly perverse about that. They would focus—they would *care*—when their pride was insulted. Or seemed about to be insulted.

Perverse especially considering what they had allowed themselves to become. Had *willingly made themselves into.*

"Sinder, you would do well to watch your tone. Remember to whom you are speaking. Remember your place. What is this *sickness* you say we aren't aware of?"

"That's just the thing," Sinder said, quiet now. "We see the fault in everything and everyone but ourselves, don't we? It's easy for us to see it in others, to alter and change and make demands of them while we hold ourselves to no such standards. It makes us feel like we have control, like we can maintain this world we've built around ourselves. This world we tell ourselves is perfect. But it's a lie. And when we are the *foundation* of that world, well." His thin smile widened, but was no less thin. "I don't think I should have to explain the problem any further."

Now, though it wasn't in their murmurings to each other, he could feel their alarm. He wasn't sure how, but he could. It was sharp and clear, like a chemical smell, and perhaps it was. Some kind of pheromone enhanced and intensified by the fluid in which they constantly floated.

"Sinder. Explain yourself. Do so now, or we will have you removed."

"The foundations of the Terran Protectorate are shaking," he said calmly. "Cracking. I am here to repair them. More than repair: I am here to *replace* them."

He lifted the hand that held the vial, thought, *Now.* And tossed it onto the floor.

Or he tossed it almost onto the floor. Inches before the vial landed, an invisible hand seemed to catch it and hold it suspended, turning it slowly in midair. The Founders were all in silent shock, their unfocused eyes snapping into focus at once.

Sinder whirled and ran.

Sinder threw himself through the doors as they swung open, silently counting the seconds. The image was so clear in his mind, as if he were still in the room: the invisible hand disappeared and the vial fell, broke, and exploded as soon as it was touched by the air.

Heat and force jetted through the crack in the door. The door had been built to withstand a blast, and that was also working perversely in his favor, but Sinder had no time to be amused by it. The heat and blast wave struck him squarely in the back, and burning pain punched through him. He cried out and went sprawling, nearly striking the edge of the fountain with his head—and then narrowly avoiding impalement by two of its fragments as it shattered. Behind the haze of agony, he was irritated. He had asked Julius to moderate his injuries—but perhaps Julius was doing just that.

The situation was, in fact, nearly perfect.

He smelled burning chemicals, hair, probably his suit—and flesh. Not his own. After a moment of lying facedown on the floor and waiting for the buzzing in his head to subside, he pushed himself up to sit, wincing at the sharp pain as the skin of his shoulders and neck stretched—burned, perhaps, and he could feel that some of his suit had been ripped away—and turned to stare back at the chamber of the Founders.

He couldn't see much through the crack in the door—the door itself halted as it closed by the force of the explosion. But he could see fire. A great quantity of fire. Physically it was contained, but suddenly it was as if it had a spirit as well, spilling sweet warmth out into the chamber and into him. A friend. An ally. It had come to him when he called it. The elements themselves were aligned with his goal. The universe was blessing him.

Beneath its roaring song, there were feeble screams, like the cries of a sick infant.

Sinder smiled and closed his eyes. What he felt—he wasn't sure he would call it ecstasy. But it was close. He reached out again to the ghost by his side.

Give them the signal. Tell all of them to move. Now.

Then he was still, simply feeling the moment. This great moment, this turning point in history, to which everyone would look back with appropriate wonder.

The rebirth had begun.

CHAPTER

TWENTY

It took three days to reach Klashorg space.

It wasn't on the edge of human-explored space, but it was close, and few people ventured near it. The Klashorg were known to be generally unaggressive, and they were only interested in maintaining their own borders. But their reputation for ferocity when provoked was a powerful one, and people were content to stay well clear.

The fleet came out of slipstream in a trickle, and while some additional repairs had been made en route, many of the ships were still badly damaged and only able to limp along. Adam stood on the top-level gallery of Ashwina's great central hall and watched the streaked white fade to starry black, and at the same time felt as if he were being tugged backward and returned to days far in the past.

A lifetime.

He and Lochlan had been together before they arrived at Klashorg, at least in the most basic physical sense; the first time they made love, if you could call something so rough and desperate *making love*, had been shortly after the clash with Cosaire's fleet that had sent them running. But it was on Klashorg that things had truly begun to soften between them. There they had started to learn each other, to trust each other. Still with some friction, still with some irritation on both sides, but the bonds that had eventually married them had taken root there.

There among the immense trees and bioluminescent flowers, and the elegant, carved wooden city of Klashorg's people. He hadn't known it at the time, but on Klashorg he had begun to fall in love with Lochlan, and he knew it had worked both ways.

Now they were returning. And while there seemed to be some doubt in the fleet about whether they would be allowed beyond the Klashorg's borders, Adam knew they would. He knew because reason told him, since they had been allowed once before and now they—and he in particular—were known even better there, and had more reason to be trusted.

And he also simply knew.

He tilted his head back and stared upward, and below him the constant, musical hum of the central hall drifted up and settled around him like a cloud. This place, this beautiful place—it wasn't his home. It never would be. He was growing more and more certain that when this was over, if he even survived, he would have no home. He couldn't. He could live somewhere, he might be able to remain for a while, but he would be drifting, and he would look back on this place as yet another part of the beginning of that. Another stop along the way. Not the beginning of a homecoming he'd never expected, but a kind of exile he'd never imagined.

Head still tilted back, he closed his eyes against the starry, endless night and let himself drift, feeling Ashwina and its people, feeling its life, feeling its fear and its hope, its pain and its pleasure, and the way—even when the ship itself was still—they constantly moved. For there was no such thing as true, perfect stillness.

True, perfect stillness was death.

The comet was swinging toward the sun. Just as it had been when it all began: a battle, flight, Klashorg... And soon would come the last step. One way or another, after this, everything would end.

The thing about orbits was that sooner or later they always returned you to the place you started from.

Eva had met Klashorg before. She had spoken to them—not extensively, but she had. She had encountered them as skilled laborers, people not particularly low in status but not especially high either. In all honesty, they had always made her uncomfortable—how their furry, impassive faces could make it almost impossible to know what they were thinking, to make even an educated guess. She didn't share the dislike—the *distaste*—for them that a lot of her fellow Protectorate citizens felt, but she certainly didn't *like* them.

Now, standing in the council chambers and looking at their border patrollers on the large comm display, she fought back her unease. They needed these people on their side. *She* needed them. She needed to adopt an attitude of complete respect and take her cues from Adisa, and she needed to not *fuck this up*.

She hadn't ever seen herself in this position. She should have had a more proactive imagination.

They had agreed that Adisa would take point. Given his history with the Klashorg, it was only logical for him to speak for all of them. He stood in front of the curved table with the rest of the fleet captains seated behind him. Nkiruka stood on his right and Eva on his left, Kyle beside her. This was the first time, Eva realized. The first time they had addressed someone else as an official group of leaders, even if they had no official rank and were only the heads of the loosest kind of hierarchy. Nothing like the highly ordered Protectorate organization most of them were accustomed to.

They were still leaders, standing as one.

But there was a gap in that unity. Rachel and Aarons should have been with them.

Adisa gave the being on the screen a deep nod—though the Klashorg would have a difficult time discerning the movement without being physically present. Their eyes were sensitive to light and movement and vague shapes, but their real sensory organs were the ends of their hair—able to detect the finest movements even at a distance, and perceive the shape of the world around them.

Perhaps that was why they felt warmth toward the Bideshi. It seemed to her that they might possess some sense of kinship with the Aalim.

But who knew?

"I'm Adisa. Of the homeship Ashwina. I've come on behalf of—"

"We're fully aware of who you are, and of your ship." Eva thought the Klashorg's voice—deeply resonant even through the comm—sounded a bit chilly. "And we can draw our own conclusions about why you and your fleet have come to us. We've been keeping abreast of events beyond our borders."

Adisa nodded again. "Of course. I meant no disrespect." He paused. "If you know who we are and why we've come, then I won't waste your time on explanations. Instead I'll address the question at hand. May we have safe passage through your space to Klashorg itself?"

Silence. It seemed to Eva that the Klashorg was staring at them—staring in almost that Aalim way, without truly using his eyes. Her sense of unease intensified. She didn't really expect to be attacked, but it could be as bad for them if they were turned away.

"We foresaw that you would come. Our leaders have already discussed it."

"I'll bow to their decision. Whatever it is."

He hadn't mentioned his friend, Eva noted. Not yet anyway. Interesting.

The Klashorg rumbled and shook himself. "You're all to be allowed entry into our space and passage to our homeworld. Whether you'll be allowed to stay and what we'll be willing to do for you is a matter yet to be decided."

Adisa showed no discernible relief. Nor did Nkiruka. But Eva felt something like a collective sigh of relief from the council behind her. It wasn't a yes, not a clear one, but at least they could all take time to rest.

"Remain where you are. Other patrol ships will join us within the hour. Then we can proceed."

This time Adisa's nod was more of a bow. "You have our sincere thanks."

The Klashorg let out another deep grumble, and the comm feed cut off into blackness.

Eva turned to Adisa. "Well." She pulled in a breath. "That could have gone a lot worse."

"Indeed it could." Adisa smiled tightly. "It still might. We have to convince their leaders to help us. In any respect."

Eva frowned. She hadn't assumed the hard part was over, of course, but Adisa sounded far less than certain. "You seemed like you were pretty sure they would."

"I was. But him." Adisa shook his head. "One Klashorg isn't necessarily an indication of anything, and there are those who simply don't like outsiders, no matter who they are. But just something in the way he was talking . . . I'm frankly wondering about the reception we'll receive."

Eva glanced back at the rest of the council, whose heads were bent together in quiet conversation. "Maybe it's because of how many of us are Protectorate? Used to be?"

"Perhaps. We won't know until we get there." Adisa laid a big, warm hand on her shoulder. "I would brush up on the finer points of Klashorg etiquette if I were you. We'll probably need all the help we can get."

Eva gave him a weak smile. But she didn't think he was joking.

When they had last come to Klashorg, Lochlan had piloted the shuttle carrying the initial diplomatic party. Now he did so again, the group this time consisting of Adisa, Nkiruka, Eva, and Kyle. He had asked for the job, and Adisa had readily granted the request. It would take Lochlan's mind off things. Or at least it might a bit, and every little bit helped.

What helped less was the fact that Adam was also riding in the shuttle, and the déjà vu was intense enough to make him dizzy. This time Adam didn't seem nervous, and this time the ride down wasn't nearly as choppy, but still. Lochlan swallowed his own unease as best he could and watched the mass of green canopy grow larger and larger in the shuttle's window.

They landed at midday, and the sun was bright and gleamed off the large leaves that swayed and danced all around the landing platform the shuttle settled on. One by one they rose and filed out, until at last Lochlan rose from the pilot's seat and turned—and there was Adam.

Maybe this had been a mistake.

Adam hesitated a moment, then came forward. "Lock . . ."

Lochlan ducked his head. Some of the pain and shame of the fight had faded, and clearly they were making their way back toward each other, but it still hurt. "I know," he murmured. What was happening now was something coming full circle, and being here would pull them together, as much a part of it as they had been at the beginning. He didn't want to stop it. He didn't think Adam wanted to either. And they had to acknowledge that it was there. Face it squarely.

Adam took Lochlan's hand. "Are you ready for this?"

Lochlan gave him a small smile. It ached like hooks at the corners of his mouth, but he managed it. It was even genuine. "Aren't I always ready for everything, *chusile*?"

"Yeah. Of course." Adam laughed softly. It was a warm laugh, and that warmth flowed into Lochlan's chest and spread through the rest of him. He wasn't afraid of this closeness and the vulnerability it brought. At least, not now. It was all right.

"Are *you*?"

Adam's brow furrowed "I don't know. I don't think so. I don't think there's a way to be ready for anything. But we don't have a choice." He leaned in and cupped Lochlan's face with one hand, kissed him. It was light and fleeting, almost chaste, but there was an intensity behind it that was impossible to miss. A heat, waiting for its time. Lochlan thought of those immense, glowing flowers that bloomed in the canopy.

They'd found each other under one of those flowers.

"C'mon," Adam murmured, pulling back and tugging Lochlan's hand. "They're waiting. Let's do this."

CHAPTER

***

TWENTY-ONE

The Klashorg's great capital city had changed not at all since Lochlan last saw it. It was a massive, sprawling collection of gracefully carved wooden buildings fitted with large glass windows that rioted with color. There were delicate spires and swooping, flowing shapes, structures that didn't seem to be separate buildings at all but one structure organically joined by wide walkways. Gondolas glided by overhead on thick woven cables, and everywhere Klashorg lumbered, worked, gathered in small groups to share a meal and talk at various open-air eateries. Klashorg lived in close proximity and in large families—profoundly communal beings.

It was strange that they would make their buildings and other creations so beautiful when their way of seeing was so different. But then again, perhaps not that strange. Couldn't an Aalim appreciate beauty? Didn't Nkiruka? Hadn't Ixchel?

The universe was a strange place.

On the landing platform, they had been greeted not by officials but by four guards armed with long, wickedly sharp *kelang* sticks. The guards had issued a gruff request for the party to follow them, and now they were leading them toward a medium-size building set back from one of the main walkways—not the central palace they had all been lodged in before.

Lochlan and Adam exchanged looks. This was interesting. And a little disquieting.

Eva must have caught their glances because she leaned in close and whispered, "What? What is it?"

Lochlan shook his head. "Let's just say this isn't exactly the welcome we received last time." He pitched his voice low.

The Klashorg had excellent hearing, but their guard wasn't close to where they were walking, and in any case, he wasn't sure what actual harm there was in being overheard. He probably wasn't saying anything they didn't already know. "Not met by anyone higher than a guard? Stashed away somewhere removed from everything? I'm not saying it means anything, but." He shrugged and let the *but* speak for itself.

Adisa, oddly—or so Lochlan thought—had asked no questions so far, and when they were led up to the door of the house and ushered inside, he went with only a polite nod. They found themselves in a central room furnished with plump couches large enough to accommodate a Klashorg, more beautiful wood carvings—tables, a couple of cabinets, sculptures, and lanterns—and a high, arched ceiling made not of wood but more colored glass, wood framed.

"We'll return shortly," a guard rumbled, and they departed without another word.

"Adisa." Lochlan stepped forward, arms crossed over his chest. He wasn't worried, not quite—but this was getting stranger all the time. "What's going on? Where's your friend? Where's Trachek?"

"I don't know. I don't know any more than you do." Adisa's mouth twisted as he scanned the room. "I agree, it's a little unsettling."

"They don't seem exactly friendly." Kyle moved over to one of the couches, pressed on it, and sat—a bit heavily, brow furrowed. "You're sure we're not in any danger, Adisa?"

"Yes. Absolutely sure." Adisa appeared to contemplate the ceiling, which sent patches of rainbow light scattering around the room. "They might berate us, certainly. Send us away empty-handed . . . I can see that happening as well. But they don't become violent without genuine cause. They won't harm us."

"Berate us." Lochlan cast a grimly amused glance at Adam—which earned him an equally amused smile. That made him feel the smallest bit better. "For *what*? They're the ones who let us into their space in the first place."

"I don't know for what," Adisa said calmly, and nodded to Nkiruka. "You should all rest, best as you can. I don't know how long we have, but we need to be ready for whatever is coming next. Nkiruka and I have to speak, just the two of us."

He and Nkiruka withdrew to a room off the central one and left the four of them alone.

"He's sure we're safe," Eva said, the skepticism clear in her tone. She stood with her arms folded across her chest, uneasily studying the room. She had seemed uneasy since they departed Ashwina; Lochlan had wondered if it was only the stakes of the situation, and if it might become a bigger problem. But she had to be here. There wasn't anyone else; he didn't think Kyle would have been especially willing to come without her, and in any case he doubted she would have let herself be left behind.

"Trust Adisa." Adam took a seat on the couch opposite Kyle. On the floor between them was a low table of mingled wood and green-blue crystal. Lochlan thought for a second of Adam's eyes. "He's never once led us wrong."

"Never?" Eva arched a brow.

"Never."

"He got us through this last time," Adam said quietly. He was standing and gazing toward the door, his expression distant. Distracted. "He'll do it again. This . . ." He turned back to them, but his distracted look remained. "Of everything we have on our plates at present, the Klashorg are one of the problems I'm *least* concerned about."

Kyle shook his head, but he was almost smiling. "You always were like that, Adam. Picking what to worry about. More like that now, though."

"No." Adam was also a few millimeters from a smile, and his gaze flicked up to Lochlan's. He knew. They both did. Whatever else had happened—however close he and Nkiruka were growing—Lochlan still knew him best. That was something. "No, I'm worried about everything. All the time now. It's just a matter of degrees."

They waited and didn't talk much. Adam wandered the room and Lochlan watched him. Kyle and Eva sat with their heads bent together, occasionally murmuring to each other, softly enough that Lochlan couldn't make out the words. But that was all right. He didn't need to. Maybe Adam was worried about everything, but Lochlan was finding a kind of tranquility, no matter how precarious their situation had become. Adisa was Adisa, and Adam was correct; Adisa had never led them wrong before. Sometimes *things* went wrong, but the direction was always true and the logic behind it quite solid.

What would be, would be. For now he had to wait.

After about twenty minutes, Adisa and Nkiruka reentered the room. Adisa took a spot beside Lochlan without a word and folded his hands in his lap, closing his eyes. Nkiruka moved over to Adam and laid a hand briefly on his shoulder, but said nothing.

Another twenty minutes or so, and the guards returned and gestured for them to rise and follow. They were led down the main walkway toward a large building some distance away—still graceful in spite of its bulk, with wide balconies and immense windows, terraces and parapets and towers. Lochlan recognized it immediately: the great central halls of the Klashorg high council, where they had been housed when they were last on this world. He had thought it beautiful then and he did now, but with the silence of the guards and the not entirely friendly looks they earned from the people they passed, it also seemed just a touch foreboding.

Adam's hand found his and held it gently.

They climbed a flight of steps and into a high-ceilinged entrance hall, and from there up a wide staircase that terminated in a door the size and grandeur of which matched everything else. Lochlan already knew what lay beyond it, and as it opened on a bright room dominated by a long table, they all stepped inside.

Around the table were seated twelve Klashorg—one from each of the world's provinces—and the four high councilors who held the most powerful status in the group. Lochlan scanned the councilors; many non-Klashorg had difficulty in telling them apart, but he had always been able to do so fairly well. He was searching for Trachek—and saw him nowhere.

He shot Adam a look and earned himself a headshake. *Stay calm. Wait.*

The group was ushered toward six empty chairs that had been set at the far end of the table. The Klashorg might not possess conventional sight, but as he and the rest took their seats, Lochlan felt their piercing scrutiny.

This wasn't necessarily *bad*, but line and orbit, it wasn't *good*.

There was a brief silence. Then one of the four high councilors—an elderly Klashorg with light green fur that indicated her age—rose and laid her large hands on the table. "We've done the bare minimum hospitality requires," she said. "Or at least, the bare minimum it requires where you're concerned, Adisa. Speak now, and tell us why we should grant you any more than that. We're willing to listen, but I'll be honest with you: you'll have to be convincing."

Adisa rose as well and gave her a low bow. "Mashkak. It's good to see you again." He cleared his throat and looked around the room. "I won't waste your time with further pleasantries. You've seen the state of our fleet, our people. I'm guessing you know who we are. What we're attempting to do."

"To destroy the Protectorate? Yes, we're abreast of what's happening beyond our borders."

"Destroy them?" Adisa shook his head, brows drawn together. "No, not destroy them. Quite the opposite. We mean to save them, if it's possible to do so."

There was a low rumble around the table—the Klashorg conferring in their own, more esoteric language. The Klashorg Adisa had addressed as Mashkak lifted her hand for silence. "Explain."

"You recall the circumstances under which we last came to Klashorg?"

Mashkak nodded and pointed at Adam. "That one. He was ill, and you were seeking a cure. The Protectorate was pursuing you, and you needed refuge and repairs for your convoy. Healing for your wounded."

"Yes. The circumstances this time are almost identical. Except this time no one with us needs the healing Adam did. Instead all the Protectorate with us carry a way to heal their own people. For Adam wasn't the first, nor was he the last. Have you heard that?"

"We're aware," said the Klashorg to Mashkak's left—a younger male with especially shaggy, deep-green fur, "that there's unrest within their borders. Something amiss. We weren't clear on what it was. It's no concern of ours, so long as it doesn't affect us directly."

"It's killing them," Adam said quietly. He didn't get to his feet, but leaned forward slightly, and beneath the table his hand once again sought and found Lochlan's. "Slowly. Not so slowly now. We can help them, but they won't be helped. Their authorities . . ." Frustration passed across his face. "Do you understand that pride can be a species of madness?"

No one spoke for a moment. The Klashorg didn't seem to use facial expressions in the way other species did, but Lochlan got the feeling that they were exchanging glances.

"We do," Mashkak said at last. "Are you saying their pride is preventing them from seeking—or accepting—your help?"

"That's exactly what I'm saying." Adam gestured at Lochlan, at Nkiruka and Adisa. "These people are everything the Protectorate doesn't want to be. They represent something that . . . I know it sounds strange, but I was one of those people—" He cleared his throat and stood a little more erect. "I *am* one of those people, and I know how they think. The Bideshi are like . . . a kind of blasphemy. They'd never put it that way, but that's how the Protectorate sees them. It's irrational, it's terrible . . . but it's how things are. They would rather let their own people die than take what we're offering. Than admit we're offering anything worth taking."

Eva spoke up, her voice soft but sharp and clear, and carrying across the table. "They won't even admit there's a problem. Not a serious one."

Another council member shook his shaggy head. "I don't understand. Why then are you trying to *save* these people?"

Adam spread his hands helplessly, and Lochlan saw something breaking through behind his eyes. Something coming together into a single point.

"They're my people."

A pause, which no one filled. Adam took a breath.

"Look, someone helped me when I was in need, when they had no reason to do so. They did it because they believed that I *was* one of them in some way. That there was a rift that had to be closed. That I could close it. Bideshi *died* to help see that happen. I can't—I can't just give that up because it's hard. And I can't walk away from my people just because they're too stubborn and too stupid to see what has to be done."

"So you'll kill them? To make them understand?" Mashkak sounded bemused. "That seems counterproductive."

"We don't want to kill anyone," Eva said. "That was never what we were doing. Our raids were about freeing people from quarantine camps. Places where they were being starved. Murdered. Experimented on and tortured. We were saving them, taking supplies and ships, growing our numbers. We always minimized casualties. Theirs as well as ours."

"But your goal was still to make war on them, ultimately. Once your strength was sufficient."

"Our goal was to force them to notice us. Force them into talks."

"Or erode the confidence of the people in their leaders," Adam said. "Get them questioning. Resisting, at least those who would if there was a chance. We've heard that's already happening, from some of the people we've picked up more recently. They're seeing friends disappear. Family. They've been given explanations, but they aren't all buying them. Not anymore. The Protectorate's political structure is already shaky. We don't think it will take more than one big push to bring the whole thing down."

Adisa cleared his throat. "But we've all been hit hard. The Protectorate's military are starting to adapt. They're anticipating our moves. They're carving away at us. We came to you to rest, to repair the damage to our ships, just as before. We've lost Kae, our principal wingleader. He's alive, but he's in no condition to pilot a fighter." His gaze flicked to Lochlan. Lochlan felt a stab of fresh pain. He had managed to let this go, for the time being. To release his hold on something he couldn't hope to control.

But now he thought of Kae back in that clinic bed, still as death, and a clenched fist rose into his throat.

"It's unclear," Adisa continued, "whether he'll ever be able to fight again."

"That's certainly unfortunate," another of the council rumbled. "But I think, Adisa, that rest and repair aren't all you've come looking for."

"You're correct." He hesitated, but it probably wasn't out of uncertainty. Adisa would have walked into this room with not only one speech planned but several, each tailored to a specific tonal shift in the conversation.

The floor under him somehow felt a little more solid. He had told Kyle and Eva not to doubt Adisa. Now he was being reminded that he shouldn't either.

"I know this is highly irregular. I know it's beyond a long shot. I know your answer will likely be no. But when one is backed into a corner, when there are no more good choices, it does little harm to ask. At least," and he cast a faint smile around the room, "when one is assuming it won't earn him and his friends additional physical damage."

Another rumble from several of the council, which worried Lochlan for a few seconds until he recognized it.

Laughter. Low and brief, but there.

"Friends—and yes, I consider you friends, to my people if not specifically to me—we believe we've come to a crucial point in the flow of events. We and the Protectorate are two lines that have been running parallel but that can now intersect at a point where neither is as bad as it might be. We've risen in strength just enough to potentially make the intersection swing in our favor. The Protectorate has begun to slide downward, but they haven't yet fallen into the sort of chaos that might result in the deaths of millions more of their people. By the same token, they haven't yet hit us as hard as they might. We have the potential ability to end this now, swiftly, avoiding much more bloodshed. We can either pressure the Protectorate's authorities into a place where they have to talk, or destabilize them to the point where they fall. If we act strongly and decisively, we might be able to avoid a war that could drag out for *years*."

"But if the Protectorate government falls," Mashkak said quietly, "won't that also create chaos?"

"Chaos within which we can place ourselves," Eva said. "Adam is known to many Protectorate citizens by now. We don't know to what degree he's regarded positively, but he's known. At least to some. There are other people with us who used to be highly placed. They have connections. If anyone can go in and help restore *some* kind of order, it may be us."

Adisa nodded at Eva. "If we were better able to penetrate deep into Protectorate space, we would have more of a chance to coordinate with anyone inside who wanted to help us, who might act as an ally. But we've been prevented from doing so. As I said, this isn't necessarily a good plan. It's barely a *plan*. But right now, it's the best we have."

There was a short period of silence. Lochlan had kept his peace so far, but now it was worth openly making a certain admission. Practically a concession.

"We've been winging this." He allowed faint, self-deprecating amusement to slip into his tone. "From the beginning. Lunging about. I'm not saying it's served us well, but." He shrugged and glanced at Adam, who was smiling at him again. "We're still here. When we should have been dead about fifty times over. That has to count for something."

"It may." Mashkak's voice was low and rough. "Make your request, Adisa. Make it plainly."

Adisa nodded. "We're at a crucial moment. We want to save Adam's people. We want to save ourselves. We want to save as many people as we can, on all worlds, of all species. The Protectorate is crumbling, and we want to bring it down as quickly as possible, but we aren't strong enough to do it alone. Your strength in war is unmatched in our histories, and your people are feared even above the Protectorate. We've come to ask you to help us. We've come to ask you to fight by our side."

This time the silence stretched out longer than any before. Adisa lowered himself back into his chair, and the six of them sat through it, waiting. Lochlan took a breath and found that he wasn't actually afraid. Not much, anyway. They had come through everything so far, and as Adisa had said, they were now in a place where their essential lack of options gave them a certain freedom.

Not the best species of freedom, but it was there.

Adam's hand was warm and firm, curled around his.

"You're right," Mashkak said at last—slowly. "This is highly irregular. *Irregular* doesn't begin to capture it. Not once in all our history has anyone outside our borders come to us with a request even vaguely like this. We eschew violent conflict. You know why. We have avoided war of any kind since the civil war that almost destroyed us. Now you come to us, requesting that we dive into it with you." A soft, growling laugh. "Yes, this is rather *irregular*."

Adisa dipped his head. "I know, Mashkak. It's beyond presumptuous. I apologize for it. As I said, I fully expect to be turned away."

Mashkak made a meditative noise and bent her head to the three others of the high council, murmuring to them. Finally she looked up again. "Why should we? Make your case as briefly as you can."

There was a sternness, a warning in her words, but Lochlan detected no anger. Nor had they been bodily thrown from the chamber. That was good. Anything but outright rejection was good. He squeezed Adam's hand again, and Adam gave him a nod.

It's going to be fine.

Lochlan let out a soft laugh. *One way or the other, eh,* chusile?

It was entirely possible that Adam could hear him.

"We're asking you to go to war with us because you hate war," Adisa said simply. "The two interstellar wars you fought, you completely obliterated your enemy. No detailed records of them even remain. You know what crushing force can do. You know how abruptly it can stop a conflict. And you've seen what civil war can do. And please believe me, this *will* become a civil war if it's allowed to continue. Even if we're destroyed . . . It won't need us to get itself going in the end, and it won't need us to feed the fire. This is a wave, Mashkak. It's not our wave. We're only riding it."

"But it's outside our borders."

"Nothing is outside your borders."

Lochlan looked over at Nkiruka in surprise; she had been silent, motionless, and he had honestly begun to forget she was there. But naturally she had only been waiting for the precise moment to speak.

"Nothing," she repeated, and while she didn't rise, she sat straighter, her hands folded in front of her and her head slightly raised. "Mashkak, you're not so foolish as that. None of you are. To think that lines drawn on a chart constitute real boundaries in the end. They're phantoms. Political fantasies. They mean nothing. Not to destruction. Not to death."

"Aalim," one of the younger councilors said, sounding a bit affronted. Lochlan thought of the day, what felt like years before, when Ixchel had forced her way into this very room and made her argument for Adam's life. Of course it would return to this now.

"You and I know that solitude has to end sometime. You've kept yourselves apart for as long as you could, but now—like us—you're at a crucial moment. You can keep yourselves separate and watch everything slowly fall to pieces as the Protectorate tears itself apart. And then when it's all over, you can find yourself alone among the ruins—and that's the best possible scenario. Or you can come out from behind your imaginary walls. Help us end this quickly. Help us save billions of lives. Even if that means we end others."

She smiled thinly. "Even if it means your *grand solitude* is at an end."

Mashkak stood there, and although she appeared motionless, Lochlan was almost certain he could see the ends of her fur twitching. At last she shook herself.

"We need to confer. The hour is growing late, and you must be hungry. Give us some time. We'll reconvene tomorrow morning."

"Our ships? Our people?" There were no courteous preambles now on Adisa's part. The time for that was over.

"You may transport your most seriously wounded down to us. We'll send you supplies for use in repairing your damaged ships. Further than that we won't go. At least not yet." Mashkak gestured toward the door, and the guards came forward, beckoning. "Please leave us now. We'll see that everything is done."

They all rose, but Adisa made no move to leave the table. "Mashkak . . . If I may. One final request."

"Adisa, you *embody* presumptuousness." But Mashkak sounded amused. "What is it?"

"My old friend, who served on the high council. Trachek. He isn't here, and we haven't heard from him. Where is he? What's happened to him?"

Lochlan glanced back at Mashkak. It was difficult to be sure, but he thought he detected a softening in her features, and when she spoke, her voice confirmed it.

"I'll see that you're taken to him, Adisa."

Adisa hesitated, then gave her a small bow. Lochlan caught only the briefest glimpse of his face, but that was all he needed to see. Adisa was already grieving.

"Come on," Adam said quietly, taking his arm. "Leave him be."

Together they left the chamber and followed the others out into the warm, fragrant Klashorg dusk.

CHAPTER

TWENTY-TWO

For a short while, Nkiruka made no move to approach the tomb. She had stayed behind as Adisa walked up the long steps that led to the Klashorg memorial halls. They were a series of enormous open spaces, covered only by a canopy of woven branches and leaves that wasn't unlike the ceiling of the Arched Halls. No one was buried on Klashorg, the forest floor being many hundreds of feet below. Instead they were carefully mummified and placed—with flowers and spices—into large caskets of carved wood. These were arranged in neat rows on the floors of the halls—thousands of them. Thousands upon thousands, lit by the last of the fading daylight and by immense lanterns that hung from the canopies. When one was filled, another was built, so the halls made up a kind of city of the dead, lonely and lovely, always growing into the trees.

Nkiruka both saw and felt the place—the tangled impressions washing over her in waves of sight and sound and emotion. There was sadness here, grief and loss, but also joy, love—memories uncountable. It was like the Halls in more than one way, but this wasn't hidden or secret. This was open to anyone, *for* anyone, in a way the Halls could never be. Nothing was concealed. No shifting paths or clearings. No journey of transition or meditation needed. Nothing between the living and the dead.

She wasn't sure whether she preferred one or the other, though she saw the attraction in both. The benefit. The beauty. Because death could be simultaneously beautiful and loving. Even when it was ugly. Even when it was horrible. Because life was all of those as well.

The guard who had led them here was also waiting with her, and Nkiruka could feel the ends of his fur extended slightly into the evening. She and the Klashorg didn't perceive the world in quite the same way, but it wasn't as far off as it might have been, and there was something pleasant about being among a species who shared a similar form of perception to hers.

She turned her attention away from the guard and let it flow out into the dusk. The sleepy buzz and whine of insects, the sound of a city shifting into a night when things would quiet but not truly stop. Soft music, conversation, the low hum of the trams as they slid past on their cables. The shimmering of lanterns and colored glass came to her like a sweet mist. The call of night birds—and creatures who might not be birds at all. A place this full of life never genuinely slept.

The guard beside her cleared his throat with a noise like a tree falling over miles away. "I have never met an Aalim." He paused. "If you'll forgive my forwardness."

Nkiruka smiled slightly. They had been treated in a brusque manner since arriving on the planet, but she had sensed that brusqueness was directed mostly at Eva and Kyle, to a lesser extent at Adam and Lochlan, and least at her and Adisa. And particularly not at her. The Aalim had always been what bound her people and the Klashorg most closely together.

The Aalim were counselors, advisors, scholars and seers . . . And, when necessary, diplomats. She had known when she accepted her place that she would have to assume a variety of mantles. Some of them unexpected.

"You're not being forward." She turned to him, her smile widening, though it was still small. "I've never been on Klashorg."

"Were you not on Ashwina when your people were last here?"

"I was. But I was only a pilot then. Barely out of training. I never actually came down with the others."

The Klashorg grunted. "Then I welcome you, Aalim."

"Nkiruka." She laid a hand on his arm, and it was like touching a furry branch of a massive tree. "And I thank you. Tell me your name?"

"I am Kegat." She felt him nod, and slight tension where she was touching him. He wasn't sure what to make of it. She lifted her hand away, faint uncertainty rippling through her; she had thought to be friendly, but he wouldn't be comfortable with that kind of friendliness from an off-worlder. Even an Aalim.

Perhaps especially an Aalim. Regardless of how much his own people might respect her. He wasn't one of her people, but all at once she felt the separation keenly. Loneliness was a pang in her chest.

"I'm glad to know you, Kegat. Thank you for bringing us here. It means a great deal to him."

"I was ordered to do so." He paused, and when he spoke his voice was lower, his tone less formal. "I was happy to do so. We know . . ." He paused again, and Nkiruka sensed his attention shift back to Adisa. "My mother knew Adisa. Not well, but she knew him. I know he's honorable. Trustworthy. And I know he and Trachek were friends."

"Yes. They were." She sighed. "We're running short of friends these days, to be honest. It's not good to have lost another one."

"You came here looking for more."

Amusement touched his voice, and Nkiruka responded in kind. "I suppose we did. Many friends."

"You expect a lot from your friends."

"We hope for a lot. That's not the same thing. We don't *expect* anything from your people."

She frowned. She had meant to keep out of the way and let Adisa handle the convincing; she hadn't wanted to overreach her authority. But now she wondered if she had lost sight of some important truths. How far she had come. Everything she had done since this all began. Everything she had gotten *right,* even when she feared getting it wrong.

She might feel alone, but she was needed. She couldn't forget that. Someone else might have thought it intensely strange that she *could* forget, but sometimes it was possible. To slip into the world inside her head—an entire cosmos. To forget that she was more than one woman now.

One girl. Because that hadn't been so long ago.

"We come to you with a request." She clasped her hands at her waist. Adisa had stopped some distance away, and his attention was fixed. Narrowing. A surge of emotion from his core. It was almost as if the lamps flared. "We know you owe us nothing. We already owe you from the last time you helped us. Many of us fully expect your people to send us away without anything at all."

"So why did you come?"

Nkiruka shrugged. "What did we have to lose?"

"No." Kegat shook his shaggy head. "Maybe some of you feel that way. Adisa spoke as if it was so. But I don't think that's the real reason. Why?"

His voice was gentle despite his persistence, and as she turned back to him, Nkiruka was smiling again. She liked him, this young Klashorg who seemed both kind and perceptive. Like all the Klashorg. Perhaps they survived and even thrived in part through the ways in which others habitually underestimated them. In spite of the reputation of their civilization as a whole.

It could be difficult to look past appearances. Even when one knew the contradictory facts.

"Because you're strong," she said simply. "And right now, we're weak. In a just universe, a place where things are balanced, the weak appeal to the strong for help, and the strong help them."

"So if we don't help you, we're unjust."

"Not at all." Adisa was crouching beside one of the caskets, a hand against its side, and she knew she had to go to him. "We're simply treating the universe as if it was what we hope it might someday be. How else is it ever going to become that way?"

She gently touched his arm again. "Excuse me, please. I'll come back."

Adisa was approximately twenty rows down, directly beneath one of the enormous lanterns. She stopped a few feet from him; his head was bowed, and his attention touched her only briefly before swinging back to the casket on which his hand rested.

Like all the others, it was large and plain. The elegant, complex woodcarving that marked so much of the Klashorg's other work was absent here. There was, she supposed, no need for it. However, there was a word etched into the casket's top. It was in the flowing script of Klashorg's standard tongue, but she could read it perfectly well. *Trachek.*

"We were caught in a skirmish on one of the frontier stations when we were both young," Adisa said quietly. He still didn't lift his head. "He wasn't in the center of it. Only pinned between the people who were. Some overassertive Protectorate peacekeepers on one side, on the other a bunch of mercenaries unhappy because they thought their business was being cut into. He and I extracted each other while pacifying the situation. *And* we managed not to kill anyone. It was a good day."

Nkiruka moved closer, a sad smile pulling at her mouth. "Let me guess, he brought you home to meet the family."

"Something like that." Adisa sighed and rested his head against the edge of the casket's top. He had been grieving—but now he seemed weary more than anything else.

She laid a hand on his shoulder. It was terrible that it came at a time of grief, but here she felt close to him, and she drew strength from that closeness. "I'm sorry."

Adisa covered her hand with his. "He was old, child. This isn't any great surprise."

"Surprise isn't the whole of pain."

"No, it isn't." He paused. "In terms of the life spans of his people, he and I were—are—almost evenly matched. And that's the thing."

He was quiet another moment, then gently shook off her hand and rose to his feet, still looking down at the casket.

"What's the thing?"

"Another one of my old friends dead. So much of the council is gone, one way or another. We lost people on the Plain. Ixchel is gone. We keep losing people now, and I know this case is not quite the same, but . . ." He shrugged and tilted his head back, and she could feel the lantern light bathing his worn face. "There's more than one kind of survivor, Nkiru. There's more than one kind of battle. The greatest one, the business of life itself . . . I keep watching old comrades falling. And in the end, not one of us will come through alive."

She let him be for a little while and simply stood behind him, her hands folded in front of her and her head bowed. If Ixchel were present instead of her, she would have been able to offer him comfort and counsel. Nkiruka had known from the first that she would never be Ixchel. That no one expected her to be Ixchel. That was all right. She didn't *need* to be Ixchel; she was beginning to truly understand that. She might be unsure, even now, but she needed only to be herself.

But she wished Ixchel was there.

At last she stepped forward and placed her hands on his shoulders, tipping her forehead against the center of his back in something not quite an embrace. "You're not dead yet, Old Bear." She smiled. "You don't get off that easy."

He laughed. "And now you truly sound like an Aalim." He turned and took her hands between both of his, kissed her knuckles. "I'm glad you're here, child. Old Mother. You are exactly where you're supposed to be."

"So I keep hoping." She curled one hand through his and squeezed. Darkness was falling faster all around them, and she sensed that his weariness was only increasing. There was much rest needed, and little time for it. "Come on, Adisa. There's nothing more for you to do tonight."

Together, side by side, they left the halls of the dead.

Later, Lochlan and Adam had separated, and had done so without a word. But Adam didn't have to ask anyone where Lochlan was. In the better part of a year removed from this world, he hadn't forgotten where they had first truly been together. As the last of the night fell and the others made their way toward their beds—large and soft and very comfortable—Adam left their lodging and made his way along a lesser-used walkway until it met with a branch thick enough to climb up and walk on.

He climbed. He walked. He went into the forest night, where the birds and the unseen climbing, swinging creatures allowed no silence, and the glowing flowers and dancing insects allowed no real dark.

He found the right branch—this one wide enough to serve as a platform—on which he and Lochlan had spent that one evening so long ago, beginning to know each other. Beginning to trust each other. To love each other, he now understood, on that evening beneath the bell of that flower, in a room where the walls and ceiling themselves had been made of low light.

But of course the flower was gone.

In its place Lochlan sat, his knees drawn up against his chest. Adam made no attempt to hide the sound of his approach, and as he stepped onto the branch, Lochlan offered him a small smile.

"Was wondering if you'd come."

"No, you weren't."

"No, I wasn't." Lochlan extended a hand and Adam moved forward, took Lochlan's hand in his, and let himself be tugged gently down to sit.

"Is it dead?"

Lochlan shook his head. "I don't know." He sighed. "Does it matter? It's gone."

"I guess it doesn't." But it felt like it did. Or like it ought to. All around them, the other enormous glowing bells dangled from the vines that wound themselves around branches as wide as the Klashorg's widest walkways and trunks as thick as their largest buildings. Perhaps the vines had simply moved. Perhaps the flower had been drawn upward or dipped down or shifted out of sight. Perhaps one of the others was theirs.

But he knew it wasn't so.

"That was a good night," Lochlan murmured, head still tipped back. His eyes were open and the flower-light shone in them.

"It was. In some ways."

Lochlan shot him a look. "In what ways *wasn't* it a good night, *chusile?*"

"Stop." Adam smiled faintly and jostled Lochlan's shoulder with his—and then left it there, leaning against him. "*You* were good, if that's what you're worried about."

"I've never worried about that."

"It was a hard night," Adam said softly—not ignoring Lochlan, but not in the mood for the banter. Lochlan employed it when he was relaxed but also when he was under the right amount of stress. Whistling in the dark. It was a little difficult to tell which this was, but it didn't matter either way. "They were all hard nights."

"They never stopped, did they?"

Adam shook his head.

"You think they ever will? If we do get through this?"

"I . . ." It wasn't an unfamiliar question. He had been asking it of himself, in one way or another, almost constantly since they had first left Ashwina all those months ago. But still . . . "I don't know."

Lochlan didn't immediately answer, and the silence flowed between them, settling around them. Pulling them together rather than pushing them apart. The source of the feeling was this place, but it was also more than that. It was this place and this *time*. A moment of peace in the chaos of existence. Gazing up at the glowing insects and the bellflowers—hanging in the night like lanterns—and the stars through the spreading branches and huge leaves, Adam realized that even the Arched Halls didn't match this place. This was something . . . not *more* powerful, no. But its power was of a different kind.

This forest didn't exist *for* anyone or anything. It wasn't carried, it wasn't a companion, it wasn't a tool, and it wasn't some kind of living memorial of an exile's past.

This forest simply was.

"I was with you," Lochlan repeated and turned his head, pulling back enough to meet Adam's gaze. He hesitated, then combed a hand into Adam's hair, gentle. Careful. At first Lochlan had never been careful with him, but that was a long time ago. "I was with you then. I want to be with you for all the nights. Whatever else happens, that's . . ." He sighed and lowered his eyes, and the sorrow that gripped him was suddenly intense and clear. "*Chusile*, I'm not stupid enough to think this is going to end well. Not for us. But if I have those nights, it might be worth it."

Adam didn't immediately answer. It wasn't that he didn't want to, or didn't know what he would say. He looked at Lochlan and he felt—again—that space between them that pulled rather than pushed, that had been pulling since Lochlan first dragged him out of the clutches of irate Protectorate peacekeepers on a station whose name he had long since forgotten. It was a space to be crossed, like the dark of the night that existed only for light to shine within it—so long as there were people to do the crossing and lights to shine.

The space between them wasn't their enemy, and it wasn't going to destroy them. Every time they reached for each other, every time they crossed it as one, they were making that first journey together all over again.

Falling in love didn't happen only once. When it was true, when it was real, it happened every moment of every day, until the last day. Until the last moment. That moment would come and it would hurt, and it might be senseless, might be ugly and marked by terror and utterly devoid of peace, but he didn't have to go into it alone.

Adam was tired of being afraid.

"I don't know what's coming after this," he said softly.

"I don't care."

"I don't know who I'll be. I don't know *what* I'll be."

"I don't care about that either."

Adam laughed, and it felt good. "So what *do* you care about?"

That space, being crossed. Again and again, until the end. Lochlan smiled at him and reached up with his other hand, framing Adam's face, tipping their foreheads together. Nothing was *all right*, maybe nothing ever would be, but everything was—perhaps—right enough.

"Let me show you."

This time they didn't need the flower to hide them.

CHAPTER

※

TWENTY-THREE

inder stood in the command center of the Palace and created a calm little bubble around himself as chaos seethed everywhere.

Or to someone else it might appear chaotic. From here the peacekeeper force in the city was controlled and directed. From other centers nearby, the other functions of the city were likewise managed: power, water, communications networks—all the basic necessities and utilities. This was the other reason he'd needed to be here from the start. The city's highest-level administrators were in shock, many of them confused, unable to coordinate efficiently with each other.

This was the time when all his favors owed and bestowed, all the networks he had spun through the Protectorate's halls of power, would be put into play. Here was Isaac Sinder, already known to be a steady and capable man, already rising quickly through the ranks, known as someone who could get things done. Here he was, ready to help despite his own shock and injuries, and he was also the only person who seemed to have any understanding of what was going on.

Here he was, with a tremendous amount of influence that no one had noticed him gathering and that no one was now in a cognitive position to question.

"I suspected this," he had said, as the EMTs—finally given something to do though they appeared ambivalent about it—saw to the burns and lacerations on his back and arms and neck. "It was why I came. A planned assassination—I couldn't trust anyone. I had to tell them myself. Treason at the highest levels . . . I know it's difficult to believe." A shake of the head, a look of haunted terror in his eyes.

"But here." He had produced a small data chip in a locked case. "All these names. I'm not sure, of course, but I think there's a distinct possibility..."

There had been rapid movement after that. Contingents of peacekeepers were dispatched to take those on his list into custody. No one demanded that he produce evidence. No one questioned him. No one *wanted* to—how skilled people could be at refusing to see what they didn't want to see. When the wheels were in motion, he watched them turn and allowed himself an internal smile. So strange and so darkly amusing: the people of this great civilization could be handled like puppets now that he had made them afraid. So it was whenever anyone powerful became complacent. Once they would have been ready for an attack like this at the center of their power, but that had ceased to be the case decades ago. There might be resistance elsewhere, certainly. But here? At the heart of everything they were?

Unthinkable. Unimaginable. And it was always what one couldn't imagine that served as one's undoing.

He would see to it that no one ever made that mistake again.

And about an hour after the initial wave of peacekeepers was dispatched, the attacks from below began.

Nothing serious, as agreed. Vandalism—broken windows, bombs of paint, minor fires. There were no deaths but physical assaults—people who lived on the lower levels were being terrorized, and that terror was rising. From the bottom of the city, people were swarming, attacking the very system that sustained and protected them. More confusion. More peacekeepers were dispatched but in some disorder. Everyone was looking to Sinder, who remained calm in spite of everything, and as he directed peacekeeper forces to the places he knew would be hit hardest, he whispered into the calm places of his own mind. Whispered to where Julius waited and watched.

He told Julius where and how to manipulate the minds of both sides to be more effective. Less effective. To create more confusion. To allow the people rising up from below to rise even farther. Rising on the wings of the promises made to them and their own advantageous lack of loyalty—in aircars and through corridors and hallways, breaking through ceilings and sealed-off stairways, up inactive lift shafts. Through all the barriers erected to divide the city into its openly secret class structure. This, too, Sinder now understood, was part of the fundamental weakness of what the Protectorate had become. It was splintered. Lacking in unity. It was fortunate that he was doing this with the best of intentions and the highest goal in mind. This was a weakness which, if it were exploited by someone with worse intentions, might prove disastrous.

Someone like Adam Yuga.

"Another breakout in the northwest sector." One of the emergency peacekeeping technicians turned back to him, face twisted with anxiety. "Mr. Sinder . . . I can't believe I'm saying this, but we're running out of peacekeepers."

Because the army is away at war in distant lands, Sinder thought grimly. *Leaving the homeland defenseless.* Aloud he said, "Send whatever you have. Do whatever you can to stabilize the situation. You don't have to stop it all outright," he raised his voice and addressed the entire room, "you just have to contain it. For now, at least."

He stooped and laid a hand on the EMT's shoulder, as if fighting a sudden wave of pain. "I have to go for a short time. I'll return. Do what you can here. I have the utmost confidence in all of you."

He shrugged off the suddenly concerned EMTs and made his way to the landing platform, where his car still waited for him.

Time for the next phase.

The ride back to his own building was short but seemed to take hours. He *was* in pain; he hadn't needed to do much acting for that part. The painkillers he'd been given had helped enormously, and his cuts and burns were cleaned and bandaged. He would naturally heal quickly, but the next week wouldn't be enjoyable. Especially not given the enormous quantities of stress he would soon be under.

Sacrifices had to be made on all sides.

By now it was midafternoon and the sun was bright, though occasionally obscured by cloud, and it caught smoke rising from below. Smoke, and the gleam of white peacekeeper cars as they flew outside of the designated civilian airlanes, downward toward the scenes of the many crimes being committed at his command. And though this was all necessary, though this was to a good end, it hurt him to see his city brutalized this way. Small brutalities, perhaps, easily repaired—the physical damage would be nothing in the end. But it was another sacrifice, and it pained him.

It should never have come to this.

Once on the landing platform, he hurried from the car—ignoring the sting and ache of his abused body—and headed toward one of the main lifts, then stepped inside and directed it down to the lower level on which Julius waited for him.

Everyone had been directed away from this level—from this part of the building—and he was glad. He had worn a mask of mixed distress and firm competence since the assassination and the attacks commenced, and now he wanted to let it slip—wanted to give free rein to both his exhaustion and his exhilaration. The Protectorate's remaking in progress after weeks of planning, and it was his sheer skill and steadfastness that had made it come to fruition in such a short time. This might have taken other people years. At a different point in history, it might have taken *him* years. But he had seen his moment and seized it with all the strength at his command, and now he was being rewarded.

Or he would be. There was a great deal still to do.

The lift opened. Sinder strode quickly to the room where Julius worked and threw the doors open.

The thing struck him in the face.

He wasn't sure what for a fraction of a second. It was as much a sensation as it was something he saw. The world went white, red around the edges, wavering like heat haze. He was standing in something like a fog that was no fog at all. And inside it was screaming, a chorus of screaming, pounding against his eardrums and destroying his balance. No words that he could make out. Only sound, relentless, crashing into him like an infernal wave.

Then the world was clear. He wasn't afraid. He wasn't even alarmed. There was no place inside him for either of those emotions. He took a slow breath and clenched his hands into tight fists.

Julius hadn't seen him.

Sinder managed to ignore the blood that painted the far right corner, the three torn things hanging from hooks fastened to cables bolted to the ceiling, the tray of stained tools atop a cart nearby. The obscene symbols painted across the floor, the walls, on the bodies themselves. He focused only on Julius, who turned toward him now, hands soaked in wet red and face flecked with the same. His white eyes were wide, his face flushed even under the blood, and he was breathing fast and heavily. With effort.

With excitement.

Sinder reminded himself that this, too, was a sacrifice. On the deepest level, in the most darkly amusing sense of the word.

The old superstitions were children's nonsense, but something they got right—had always gotten right—was that when you wanted to make extraordinary things happen, you needed blood.

Julius gave him a jerky nod and a faint, unpleasant smile. "Isaac."

Sinder didn't return the greeting. He stepped forward, head back and shoulders up. He had never been squeamish. This was the worst he had ever seen of Julius's *rituals*, but he wasn't going to start quibbling with it now. "Things are proceeding."

"And proceeding well, I take it."

"About as well as can be expected." Sinder paused, then decided not to attempt to hide his irritation. "You could have protected me just a *little* bit better."

"Wasn't it convincing, though?"

Sinder shrugged and then winced, immediately regretting it. Julius seemed to smile a little wider. "Never mind. I appreciate your assistance in any case."

Julius dipped his head. "Can you give me any estimate regarding how long you'll need me to maintain this level of control?"

"Can you give me an estimate regarding how much time you get out of each subject?"

"It depends."

"On what?"

Julius shrugged. "Pain tolerance. Alertness. Physical condition. The longer they remain alive and aware, the more suffering I can extract, and the more suffering I can extract, the longer I'm able to sustain my control. Each one . . . two to three hours? Slightly more than three at best. But as I said, it depends on a number of variables."

"Then sustain it until I signal you to stop. Or until you can't continue."

The unpleasant smile returned to Julius's face. "With the right flow of energy, my friend, I can continue almost indefinitely. I could do with food, though. Perhaps chemical stimulants. I don't anticipate those interfering with my work."

"I'll see that some are sent down."

Julius arched a brow. "By trustworthy people?" He gestured to the mutilated corpses. "You have those you trust enough to let them see this?"

"They'll have to see it in order to dispose of the bodies anyway." Sinder met the smile with his own grim version. "They'll see it and draw inferences. Fear is a powerful motivator. You know that as well as I do. Perhaps better."

"To my advantage or disadvantage. It was the fear of my once-people that led to my exile. Still." Julius let out a breath and drew himself up. "I have confidence in you. You haven't yet led me wrong."

Sinder gave him a nod. "Proceed, then. I'll do the same. At some point I'll need to sleep, like you. Tomorrow we move into what comes next."

"The rest of Terra. The other Sol population centers."

"Yes. The effects there won't be as severe as they will here. It won't be necessary. The groundwork has been laid. Or rather, undermined. We're almost ready to lay down our own. Then the real work begins."

"And then we discuss my compensation."

"Naturally." Sinder turned to go. "Like you just said, Julius. I haven't steered you wrong yet. I won't do so now. We've already established that I don't forget my friends."

Nor, he thought as he stepped back into the corridor and closed the doors behind him, did he harbor any illusions about who his true friends were. Or weren't. Bringing Julius to heel wouldn't be an easy task. Keeping him there would be even more difficult. But it could be done. Superstition or no, divinity *did* exist, as did its power, and he was moving according to divine right. In the path of righteousness.

Halfway to the lift, he fell against the wall.

He clutched at his chest, squeezed his eyes shut. Curled his arms around his middle. His core swung from hot to cold and back again.

The room tilted, spun. When he opened his eyes, lights that had been gentle and pleasing were suddenly glaringly, painfully bright. He shivered. Shuddered. Clenched his teeth. He wasn't going to be cowed by this weakness. It was a mirror to the weakness that lay beyond these walls, the one he was exploiting in order to end it. Cut it out like the cancer all those centuries ago, the cure that had led to the birth of this civilization that he loved above everything else in the universe.

He was a surgeon. *Physician, heal thyself.*

He would, naturally. Once he was done healing everything else.

He stayed where he was, forcing his breathing into a regular pattern, until the fit passed. Then he pushed away from the wall and smoothed his hands over his suit before shaking himself. Already he felt better. Refocused. He couldn't afford to waste time on this physical frailty. He had to get back to work.

He returned to the lift and took it up to the landing platform level. On his way, he stopped off in his office and went to a beautifully carved chest of locked drawers at one end of the room. This was slightly distasteful, but he had accepted the necessity of distasteful things, and he didn't hesitate as he keyed open the lock and withdrew a small injector, fitted it against the side of his neck, and depressed the end. Warmth flowed into him, and instantly the world around him sharpened.

He hadn't needed this drug before—one of the purest kinds of stimulant available to anyone. It had some potential side effects. But now it might be worth it. In fact, there was no *might*; it was definitely worth it. The drug would steady him, strengthen him, prepare him for what was next.

He placed the injector back into the drawer and returned to the platform, moving past the scatters of alarmed people rushing to and fro without sparing them a glance. They would all understand soon enough.

He boarded the car and returned to the Palace to oversee the rebirth of an empire.

All through the night, the foundations of the Terran Protectorate literally burned.

The damage wasn't severe—not the physical damage. The damage to the collective psyche of every authority on Terra was more significant: The confusion, the disbelief. The rising sense of disorder, of loss of control. The capital was still in chaos; before long, reports from other cities rolled in. Unrest there as well. No one understood what was happening. People taken into custody gave no explanation but demanded legal representation. For many, none could be obtained; there simply weren't enough advocates to spare. But even those who received them continued to keep silent. Then, in smaller and less secure detention centers, attacks from the outside and inside led to mass escapes. More vandalism. More assaults. There were only a few deaths, and as far as anyone could tell, they were accidental— except in a few places, where the peacekeepers appeared to have grabbed desperately for any sense of control. They were now firing lethal ammunition rather than using the tranquilizing and pacifying weapons they usually carried—designed for infrequent violent crime, because violent crime was everywhere extremely infrequent.

But this only increased the chaos.

No one was prepared. No one had imagined this was possible.

Sinder watched it all from the Palace command center until he was too tired to continue, and then he returned to his apartment to rest for a few hours. He promised to return. Yes, if they really wanted him to, he would continue to oversee matters. He knew he appeared to be one of the few truly calm administrators around. Even if his assumption of authority wasn't in keeping with the formal chain of command, those higher up on that chain seemed prepared to trust him.

He had received reports that order was slowly being restored in scattered areas. Restored as Julius began to lighten his control in some places and exert it more strongly in others.

All would be well.

Just as Sinder was undressing, shaking gripped him again and he almost fell. The world tilted sharply to the side, every shape dissolving into bright, indistinct ghosts. He sat down on the edge of the bed and breathed deeply until the fit released him. He was very tired. That was making him more susceptible to the attacks. He would sleep, and in the morning he would feel much better.

He slept, and in the morning he did.

On returning to the Palace, he was informed that the unrest on Terra had been further subdued—though not eliminated—but now it appeared to have spread to colonies and population centers throughout the Sol system. How was that possible? How could so many people strike back at the established order that had served them so well for so long?

Sinder was grave. Clearly the conspiracy ran deeper and wider than he had ever imagined. A strong, swift response was needed. He ordered the dispatch of the remaining peacekeepers to the places where there were none, and to areas where their numbers were inadequate. The violent force was regretful, but if they wanted him to stay where he was, to use what he knew—and he did know much, and had received even more information from his sources just before returning to the Palace—he would have to be given a greater degree of authority. As he communicated this to his superiors, they readily agreed, many before he had finished speaking. He should do whatever was necessary. They would back him. He should remain in constant contact with them. They would all have to work together if order and peace were to be restored.

Of course. He would accept nothing less. Whatever was happening, they would end it and then they would see to it that every poisonous tentacle of whatever was responsible was rooted out and destroyed. This would never happen again.

He spoke the complete truth, and with absolute conviction. He could tell they felt it and it calmed them, raised their confidence. Their confidence in him was clear on their faces in person, on comm screens. Clear in their voices when there was no visual feed.

They were like children, he thought with equal parts dismay and affection. They were like children when the chips were down, when they were faced with something entirely unprecedented. The greatest civilization the galaxy had ever known, and they were reduced to chaos now. It was pathetic in every sense of the word.

He would be their father. He would guide them and show them love. Standing at the center of it all, taking power into his hands and finding the strength his people had given him, Isaac Sinder smiled the beatific smile of a humble savior. He glanced down at himself and saw light gathering around him. Illumination of the most literal kind. Even with his bodily weakness, in this act, he was being perfected.

And behind and beneath him, Julius—once Julius d'Bideshi—spun his blood-soaked magic.

Sacrifices. Blood was always needed.

CHAPTER

※

TWENTY-FOUR

The early morning light streamed through the windows of the Klashorg council chamber and cast a shimmering glow over everything, catching the fur of the assembled councilors in a way that was both arresting and strange. Eva was having the smallest bit of trouble focusing. The night before, she had lain awake for a long time with Kyle curled against her, their legs tangled. He had seemed to sense her tension and had made love to her, slowly and very sweetly, and for a time she had forgotten herself in the circle of his arms and the oncoming waves of pleasure he'd given her—from the start he had been good to her like that, attentive, so concerned with satisfying her. And he had, and it had been wonderful, and for a little while after, they had remained awake and talked together, and she had watched one of Klashorg's golden moons as it proceeded across the sky and its light spilled across their bed.

But when he fell asleep, she couldn't follow him. At last she gave up trying and let her mind wander in circles, waiting for it to tire itself out. There had been no sense in trying to fight it. It would only frustrate and distress her.

In the small hours, she had heard Nkiruka and Adisa conversing in low tones out in the central room. She had considered joining them, then had decided against it. They were close, and no matter how much they clearly liked and respected and trusted her, no matter how much they brought her into their counsels, she would never truly be one of them. Better not try to insert herself where she hadn't been invited.

And they would have their own way of approaching the Klashorg. Whatever she needed to know, they would tell her.

Now she sat at the end of the council table, in the seat she had occupied the day before, gazing down at the breakfast that had been brought to her. It looked profoundly unappetizing—a dish of slimy brown and gray-green stalks on a plate beside it—but Adam had assured her that the taste more than made up for the appearance, and the others were eating heartily. It made sense. With how Klashorg senses worked, when it came to something that wouldn't last, other things would take priority over presentation. For someone with human sight—or any sight like it—appearance enhanced the experience. But not for them.

She closed her eyes and took a cautious bite of the brown stuff. It really was extraordinarily good—a deep, rich flavor somehow treading a perfectly placed line between sweet and savory. The texture, far from being slimy, was pleasingly smooth. Almost like well-prepared noodles.

She ate, realizing as she did so how hungry she was. And as breakfast concluded and the dishes were cleared away, it became obvious by how the council was settling themselves that discussion was about to begin.

The assembly waited. Eva wished she hadn't eaten quite so much and so fast. Suddenly her nerves twisted at her belly.

As she had the day before, Mashkak stood and laid her big hands on the table. "I'll come straight to the point," she rumbled. "There's no sense in delaying. Adisa, I regret to inform you—sincerely, I do—that it is the decision of this council that we won't assist you in any military capacity."

Eva closed her eyes as her stomach stopped twisting and dropped a few inches. She wasn't surprised. It was exactly what she had expected. But she had hoped. She hadn't wanted to hope, but she had trapped herself into doing so anyway.

They needed help. There was no sense in denying it, especially not to herself. *She* had needed this.

She shot Adam a glance, then Adisa, Nkiruka, but their faces were unreadable. Beside her, Kyle whispered, "It's going to be okay."

"We don't want to send you away with no assistance at all," Mashkak was continuing. "We'll render you whatever medical aid you desire that we can reasonably provide. We'll see to it that you have whatever parts we can give you for the repair of your ships. You can remain with us until you're ready to go on. We have to place certain restrictions on how many of you we allow in our city at one time, but within those restrictions, your people are free to visit us, at least for short periods. We still consider you our friends, Adisa, and your Protectorate people are friends by extension, though of course not nearly as close. Allies, if you will." She took a breath and looked around the room. "We want to be generous. But there are lengths to which we aren't prepared to go. To which we refuse to go. We trust you understand."

She fell silent. None of the other councilors spoke. After a moment, Adisa rose to his feet and gave her a bow.

"Mashkak. We are profoundly grateful, and we respect your wishes. We would appreciate it, then, if we could commence as soon as possible."

Mashkak nodded. "If you'll leave us, we'll make immediate preparations. We'll speak to you shortly regarding logistics. In the meantime, rest and further refresh yourselves. I think, though you're all here to rest as a fleet and a people, you specifically—and your companions—will have much work to do."

"Well," Lochlan muttered as they were ushered out. "That could have gone better."

"It also could have gone a lot worse." Adam touched his arm and shot Eva a steadying look. He must have seen her disappointment. She had never been particularly good at hiding strong emotions. "They're giving us a huge advantage. We'll be in a much better position once we leave here. We might even be able to get some resources to trade. To give us more leverage if we decide to look for others to bring in on this."

"It's something." Kyle sounded tired. Felt tired, walking close to her as they exited the entrance hall and went out into the warm sunshine. "We better get started with our own planning, then. Our own logistics. I don't think we're going to have a whole lot of time to *rest and refresh ourselves*."

They didn't. For a few hours they did what they could, though Adam and Lochlan went wandering, and the others were content to let them be. Eva didn't particularly want to ask Kyle for details, but it was clear that they were working some things out between them. Adisa and Nkiruka went into more quiet consultation, sitting on a bench under the shade of a low-spreading tree outside their lodgings. Eva and Kyle were once again left alone, and she decided she wanted to do some wandering, see this city and these people about which she had been so uneasy.

Hand in hand, she and Kyle walked the wide thoroughfares, looking at the rows and levels of lovely houses and commercial buildings, places obviously set aside for woodworking, hanging gardens of flowers and fruit. The city wasn't on one level but several, above and beneath them as the canopy allowed, places of bright sun and deep shade. Vividly colored, birdlike creatures as small as her hand and as large as herself flew both low and high overhead, fluttering, circling, calling to each other. Klashorg moved past, most seeming to ignore them, but a few younger ones were clearly puzzled, tugging at their guardians' fur and gesturing wildly, talking in excited tones.

"They've probably never seen an off-worlder." Kyle's voice was rich with amusement. "Aliens."

"At least they aren't afraid." Eva closed her eyes briefly against the sun. It felt good to be here, if she pushed aside her lingering discomfort and the disappointment that still weighed heavy on her. She wasn't angry. Wasn't resentful, and that was a relief. Why *should* she be angry? Adisa was right. *Adam* was right. Given the Klashorg's general attitude toward anyone from outside their own species, they were being remarkably generous. Likely more than she should expect. And it would help.

"Are you all right?" Kyle squeezed her hand, and she glanced at him, smiled. It was a smile she felt, and relief at it loosened her. Maybe she was frustrated with herself for admitting hope into her mind regarding the level at which the Klashorg would help them, but hope in general . . . That might still be worth having. Things were looking better for them now. Maybe not ideal, but how would they ever have been ideal?

She had to be realistic. She had to value good turns of fortune when and where they came. Otherwise hope would be harder and harder to hold on to, and while hope was dangerous . . .

It was necessary. Especially now.

"I've been thinking," she said suddenly.

"About what?"

"About our options. About fighting versus running." She sighed and glanced around at this lovely city these strange people had built. This little . . . not a paradise. But people here were plainly happy. "I'm not so sure fighting is the right decision."

Kyle tugged her to a stop and faced her. An especially large Klashorg carrying a crate on her back almost collided with them, muttered, and lumbered around them. Kyle didn't seem to notice. "What do you mean, you're not sure? I thought that was all settled."

"So was I. But Kyle . . ." She tugged him gently out of the center of the walkway. "That was before we got here. The Klashorg . . . They're already being generous. Adam is right. And think about what they have here. I know Nkiruka said they can't hide behind their borders forever, but what if everything was different? What if they could? What if their homeworld was far away from the center of the Protectorate? What if they were on the very edge? Out of the way? What if they had the luxury of being uninvolved?"

She paused, fumbling for the words. Kyle was frowning, tensing, but he didn't try to interrupt her, so she pushed on. "They're going to give us supplies. Maybe we can get them to be even more generous there. We know the Protectorate is about to tear itself apart—maybe we should let it happen. Maybe we *should* run, find somewhere to settle, build our own lives. Our own world. Forget where we came from, put away the past."

Kyle slowly shook his head. "Eva . . . What about all the people we were trying to save? All those people who would die?"

"I know." She took a breath, an edge of guilt digging into her. "But perhaps we can't save them. We might have already done our best. What good does it do our *species* if we just get ourselves killed anyway? And what the hell do we owe the Protectorate itself? Those people who are standing by and letting this happen? *Making* it happen? They rejected us. They tried to kill us. I know the civilians aren't so much to blame, but as for the ones on top, *fuck* them. I say let them die."

"The Bideshi," Kyle said quietly. "The people on top are going to go after them. They're going to lash out at anyone they can, just to distract them from what's happening to them at home."

"The Bideshi can take care of themselves. They always have."

"Eva." Kyle framed her face with his strong hands, and his eyes were so warm, so loving, and so sad that abruptly her throat clenched and her eyes stung. It was too much. She was too weak for this. She always had been. "You're tired. We all are. I don't think we should be making any decisions right now."

"I'm not making any decisions." For a few seconds she wanted to shake him off. Then she lifted a hand and covered his. "And even if I was . . . there aren't going to be any *good times* to decide something like that. But I—" She dropped a hand to her belly. "I want to give this kid a chance. A real chance. I don't—I want to keep it, I do, but I don't know what kind of chance I can give it like this."

"No one does." He pulled her in then, pulled her against him, and the rest of the world melted away as she curled her arms around his broad shoulders and pressed her face against his neck, letting the tears come. She hadn't known how tired she really was until now. But she wasn't alone. She kept thinking she had to prop herself up without help. And it wasn't true. Even in the worst depths of his sickness, after they had given up all hope of the cure Adam had found, there had been strength, and she had leaned on it. "This is awful. The whole fucking thing, it's just— It's *awful*. No one is denying that." He combed a hand through her hair, slow and gentle. "And you know what? If you want to leave, if you want to pull out of this and just go . . . I'll come with you. I won't pretend to like it, but I'll come. And I promise I won't resent you for it. Never. Wherever you want to make a life, I'll be there with you."

He pulled back and looked into her eyes again, smudged away the track of her tears with the pad of his thumb. "But that's just us. I'm not convincing anyone. The rest of them made their decision. If you choose this, that's for us and us alone."

Eva said nothing. She simply stood there and let him hold on to her, this man who had somehow come to mean everything to her, and she knew she couldn't fight any of what he was saying. Didn't want to. Not now.

She nodded.

"Let's go back," he said softly, pulling her against him again. "You *do* need to rest. If you can."

She let him guide her back to their quarters, and she tried to rest. But barely an hour later, they were summoned to the council, and then all choices were snatched away from her.

Lochlan and Adam were heading back when Adam stopped dead.

He wavered. Gripped at Lochlan's arm. Lochlan spun and seized him by the shoulders, all instinct and shock. Fear. Terror. He peered into Adam's face—it was bloodless, eyes half rolled back into his head, lids fluttering. *Not this. Lines, not now.*

Is this how I lose him? Something this senseless? Something just kills him, randomly, and he dies in my arms like he nearly did on the Plain?

"Adam." Adam slumped against him, breathing but heavily, shallowly. Lochlan glanced frantically around for any assistance. No one was in evidence. But he couldn't be sure.

"Someone! Anyone, we need help here!"

"Lochlan."

The word was slurred, consonants and vowels running together, and Adam's eyes were still only half-open and half-focused. But there was a little more muscle tension in his body now. He felt more *there*.

"*Chusile*, what happened?"

"Something…" Adam pushed at him, seeming to solidify both in body and aspect. "Lock, I'm all right. Let me go."

Reluctantly, Lochlan did so—pausing for a fraction of a second to consider refusing—and Adam stepped back and dropped his face into his hands, pressing the heels of his palms against his eyes. "Just give me a—a moment—"

"I don't want to give you *any such fucking thing*." Lochlan gripped his shoulder—not hard, but firmly enough to catch Adam if he started to slip again. "Adam, what *happened*?"

"That's what I'm trying to figure *out*." Adam shook him off and stepped away, half turning. He dropped his arms, clenched his hands into fists, appeared unsure of what to do with them.

He still wasn't entirely *there*.

Lochlan waited, fighting a terrible helplessness.

"Something happened."

"Yes, we've established that." Adam's pupils were dilated, practically eating up his mismatched irises. "Talk to me. Tell me what's going on. What did you feel?"

"Not close. The Protectorate. No. It's . . ." Adam closed his eyes, breathing deeply. More slowly. "The center. It's all—it's unbalancing. But it's spreading. It's expanding, it's like something big collapsed and now there's a shock wave. But I can't—"

His eyes flew open, and they were hard. Keen as the points of twin blades. "Lock, it's Terra."

Before Lochlan could ask anything else, *do* anything else, Adam had whirled and was striding rapidly away. Lochlan rushed after him, calling his name. Confusion was battling to overtake his helplessness. Nothing had been *good* before, but it had at least been *clear*.

That was over. He was sure. Why, how . . . those were questions for later.

Now, practically jogging along the walkway past the quizzical looks of the Klashorg, it was all he could do to keep up, in body *and* in mind. Whatever happened now, there was no turning back.

Then again, there never had been.

Nkiruka met Adam on the steps of their lodging house and reached for him as they nearly fell against each other. "I felt it too," she was saying, breathless. "But I didn't— Adam, I felt it *through* you. That means—"

"We don't have time for what it means. We have to tell Adisa."

"He's inside. He was with me so he already knows something isn't right. I didn't have time to explain."

"We'll explain now." Adam glanced over his shoulder as Lochlan drew up behind him. The look he gave his husband was apologetic— but still distracted. He couldn't help it. He was being torn in two directions in a more visceral way than he had ever expected, his gut literally twisting. His core had been dragged across incredible distances to the home of his birth—where everything was wobbling. Tipping.

Not in its slow, inexorable course as before. Someone was purposefully bringing it down.

An ally? Unknown but powerful?

No time. *Why* there was no time, what they had to grab for wasn't clear. The first priority—as seemed so often to be the case—was to move. Then they would figure out the details.

He fought back a laugh as Nkiruka tugged at his arm. "Come on."

The others were inside, talking in low, agitated tones; they ceased and looked up as he, Nkiruka, and Lochlan entered. Their expressions were expectant and worried. Eva's eyes were wide, her hand on Kyle's shoulder. Adam stepped forward, Nkiruka close beside.

"No, it's . . ." He took a breath. "It's not bad. Or I think it's not. Whatever it is. It's—"

"It's more complicated than that," Nkiruka said, and he was grateful to her. He *knew* what was gripping him, but it was resisting his efforts to put it into words. Though he had to try. These were his *roots*: every star and every part of his code, every line and every orbit that bound him to the planet from which his people had come—Protectorate and Bideshi.

Terra was the center. *Earth*. Its ancient name, because it was an ancient place. As powerful in its way as the Plain of Heaven.

"Complicated how?" Adisa's voice was low and calm, but there was an urgency beneath its surface. "Slowly. Tell us whatever you can."

Nkiruka cast Adam a glance. As she did, he felt Lochlan's hand on his back, gentle and solid. Adam's gratitude spread to him like a warm wave. He loved Lochlan. Would always love him, until the end.

"I don't know how and I don't know who," Adam said quietly. "And I don't know why. I don't even know how I know it. But someone on Terra has started a revolution."

Once more he inhaled slowly. Because this was the part that meant everything.

"And they're succeeding."

CHAPTER

TWENTY-FIVE

Just over twenty-four hours after the second phase had begun, Sinder was almost ready for the third.

This was the most difficult part. Before he began this work, he had believed the early steps would be the hardest, just as the first steps of a child were the clumsiest. He'd thought that once those were taken and the project was begun in earnest, the rest of it would fall into place. Nearly everything he'd asked for had been given to him: every element of control, every piece of information. The leaders of most of the large Terran cities—there were only a few—and the largest Sol population centers were looking to him for direction. With them on his side and willing to see his *suggestions* put into practice, the others had followed.

Now unrest had increased in just the right places and been brought under control in the others. The balance of confusion and fear was being carefully maintained, while the evidence that he was the person to trust stacked up ever higher.

But now all those agents of unrest he had engaged with every piece of capital at his disposal needed to be brought to heel. More than that. It was time to do what everyone else expected him to do. To make possible.

It was time to target those violent criminal elements and crush them.

But he couldn't attend to that properly if he was crippled by weariness. He slept a few hours—

An impact to his side and back slammed him out of sleep, and he hissed a curse, more out of surprise than anything else. He blinked, tried to pull in the breath that had been knocked out of him, to see where he was. What had hit him.

What had hit him, as it turned out, was the floor.

He tried to push himself up, caught sight of the bed and the tangle of sheets that hung over his side. Then a fierce shuddering gripped his arms and shoulders, and he fell again, the polished floor shockingly cold on his bare skin. He hurt all over, every muscle wrenching, and it wasn't just from the fall. Once he might have tried to convince himself of that, but now he knew better. He lay there and tried to breathe regularly and felt such dim pity for the man he had been. The man who hadn't been willing to face the truth.

And spit at its feet.

He closed his eyes and focused on the here and now. He fixed his mind on the strength that lay deep within him, strength greater than any insidious disease. The body of the Protectorate and his own: they were one and the same. He would see both healed.

He saw the future. He saw its elegance, that tree-like shape growing and thriving in front of him, watered with his sweat and blood. It bent its boughs over him, curling its roots around his body and cradling him. He closed his eyes and let himself sink into it—its light and its beauty, its inevitability. He could feel its cool smoothness under his hands. It was unmarred. Every part of it was in perfect harmony with every other part. It was fully itself. It was beyond life and death. It simply *was*.

It accepted him.

Gradually the shaking stopped and the pain faded. He pushed himself up to his knees and then slowly to his feet, rubbing his eyes. His bedroom was bathed in the gray light of predawn. It was time— time to move, time to carry things forward.

He stumbled over to the table by his bed, bent and unlocked the little drawer set into its black glass front. Inside was another injector, and he placed it against the side of his neck and pressed the drug through his skin. He stood for another moment and waited for it to spread through him and soothe his nerves.

It would still be better to use as little of the drug as possible. He had plenty—he wasn't worried about that—but there were the side effects. He had to keep his wits as sharp as his body. The potential for the situation to slip out of his control remained far too great.

He bathed quickly, dressed, and went to see Julius.

Eight subjects remained. The room had been cleaned and Julius was sitting on a low, cushioned platform in its center, eyes closed. The overhead lights had been switched off, and the only illumination was a small oil lamp of beautifully shaped brass. Sinder recognized the shape: a tiger, an extinct Terran predator. A noble beast. It could have been cloned, but the Terran authorities had long ago decided that what had gone extinct should stay extinct. Life itself had decided to discontinue those lines. One had to accept it.

But one could still admire.

"Isaac," Julius said softly, and opened his milky eyes. Of course he hadn't been sleeping—or if he had, his awareness likely remained sharp. "I trust you're doing well?"

"I am. And you?"

"Very much so." Julius rolled his shoulders in a stretch, making a low sound of pleasure. "I'm refreshed and ready to do whatever you require of me."

There was subtle mockery in that, almost certainly. But by now Sinder was used to it; it wasn't of any consequence. "What I require might be the greatest test of your abilities yet."

Julius's brows lifted. "Do tell."

"You recall what you did on Koticki?"

"The Kitchit separatists? How could I forget? It was exhilarating. A pleasure to discover one's own power."

"How many of them did you actually kill?"

"How many?" Julius stroked his chin. "I can't be sure of the exact number, but I think it might have been as many as fifteen thousand? Call it between fourteen and fifteen thousand."

"Do you have any idea how many you could manage at this point? With the proper resources?"

For a long moment Julius simply regarded him without speaking, his face unreadable. Sinder waited. He wasn't worried. He wouldn't have asked the question otherwise. And he was confident he would get the answer he wanted.

He had chosen Julius d'Bideshi for a reason.

"With the proper *resources*," Julius said finally, "I think I could manage three times that many. Perhaps four." He cocked his head, curiosity flitting across his features. "How many do you think you would need?"

Sinder smiled. "As many as what you have in this room will make possible."

"Three times," Julius said immediately, and though he didn't return Sinder's smile, the hint of it was there. "I doubt more than that." He paused, head still tilted to one side. "Would that be enough?"

"How far off-world?"

"I don't know. Possibly some distance. It would depend on how you want me to divide my energies."

"The targets on Terra are first priority. After that, the priority decreases the farther away you get."

Julius nodded once. "Yes. Well, then . . . You indicated to me when we began this little venture that you would need me to exert myself to my utmost ability for this penultimate move. Tell me what you have in mind, and I'll see what I can do."

"Everyone I engaged in sowing unrest. All the connected underclass. All the black marketeers." It was good to say this. It was the beginning of a final cleansing. But it also once more brought home to him, with the sensation of a slow-motion blow to the gut, how far he had gone. How far he was still willing to go. *Would* go. "All of them. I want them dead. I don't know how many there are, but on Terra . . . I would estimate their numbers, in our seven largest cities, at around thirty thousand. Give or take a few."

Julius glanced around the room, and Sinder sensed that he was doing a kind of internal calculation. Feeling his way through what was there and everything it could give him. Once again he waited patiently. He had to move quickly now, but here, in this moment, he could spare all the time necessary.

"I can do that," Julius murmured, and smiled widely. "Yes, Isaac. I can do that for you."

"Then," Sinder said, and everything in him burst into righteous flower, "I'm ready."

It didn't happen all at once. But nearly so.

Sinder returned to the command center and asked that every peacekeeper comm feed on Terra be patched through, or at least to the extent where the noise wouldn't descend into chaos. For the first five minutes, it was business as usual: status reports from dispatched units, calls for backup, announcements that an area had been pacified and they were returning or reporting to somewhere else. Complaints, curses. This last wasn't so commonplace, for peacekeepers were trained to the highest standard. But even second nature could slip when one was confronted with unprecedented chaos.

Then the feed changed.

Confusion, but no more frustration from the reports. Exclamations, amazement. Cars were dropping out of the sky. People were falling lifeless in stairwells, on walkways, on balconies. Everywhere, the insurgents died without explanation. They hadn't been shot. There were no signs of injury at all.

They were just dead.

From city after city the news rolled in, moving from the peacekeeper feeds to the common civilian ones. There were rumors here and there—an experimental weapon being deployed in the field for the first time, a highly controlled release of some kind of nerve agent—but no concrete information beyond what the peacekeepers themselves knew.

All over Terra, order was suddenly and very lethally restored.

The officers in the command center appeared dazed. Officials and authorities elsewhere checked in, confirming what had already been reported. And as they did, the news from off-world began to arrive: all the same story. Luna, Mars. Europa, Ganymede. Titan. The three large residential stations between. On the further of these, the massacre of the troublemakers hadn't been total, but with so many dead, it had been a simple matter to subdue the remaining ones.

Once again, all attention gradually swung back toward Sinder. Within a matter of hours, people were asking new questions. Did he know anything? Did he have any explanations?

As a matter of fact, he did.

CHAPTER

TWENTY-SIX

"So you know what's happening in your system," Mashkak said—with exaggerated patience, as if she were talking to an excitable child. "You're sure of it, and we're supposed to accept that. Because . . . because we're supposed to believe you both had a vision?"

"Is that so difficult for you people to believe? You trust the Aalim, you trust their sight. Or I thought you did. Why are you so reluctant to trust mine?"

Lochlan winced at the snap in Adam's words, and wondered how long the Klashorg would push back before Adam actually started throwing insults.

"Frankly, it's a little hard to accept that you would know something at such a distance and with such precision, especially when that's so convenient for you at this point in time."

Adam bristled and Lochlan touched his hand, trying to steady him—and considering the merits of simply yanking him down into his seat. But Nkiruka spoke up, and she also didn't sound pleased.

"It wasn't him alone. I felt it too."

Mashkak turned to her and gave a small bow, but when she spoke, the skepticism in her tone remained. "Aalim, you know we hold you in nothing but the highest respect, and we know your people possess significant abilities. But Terra is far enough away that we're still skeptical. And this one." She gestured to Adam. "When he last came to us, he was gravely ill. Your people were doing an admirable job of caring for him, and he appears to have made a full recovery, but should we really count him reliable in this? He's not even an Aalim."

Irritation tightened his gut. The thing was—possibly most infuriating—Mashkak was *right*: this was unprecedented. Potential

Aalim often showed a rudimentary aptitude for their skills, and that was how new Aalim were often chosen. Kae was in fact one of those—and that memory sent a lance of pain twisting through him. But still, that aptitude had never gone as far as this.

That Adam was becoming more like them was yet another thing to be frightened of. Adam wasn't going to become an Aalim, not like *that* . . . But Aalim couldn't allow themselves to love. Not as lovers. One more thing looming, one more thing suggesting an end that gripped him and shook him and made him sick with helplessness.

"I don't know how to prove it to you," Adam said, clearly still tense. "Not on my own. But if what's happening is as big as it feels, there should be something about it on the feeds. Soon if not now. Check. See what you can verify. You'll see it's true."

Mashkak's features shifted, and she beckoned over one of the attendants who waited by the door and said something in a voice too low to hear. Adam sat and Lochlan tugged him closer.

"*Chusile*, are you all right?"

Adam breathed a terse laugh. "What do you think?" Immediately his breath caught and he shook his head. "Lock . . . I'm sorry. I can't . . ."

"I know you're frustrated." Lochlan found Adam's hand and squeezed it. "Just promise me you'll explain it better after this. Mashkak . . . Look, she's not wrong. This just doesn't happen. I don't need to understand it to believe it, you know that. But I still want to."

"I'm changing. I told you." Slow words, each one articulated carefully. Every consonant, every vowel. "More than I've told you. And it's not over. It's—"

"We'll do as you say," Mashkak cut in, turning to face the table. "As I said, we respect you, Aalim. We can't discount what you claim. But in the meantime we should have other matters clear." She swung her attention back to Adam, and Lochlan was once more gripped by a wave of protectiveness, a desire to rise and say some sharp words of his own, whatever the consequences. Once, he would have. But that had been another life.

For the first time, Adisa spoke. "Speak plainly then, Mashkak. We'll tell you what we can."

"What we want to know is simple," Mashkak said. "Why bring this to us? Aside from just generally sharing information, you're talking as if this has particular implications for our relations, but you haven't told us what those are. I have a feeling you were coming to that point anyway. That's why you're here. Come to it now."

Lochlan expected Adisa to answer, or perhaps Nkiruka, but instead, once again, it was Adam, and this time his voice was steady.

"At this moment the Protectorate is weak. Significantly weaker than they were. I can't be sure, because I only felt what I felt for a short time, but I believe their entire command apparatus is wobbling. Ready to fall. Someone is pulling it into a different shape. I don't know how long it'll take them to succeed—*if* they succeed. But right now, if someone came in and helped whoever is doing it, struck the Protectorate at their center, struck them hard . . . I don't think it would take much to bring them down. Possibly while minimizing casualties.

"I'm asking you to reconsider helping us go in, make contact with whoever's doing this, and take Terra under full control. If we do that, this is all over. Mostly, anyway."

A chorus of rumblings at the far end of the table. Klashorg leaned their heads close, conferring. Mashkak glanced up. "You realize few of the variables of your circumstances have changed."

"I do." Adam shot Nkiruka a glance, and she nodded. A chill ran down Lochlan's spine. Back when this had begun, he wouldn't have predicted a relationship like this between someone like Adam and an Aalim. It was strange. Unique. Close enough to be uncomfortable. Nearly equal.

Nkiruka had made her own sacrifices.

"Then what do you have to say in defense of your request?"

"It isn't the number of variables. It's which ones have changed. What they mean."

Another deep murmur circulated through the council, and Mashkak cocked her head. "What do they mean, Adam Yuga?"

"That crucial point we were talking about? It really is here. That's what this means. It's more crucial than we thought." He leaned forward, fists braced on the table, and once again Lochlan would have sworn the phrase *blazing eyes* was literal in his case. His eyes glowed with inner light. "Since this began, something—or someone—has been guiding it. I don't know what. But I know it's true." He paused and smiled thinly. "And no, I can't tell you why. I can't prove it. At all. You'll just have to make up your own minds about whether or not you believe it too."

No one spoke. The Klashorg actually seemed a bit stunned, sitting up straighter, focus locked on Adam. Lochlan got the distinct sense that they weren't sure what to make of him.

"We're being swept along," Adam continued. But just as sharp, every word like the stab of a knife. "We're done resisting. Once I got pulled into this, what's happening now couldn't have been avoided. I was the catalyst. I'm no hero, I'm no leader, but I look at this and I *do* know my place in it. Finally. I'm going to see this thing through to the end. You helped us once before. Helped *me*. It's up to you what you do now, but whatever you choose will set *your* place in it, whatever happens after this. What role do you want that to be? The people who stood by and let us make all the sacrifices, when they could have saved potentially billions of lives? Or the people who helped end this?"

"History will judge you," Nkiruka said, even softer than him. Just as sharp, and as Lochlan turned his gaze to her, he fought back a shiver. Because he didn't see her anymore, or not just her. It was as though there was another woman occupying the same space, forming a cloak over her, a mask. A face overlaying hers. It was deeply familiar.

Ixchel. "You may be able to live with that, and do so comfortably. But I promise you, whatever happens after this, whatever becomes of the Protectorate and its people, whatever becomes of mine—for the two *are* connected and you know that as well as any of us—history will be kept. Histories are always kept. And your story will be told."

She arched a brow, and there was just a hint of sardonic humor in it. So essentially Ixchel, and Lochlan smiled, sudden strange love jumping in his heart. "What kind of story do you want to be?"

Utter silence fell. Out of the periphery of his vision, Lochlan studied the others: Adisa, Nkiruka, Adam. Kyle and Eva. He expected at least a little nervousness, a little trepidation, especially from the last two, but he saw none. Strength had settled over them, a strength plain to see in their direct gazes, their erect postures. Strength and composure.

He was still smiling, the curve of his own mouth a pleasure to him. And beside him Adam returned it, tiny but clear and warm.

"We will discuss it." Perhaps it was Lochlan's imagination, but it seemed to him that Mashkak's deep voice wavered almost imperceptibly. "And we'll investigate your claims, evaluate their truth. Leave us. We'll call you back in when we know something."

Calmly, they rose and left without waiting to be escorted. But as they passed one of the Klashorg guards, Lochlan marked the way Nkiruka caught his attention, and when she smiled at him—though it was difficult to spot a Klashorg smile—he was sure the enormous creature returned it.

Then there was nothing to do but wait.

Something had come over all of them; Lochlan felt it as directly and as vividly as sunshine—not exactly light, but a partial suspension of the darkness that had been threatening for weeks. They returned to their lodging and found their own places. Kyle and Eva retired to the room they had chosen, Adisa went outside, and Nkiruka took a seat on one of the couches and clasped her hands in her lap, appearing to slide into a deep meditation. Adam sat across from her, his attitude the same, and when Lochlan sank down beside him, it seemed like Adam had followed the Aalim into whatever inner stillness she had found.

But when Lochlan touched Adam's arm, his eyes opened and focused, clear and aware.

Lochlan leaned closer. What lay between them now wasn't *comfortable*, but neither was it as disquieting as it might have been. The darkness was suspended; he could do the same with fear. "Any news, *chusile*?"

Adam shook his head. "It was only that one flash. Like a blow to the head." He gave Lochlan a wan smile. "Almost knocked me down."

"But you saw that much? Enough to be sure?"

"That much." Adam sighed and pinched the bridge of his nose. "It wasn't *seeing*. It was more like . . . everything. Sight, sound, the sensation of being in those places. Running people. Cars dropping out of the sky. Burning, smoke, explosions. Screams. I don't—" He squeezed his eyes shut, and when he spoke next, his voice trembled. "There are a lot of people dying. I don't know how, and something about it . . . It doesn't feel right." His eyes flew open again, and this time there was fear in them—a flicker behind the steadiness. "There's someone there. Greater than . . . Power. A lot of power. I've never felt anything like it. It's dangerous. No, worse than that. Lock . . ."

His hands suddenly gripped Lochlan's hands, nearly to the point of pain. Lochlan stared down at them, at Adam's pale knuckles, and back up at his equally pale face. "Lock, we have to go, but it's . . . it's bad. It might be worse than anything else we've ever dealt with."

Lochlan's eyes widened, dismay a dull weight in his chest. "*Chusile* . . . Why didn't you say anything about this *in there*?"

"Because I didn't *know* it until just now," Adam hissed, then cut himself off, clearly trying to collect his thoughts. "I mean . . . I did. I knew. I just didn't have the words. I was sounding crazy enough without babbling about something I couldn't begin to explain. And I was *already* babbling about things I couldn't explain."

"All right. All right. Adam." Lochlan cupped a hand against his cheek and bit back a wince; Adam was hot, almost feverish. "So there's something worse. Does that mean whoever is behind this isn't an ally?"

"I don't know that either. Lock, there's *so much* I don't know. All I'm sure of is that whoever it is, they're there, and they're sentient. They know what they're doing. This isn't some kind of natural disaster. This is a person."

"And if we go to Terra like you're saying we need to . . ."

"We're going to run into them. And it's probably going to be bad." Adam frowned. "And I'm not *saying* we need to. *We need to*."

"So there's no escape." Lochlan's smile didn't feel much like a smile at all. "Well, then. How many times have we been in this situation now?"

"Like this?" Adam returned the smile. "Actually, we never have."

"That's very comforting." Lochlan paused a moment. Neither was this next subject comforting, but with whatever this was so close, and with the certainty that—with or without the Klashorg—they were indeed going to Terra to face the unnamed danger of which Adam was speaking, he had to broach it again. Had to ask. Had to *know*.

"You felt it. What happened. So did Nkiruka, and she's an Aalim of course, but even she . . . Our people just don't do that, Adam. Aalim have intuition, and they get premonitions, and they even have ways of knowing things no one else could know, but not like that. Nothing that clear from that far away. And you . . ." His stomach twisted. God, he couldn't recall feeling fear like this. "You said you were changing more than I knew. I believe you, I sense it, but . . . What did you mean? Tell me now."

Adam didn't answer immediately. He flicked his gaze away, across to Nkiruka, who hadn't moved. There was no indication that she was listening, but she was likely aware of everything around her. Lochlan wondered what she was thinking. What she might say if she cared to say something at all.

Because she knew about this. She knew more than anyone except Adam.

"I can heal people now," Adam said softly. "Like Ying."

Lochlan blinked. "What?"

"You heard me. Like Ying. When people were making repairs to Ashwina, after we—after we fought. I went down to the bottom of the ship. There was an accident, a fire. A woman was burned. She would have died, but I saved her, and I did it the way Ying does." He spread his hands against his knees, palms up, as if cupping something invisible. "First there was what happened on the Plain. Then what I did in the camp, with Rachel. Then on Peris with Lakshmi and Nkiruka. What I've done with Nkiruka since then. Now this." He locked his gaze with Lochlan's once more, and it was so brilliant and so terrible that Lochlan nearly had to look away.

"It's only getting worse. There's more and more of it all the time, all these different parts of it, and I—I'm already slipping. I still don't know what this power is, but I feel like it's *for* something, and I can't shake that. And if there's someone waiting for us on Terra . . . and somehow I'm meant to be there, and I'm something . . . *else* . . ."

He shook his head. "Lock. Lochlan d'Bideshi. No, I won't say the rest of the names. You know I can't even remember them." Adam smiled again, and this time it was sweet and sad. "*Chusile.* I love you. I love you more than I ever expected to love anyone. I believe . . . I believe you'll be with me at the end of all of this. I know you'll come with me as far as you can. But I can't turn back now. I never could. I tried, so many times, and now I know I can't."

He took Lochlan's face in his hands and leaned their foreheads together. Close by, closer than her proximity accounted for, Lochlan sensed Nkiruka watching them—and he felt her sorrow.

"Come with me to Terra. My home. My *real* home." Adam lifted his head and kissed Lochlan's brow, and all at once Lochlan felt small, weak, in the presence of something much larger and much older than he was. Larger and older than anything in his experience. It wasn't Adam. But it stood behind Adam. It stood behind everything, and it spun the threads and lines and orbits of fate and chance through its hands.

"Come with me," Adam whispered, "and let's finish this."

When they were called back to the council chamber, Adam didn't sit.

None of their group did. They ranged around the end of the table, standing straight, strong, and Adam felt them close to him in a way that had nothing to do with their bodies and his. Their spirits were with him. He didn't believe in a god, or gods, or any conscious entities controlling their destinies with any specific intent. But he believed in something greater than himself. He had been brought mind to mind with it.

It bore him up, and it bound him to his friends. His family. All these people who would stand with him at the end just as they stood with him now.

Mashkak rose, as she had before. Her fur was rippling slightly, in a way he hadn't seen, and he suspected it indicated consternation at their refusal to sit. But she seemed unwilling to make an issue of it, because she leaned forward, bracing herself over the table with her powerful arms.

The rest of the council sat wordless, their expressions unreadable.

"We have examined the feeds," Mashkak said slowly. "We have looked for any evidence that supports what you say." She paused and lowered her head, appearing to gather herself, and then looked up.

"What we have found isn't conclusive. Reports of unrest and violence in the Sol system are rough, vague. But they're present. We aren't sure how you know what you claim to know, and there are those among us who suspect you might have manufactured the direct claim behind your request, inspired by the feeds. But others of us think that's unlikely. Because as far as we can discern, these reports came across the feeds only within the last couple of hours."

As usual, it was difficult to tell, but Adam was getting better at reading Klashorg body language, even after a relatively short time among them, and he sensed that her attention was locked not on Adisa, or even Nkiruka, but on himself.

"Adam Yuga, we've considered your argument. We've considered it carefully. There were many among us who spoke against it. But I considered it myself, and I tell you plainly..." Her mouth twisted. "No one alive remembers the civil war that nearly destroyed our species. It was long ago, and so destructive that few records from that time even remain. To this day no one is certain what started the conflict, or why it became so vicious. What we remember is that it was awful, that it nearly wiped us out, and our entire society has been founded on the conviction of peace within our borders. Peace on our world. Peace at all costs, which is why for many years we've turned our faces away from other species and their business.

"But the war happened. And when I meditated on your plight, I thought about how civil wars are always the most terrible wars, about how violence is always most terrible when siblings set themselves against each other. Because there is so much love, and so much likeness.

"Our species owes yours nothing. We have no practical reason, here and now, to care what you do to each other. But are not all of us sentients, who know each other and share this part of space... Are we not all siblings, in a sense? And I look at your people, your plight, and I think: Adam Yuga, the Bideshi did not abandon you in your time of need because Ashwina's great and wise Aalim understood that you were as much their brother as anyone. That you might be the first step toward a greater reconciliation. They welcomed you. They fought for you. Sacrificed for you.

"Many of my people may not agree. I *know* they don't agree. But I also don't think I could ever rest easy if we were to abandon you all now."

She bowed her head again. Adam stood in the quiet and let her words sink into his mind, his heart. They had warm weight, and he closed his eyes and was glad.

The work Ixchel had begun, the great reunification she envisioned, was nearly completed.

"We will send aid with you when you travel to Terra. Ships. And we have technology that will shield you from easy detection. We will give you what we can." Mashkak pushed herself up to stand erect, and spread her hands as if offering a benediction for them all. The sun was setting, and the light colored by the windows caught her green fur and sent it dancing into other hues that shifted with every movement. "We will fight with you. With you, we will see this through to the end."

CHAPTER
TWENTY-SEVEN

"They're coming."

Sinder started and whirled. He had been standing in his office in a moment of rare quiet, contemplating his next actions. The list he had accumulated of the people who might become problems for him, who were outside the range of his influence—they would have to be dealt with. He had been gazing at the ruddy sunset over the city's towers without seeing any of it at all, lost in meditation.

And now Julius was standing in his doorway, his face awash with excitement and fierce anticipation.

"Who? Who's coming?"

"Your insurgency. Your little pesky battle fleet. The ones you mean for me to destroy, when the time came." Julius grinned, and his teeth appeared very long and very white. Like that tiger in his room. Extinct but resurrected in brass. "The time is coming, my friend. Sooner than you expected. They're coming here, and they don't intend the visit to be a peaceful one."

They were . . . Sinder shook his head. He couldn't remember the last time he had felt so confused. The room spun, and he wasn't sure what to do with his hands. White patches floated in front of his eyes like thin clouds.

He battled it back, his lungs emptying themselves of air and his diaphragm clenched.

"They can't be. This is *Sol. Terra.* They wouldn't *dare.*"

"Oh, they dare." Those teeth seemed longer and longer all the time. With the bloody light, with Julius's white eyes, this was taking on all the aesthetic and feel of a nightmare. "They dare very much. They're coming, and your pet Adam Yuga is leading the pack.

And he . . ." Julius closed his eyes, his features smoothing into something like ecstasy. "He's been busy. Made some changes. He's making more. He touched me—me and that girl who fancies herself an Aalim. I have to say, I'm looking forward to meeting them both."

Those might be the ravings of a lunatic. They might be. But with a cold knot in his gut, Sinder knew they weren't. Julius was many things; a madman wasn't one of them.

And . . . this cold knot, this numbness . . . it was fear. *Fear.*

Why was he afraid? What possible reason did he have to be so?

"When will they arrive?"

Julius shrugged. "I don't know. Soon. Within the week, almost certainly."

A week. Maybe less. Sinder gritted his teeth and shoved the numbness and the shaking in his hands and the fucking *fear* aside. He didn't have time for it. He didn't have the luxury of weakness, of giving in to the shameful faults in himself. "Well. We have time. And when they arrive, you'll be ready for them. Of course. A simple business."

"Of course," Julius repeated, but the wild conflict of emotions on his face had reached no accord. "But I'll need new resources. Very soon. I assume you can deliver those."

The people he was going to have removed. Yes. Yes, now he had some use for them. That was fortunate. "I'll see it done."

"Good. I don't foresee a problem. Then again . . ." Julius added, and now the expression twisting his face was worryingly like glee.

Glee and that awful vein of fear.

"Then again *what*?"

"Oh," Julius said and grinned again. "Nothing. Nothing at all."

"You'll be ready."

Nkiruka had been waiting for him by her fire in the Arched Halls—where it seemed they always found each other in the end—and she reached for Adam's hands when he got to her. He knelt and gave them to her.

After three days of riding high in slipstream, they had one more day to go before they exited just beyond the bounds of the Kuiper

Belt and began their progress through the outer system of Sol. Repairs had been made quickly, and not all of them to an ideal extent, but they were battling time, and their Klashorg companions—a full complement of thirty battle cruisers—afforded both disquiet to some of the fleet and cautious, slightly anxious confidence on the part of others. But everyone knew they couldn't afford to be picky regarding allies.

And everyone knew they were heading, one way or another, to an end.

"I can feel the whole fleet," Nkiruka murmured. "All of them, everything they are."

Adam's hands were warm and solid in hers, and for once she banished her higher senses and felt only his touch and heard the sound of his breath and his heart and the strength of the connection between them. He would never be fully one of them. And it wasn't his task to save them. Yet it was. Not to be the only one, but to be the first.

What he was going through . . . It wasn't as if she could truly comprehend it. But she could sympathize, a little.

With whatever wisdom she could find, she had been guiding him toward the next phase of his task. Not always well, maybe, and she hadn't been able to help him as much as she wanted to, hadn't been able to spare him pain . . . But that wasn't for her to do. She had been there for him, and now in these last days, she was beginning to understand that it had been enough.

It had been all she could do.

Adam pressed her hands together in his, lifted them to his mouth, and kissed them. "And what are they?"

"Afraid. Angry. Determined. They're shedding old misgivings and old resentments and finding strength in themselves. In each other. The way we always knew they would. The way we can, when we're willing." She ran her fingertips down his face, feeling the line of his brow, his closed eyes, the fine structure of his cheekbones and nose, and the delicate curve of his mouth. "They're returning home, to their center. It was what they needed, even if they didn't know it. Don't we all, someday, have to return to the land of our birth?"

She raised her hands and spread them like the branches of the trees above, rich brown, with shining green beaded bangles at her wrists.

Leaves. She could picture that tree, even if she couldn't see it. She was finding herself inside it; she had felt isolated, but she was part of these Halls, her Halls, and had become so the day her sight had been taken from her and her deeper sight had been bestowed—except no. No, it had begun earlier than that. From her birth. Before her birth.

It all came to the same in the end. Root and star. From one to the other and back again. And now, falling from the stars toward the ground within which the roots lay . . .

A blade. A sword. War, and though the thought of this final homecoming clenched a fist of hot, brilliant joy in her heart, grief was a ball of ice in her belly. That it should have to be this way.

But when the Bideshi had first left Terra, first rejected what would eventually become the Protectorate and taken the mantle of their self-imposed exile . . . There was no other way it could be.

Brother set against brother.

But, she thought, *we will come together to bury our father.*

In the end, one way or another, we will come together to bury our past.

"We're going home, Adam," she whispered, and to her own ears she sounded like a child. Full of wonder and joy and fear. "Can't you feel it? We're so close, and they all know it. We're going home."

"Yes." When she touched his face again, she felt his tears. "Nkiruka, I . . ." He let out something between a moan and a sob, and her heart wrenched for him. She would be with him in every way she knew how, but at the final moment—however it would come—he would still be alone. "What am I? What's going to happen to me?"

A child like her. The two of them, little children lost in the woods, beneath the stars. She no longer saw any conflict in being both an Old Mother and a child. Children possessed wisdom. Sometimes a great deal more than their parents.

"I don't know," she whispered, and she folded him into her arms and held him while he wept.

Sorrow lurched through him and into her—he was mourning. Mourning for the people who would likely die. Mourning for the world, because after this it would be forever changed. Mourning for himself, because he would never be the same.

The fire burned lower and stillness descended. Adam quieted, his body softening against her. His arms were curled around her, and she took her own comfort in them. He was strong too, after all. In his own way, he was as strong as her.

Movement, close. Someone coming; she already knew who it was. Adam pulled gently away from her and turned his head, though he still held her hands.

"Lock."

Lochlan's heart was pounding. She felt it from where she knelt, still yards away from him. It thudded practically in her own chest, as if he had been running and was now embracing her. She tugged one hand free from Adam's and laid it over her breastbone.

"Adam," Lochlan breathed. His voice was hoarse, thick, and Adam rose and went to him, cupped Lochlan's face in his palms. Nkiruka felt this too: warm skin against warm skin. "It's Aarons. He's awake."

Adam drew in a sharp breath, and Nkiruka bowed her head. This, she hadn't felt. But with the certainty of having been there herself, she knew what was coming next.

"So is Kae."

Aarons wasn't only awake. Aarons was *walking*, though not steadily, and Rachel had helped him into a chair by Kae's bed. Lochlan's chest seized all over again as he and Adam walked through the clinic doors: Leila, Rachel, and Aarons were hovering over the bed . . .

Over Kae. Head still bandaged, still appearing bloodless and gaunt—far closer to a corpse than a living man—but propped up and awake, looking around at them, a slightly dazed expression on his face.

If the worst he feels is slightly dazed, Lochlan thought, *we're all doing very well indeed.* Leila was seated on the edge of Kae's bed, and she raised her head as Lochlan and Adam approached, smiling, her cheeks still streaked with the tears she had been shedding when Lochlan left her, barely fifteen minutes before. She reached out a hand.

"Adam."

Adam went to her and Lochlan let him go, standing back for the moment. He had been the first person Leila had sent for, and he had taken his turn visiting already—gently, because Kae was still a weak man, and likely would remain so for at least the next fortnight. No fighter wing for him.

He'll be disappointed to miss the fun. Lochlan again felt the urge to laugh.

Adam was saying something to Leila, bending over Kae and grasping his hand. Kae was smiling, though it was a faint smile, and though his lips moved, it was impossible to make out his words. That was all right. This moment was for Adam. He deserved to have it to himself.

Kae was his brother too.

"Can't kill him even if you shoot him in the head, huh."

Lochlan started; he had been so focused on Adam and Kae that he had missed Aarons rising from his chair and coming to join him. Aarons flashed a grin—warm, though a touch grim. "Tough bastard."

Lochlan shot the man a small smile. "You have no idea."

"Actually, I think I do, now." Aarons was quiet a moment, and Lochlan studied him. He appeared to be in a considerably better state than Kae. His own bandages were gone, and he looked merely like what he was: a man who had gotten up after an extended period of bed rest and was now testing his long-disused legs.

"Are you doing all right?"

Aarons grunted. "They said I was out longer than they expected. Figure it just means I came out in better shape. Him . . ." He nodded at Kae, and though his face was as rough and scarred and pitted as ever, a softness came over his features. "They say they didn't know if he would come out of it at all."

"Like you said." Lochlan shook his head. It was actually a little difficult to keep his attention on the scene in front of him. Watching them hurt—with sorrow, with relief, with a hundred other confusing emotions. "Tough bastard."

Aarons grunted again, and when Lochlan glanced at him, he was studying Lochlan with his half-bionic gaze. "Apparently I missed quite a few things. We're going to Terra?"

"Be there in a day." Lochlan allowed himself a short, wry laugh. "*Mitr,* believe me, *missed quite a few things* is the understatement of the decade."

"To assist in some kind of revolution?"

"As far as we know. Fact is we're not sure *what's* going on there."

"Because Adam fucking Yuga had a vision."

"Basically."

"And suddenly the Klashorg are our brothers in arms."

"Again . . . yes, basically." More laughter bubbled up, and this time Lochlan made no attempt to fight it back. It was soft, not in the least hysterical, but it had a wavering edge to it all the same.

"And . . ." Aarons's voice dropped, the focus of his organic eye flicking to Rachel, where she stood slightly apart from the rest of the group. She didn't seem to know anyone was watching her, and her arms were crossed over her chest, her brows drawn together and her attention appearing to drift between them all. She looked somehow lost.

Lochlan nodded, already knowing what was coming, but Aarons continued. "There was a traitor. That was why. That was how. And she—" He jerked his chin at Rachel. "She *took care* of it."

"Yeah." Lochlan hesitated, then laid a hand on Aarons's shoulder, the muscle as solid and knotted as the trunk of an old tree. "She did the best she could. She just—"

"We each have our breaking point," Aarons said quietly, and Lochlan couldn't remember ever hearing him sound so gentle. He couldn't remember hearing him ever sound gentle at *all*.

Except for the crash on the quarantine planet. When he had put Kerry out of his misery. He had been gentle then. Aarons was capable of profound gentleness. More than anyone would expect, seeing him.

Rachel would be all right.

"I'll take care of her," Aarons said, still quiet. "She was—she was always so damn strong. She forgot she didn't always have to be."

"None of us always have to be." Suddenly he could see nothing but Adam leaning over Kae, nodding as Kae said something to him. Adam, so strong and so weak at once. He turned back to Aarons, still resting a hand on his shoulder. "Bristol, you should sit this out. Sit it out with her. I'm not saying run, but . . . Only fight if you have to. You've both given enough."

He was expecting an argument. Sure he was going to get one. Bristol Aarons was a goddamn bulldog, had been through hell and back five or six times and had never given any sign that he had anything left to fear. But of course this wasn't about fear, so he wasn't altogether shocked when Aarons nodded.

"I've been around long enough to know when it's time to pack it in. We'll wait in the reserves. We'll stay here, do what we can on Ashwina. But we won't be leading the pack. And I don't think we'll be doing much in the way of *generaling*."

"Eva and Kyle seem to have that in hand."

"Good people. Both of them. I'm not worried. Not about them, anyway." Aarons cocked a scarred brow at Lochlan. "You, on the other hand. That boy of yours. You're going to be all right? Because he wasn't looking so great before, and you now . . . Don't take this the wrong way, *mitr*, but you seem a little shaky."

"That's because I am." Lochlan turned the full force of his smile on Aarons—the curving of his mouth familiar, the smile he had frequently worn in a life before Adam Yuga, when everything had, at least on the surface, been much simpler. A cocky smile, one that gave him confidence when he wore it. It felt like a mask, with all the protection a mask afforded.

A mask that was still, in every important respect, part of him.

"I'm *extremely* fucking shaky. And him?" He jerked a thumb in Adam's direction. "I have no idea about him. I have no idea if we're going to be okay. To be honest, I strongly suspect not." He shrugged. "But hey. Here we are, here we go. Am I right?"

Aarons grinned his twisted scar-tissue grin. "That you are, Bideshi. Right as you've ever been."

CHAPTER

TWENTY-EIGHT

Sinder had made the peacekeeper command center in the Palace his formal base of operations, and now he was regretting it.

In logistical terms, it had made sense. He had been overseeing the situation from there since he put his coup in motion, plus the center's personnel now knew and trusted him implicitly, and it had all the communications equipment he needed, as well as direct access to the entire arsenal of planetary defenses. Maybe it had once been only a military center for a planet that hadn't needed much in the way of military or even domestic policing in quite some time. But with a little judiciousness, Sinder had made it effectively the center of everything.

But now it was claustrophobic. He wanted to move about, to pace, but people were coming and going, delivering reports. The conversation was a nearly constant hum, and it was making his already pounding headache pound even harder.

He could duck into a secluded corner or side office and make use of one of the three injectors he carried in his inner suit pocket. But he was beginning to suspect that the substance in the injectors might be just as responsible for producing his headache as anything else.

Things were going well. They were. All Protectorate vessels in the sector had been recalled to Sol. All defensive installations in the outer and inner system were on standby and ready to go into action at a moment's notice. Terra was well equipped to defend itself; thankfully its weapons hadn't fallen prey to the same systemic weakness as its leaders.

They could handle a small, battered fleet of rogues and refugees and renegade Bideshi.

But Julius had grinned at him, that horrible grin, and said *Of course* . . . He hadn't seen Julius since. Hadn't heard word from him. He had sent him updates, and as certain undesirable people were *collected*, he had sent them down to serve in their new capacity, but otherwise there had been no communication at all.

He didn't doubt Julius's abilities. And he didn't doubt his willingness to do what needed to be done. But as far as the man himself went, as far as his stability went . . . though Sinder still believed he wasn't actually insane . . .

Sinder shook himself. He was waiting for word to come in regarding the battle readiness of a peacekeeper post in orbit around Uranus, and then he could step out onto one of the wide balconies on this level to take in the air, clear his head. It wasn't known when exactly the fleet would arrive, but contact with a border patrol had been abruptly lost less than a day ago, and while it was strange that it would have happened so quickly, with no other word since then . . .

It was difficult to believe that a ragtag group of ships like that would be able to travel so far undetected.

But there was Adam Yuga. Who was, as he had observed so long ago, a wild variable.

He closed his eyes and pinched the bridge of his nose. His hand was shaking slightly; gripping something helped to bring the trembling under control. And when the room tilted again, seemed ready to fold in on itself, the grip kept that at bay as well.

"Sir."

It was Commander Carson, the officer whom Sinder had adopted as an informal second-in-command—a silver-haired woman with smooth brown skin and a piercing black gaze. She appeared constantly composed despite significant pressure. But now even her low, pleasant voice was an irritant. "Commander?"

"We've received a message from one of our listening posts just beyond Neptune. We didn't get a clear reading, but we're fairly certain it's them. Sir," she added, and her voice dropped, "I don't want to make something out of nothing, but I think there might actually be cause for concern."

Sinder lowered his hand and his eyes snapped open. "Concern?" The word came out more sharply than he intended, and some junior officers in earshot gave him alarmed glances. "After how hard we hit them, they should be half in pieces. And even if they're not . . . Why in all the worlds would we need to be *concerned*?"

"Because," Carson said, her voice still calm but now edged with a tone a good deal less so. "We suspect we may not have gotten a clear reading because they're using sensor-obscuring technology. Which would explain why they've managed to penetrate this deeply into our space without being detected."

Sinder stared at her. For a few seconds he wondered if the headache was impairing his hearing. "That can't— We've kept up with any sensor-obscuring tech out there. None of it works on ours. So unless they've managed to find a prototype somewhere we don't know about, how can they—"

"But we *haven't* kept up with every kind in existence. There's still one."

Sinder was opening his mouth to lodge another protest. Then he stopped, lips parted, staring at nothing. It was a ridiculous conclusion, well outside the realm of reason, and at any other time he might have rejected it out of hand, but now . . .

"The Klashorg," he murmured, and Carson nodded. He laid a hand on her arm and tried not to squeeze. "How sure are you?"

"We aren't sure at all. It's just a guess. But it's a more probable guess than we might hope. The listening post also picked up what we thought at first was only a sensor ghost. But we ran it through a couple more rounds of analysis, and now a couple of the techs are thinking otherwise. Sir, I want to stress that we have no hard evidence of *any* of this, and it could all be a misinterpretation of something completely innocuous. But those techs are swearing up and down that it looks like the sensor signature of a Klashorg battle cruiser."

Sinder shook his head. In his pocket, he was fingering one of the injectors. The headache, dulled for a moment by his surprise, was back and hurling itself against the inside of his skull. "We've only ever spotted—"

"Only ever spotted one of those outside their territory. Yes, sir. So we're working off our records from that sighting. But still . . ." She gave him a half shrug. She, at least, didn't appear concerned. "The techs, the ones who claim to be sure . . . They seem *very* sure."

Sinder closed his eyes again. He focused on the red, swirling darkness of the inside of his lids. This was ridiculous. Absolutely ridiculous. Not even worth entertaining. The upstart little insurgency would have to be insane to try to push this deep into Protectorate space—to the *heart* of it—and the Klashorg would have to be twice as insane to throw themselves into an interstellar conflict the size of which this might become. It had to be a mistake. There was no other explanation.

Of course . . .

"Those techs." He opened his eyes and pressed close to Carson, his voice at a low growl, his teeth clenched. "I want to talk to them. *Now.*"

Ashwina's council chamber was barely recognizable.

At least to Eva. She watched people hurrying to and fro, double-checking comm units, calmly making sure the runners who would physically carry messages when needed knew their routes, coordinating with the fighter wings ready to launch. She gathered that practically everyone else had seen this before. Adisa had spoken to her not long after she came with Kyle to the chamber and had—in the process of explaining things—mentioned that drills were frequently run for this specific scenario, and that what looked like chaos was in fact deeply established order.

But it still looked chaotic.

The council seats were now occupied by only a few council members—Adisa and three women who weren't much younger than he was, as well as Nkiruka—Kyle, and her. Adam had put in a brief appearance, but he and Lochlan had vanished shortly thereafter, and their whereabouts weren't clear. Kyle had observed that finding them probably wasn't necessary. He and Eva were present to help coordinate the Protectorate part of the fleet. The Bideshi were there to coordinate Ashwina with the whole. And the Klashorg would keep in touch through the comm.

It all felt so unreal. She sat there, staring at everything, wondering when it would make sense.

When it was over, possibly.

Abruptly there was silence. Adisa stood and raised a hand, as if to signal the quiet that had already fallen. "Gen," he said to a small blond woman who had taken charge of communication with the Protectorate ships. "Are we ready on your end?"

Gen looked up from her console and nodded at Eva and Kyle. "Just say the word."

"Vashni, report." A pale, silver-haired man with a beaked nose who was the go-between with the Klashorg ships, given a history of trading with the species. He signaled an affirmative. "They're saying we should keep the sensor jammers up until we pass Mars. After that they advise that we drop them and send out a general hail. See who's in charge on Terra, make it clear that we don't want any shooting if shooting isn't necessary. Make it clear that we *will* shoot if we have to."

Adisa nodded and glanced at Eva and Kyle; Kyle returned the nod. "Like we went over. If they identify the ships as Klashorg," he said, "which, how could they not? They won't open fire. Not right away. Not unless something is *seriously* wrong down there. If they've suddenly become friendly—or at least less than hostile—they'll want to talk. If they haven't, they'll *still* want to talk."

Eva drew herself up a little straighter in her chair. "Exactly. No one has even *seen* a Klashorg battle cruiser this side of their border in . . . I don't even know. Long enough that the shock alone should be sufficient to get some talking going."

"And once we're talking, we have leverage." Adisa sighed. "When do we pass Mars?"

Another woman at a console glanced up. "At this speed, approximately an hour."

"Sir." Vashni was frowning slightly. "Word from the lead Klashorg cruiser—they were reviewing some of their own data, and they want to let us know that it's possible we've already been spotted."

Adisa's brows lifted. "How?"

"When we passed a listening post near Neptune. There was a minor power loss on one of the jammer ships—only a few seconds, but they think it might have been enough to tip someone off that we're coming. If anyone is looking for us."

"Which they may be," Eva murmured. "Or they may not be." She gave Adisa a tight smile—tight as she felt. "Nothing to do about it now."

"Right you are." Adisa turned back to Vashni. "Tell them it's noted. And inform them that we're ready to patch them through on the main screen in here if necessary."

Vashni nodded. He and the others assigned to the makeshift battle bridge lowered their heads and continued their preparations, and Eva took a breath. This was supposed to be simple. It had *seemed* so simple on paper. Many of the Protectorate people she had talked to had appeared optimistic about the possibility of carrying out the entire plan without bloodshed. But she had caught the way Lochlan and Adam were talking about it, some of the things Nkiruka had said to Adisa, and especially snatches of conversation between Aarons and Rachel, and she didn't share that optimism.

Nothing about this felt right. Nothing.

She wasn't an Aalim. She couldn't do what they could do. She had no special intuition. Sure, she had healed Kyle, but that had been . . . That wasn't the same. She wasn't even like Adam. But there was a tickle in the back of her mind, a tickle that was sharpening into a scratch.

She touched Kyle's hand and he turned to her, brows knitted together. "What?"

She shook her head. "I . . ." But she didn't know. She couldn't operate merely on the basis of nerves. She closed her fingers over his and gave him a tiny smile. "Nothing. Just tense."

"We all are." He squeezed her hand. "Just hang in there. We'll be fine."

Sure, Eva thought, looking at the chamber, at the preparations to open fire on her homeworld. The world she had quite literally take an oath to defend. And whatever else she had left behind when she abandoned the rest of that oath, there were a few parts of it she had intended to carry with her for the rest of her life. And now.

Absolutely fine.

CHAPTER

TWENTY-NINE

S inder stared at the screen as the room around him fell silent and stared with him. The people there, looking back at him. Not Adam. Not that Bideshi lover of his. Not Bristol Aarons, nor anyone else he might have expected to see.

Kyle Waverly and Eva Reyes. Standing there and talking to him like *they* could dictate terms.

Given who they had brought with them, they probably thought they could.

"—know you don't exactly have the best history with our people," Reyes was saying. "Adam has filled us in on what happened. But we swear, we don't want bloodshed. We came to offer you help. We know you need it. We were healed; we can heal you too. All of you. We don't even want anything in return. Just meet with us, we'll share what we know, and none of us have to—"

Sinder held up a hand. He had been worried; he would admit it now. Definitely upset. Their actions had been unexpected—the audacity, the stealth, and the *Klashorg*. A lesser man might have been scared. But now, seeing them and knowing what was waiting on the lower levels of his building . . .

He was simply annoyed. And he couldn't escape the feeling that everyone in the room was scrutinizing him.

"You're a traitor, Reyes. You, Waverly, every one of you. Traitors, and you've sullied everything you are by allying yourself with the Bideshi." He spat the word out "The *Bideshi*, of all people. Does none of what you were born to mean *anything* to you anymore?"

"It *does*," Waverly insisted. He sounded just a bit desperate. Good. "Don't you understand? That's why we're here. We wanted to—"

A low murmur was beginning to make its way around the room. Beside him, Commander Carson gave him a raised brow. Maybe he had come to trust her somewhat, yes, but he didn't like the way she was *looking* at him, and it was somehow worse than usual. She seemed to be evaluating him. Like she was waiting to see what mistake he might make. Perhaps depending on her like this hadn't been so wise.

He raised a hand again and hissed, "Quiet."

Silence dropped, and in it Sinder allowed his mind to spread. In a few seconds he did the calculations. They were easy. The solution was really quite simple. It just required some minor adjustments.

He would take care of this.

"You want to talk? Very well. We'll talk. Give us half an hour to confer, and we'll be in touch."

"Take all the time you need." Waverly sounded perfectly amiable now that he might be getting his way, but he shot Reyes a glance that, to Sinder, felt weighted with meaning, and added, "Please keep your planetary defense systems inactive. We'll be able to tell if anything is coming at us. We're reluctant to open fire, but the Klashorg . . ." He shrugged as if to say, *I can only do so much.*

Sinder showed his teeth. "As I said. We'll be in touch."

The screen went blank.

He turned away, ignoring Carson's questioning look. No, the planetary defense systems wouldn't be necessary. Not at the moment. He would leave them inactive, as Waverly had so *politely* requested.

The conventional defense systems at least.

The less conventional ones, however . . .

"Commander Carson," Sinder said without turning.

"Yes, sir."

"I have a task of the utmost importance, and it requires a degree of discretion. Can I trust you?" And if he couldn't . . . Well. He had a way of handling that scenario.

"Of course, sir."

"There's a man named Julius lodged on a lower level of the building where I keep my offices and apartments. I need you to go and fetch him for me. I need you to bring him here as quickly as you can. I need you to do it *now*."

"Sir."

He felt the slight displacement of air as she moved past him, and he watched her receding back. Could he trust her? He didn't know. He didn't know *who* he could trust now. He scanned the room, and while everyone seemed engaged in their tasks, their heads bent together or over their consoles, he *still* couldn't escape the intensifying feeling that they were all looking at him. Looking at him and *judging* him and finding him wanting. Their eyes, all turned toward him, flicked away before he could catch them. *Growing eyes*, he thought, *bigger than eyes should be.* But narrowed. All of them, a silent and hostile audience. Like vultures.

Like Carson, waiting for him to make a mistake. A single crucial mistake. Then they would close in and try to devour him.

He had believed there was a conspiracy. Had made *them* believe there was one. Then he had purged the list of "conspirators," or he had made a tremendous amount of progress in doing so before this particular wrench had been hurled into the works. But had he? Had he made any progress at all?

Who *were* all these people, really? How could he trust them to do *anything*? How could he trust them to remain loyal to him—or to the vision he was trying to see to fulfillment? That *had* to be seen through.

He fumbled in his pocket for one of the injectors, and without moving from where he stood, he pressed it to the side of his neck. The drug flowed into him, and with it, calm. The rest of the room became muted. Faded. Distant enough that he knew he was safe.

It didn't matter who they were. Any of them. Didn't matter what they did or didn't want. He was going to see this *fixed*.

And then he was going to see the rest of these people, all of these untrustworthy people, all of these weak links in the Protectorate's great chain . . .

He was going to see them fixed too.

Sinder met Julius on the landing platform. For a moment he merely stared at the man coming toward him from the shuttle, who strode forward with his head up and a cheerful smile on his face.

Behind him, sprawled on the platform, her head lolling, eyes open and bulging, and with blood running from her nose and mouth, was Commander Carson.

"Isaac." Julius's hands were bloody. His clothes were bloody. His face was spattered with it, and red streaks stained his hair. Sinder wasn't sure whether he was afraid. He wasn't sure *what* he was feeling.

Nothing. He felt nothing. He was almost sure of it.

"Julius."

"It's *wonderful* to see you. Wonderful to finally be here." Julius stopped in front of him and bowed slightly, then clasped Sinder's hand in his. They were slick and sticky. Behind him, the sky was bathed in the deep red of late sunset. The first stars were beginning to shine.

Sinder gazed at all of this, looked down at his own hand—now smeared with blood—and knew that he had been wrong.

Julius d'Bideshi was completely and utterly insane.

And are you really so surprised?

Are you sure he's the only one who is?

For the sake of your code, Isaac, look at what you've done.

He shoved it away—that tiny, unwelcome voice. It wasn't his. He had no idea where it came from. Everything was as it should be. This man, this bloody, insane man . . . He still possessed the abilities Sinder had chosen him for. He could still make this right.

And here, in a tower full of people—all of whom were now under intense suspicion—Julius would have the resources he needed.

"Isaac," Julius said and nodded toward the door, eyes flashing eagerly. "Let's get down to business, shall we? Tell me who you want me to kill."

"So here we are again."

Adam shook his head, a smile tugging at the corner of his lips. "We've never been here, Lock."

"Yes, we have." Lochlan slid his fingers through Adam's hair and leaned in, kissed him—not deep, but slow—and felt the kiss ground him. Settle him. "We keep splitting up at these epic moments. Aren't we supposed to ride into battle together or something?"

"You never taught me how to do any riding into battle." Adam closed a hand over a fold of Lochlan's flying tunic. "You promised."

"That was before you went all Aalim on me." Keeping things light was a survival mechanism, and Lochlan also sensed it wasn't helping only him. Everywhere, pilots were heading toward their ships—and Kae wasn't among them. It hurt to think about, so mostly Lochlan was trying to avoid doing so. "Anyway, you *will* be with me. Won't you?"

"And the others." This time Adam actually grinned—quickly, but it warmed Lochlan from the heart outward. "I'm not very faithful."

"As long as there's enough of you to go around." Lochlan pulled him in again, and this time the kiss was deeper, and there was just a hint of desperation in it, which Lochlan didn't entirely succeed in keeping back. People were saying it might not be so hard, that it was possible no one would have to fire a shot. But neither he nor Adam believed that.

They had been clear about that with each other. As clear as they could be. Yet now, this lightness.

All those solemn words had been said. Now there was nothing to do but wait to see which way things went.

"I should get up to the Halls and meet Nkiruka," Adam said quietly—more seriously. "They'll be sending that hail any minute now, and . . ." He shrugged. *Who knows?*

"So hopefully we'll see each other again soon. When we get down there, *mitr*, I expect you to show me all the sights. Buy me a drink or forty."

Adam rolled his eyes as he disentangled himself from Lochlan's arms and stepped back. "Sure, just like you—"

He stopped dead, blinking, his eyes gone huge and unfocused. Lochlan pressed in, arms around him again, anticipating a fall—like before? Was this another message from somewhere, another glimpse of something? *What?* He shook Adam gently, lifted a hand, and pushed back his hair. "Adam? Adam . . . C'mon, come here. Adam."

Adam's eyelids fluttered and closed, his head lolling. A few passing pilots were coming toward them, asking what the matter was, pulling off their helmets and offering to call for a medic. Lochlan tried to ignore them as Adam began to go limp against him—Ying might be a good idea, but he just had to—

His calm abruptly tore open. Adam jerked in his arms, spasmed, his eyes wide and staring and his face twisted with agony. Lochlan stared, everything around and inside him gone blank. This wasn't like before. This wasn't *anything* like before.

"*Chusile.*"

Adam screamed.

"Nkiruka!"

She was aware of her name. Her name, it was hers . . . It was hers, it belonged to her, but nothing else did. None of her was hers. It was being taken from her, a ravaging, clawing, tearing hand reaching into her and ripping it away. Somewhere she had fallen, and in that distant place she had hit her head and warm wetness was spilling down her face, but it didn't matter. It wasn't here, in this place inside her that was made entirely out of pain.

She was being eaten away. She was being consumed.

Her name. That was hers. She whirled in red darkness and beat against it with her fists, with her body, with her mind—those parts of her that were now no longer hers. The invader was laughing at her, delighted by what was happening—what *it was doing to her*. It was all demonic glee, all pleasure at finally having her.

But it wouldn't. It would *not*. She wrenched herself away, spread everything she was into a shield over herself, made her very being into a sword with which to strike at this *creature* that was trying to destroy her.

I am Nkiruka. Nkiruka d'Bideshi. I am Aalim of my people, death-dancer, star-daughter, reader of the lines and rider of the orbits. I hold the threads of fate and chance in my hands and I weave them into the tapestry of creation, as all my mothers have done before me. I am a blade in the dark. I am a star in the night. I am Nkiruka, and you will not have me.

More laughter, sharp and infernally cheerful, and though she hated herself for it, the sound sent fear stabbing into her like a needle of ice.

She was all of those things, but she was also a scared child, and she was alone and lost.

Well-met, Nkiruka d'Bideshi. It's good to see my old brothers and sisters again. And you, little girl. What present have you brought me? I see him down there. He's new, isn't he?

I'm also a new thing. Before we two get better acquainted, I think he and I . . .

He and I have a great deal to discuss.

CHAPTER

THIRTY

Nkiruka collapsed barely seconds after Sinder's image had vanished from the screen. Eva tried to reach her, but was shoved back as others rushed forward—including Adisa, who knelt, pulling the still-convulsing woman into his arms. Kyle grabbed her hand, tugged her back—*"there's nothing you can do, let them"*—and then Vashni spoke.

She whirled. "Say that again."

Vashni cleared his throat and spoke louder. "The Klashorg flagship. They're saying they just lost contact with five of their cruisers. Total communications blackout."

Eva started toward him. "Can they talk to us directly? Can you put them on screen?"

Vashni nodded and tapped in a few commands. The large central screen flickered to life and showed an older female Klashorg sitting on a dimly lit bridge, leaning forward as other Klashorg lumbered around her.

"—lost all communications, as I was saying," she said. "Are we—Ashwina, yes."

Silence fell as the people around them stood, turned, looked at the screen. Those gathered over Nkiruka stayed where they were; her screams seemed to have quieted for the moment.

"Yes," Kyle said. "We're here. Go ahead."

"We've lost touch with five of our ships. We have no idea why. We're trying to find out as much as we—" There was a commotion offscreen, and the Klashorg captain turned her head, mouth open as she listened. "That's—" she started, and after a few seconds she faced the screen again. Eva didn't need to be able to read Klashorg body language to tell that she was shocked. "We just lost two more. It appears that all seven of them are dead in space. Total power failures. Ashwina, we don't know what's happening on our end, but we need to figure it out, and we need to do so *now*."

Eva looked from the screen to Kyle, then to Adisa and Nkiruka—who was pushing herself up, nudging people aside. She was shaking, trembling so hard Eva wondered if she would be able to stand, but rather than trying to make her lie down, Adisa took her hand and shoulder and steadied her.

"There's a man on Terra," Nkiruka's tone was almost calm. "He's going to try to kill us all. *Toy* with us first, but in the end—"

Eva's mouth felt like it was coated with ash. "Sinder?"

"No." Nkiruka shook her head and took a long, shuddering breath. "Not Isaac Sinder. Another man. A worse man." She took a step closer, still supported by Adisa. Tears were running down her cheeks.

"He's much worse than any of them. And he's—God, Adisa." She let out a sob, deep and bone-shaking, and she sounded not like an Aalim, not like a woman, but like a frightened child. "He's one of *us*."

Sinder watched Julius cut a bloody swath up toward the command center.

The first person they encountered, just inside the door from the landing platform—a young Protectorate officer, a man clearly on some mundane errand—had broken his back against the wall when Julius flung him into it with a careless wave of his hand. Then, as he lay on the polished floor, screaming, Julius snapped the man's femurs with a couple flicks of his fingers. Then, speaking of fingers . . . Each of them broken, one at a time.

The man, Sinder thought as he observed numbly, should have passed out from the pain immediately. But it took Julius fully ten minutes to kill him, and by the time he was done, the shattered sack of bone in front of them barely looked like a man at all.

"You see," Julius said with considerable satisfaction, "I don't have to bleed them anymore. It's more than enough to just kill them like this. I don't even have to *touch* them. Don't you think that's marvelous, Isaac? And I have you to thank for it."

Sinder merely nodded. He didn't particularly care how happy Julius was. He was having difficulty focusing on anything, yet he couldn't tear his attention away from what was happening right before his eyes. He had never actually *seen* this done. He'd known what was going on, known what fate he was sending those *subjects* to, but now that it was in front of him, an awful blankness was descending in his mind. He was fumbling for his purpose, and that was everything. He *had* to hold to it. "But can you eradicate them *all*?" He was now leaning back against a wall and watching as Julius slowly tore the ligaments in a shrieking woman's legs. "Julius, I need *all* the Klashorg dead. You can take every fucking person in this building; I don't care. Hell, you can take every person in this entire fucking *city*. But I want the Klashorg dead. I want the Bideshi dead. I want those fucking traitors dead. I want *everyone fucking dead*."

He stopped, breathing hard. He hadn't been aware that he was yelling until he heard his own voice echoing off the elegant silver and gold of the hallway they were standing in.

Abruptly the woman stopped screaming. There was a soft thump, and when Julius stepped away and left her in plain view, her head was twisted completely around.

Her face wasn't visible. Somehow that was horrible, worse than if he had seen it. He stared at her, numbness pulsing through his body.

The blood on Julius's hands had dried to scales, and some of it flaked off as he rubbed them together. "Isaac, you really do need to relax. I've taken care of seven of them. I'll take care of the rest as soon as we find some more *pain* for me to eat. You know how this works. Come on." He laid a hand on Sinder's shoulder and ushered him down the corridor. Grudgingly—a little wearily—Sinder let himself be ushered.

His headache was back. And it was intensifying. It had returned as soon as Julius had joined him. Could it be Julius? Was Julius doing this to him? Was he being attacked even now?

He couldn't reveal that he suspected anything.

"Look." He stopped, turned, and laid a hand against Julius's broad chest. "Do you need me here?"

Julius shook his head, smiling. "No. But I do enjoy your company."

"Then I'm going back up to the command center. If you can take care of the Klashorg, I can call in all reinforcements in the area. I can engage the planetary defenses. If we work together, Julius, this can be over in less than an hour." It took everything he had to keep from snapping his fingers in front of the man's face to make him focus. "Understand?"

Julius's face darkened. "I understand," he said icily. "Just as long as you do."

"Good." He headed swiftly for the door; he didn't have time for this. He didn't have time for his own doubts. He didn't have time to watch Julius amusing himself with murder. He didn't have time to *keep him company* while he did it. He had his own problems to worry about.

He was almost to the lift when his legs gave out from under him and he went sprawling.

He hit the floor hard, knocking the air from his lungs, and for a moment he just lay there, half pushed up on one elbow, staring at his own blurry reflection in the shining golden floor. It was warped. Mutilated. It didn't look anything like him.

Nothing looked right.

He fumbled for an injector.

"So, Isaac," Julius said from behind him. He sounded amused. "You don't seem well at all, do you?"

Adam wrenched himself away from the seething void.

It felt like he was clawing his way up from the bottom of a living pit—a thing more like a mouth, lined with vicious teeth and many tongues, all grabbing for him, biting into him, trying to drag him down. He beat at them, hauled himself up toward the light—Lochlan's face there, like a man peering over the edge of a well. He reached, groped—

And Lochlan's hand was in his, arms around him.

He was here. He was himself again—for the moment. He gasped and shuddered, curled against Lochlan's chest.

He knew what he had to do. And it was horrible.

And there was no way Lochlan was going to let him do it.

"*Chusile?*" Lochlan was staring at him, eyes wide and terrified. "Adam, what the fuck just—"

"I have to get down there."

For a few seconds Lochlan simply gaped at him, but before he had a chance to say anything else, klaxons began to blare. Pilots jerked their heads up, slapped each other's shoulders, and then ran for their fighters. Lochlan looked up with the others, but barely seconds later. He bent over Adam again, stroking his hair away from his face, trying to slide an arm more securely under Adam's back. "C'mon, *chusile*. I'm getting you to Ying."

"No." It didn't take much. At least, not nearly as much as he'd expected. Adam shoved Lochlan back and got shakily to his feet. Lochlan rose at the same time, and he appeared less steady than Adam felt.

At any other time it might have been funny.

"The fuck do you mean, *no?*"

"You're going to give me your fighter," Adam said calmly. He *was* calm. The pain was gone, the fear was gone, and he knew exactly what he was doing, and that was good. It was good to cling to certainty, as one went to one's death. "What's going on out there will give me enough cover to break the atmosphere. I'm going down to the capital."

Lochlan blinked at him, mouth hanging open. Adam blinked back at him as the room wavered again and he had to catch himself on Lochlan's shoulder. Which knocked Lochlan out of whatever trance he had slipped into. He took Adam's hand, yanked him close again.

"Like *hell* you are."

"Yeah. Like hell." Adam sighed. Of course this was going to be a fight. It was always going to be a fight. "Lock . . ." All he could do was look at this man, this man who meant everything to him, who was his dance, his heart. Look at him and try to find a way to say good-bye. "The man who's doing this, doing all of this . . . It's not Sinder. It's someone else. Someone *with* Sinder. Someone worse. Sinder means to do good. It's horrible what he's willing to do, but he still wants to do what he thinks is *good*. This man . . ." He let out a breath, briefly closing his eyes. "This man just wants to eat the universe. If he ever had any other purpose, he forgot it a long time ago."

"And you're going down there . . . To *what*? *Feed* yourself to him?"

"Yes."

"*Chusile*." Lochlan gripped his shoulders. "Listen to what you're *saying*."

More klaxons sounded. All around them, Ashwina's great fighter wings were taking to the night. Beyond them were the huge white Protectorate battleships, small pale fighters. The elegant winglike ships of the Klashorg. The patchwork fleet cobbled together out of broken parts and broken people. It was in gas-fed flame, bright streaks of weapons fire, explosions like lethal fireworks. He didn't need to see it to know it, because it always came back to this in the end.

And it needed to stop now. All at once. It would take overwhelming force—force he could feel, inside him. A seed, planted long ago on a dusty plain, rising into the sun and beginning to unfurl its leaves. The well-mouth was still there in his core, threatening to swallow him, but something else was there too. Had always been there, showing itself to him when he needed it. Helping him heal. Protect. Save.

Now it was here for a different purpose.

And I'm not the only one. It's in all of us.

I'm just the first.

"Lock," he whispered, and didn't try to pull away. "Look at me. Just . . . look at me."

Lochlan did.

He didn't know what Lochlan saw. He would never know. Lochlan's eyes were on his for seconds that seemed to stretch out for hours, days, lifetimes. Adam couldn't breathe, couldn't move, his chest seizing up as if his heart had lost its ability to beat, and still Lochlan stared at him. Into him. Seeing everything.

And finally he nodded and stepped away.

"Lock," Adam whispered, and reached for him one last time, but Lochlan held him back and shook his head.

"No time for that, *mitr*. Much as I'd like it." He took Adam's hand and began to pull him toward the few remaining fighters. "C'mon. We have a ship to catch."

"Lock . . ." Adam was too stunned to resist Lochlan's tugging arm, but then he understood and grabbed for it, trying to stop them both. "Lock, no, you can't—"

"Adam." Lochlan stopped, whirled around, pulled Adam in tight and hard and close, hands against his cheeks. "Look at *me*."

What Adam saw there was enough.

CHAPTER

THIRTY-ONE

"I need to stay here." Nkiruka shook her head, face tilted up to meet Adisa's. She could feel the strength of that gaze, the pressure of it, and the way it saw all of her. Loved all of her. He wasn't going to fight her, no matter how much he wanted to, but she needed to make this plain. "I need to. I have tasks here. Ying can't help me. There's nothing to help."

Around them was true chaos, *real* chaos. Contact with more Klashorg ships had been lost, including the flagship—it was now unclear how many were still with them. And just as the comm feed with the flagship had cut off for the final time, what seemed like every piece of the Protectorate military in the area had leaped out of slipstream, launched from nearby bases, scrambled fighters, fired weapons. Everyone in the room was reeling, trying to untangle hopelessly tangled lines of communication, Eva and Kyle working frantically to coordinate with the Protectorate ships in their fleet. All their plans—such as they had been—were burning away before their eyes. How many people would die today?

How many had died already?

But here, with Adisa, she had made a tiny pocket of calm for them both.

"This is the end," she said softly. All around them, bad news was pouring in. Three of their ships had gone. Fighters were getting swatted out of the sky. The Klashorg, *what has happened to the Klashorg*? "But the war doesn't end here. With us. We have to keep it in motion for as long as we can. It's Adam. Do you understand?" She laid a hand against Adisa's weathered face, and her lips pulled into a smile. "It began with him, and it's going to end with him. And begin again. We have to give him a chance. That's all we have to do. That's our only task now."

She closed her eyes and let herself flow into him. Flow out of herself and through the horror outside and into everyone, everyone fighting and running and screaming, crying, afraid, angry, killing, praying to be allowed to live, dying. She touched them, giving them her strength—because she possessed strength, and it was both her own and not her own at all. What she could give them, she had drawn from them. The horror she had been dragged into was a lie: she *wasn't* alone. She never had been. No voice in her head was going to change that, or change who she was. She *was* herself, *owned* herself, and belonged to no one but her own people.

Whatever monster was waiting on the planet below . . . It was a thing out of a nightmare.

And in the end, nightmares were always devoured by the light.

The journey upward had been made through a thundering, seething cloud of confusion, which hadn't improved when he reached the command center. Sinder had lost Julius, lost everything but the floor under his feet, and had barely managed to hold on to that. The fit was worse than it had ever been. He recalled the injector tumbling from his fingers, recalled hearing it clatter. Then the fog had closed on him again, and he had pushed on, no longer sure why he was doing so. He was weak and no more strength was coming to him—it was as if the man beside him was devouring him, burning away his conviction. What was he attempting? What was this all *for*?

Why had his purpose left him?

Now he was with this horror of a man, surrounded by death. In a sense he already had been, with Julius, but now everything had reached a crescendo, and the confusion and exhaustion were abruptly smothering him. The wreckage of human bodies. The way he had delivered them to be destroyed. He had told himself it was worth it, but he . . .

He wasn't certain. A *bang* ripped through the air, and Sinder turned just in time to see the door of the command center blown inward. Flying past him through the air, it struck an officer and pinned her against the wall, crushing her from the waist down; blood rushed from her mouth and she died, still gazing wide-eyed at the man who had killed her.

Julius stood there. Of course he did. He stood there smiling that same cheerfully insane smile, and when he raised his hands, Sinder did likewise, lowering his face into his cupped palms.

He thought Julius might be nearly done. Then, as screams and the sound of crunching bone filled the room and echoed off polished consoles and panels, he knew he was.

Things were becoming very difficult.

"Sinder," Julius said softly. "Isaac. Look at me."

Sinder dropped his hands. What he saw was nothing new. Nothing impressive. Nothing interesting. He stared dully at Julius d'Bideshi, mad Aalim exiled for crimes too unspeakable for his people to name or record, a creature he had thought he could make use of and who, he now saw—

No. He had seen it from the beginning. He simply hadn't wanted to *look*.

"My payment, Isaac." Julius stepped into the room, hands still raised, blood-streaked smile still mutilating his mouth. "I've come for my payment. My sacrifice. And unlike Abraham's capricious sadistic *God*, I won't be providing any last-minute rams. I want what I want. And you said I could have it."

Sinder wearily scanned the room. The floor was covered with broken, motionless, bleeding dolls. He turned back to Julius and let out a thin laugh. "What you *want*? Look around you, you *stupid fucking Bideshi*. There's no one left for you to kill."

"Oh, there are. There are lots of people. This city, for example." Julius practically strolled toward him, as if he had all the time in the universe. Perhaps he did. "This planet. This system. This sector. The list goes on and on. But I'll settle for this planet to start with. I'm *becoming*, Isaac. No one is going to stop that. I'm becoming something *more*. Killing isn't enough now. I need to *destroy*. I need to devour worlds."

He stopped just feet short of where Sinder stood, and cocked his head. His smile had, if anything, widened. "You have the planetary defense system activation codes. You're going to give them to me."

Sinder shook his head—but in incomprehension. The defense codes? If Julius wanted Terra, if he wanted it in the way Sinder was sure he meant, why would he—

Then Sinder got it. *Destroy.* Not the lives of the people on Terra. Not the lives of the people in orbit around it, not the lives of those others within his reach, scattered around the system.

Everything. With those weapons turned outward, he would destroy everything in orbit. Then, when Julius was ready, turn inward on themselves.

A final sword of righteous, furious *strength* flashed in him and presented itself to his hand.

"No."

"Yes. A ship—which I certainly don't need you to give me—and the codes, which I do."

"No." It was an easy word to say, really. He should have said it before. He turned it over in his mouth, feeling its shape, how it fit on his tongue. A good word. *No.* He could have been telling himself no when he'd demanded things of himself, of others, that some tiny part had known were wrong. *No, this is too far. No, this isn't worth it. No, the lives of all these people aren't worth it. No, your soul isn't worth it.*

No, there isn't only one way to fix this.

Julius laughed. It was a gentle, almost affectionate sound, and when he raised a hand and touched his finger to the underside of Sinder's chin, that was affectionate as well. "You can't say no to me, Isaac. I've bound you. You belong to me."

"No." Now that he had started, it seemed difficult to stop. "I don't. None of this does. None of this should have happened, Julius. None of it ever should have happened." He lifted his head slightly, and as he did, the pain and the shaking in his joints and muscles and bones faded. He was all right. He could still honor his cause. "Just kill me. We both know you're going to. You were always going to. Do it now and save yourself time. I'm not giving you the codes."

Julius looked him over speculatively. "You know it would be the work of a moment to torture them out of you."

"Get to it, then."

Nothing. No movement. Sinder wasn't sure he was even breathing, and was positive Julius wasn't. There was no life anywhere around them. Maybe they were both already dead.

That might be a relief.

But then Julius grinned, as if he had just thought of the punch line to some especially amusing joke. "No."

And he tore Isaac Sinder's mind apart.

CHAPTER

THIRTY-TWO

Adam stopped dead inside the doorway, Lochlan just behind. They had seen some horrible things in their journey through the Palace, but this was somehow the worst.

They had passed broken bodies, shredded bodies—people who had clearly died in fearful agony. A windstorm of death had swept through the place, and through all the halls and corridors, they found no one alive. Adam had folded his fingers around Lochlan's, and they had walked hand in hand through the charnel house that the greatest center of Terran power had become.

All the while Adam had been following a tugging in the back of his mind—a voice from the bottom of the well-mouth, the pulling of a tentacle-tongue that longed to drag him down and finish him. But in truth they might as well simply have followed the trail of death.

And here it would have led them, to the horror's center.

Sinder was standing, his face frozen into a rictus of pain and terror, a runner of drool dangling from his chin, his eyes bloodshot and unblinking. His hands hung loosely by his sides. The crotch of his perfectly tailored suit was wet.

He was still alive. For whatever that kind of life was worth.

The man who had done this to him turned, and Sinder crumpled to the ground and stared up at the ceiling.

Adam saw none of the dead. Even Lochlan was now distant and indistinct. As soon as Adam entered the room, he had stepped into another world, a pocket world, where only he and this man could exist. This handsome man of full years, blood-soaked, mouth pulled into a happily mad smile, and his eyes the milky white of an Aalim's.

Of course. There was a story here, and Adam didn't need to know it. He already knew everything necessary.

There wasn't a great deal for him to do.

"I'm going to kill this entire planet," the man said as if they were conversing about the weather. "Yes, I think that's what I'd better do. But first . . . You're *very* interesting, aren't you?"

Adam walked slowly forward. Behind him, light years away, Lochlan gasped and whispered his name. Adam ignored him. Had to, now. "I suppose."

"You're like me." The man stepped closer, and Adam felt that they were two beasts circling each other, looking for an opening.

"How so?"

"Why, we're both different. We're both *becoming*. But they exiled me for that. Stripped me of everything. You're not even Bideshi, and what have they given you? Yes. I can feel it in you. They gave you a *Name*. They gave you a *home*. You could have stayed with them, and all those people dying up there would still be alive now. Yet here you are. Because you had to come. Because we're the same. We transcend both." He stopped. "We are neither."

Adam shook his head and allowed himself a smile so thin he could barely feel it. Once these words would have articulated a deep and foundational terror. Once they would have been a vicious stab into his core, piercing something he had tried to keep hidden and releasing poison into his mind. But none of that mattered now.

Maybe the man was right about this much: he *was* becoming. He still didn't know what. Whatever it was, it wasn't Protectorate. It wasn't Bideshi. He didn't belong anywhere.

Maybe he truly was here because he couldn't be anywhere else. "We're not the same. I don't care what your name is. I don't care who you think you are. I don't care what you think you'll be. I don't care about any of it. I want it to end." He spread his hands, tilted his head back. *Come and get me.* "Just let's . . . let's end it now."

I'm tired.

The man regarded him with faint curiosity. Then shrugged. "Suit yourself."

Lochlan screamed. "Adam, *no!*"

And the man slammed himself into Adam Yuga's soul.

Nkiruka dropped to her knees, clutching her head. No scream this time, but she felt him now, in so much pain and so much fear, being dragged toward a blackness beyond imagining, and she gathered whatever she had left and hurled herself through the war still raging outside, down to the planet below. Down to her son, her brother.

Her friend.

And she didn't go alone.

On Ashwina she turned. In midflight she turned. In the minds of every pilot and every fighter in every battling ship, she turned and saw what was coming to them now, flashing out of slipstream and into glorious being. Hundreds upon hundreds, all come to join them at last—she felt them, their fresh determination, the strength in them. They were *with* her. *We heard. News travels, when it has to. We heard and we couldn't stay back. Not when it's our own in the fight. Not when it's our blood.*

She raised her voice to them, singing a welcome, and in Ashwina's council chamber they all heard and saw and were amazed.

All the homeships. All come home.

This was death.

Adam had thought he knew what it was. On the Plain, surely, he had known death, and he had seen it elsewhere since. So much death, all around him. Death everywhere. Death had dogged his track—or he had left it in his wake. Left a trail, like the one he and Lochlan had just followed. It was simply a feature of his nature, what he was *for*. This, to be here, and as far as the universe was concerned—the cold, heartless universe—every one of those corpses scattered behind him was merely collateral damage. It was possible that he wasn't so unlike this man.

But no. *This* was death. Countless people killed—even if it *had* been his fault, those deaths had still only been the ending of life, and all life had to end.

This was so much worse.

It tore at him. Ripped at him. He was being flayed away, layer after layer of skin grated and stripped. His muscles were raked with long forks, serrated knives. Every nerve in his body, each a sparkling wire, was dragged out of him. He writhed in the grip of that demonic blackness, that living *pit* that only wanted to eat and eat and eat, and it bathed his raw being in acid, and was all *teeth*.

This had nothing to do with his physical body. His body was probably fine. This was inside.

In his roots.

He had to fight. He hadn't come here just to be eaten. He hadn't come here just to be a sacrifice. To die, yes, but to go with company. He had to *fight*. He tried to struggle, to strike back, but he had nothing to strike with. It had all been taken from him.

It had been taken from him and he was going to fail.

Adam.

At the name, the hungry mouth froze in midchew, and the blackness was pierced with one bright beam. *A sword*, he thought as he stared at it, entranced.

A star.

It was not a single voice speaking now, but a chorus of them singing his name, reaching for him, hands bearing him up—here where before there had been only a void. Suddenly he remembered the Plain, of how the Aalim had helped him then, had given him their strength, but this was so much more than that. Not hundreds. Not thousands. Hundreds of thousands, perhaps more, beating back the darkness, singing the light into being. Dancing toward him, lifting him, placing the weapons he needed into his hands.

Welcome home, they sang. *Yes, we are all most welcome.*

Him. Them. He *wasn't* like this man. He *wasn't* homeless, wasn't so locked between two extremes that he would never have any purpose but this last fight. He had been made to be here, made to do this, was *becoming* . . . But not becoming an end.

He was something new. He was the first. And if he had changed from who the Protectorate had made him, transformed into something different from what the Bideshi had helped him to be, it was so he could make *life*.

Life, which was at the core of everything. Coded into the roots.

This is who you are. They took him, held him, turned him toward what he needed to do. A child, leaving the hands of a parent and beginning to walk unaided. In front of him was the churning, mutilated horror he had to end, and it wasn't like him. It was *nothing* like him.

This is a dark mirror. Break it. Break it and become.

Break it at its core. Rip it out by the roots and cast it away.

It had reared back, but now it was whirling, coming for him, maw gaping and tongues lashing like the heads of an immense hydra with row upon row of serrated teeth ready to dismember him strip by strip. He faced it and knew he was weak. He had always been right about that: he was just one man, and he couldn't do anything alone.

He wasn't alone.

You are not welcome, Adam said, with hundreds of thousands of voices in his own. He felt their hands in his, their hearts beating in his chest. Their souls—how could anyone ever be so full of life and still live? *We are all welcome here. You are not.*

The hideous thing howled and flung itself at him. Carried by countless hands and crying out with countless voices, with all the force of the healing power in his roots and his code, Adam rose to meet it, and it swallowed him whole.

And he plunged into the monster's throat. He found the roots and tore them up with everything he had been, and was, and would become.

CHAPTER

THIRTY-THREE

Here they were again.

Lochlan would have laughed if he could have found laughter. As it was, he could barely find tears. Here they were once more, surrounded by the dead, and he was cradling Adam Yuga's body in his arms.

Only this wasn't like before. Because now, when he felt for a pulse, for breath, for even the softest beat of a heart, there was nothing.

"*Chusile*," Lochlan whispered, then swung his gaze over to where the Aalim lay a few feet away—as lifeless as Adam.

Lochlan had put a bullet in his head just to be sure.

"*Chusile*, was it worth it?"

Well, was it? Everything they had gone through, everything they had lost, and *Adam*, Adam slipping away from him a long time before now, going somewhere he couldn't follow. He had always known, in some cold, bloodstained part of himself, that that place was here. He had found Adam only to lose him to *this*, and there was nothing he could do. Nothing he ever could have done.

Caldor, his family bleeding out on the deck while he ran and hid. The Plain and everyone dying, no matter what he did. Every battle after that, and all the time Adam had been leaving them. Leaving him. Becoming.

Now this, while Lochlan stood by. Useless. Like he always had been. When it came right down to it, he never fought. He gave in, gave up, surrendered, and *should* he have? Was the fighting worth it? *Was it*? Were people still alive up there? How many were dead? Was any of it really worth this? *Fuck* the selfishness, *fuck* the good of the many. Chusile, *was* anything *worth what's happened here*?

There was no answer. There was only Adam dead in his arms, and beyond these walls, somewhere, the dawn.

"If I were you," Lochlan whispered, pulling Adam closer and smiling against his brow. "Now, *chusile*, if I were *you*, I would do something clever with magic. You probably wouldn't call it magic, would you? But I'm not clever. I don't know magic. I just . . ."

He stopped and tried to breathe. He could do that. That was simple. He could hold Adam and breathe, because one of them should be able to.

"I don't know anything." He tilted his head back, one hand combing slowly through Adam's hair. "I never did, Adam. I never did. Except . . ." He laughed softly. "I was always so *shit* at good-byes."

But this is hello, a voice whispered in his ear. *Can't you hear it? Listen.*

Lochlan started, glanced around. No one was there. All were dead. There was nothing here, nothing left. His imagination—he was exhausted in every possible way. He was—

Listen, Lochlan d'Bideshi. Everyone has come home, child. Come home to bury their father. And you . . .

Not a single voice but a chorus. And every single voice in the chorus seemed to be smiling.

And the loudest? Oh, yes. He knew that voice.

He was never the only one, you horrible child. Don't you know that? You really think he was so special? He was never the only one.

He is only the first.

Adam was heavy in his arms. Still warm. Solid. Real. Something he could touch, no matter how distant Adam had become. The man he had sworn to be with through every trial was *here*. Part of Lochlan didn't want to take the risk, was still shouting *was it worth it*, but a body he could touch was a body he could *reach into*. He was strong enough. He had to be. Through everything they had suffered, all his fear and his doubt, Adam was still the man he had pledged his life to. Lochlan had never stopped loving him.

He closed his eyes and let himself sink into the darkness.

And at first darkness was all there was. He waited, and when nothing happened, he tried to move, twisted, though he could feel nothing holding him. This wasn't working. He wasn't strong enough, and Adam was too far away. He hadn't gone into this with much faith to begin with, but it had been there, and now it was crumbling. He was *failing*. Anger dug its claws into him—what the hell else was he supposed to do?

He was alone.

But then, abruptly, he was traveling deeper and deeper into the darkness at ever-increasing speed, and at last, ahead of him, a tiny light flickered and winked, a candle flame being carried into a dark corridor. Not quickly. It wasn't being stolen. It was merely leaving. It had somewhere else to go.

Except no, it didn't. The light had all his attention, and now—after the rage and the pain and every part of him ready to give up and lose itself—Lochlan was merely irritated. Because the light's intention to leave was ridiculous. It certainly *didn't* have somewhere else to go. It was needed right here.

Grab him and drag him back, you idiot.

But what was meant to happen? He couldn't forget the change they'd known was coming. The change they couldn't stop. *You knew that by the end, he might have moved too far beyond you. You clung to him for as long as you could—is this where you fail? Can you reach him now? Or has he gone where you can't follow?*

How much had changed in the last few minutes? How far away was Adam, truly?

Would his heart be enough to cross that distance? To overcome whatever separated them now? He quailed, a tremble rolling through his core. He'd been so afraid, and now it was like a vise around him. He began to reach, flexed his hand, and it was small. Weak. He drew it back in.

But a new voice rose then, whispered, and he couldn't tell if it was Ixchel's or Nkiruka's... or his own.

You love him, don't you? Doesn't that bind you to him?
Maybe it's enough after all.

He didn't know if it was. He didn't know if he was strong enough. In this moment, none of that mattered. He had never known what would come when he joined with this man. His decision to do so had been entirely faith, and he could have faith now. He could *do* something, was *here* to do something, and he would do it, and even if he failed, it would be . . .

Well. It would be better than nothing. Wouldn't it?

He reached out, and it wasn't too far. It never had been. Adam would never truly have left him, even in death. He cupped his palm around the little light, drew it to him, and carried it back up into the world.

For a moment he merely sat, Adam still limp against him. What had just— He looked down at his hand as if he half expected to see a flame burning there. A little light that he had collected and brought back as simply as catching a glowbug in the Halls, as he had done so often as a child.

Just reaching out and taking it. He frowned, confusion driving away his grief. He had been positive he had . . . And there had been . . . But how could it possibly have . . .

Adam Yuga opened his mismatched eyes and smiled.

The cease fire was sudden and complete.

No one surrendered. There was no final communication that stopped the fighting. There was no coordination whatsoever. All across the battle, moving as one, everyone stood down. Guns stopped firing. Fighters rejoined their wings and flew in simple formation. On board battleships and cruisers, people stood still and stared at each other, at the people around them, as if seeing everyone for the first time.

The change had begun in a chamber full of death on the planet below. It had been a tiny flame that burned back on every consciousness that was bound to it, eating up those tethers like fuses and bringing an explosion of peace in its wake. It swept over each mind, wrapping them up in itself. Even the wounded quieted, their pain fading. The dying closed their eyes and slipped easily into whatever waited for them.

Protectorate and Bideshi stood on either side of a divide and gazed at each other, and when they reached out, the divide closed as immediately and as completely as if it had never been there at all.

The remaining Klashorg watched the sudden peace on their screens and sensors with incomprehension and awe—and the deep certainty that they were seeing something beyond understanding.

That they had been brought here for this. Not to fight, but to bear witness.

Later, things would once again be difficult, confusing. There would be clashes and there would be argument. There might even be violence. Two siblings so long at odds wouldn't return to each other so easily.

But this was the first and greatest step. And on Ashwina, Nkiruka stood within it and smiled. She was herself, with these people. She could feel them all, in a way she never had. A kind of communion closer than had ever been possible—their hearts and their dances beating and spinning around her, each of them orbiting the other. All of them stars, all of them a galaxy of people. An immense human family, finally reunited.

Below them, a man who was the first was stirring in the arms of his beloved, both of them joined. Enmeshed. Inside each other, part of each other so completely they could never be separated. Not one of them reaching for the other but both reaching together, Lochlan finally discovering his own truth: Adam wasn't the last.

Neither was Lochlan.

Every human being carried the seeds of their own destruction. But they carried other seeds as well. For death, healing. For war, peace. For violence, beauty. A blade and a light to cut through the darkness.

Yes, Ixchel murmured—to Nkiruka, to them all. *You see now. In each of you. A sword and a star.*

What kind of story will you be?

EPILOGUE

They didn't say good-bye on any of the landing platforms of the Palace. They didn't say it on Ashwina, or any of the other homeships or Protectorate vessels. They met on a high, grassy hill, far from any human-made structure. There, it was as if they were on Terra in its earliest millennia, long before the birth of their species. A warm wind blew and ruffled the grass. In the distance, a low blue-purple range of mountains lined the horizon. A copse nearby whispered with birds. The sun was sinking on toward evening. The death beyond and above them might as well not have been there at all.

They might have met anywhere. But this felt right. Like a beginning as much as an end. When they had agreed on it, Adam had looked at the images of it taken from low orbit and had sensed a peace beyond anything he had ever known.

He still didn't fully understand where he had been. He didn't know how to understand the way he had returned. But those questions had waited and could continue to wait. This part of the story was over, and a new part was coming. It had to be birthed in its own time and its own place, and in the end no one person could select those things of their own accord.

Two ships sat on the hill, one smaller and clearly of Bideshi origin in its chaotic construction, made according to what could only loosely be called *design*. The other was a Protectorate shuttle, battered but serviceable. Between them was a small group of people divided into twos: Rachel and Aarons, Kyle and Eva, Kae and Leila, Adisa and Nkiruka, Lochlan and Adam. Kae was standing, though he was still supported by Leila's shoulder. He had insisted, gently, on coming. It was only a week after the battle that had ended every battle, but they had to say their farewells, and this was the last time they might all be gathered together.

For a few moments they merely regarded each other in silence, studying each other as if to fix every face in their minds. There might be images they could record, might be some other way of making these memories, but these were the ones they wanted to keep closest. Carry them until their own ends.

At last Nkiruka spoke, and her tone was soft, close, intimate, but it had all the formality and steady cadence of ritual. "What will we do now?"

Leila and Kae exchanged faint smiles. "I think it might be interesting to stop moving for a while," Leila said. "We don't have to be bound to anything. Not in the way we all feared. But this is our home. No matter where we go or what we do, I think it still is. Kae and I—"

"We've been wondering what kind of home it really is," Kae finished. "Not the capital, but . . . nearby. Somewhere open. Where we can breathe. See the sky. And Kyle and Eva are going to have a lot of work to do and that won't end anytime soon. It might be good to stick close."

"Same," Aarons said, his voice gruff but less so than usual. He was holding Rachel's hand, and as he spoke, he squeezed it gently, and the warmth of a slow smile spread over Adam's face. Rachel was half-pulled into herself, her eyes downcast and the hint of a frown constantly wrinkling her brow. But she seemed better than she had been. As Aarons spoke, she looked up and offered them all a small smile. "Rachel has her kids. They've been moving around for far too long, and they should have some space to be kids again. But we need to be ready to do whatever we have to do. What's coming next . . ." He shook his head. "It's not going to be easy. I don't think anyone has any illusions about that."

"Rebuilding is our task." Nkiruka's strange, blind gaze swept around to each of them in turn, and when she reached Adam, it felt like a gentle touch on his cheek. He briefly closed his eyes and gave her a nod. "It'll be a hard task, and long. Centuries of destruction have left their legacy. The Bideshi can't just ignore it and try to move forward. We have to face it. Prepare it for its funeral. We all have to come together to give it a proper burial. That's why we're all here. Adisa and I . . ." She touched the man's arm and he caught her hand, covering it with his own. "We have our own part in it. We're still leaders, and leaders are caretakers. First and foremost, above everything else."

Adam looked at the two of them, looked for a long moment. It wasn't just about fixing their faces in his memory. It wasn't just about saying good-bye. Joy and sorrow, bittersweet, washed over him and tied a knot in his chest, stung the corners of his eyes. There was no saying good-bye to people who had meant so much to him. Done so much for him. Any of them. The thought of leaving them now . . .

So don't, a voice deep inside him whispered. *Stay. You don't have to leave. Stay and rebuild with them.*

But he couldn't. He had given everything to this fight. Everything he had to give. They still had work to do, but his own work had ended on the floor of the Palace command center. It had ended with his death, and he had been reborn as something new. There was nowhere for him here now.

He was free.

And Lochlan would follow him anywhere. Everywhere.

"I don't want to go," he whispered, and Lochlan's hand brushed his. "I mean . . . it's not what I would have chosen, all things being equal. But you know . . ." He tipped his head back, staring up at the sky, and closed his eyes once more. Not against the tears. He had no reason to keep them from flowing.

"They know, *chusile*," Lochlan said, just as softly. "You don't have to say it. You know they know."

And he did.

Lochlan curled his arms around him, and Adam pressed close, gratitude a sweet ache inside him. He wasn't alone now. He never would be again.

No one would.

For a while everything was quiet. The sun hovered above the horizon. The calls of the birds grew louder, and the wind picked up.

"Well," Lochlan said at last, and he sounded just a little like old Lochlan, cocky Lochlan, Lochlan who eschewed responsibility and didn't seem to understand why everything he did annoyed everyone around him. Infuriating Lochlan, who had made Adam's life hell when he first came aboard Ashwina, and who had unbent and softened and transformed into something else under the heat and pressure of love.

He sounded like that old Lochlan, but he also sounded nothing like him at all.

Kae arched a brow. "*Well* what, wingbrother?"

"Well, we'd better get going. We have a star to catch." Lochlan stepped away from Adam and Adam let him go, but didn't release his hand. He needed it. He wasn't going to fear that need.

And yes, he also needed to fly again. He wasn't Bideshi—but he was. They all were. He needed to *move*.

The embraces were close, firm, but they didn't linger too long. *This kind of farewell shouldn't linger. Especially not when*—he suddenly suspected—*it might not be a final one.*

There might be no such thing as *final*.

If any of Adam's embraces truly lingered, it was Kae's. Kae held him gingerly, clearly still in some discomfort, but when he leaned close, lips against Adam's ear, Adam could feel his smile.

"Take care of him," Kae whispered. "He certainly can't take care of himself. Take care of him, brother, because I love him."

Adam only nodded.

At last the two of them left the others and boarded the smaller ship, and it rose swiftly into the darkening sky. Adam considered trying to catch a final glimpse of the people below, but thought better of it. There shouldn't be any turning back. Not now. Now there was only the sky above them and the stars beyond.

"So," Lochlan asked after a few minutes of silence. "Where *are* we going, *chusile*?"

Adam laughed. It went on for a long time, rolling and deep and wonderful, clenching his muscles and stroking his heart. It felt as if it was lifting them, the force that propelled them upward, flight attained through pure joy. And sadness. Sadness would always be part of it.

But for now the joy was the greater part.

When he glanced at Lochlan again, he was met with an arched brow and a crooked, well-loved smile. He didn't have to fix this face in his memory. He knew, somehow, that whenever the end came, it would be the last face he would see.

"What's so funny?"

Adam shook his head. "You know . . . I really have no idea."

"And our destination, *captain*?"

Another easy answer, and it was a pleasure to say.

"I don't know, Lock." He grinned and took Lochlan's hand. "I just . . . I don't know. I don't know anything at all."

There was nothing to know, except for that hand, and then the mouth that closed over his and the heart and the dance that joined with his own rhythm. Those things, in their way, eternal.

And the night that went on forever.

GLOSSARY

Aalim . . . . Bideshi scholar, teacher of laws and traditions, one possessing great wisdom

Chere . . . . Stars, used as an exclamation

Chusile . . . "My dance", "my heart." A Bideshi endearment.

Durak . . . A large, unintelligent land mammal, primarily kept for its hide and meat. Rather like a cow.

Fuguri . . . Balls, testicles, guts

Habibi . . . Beloved, as said to a male person

Habibti . . Beloved, as said to a female person

Khara . . . . Shit

Kutub . . . . The ancient holy books of the Bideshi

Lovina . . . Strong, rich Bideshi liquor

Mitr . . . . . . Friend

Raya . . . . . Landowner, with intensely negative connotations of being the possessed rather than the possessor

Shala . . . . . Hallucinogenic drug derived from the roots of the Bideshi's ancient trees

Voel . . . . . . Bird, with racier connotations in slang; a cocky person

Explore more of the *Root Code* series:
riptidepublishing.com/titles/series/root-code

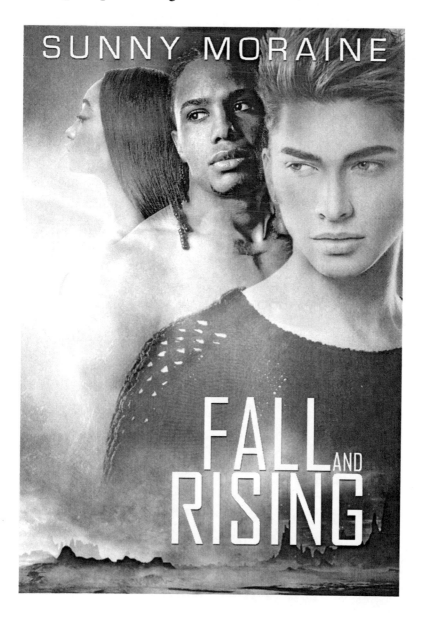

Dear Reader,

Thank you for reading Sunny Moraine's *Sword and Star*!

We know your time is precious and you have many, many entertainment options, so it means a lot that you've chosen to spend your time reading. We really hope you enjoyed it.

We'd be honored if you'd consider posting a review—good or bad—on sites like **Amazon, Barnes & Noble, Kobo, Goodreads, Twitter, Facebook, Tumblr,** and your blog or website. We'd also be honored if you told your friends and family about this book. Word of mouth is a book's lifeblood!

For more information on upcoming releases, author interviews, blog tours, contests, giveaways, and more, please sign up for our weekly, spam-free newsletter and visit us around the web:

Newsletter: tinyurl.com/RiptideSignup
Twitter: twitter.com/RiptideBooks
Facebook: facebook.com/RiptidePublishing
Goodreads: tinyurl.com/RiptideOnGoodreads
Tumblr: riptidepublishing.tumblr.com

Thank you so much for Reading the Rainbow!

AnglerFishPress.com

ACKNOWLEDGMENTS

Thanks as always go to my husband, for continuing to stick with me despite all the excellent reasons not to—many of them having to do with what happens when I try to write a book. Thanks also to my family, who supported this endeavor from book one; my fellow denizens of Darrow, AO3, and Tumblr, who kept me sane through this whole process; to Max, Marco, and Natalie for the sympathetic ears and general encouragement; and to the cats for being the cats. Thanks finally to all at Riptide for taking a chance on this series and allowing it to finally come into the world.

All stories end, except for how they never really do.

ALSO BY SUNNY MORAINE

Labyrinthian
Lineage (coming soon)

Root Code
Line and Orbit
Fall and Rising

Casting the Bones
Crowflight
Ravenfall
Rookwar

ABOUT THE AUTHOR

Sunny Moraine's short fiction has appeared in *Clarkesworld, Strange Horizons, Nightmare, Lightspeed, Long Hidden: Speculative Fiction from the Margins of History,* and multiple Year's Best anthologies, among other places. They are also responsible for the novels *Line and Orbit* (cowritten with Lisa Soem), *Labyrinthian,* and the *Casting the Bones* trilogy, as well as *A Brief History of the Future: collected essays.* Their first short fiction collection, *Singing With All My Skin and Bone,* is forthcoming this summer. In addition to time spent authoring, Sunny is a doctoral candidate in sociology and a sometime college instructor; that last may or may not have been a good move on the part of their department. They unfortunately live just outside Washington, DC, in a creepy house with two cats and a very long-suffering husband.

Sunny is @dynamicsymmetry on Twitter.

Enjoy more stories like *Sword and Star* at RiptidePublishing.com!

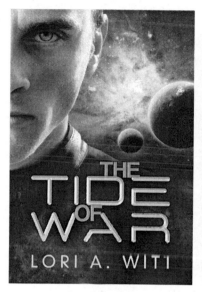

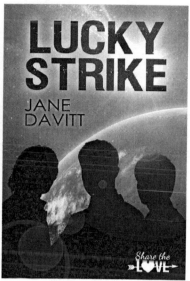

The Tide of War
ISBN: 978-1-62649-265-3

Lucky Strike
ISBN: 978-1-62649-195-3

Earn Bonus Bucks!

Earn 1 Bonus Buck for each dollar you spend. Find out how at
RiptidePublishing.com/news/bonus-bucks.

Win Free Ebooks for a Year!

Pre-order coming soon titles directly through our site and you'll
receive one entry into a drawing for a chance to win free books for
a year! Get the details at RiptidePublishing.com/contests.

CPSIA information can be obtained
at www.ICGtesting.com
Printed in the USA
LVOW12s1709260716
497852LV00008B/508/P